"The only thing I can hope for is that the scandal attached to my name will eventually fade so I can trap some poor fellow into marrying me, despite my many faults." She wrinkled her nose at him, turning her complaint into a jest. The last thing she wanted was his pity.

He took a step closer, so close that she had to tip her head back to look at him. "Any man with a brain would consider himself lucky to call you his wife. I know I would."

His deep voice seemed to rumble through her, like a small earthquake. It rather made her knees quake, too, and she could feel herself blushing like a schoolgirl. She'd heard hundreds of fulsome compliments over the years, calculated to set a girl all atwitter. But his unvarnished statement sent her poor heart thumping even harder. Her body's response told her she stood at the edge of a precipice.

"Perhaps you can write a letter of reference for my former suitors," she said, trying to hide behind the joke. "I fear they've quite forgotten my ample charms."

When his gaze dropped to her bosom, she felt herself going from warm to hot. She'd certainly walked right into that one.

"Perhaps I'll keep you all to myself instead," he murmured in a voice that spoke of dark nights, velvet caresses, and a man's knowing hands on her body. . . .

Books by Vanessa Kelly

Published by Kensington Publishing Corporation

HOW TO MARRY a ROYAL HIGHLANDER

VANESSA KELLY

ZEBRA BOOKS
KENSINGTON PUBLISHING CORP.
http://www.kensingtonbooks.com

ZEBRA BOOKS are published by

Kensington Publishing Corp.
119 West 40th Street
New York, NY 10018

All Kensington titles, imprints, and distributed lines are available at special quantity discounts for bulk purchases for sales promotion, premiums, fund-raising, educational, or institutional use.

Special book excerpts or customized printings can also be created to fit specific needs. For details, write or phone the office of the Kensington Sales Manager: Attn.: Sales Department. Kensington Publishing Corp., 119 West 40th Street, New York, NY 10018. Phone: 1-800-221-2647.

Zebra and the Z logo Reg. U.S. Pat. & TM Off.

First Printing: July 2015
ISBN-13: 978-1-4201-3128-4
ISBN-10: 1-4201-3128-1

First Electronic Edition: July 2015
eISBN-13: 978-1-4201-3129-1
eISBN-10: 1-4201-3129-X

10 9 8 7 6 5 4 3 2 1

Printed in the United States of America

ACKNOWLEDGMENTS

As always, my love and thanks to my husband Randy—a great life partner, critique partner, and writing partner. He also does a mean load of laundry. My gratitude as well to Debbie Mason, my pal and critique partner, who never fails to be there when I need her—even when I'm whining. My writing sisters at The Jaunty Quills and Rock*It Reads are also inestimably kind, and I'm very thankful to have them in my corner.

I'm in serious debt to the wonderful folks at Kensington, especially Vida Engstrand, Alex Nicolajsen, Jane Nutter, Michelle Forde, Karen Auerbach, and Ross Plotkin. A special shout-out to the Kensington Art Department, who always give me the most amazing covers.

Finally, my deepest thanks to my agent and to my editor, Evan Marshall and John Scognamiglio. They have provided me with thoughtful, kind, and intelligent guidance and support, and I'm so grateful for their help.

Chapter One

London
November 1815

It was turning out to be the worst day of Edie Whitney's life. If she'd harbored any doubts, her family's reaction to the unfortunate events at Lady Charlfort's ball last night had dispelled any illusions.

She halted midpace when she heard the hurry of footsteps in the hall. When the door to her bedroom opened, and her twin sister rushed in, Edie almost collapsed with relief. Evelyn had moved out of the Reese family town house after her marriage a few weeks ago, and the empty bedroom next to Edie's seemed to echo the sense of absence she now felt in her life.

Since they were little girls, the sisters had lived in each other's pockets. She and Evelyn shared not only their looks but their thoughts, emotions, and secrets of the heart. Edie had always known that marriage would someday separate them, but she'd never truly prepared for it. When Wolf Endicott had waltzed back into Evelyn's life a few months ago, it had changed everything.

Grateful that her twin had finally found happiness with

the man she'd adored for years, Edie still couldn't help feeling that the most essential element of her own life had gone missing. That made her feel like the most selfish wretch on the planet. To say that her emotions were in a muddle was a capital understatement.

"Dearest, what's going on? Why is Mamma in such a tizzy?" Evelyn asked, stripping off her gloves to grasp Edie's hands. She frowned. "Your fingers are like ice, and you look positively whey-faced. Are you ill? You never fall ill."

Edie let the familiar pressure of her sister's hands establish its calming hold. She tried to dredge up a bracing smile. "I'm fine. Better than fine. It's everyone else who's gone batty, not me."

Her twin drew her to the silk chaise in the window alcove. "You know you can't fool me. What did you do now?"

Edie flopped onto the chaise. Evelyn settled quietly next to her, as precise as a pin in her perfectly tailored carriage dress, her spectacles lending their usual air of bluestocking gravity.

But Evelyn also glowed with happiness, which polished her unassuming beauty to a high gleam.

"I've made a regular cock-up of things," Edie said with a sigh. "Even Mamma is furious with me."

"Surely not. Mamma is never angry with you."

"She's been banging on constantly since breakfast about how I'm the straw that finally broke the camel's back. Surely she said something to you about my *fatal transgression,* as she keeps calling it."

"No, I wanted to see you first before speaking with her. I sent Will into the drawing room to take the first volley." Evelyn flashed a quick grin. "You would have thought I was sending him to face a regiment of bloodthirsty French dragoons."

Edie couldn't hold back a snicker at the idea of her brawny brother-in-law, a former military spy, quailing before their mother. While Wolf had known Lady Reese his entire life, he still found her an intimidating presence, as did most everyone.

Everyone except Edie. She'd always been able to manage Mamma, and everyone in the family depended on her to do just that in order to keep the peace. Lately, though, she seemed to be losing her touch.

"Don't worry," she said. "Mamma is quite enamored of Wolf these days. She keeps referring to him as her favorite son-in-law."

"He's her only son-in-law," Evelyn replied drily, "but never mind about that. Tell me what's wrong."

Edie bolted up from the chaise, too frazzled to sit. She'd slept little last night after *the incident*—to use another of Mamma's melodramatic turns of phrase. But despite Edie's determined efforts to downplay the events of the previous evening in her own mind, a sense of near panic had kept her awake long into the night.

She took a hasty turn around the room before returning to stand in front of her sister. Evelyn sat quietly, clearly as ready as ever to do what was necessary to support her twin. It gave Edie the courage to blurt out the whole sorry mess.

"Well, you see . . ." She never got tangled up in words, but now her tongue was tied in ten thousand knots. "I, um, was at Lady Charlfort's ball last night, as you know, and I was caught in a rather . . . awkward position."

A look of foreboding crossed Evelyn's face. "How awkward?"

"I went for a little stroll down the hall, the one that leads to Lady Charlfort's orangery. It's rather out of the way, as you know."

"Please tell me you were alone, or at least went with someone respectable."

Edie wrinkled her nose. "I was with Sir Malcolm Bannister."

Evelyn looked horrified. "You didn't!"

"I did," Edie said with a sigh. "And we got caught, too."

"Doing what, exactly?"

Edie waved her hand impatiently. "Kissing, of course. Why else would one wander down a secluded hallway with a notorious rake?"

Evelyn slapped her hand atop her chest, looking like a scandalized virgin, though her sister certainly now had more experience when it came to intimate relations between the sexes than Edie. A great deal, if her twin's vague hints were any indication.

"You were kissing Sir Malcolm right there in the hallway?"

"Well, we were in a window alcove. One does want a little privacy in these matters, after all."

Actually, what she'd wanted was to get back to the ballroom, since she'd immediately realized what a colossal mistake she'd made. Sir Malcolm, unfortunately, had had other ideas. Edie had been about to land a hearty kick to his shins when their doom had appeared in the form of Lady Charlfort and her gossiping old harpy of a mother, Lady Morgan. Both had, apparently, wanted to take a stroll down the hall at the same time.

Evelyn let out a disbelieving laugh. "I'm assuming someone caught you."

"Obviously," Edie said sarcastically.

Her twin winced. "Sorry. Of course someone must have caught you."

Edie sighed. "No, I'm sorry. I had no right to bite your head off." She sat down again on the chaise. "I'm just tired and out of sorts."

Evelyn took her hand in a comforting clasp. "Goose, as

if you ever need to apologize to me. You've never done anything but take care of me and protect me."

Edie had done her best to take care of Evelyn over the years, shielding her from their mother's incessant carping and blocking anyone who tried to take advantage of her sister's shy nature. But, in truth, it was Evelyn's loving presence that had given Edie the courage to stand up to those who tried to lord it over her sister. People believed that Edie was the strong and fearless twin, ready to challenge the world, but she knew better. Evelyn had true courage—inner steel that enabled her to stand up for things that really counted.

"Who found you?" Evelyn asked. When Edie told her, she grimly shook her head. "Lady Morgan is the worst gossip in London."

"Don't I know it," Edie gloomily replied.

"Just how compromising was the position?"

"He was kissing me rather vigorously, I'm sorry to say." In fact, the dreary man had shoved his tongue halfway down her throat. Edie had been kissed a few times before, but she realized now how tame those earlier embraces had been. Sir Malcolm, in contrast, had acted like a starving man attacking a slab of rare roast beef.

"But you were fully clothed at all times?" Evelyn asked anxiously. "There was nothing exposed?"

She punctuated her question by waving a vague hand at Edie's bosom. Fortunately, Edie had managed to keep Sir Malcolm's wandering hands from latching on to that portion of her anatomy.

Edie held up a hand, as if taking an oath. "Not a ribbon, button, or pin out of place. Unlike some people I could mention who found themselves in a similar situation."

Evelyn acknowledged the hit with a wry smile. "Thank God for that, at least. Once that happens, the outcome is usually fatal."

Fatal, as in an inevitable trip to the altar. A similar situation had befallen Evelyn and Wolf some months ago, although everything had turned out perfectly in the end.

"You'd think Mamma would agree," Edie said, "since it was really nothing more than a stupid kiss. And not even a very good one."

"I'm assuming you have no wish to marry Sir Malcolm."

"Absolutely not. Nor does he wish to marry me. He bolted out of the house as if his coattails were on fire."

When Evelyn's only response was a frown and a slow, thoughtful nod, Edie let out a resigned sigh. "Evie, I know that look as well as I know the back of my hand. You might as well just say what you're thinking."

Her twin gave her an apologetic smile. "Dearest, you know I would never criticize, but why would you put yourself in such a perilous situation? Especially for a cad like Sir Malcolm."

Edie started fiddling with the end of the satin ribbon that trimmed the waist of her gown. But Evelyn had an endless supply of patience, and Edie knew her twin would wait her out. She tried for a less direct approach. "Evie, did you ever want to a kiss a man before Wolf? I mean *really* kiss him."

"There *was* no man before Will," her sister said wryly. That was true enough, since Evelyn had been in love with Wolf since she was a young girl.

Still, Edie needed something more to go on. "So, you never wanted to kiss anyone else, not even Michael? You were practically engaged to that poor man for almost two years."

Everyone in the family had been convinced that Evelyn would marry Michael Beaumont, a kind and gentle man who'd been very fond of her. Wolf's return home after the war had put the boots to that idea within a matter of weeks.

Her twin pondered the question. "I didn't loathe the

idea of kissing Michael," she finally said, "but it didn't make me jump for joy, either."

"And I take it that Wolf's kisses do make you jump for joy?"

Evelyn's cheeks turned pink. "That's one way of putting it."

Edie huffed out a disgusted snort as she jumped up and started pacing the room again. "It's just so unfair. I'm twenty-five, and I have no idea what you're talking about."

Her sister's gaze lit up with understanding. "I see. You were experimenting. I suppose in that context it makes sense you'd pick Sir Malcolm. One would naturally assume that a handsome and notorious rake would be good at it."

"One would assume wrong," Edie said, coming to a halt by her bed. She braced a shoulder against one of the posts. "I know my plan was demented, but I'm beginning to wonder if there's something wrong with me. I can't seem to find anyone I'd really enjoy kissing, and . . . doing all those other things one does."

"You just haven't found the right man yet. It's easy as anything once you do." Evelyn studied her. "Although I could swear there's someone who—"

Edie held up an imperious hand. "Do not even dare to whisper that man's name."

Her twin cut her a sly grin. "I clearly don't need to, do I?"

Edie felt herself blushing. But Captain Alasdair Gilbride, the most attractive and the most infuriating man she'd ever met, flustered her beyond all reason. Since Edie made a point of never getting flustered, it was very disconcerting. "Evie, I'm warning you."

An annoying little smile curled the edges of Evelyn's mouth. "Yes, dear. Whatever you say."

A quick tap on the door interrupted them, and a moment

later their lady's maid—or, rather, Edie's lady's maid now that Evelyn had married—came into the room.

"Lady Reese wants to see you both in the drawing room, Miss Eden," Cora said. She directed a critical eye at Edie's coiffure and then let out an exasperated sigh. "Your head looks like you stuck it in a rose bush. I told you not to tug on your curls."

"I've been doing no such thing," Edie protested, "and you needn't speak to me as if I were a little girl."

The maid steered Edie to her dressing table. It took her only a few tweaks to restore order to her thick locks.

"All better," Cora said, giving Edie's shoulders a reassuring squeeze. "We don't want to give Lady Reese anything to complain about, do we?"

"You mean on top of all the other ammunition I've given her?" she replied sardonically.

"Everything will be fine," Evelyn said, coming to her. "Mamma never stays angry with you."

Edie rose to her feet. "I don't think so. She was mad as blazes last night. She even yelled at me when we got into the carriage, and she's never done that before."

Evelyn and Cora exchanged startled glances, which didn't make Edie feel any better. She'd always been her mother's favorite child, the one who never got more than the mildest of scolds for any infraction. But last night even the plumes on her mother's turban had vibrated with anger.

Evelyn took her hand. "We'd better go down and get it over with."

"Good luck, miss," Cora said, grimacing.

She gave her maid a weak smile before she and Evelyn proceeded in silence down the hall to the staircase. Edie could tell her twin was getting anxious.

"I'm not going to the gallows," Edie said. "There's no need to measure me for a casket just yet."

"I'm sure everything will turn out just fine," Evelyn said. "More than fine. Splendid, in fact."

"Good God," Edie said with a sigh.

She carefully held on to the banister as they made their way down the stairs. She'd adapted years ago to her wretched eyesight. Though she didn't wear spectacles like her sister, she never took unnecessary chances. The last thing she needed today was a tumble down the staircase.

Their butler, Parkins, was stationed outside the drawing room. As he opened the door, he gave her an almost undetectable grimace of sympathy. Everyone in the household depended on Edie to manage Lady Reese out of her moods, but the servants had clearly realized that their champion had been knocked off her perch.

Squaring her shoulders, Edie followed her sister into the spacious drawing room. She squinted slightly to see her family scattered around the large space, obviously sitting as far away from Mamma as they dared. Evelyn's husband was there, lurking at the back of the room like a timid youth instead of the strapping soldier that he was. Wolf Endicott was no coward, though. He came forward to take Edie's hand while flashing his wife a loving smile.

"Good morning," he said. "Why don't you both have a seat on the sofa?"

Edie ignored her mother's irritated huff as Wolf led them to the sofa near the fireplace.

Mamma was ensconced in one of the elegant Queen Anne armchairs directly across from them. Papa sat next to her, although he'd clearly edged that chair farther away. When he gave Edie a morose smile, it made her heart plunge with a sickening combination of guilt and dismay. Papa was the kindest of fathers and a truly estimable husband as far as she was concerned. All he asked was to have a relatively peaceful household and to be left alone when it came to domestic matters. Normally, Mamma complied with his wishes, but this morning she'd obviously pulled out the big guns.

Her brother, Matthew, had squeezed his rather large bulk onto an undersized bench in a window bay across the room and was doing his best to appear invisible. Fortunately, he'd shown the good sense to leave his snobby new wife at home. Mary never missed an opportunity to snipe at Edie and Evelyn, and she would have loved to lord it over everyone on such an occasion.

Mamma waited for them to get settled, her handsome, aristocratic features stony. As always, she was impeccably garbed, her tall, willowy figure and dark chestnut hair set off to advantage by her bottle green, merino wool morning dress. None of her children resembled her to any degree, instead taking after their golden-haired, sturdily built father. Mamma had always deplored the fact that her husband's yeoman stock had prevailed in her children's looks. Not that it had held them back. Both Evelyn and Matt had married well, and Edie had no shortage of suitors.

Although that might very well change after last night.

"Now that we are gathered," her mother started in a voice that presaged doom, "it's time to decide what to do about Eden's fatal transgression."

"Oh, for God's sake, Mamma," Edie said. "That's doing it rather too brown, even for you. My error was surely not *fatal*."

Her mother's lips went tight and pale. But before she could snap back, Papa reached over and laid a gentle hand on his wife's arm. Mamma cast him an angry glance, but held her tongue.

"I'm prepared to put up with quite a lot from my children," Papa said in a stern voice. "But I will not allow them to disrespect their mother. Your outburst is both unhelpful and unwelcome, Eden. I expect better from you."

Edie winced. Her outburst aside, her father's reprimand meant that the situation was probably as bad as Mamma thought it was.

"I'm sure Edie didn't mean any disrespect, Papa," Evelyn said, casting a worried glance at their clearly irate mother.

Edie squeezed her sister's hand. "No, Papa's right. I was disrespectful." She smiled apologetically at her mother. "I'm sorry, Mamma. Truly I am."

Her mother's flinty gaze narrowed until she finally moved her head in a frosty nod of acceptance.

"As I was saying before I was interrupted," her mother continued, "we must find a way to deal with the consequences of Eden's extremely unfortunate behavior last night. Those consequences were made even worse by her choice of a grossly unsuitable partner for her escapade. If she'd been found in such circumstances with a respectable man, we might have been able to manage the scandal in the usual way of things. Sir Malcolm, however, is *not* a respectable man, and one cannot depend on him to take the honorable course of action."

Thank God for small mercies. If Edie had been stupid enough to get caught with one of her real beaus, Mamma would be trying to frog-march her to the altar within days. Sir Malcolm was not only a rake; he was possessed of a very modest fortune and that, in Mamma's eyes, might be a greater sin than his deplorable reputation. If nothing else, her mother was a very practical person.

"My dear, are you sure the situation is as bad as you believe?" her father asked. "Since Lady Charlfort is a particular friend of yours, surely she won't spread any nasty rumors."

"No, but her mother will suffer no such compunctions," Mamma replied. "Lady Morgan may be a dowager countess, but her conduct has always been exceedingly crass. I suppose that's not surprising given that her father was a member of the mercantile classes."

"Horrors," Edie muttered under her breath. Her sister dug a warning elbow into her ribs.

"Despite my best efforts last night," Mamma went on, "the worst sort of gossip is already making the rounds. By the end of the day, Eden's reputation will lie in tatters."

"Oh, bad luck, that," Matt unhelpfully blurted. "Really, Edie, what were you thinking? Sir Malcolm is a complete bounder."

Though Edie was tempted to fire back at him, her brother was right. "I know. It was stupid. And he was even rather sloppy about the whole business, too."

It seemed manifestly unfair that on top of everything else, kissing Sir Malcolm had been akin to getting one's face licked by an overly enthusiastic mastiff.

"We do not need the details," her mother snapped.

"Of course not," Papa hastily said. "And I'm sure you have a plan to deal with this awkward situation, my dear, don't you?"

Edie repressed a sigh. Not for the first time, she wished that her dear father would be a little more assertive when it came to family matters. God only knew what Mamma would come up with in her present state.

"There is only one possible plan," her mother said. "Edie must rusticate."

"That's the ticket, Mamma," Matt said immediately. "A little time in the country should do the trick. After all, we'll all be toddling down to Maywood Manor in a few weeks for the holiday season. And Edie likes the country, don't you, old girl?"

Feeling almost weak with relief, Edie smiled at her brother. She didn't much like the idea of leaving town in disgrace, but there were far worse things than going home for a long spell. And her brother was correct—they'd be leaving London in November in any case. If a little early rustication were her only punishment for last night's stupidity, she would count herself lucky.

"I'm sorry to disappoint you, Matthew," Mamma said, "but Eden will not be going home to Maywood Manor."

Edie jerked upright, as did Evelyn.

"I won't?" Edie asked in a disbelieving voice. "Why not?"

Her mother's basilisk-like regard returned to her. Edie could imagine herself turning into a pillar of salt under that hard gaze.

"Because I will not reward your bad behavior," Mamma said. "And it wouldn't address the problem in any case. Maywood Manor is hardly out of the way, and there is always a great deal of visiting and socializing at that time of year. Short of locking you in one of the attics for the winter, you would still be very much in the public eye."

"Well, we certainly cannot have you in the attic. The neighbors would talk even more," Edie's father said, trying for a little joke.

Mamma glared at him for a few seconds before answering. "Eden should spend the winter with Lady Torbeck, in Yorkshire. Aunt Eugenia has not been in the best of health, and I'm sure she would benefit from some younger company. Besides, it will do Eden good to be of use, for once, instead of flitting about London like a deranged butterfly."

Edie stared at her mother in horror. The idea of spending the winter in the wilds of Yorkshire, especially under the nose of a veritable tartar like Lady Torbeck, appalled her. She might as well hang herself now and get it over with.

"Good God, Mamma," Evelyn said, sounding as horrified as Edie felt. "You might as well bury poor Edie alive."

That gruesome but surprisingly apt image propelled Edie to her feet. She hurried to her mother's chair and sank down, sitting back on her heels.

"Mamma, I'm sorry for what I did. Truly I am." She propped her folded hands on her mother's knee, just as she used to do when she was a little girl and needed to wheedle her way around Mamma's anger. Because that anger had usually been directed at Evelyn, she understood in a visceral way how awful it must have been for her twin to be on the receiving end of their mother's temper.

"And I swear I'll do just as you say and not make any more trouble," she continued, staring earnestly into her mother's cool green eyes. "I'll be quite the reformed character, you'll see. Just don't send me away from everybody."

She hated the little catch in her voice and knew that Mamma would hate it, too. Her mother was never one for excessive displays of emotion—at least the more sentimental ones—and she would no doubt feel that Edie was trying to manipulate her.

But Edie wasn't. The idea of spending the winter in lonely exile in Yorkshire made her feel like the world was crashing down on top of her.

For several fraught seconds, her mother's gaze remained cold. Then, she blinked, and a small, weary sigh passed her lips.

"My dear, I don't do this simply to punish you," she said, resting a slender hand on Edie's clenched fists. "You believe that your popularity will allow you to weather the worst of the gossip, but I assure you that such is not the case. The *ton* is unforgiving in these matters. Your friends will snub you, and your suitors—the eligible ones, anyway—will avoid you. People will lie about what you've done and won't care that they are lying. Your reputation will be irrevocably stained."

Though her mother's features had softened with sympathy, her words were like a giant hammer pounding Edie down onto the carpet.

"I'd like the chance to try," she said. "To face it head-on and see if I can get through it."

All sympathy leached from her mother's gaze. "I will not allow you to put yourself or this family through such a doomed enterprise. It would only make matters worse."

Edie heard the soft rustle of her sister's skirts behind her. A moment later, Evelyn's comforting hand rested on her shoulder, and Edie had to blink back tears. Evelyn was always there for her, and the idea of so long a separation from her twin was gutting.

"Mamma, must it be Yorkshire?" Evelyn asked. "Surely there's some other alternative."

The sound of a masculine throat being discreetly cleared had Edie turning around. Wolf had been so quiet up to this point that she'd forgotten he was in the room.

"I don't mean to be interfering," her brother-in-law said. "But I have an idea about that."

He directed an apologetic smile at Mamma. He looked absolutely harmless, which was truly ridiculous. Until recently, Wolf had been a spy for the Crown, and Edie knew he was more than capable of doing whatever needed to be done.

Mamma had grown quite fond of Wolf since he'd come back into Evelyn's life—partly because he was the son of the Duke of York. Even though he'd been born on the wrong side of the blanket, Mamma found it rather grand to have a son-in-law with royal blood running through his veins.

"Yes, William?" Mamma asked with an encouraging smile. "What would you suggest?"

When Wolf glanced at Edie and smiled, a dreadful sense of foreboding stole over her.

"What would you think," he said, "of spending the winter in Scotland?"

Chapter Two

Captain Alasdair Gilbride, late of the Black Watch, eyed Aden St. George with distaste. "So, if I don't return to that benighted castle, Dominic Hunter will haul my arse in front of Prinny and have me ordered back to the Highlands. Do I have that right?"

His cousin lifted the glass holding a generous portion of scotch, admiring the rich amber hue within the sparkling cut crystal. "You do. By the way, Alec, this is a very fine whiskey."

"It should be. It came from one of the oldest distilleries in Scotland." He didn't bother to mention that his family owned the distillery. "But you're dodging the issue, Aden. I refuse to believe that there isn't some mission you could send me on. Surely there's still a need for spies, even after we put the boots to Boney."

Aden's heavy sigh sounded more like an expression of sympathy than exasperation. Not that sympathy was likely to get Alec where he wanted to be, which was anywhere but Scotland.

The library of his grandfather's London mansion was a gracious and noble room, if one's taste ran to styles favored over half a century ago. Although the house was kept spit-cleaned and polished by a small but capable crew of servants, it hadn't truly been a home in years. Alec couldn't remember the last time his grandfather had visited London. The only reason the Earl of Riddick had kept the place was for Alec to occasionally camp out there during his infrequent trips from the Continent during the war. As such, the house seemed trapped in another era, even down to the books. Alec was willing to bet that no new volumes had been added to the library since the previous century.

"There will always be a need for spies," Aden said, "but that doesn't mean we need *you* to be running around in disguise, rooting out conspiracies and killers. We have plenty of agents on hand, so we do not need the heir to an earldom risking his life on dangerous missions. You're getting too old for that, anyway."

Alec scoffed. "Good Gad, I'm only twenty-six, you idiot. Considerably younger than you."

"Then it's time you listened to your elders. *And* to your superior in the service, I might add. I'm giving the orders now, Alec, and I'm ordering you to go home."

Alec scowled at his cousin. When Dominic Hunter, the best spymaster England had seen in a generation, had retired, Aden St. George had stepped into his place. He now ran a significant portion of the Intelligence Service, and his word determined whether Alec would stay or go.

Aden stretched out his booted legs and dangled a negligent hand over the arm of one of the leather club chairs that faced Alec's desk. To the casual observer, he looked like the average Corinthian, entirely at his leisure until he lounged off to a cockfight or to his club. But Alec knew how false that impression was. His cousin was still one of England's most effective and lethal spies. Neither marriage nor his promotion to head of mission had changed that.

"Alec, you've earned the rest," Aden said. "You spent

ten years fighting. You're heir to one of the most powerful titles in the Union. You have a place in the world and a role to play, and it's time you faced up to that. And perhaps you could try, for once, to enjoy the privileges inherent in that position instead of running away from them. Most men would kill to be where you are."

Alec almost inhaled a snort of whiskey at the idea that he would actually enjoy the obligations that awaited him back at Blairgal Castle. And as for whether he had a right to the attendant privileges that remained to be seen.

"Some might not agree that the earldom actually *is* mine in the first place."

"You mean *you* might not agree," his cousin replied. "To anyone that matters, you are the legitimate son of Walter Gilbride and his wife, Lady Fiona, the only child of the Earl of Riddick. And since Scottish earldoms can pass down through the female line, that makes you Riddick's heir. Anyone who says otherwise will not just have your grandfather to deal with, but the Prince Regent."

That was true enough. His grandfather had always stood by his daughter, even after her brief, adulterous affair with Prinny's brother, the Duke of Kent. And so had Walter Gilbride, her husband and, for all intents and purposes, Alec's father. Walter insisted that Alec was his true son, and the old earl was just as adamant that his grandson was the rightful heir to Riddick. Alec's relatives had never been anything but steadfast in their loyalty to him and to his mother's good name, denying any rumors or gossip that suggested he had been born on the wrong side of the sheets.

Too bad all that loyalty made him feel guilty as hell.

"Alec, it's time to go home," Aden went on. "If you give it a chance, you might find it easier than you think."

"Easy for you to say," Alec said absently as he swirled the last bit of whiskey in his glass. When he glanced up to catch his cousin's ironic stare, he winced. "Sorry about that."

In fact, it hadn't been easy for Aden St. George to come out of the shadows and rejoin his family. Everyone knew that Aden was Prinny's bastard, just like they knew that his mother's husband had resented the cuckoo in his nest. Aden had been estranged from his mother for a long time, and only his stepfather's death had allowed them to reestablish a relationship.

"You know how bloody difficult it all is," Alec said. "Families are a royal pain in the arse."

Aden laughed as he came to his feet. "With the emphasis on *royal*. But I've found it to be worth the effort."

Alec rose and strolled around the desk. "And how is your wife? I trust Lady Vivien is no longer reaching for a basin every ten minutes."

His cousin unleashed a grin that on a less imposing man would have looked almost fatuous. "Fortunately, Vivien seems to have gotten over that. Now she's simply hungry all the time. I suppose she's making up for two months of bland food and gruel."

"I'm glad to hear it. I hope the rest of her pregnancy continues without further incident."

"I'm sure it will. Let me know when you plan to leave London. Vivien and I would like to see you again before you go."

"You'll be the first to know," Alec responded in a dry voice.

Never would be the answer if he had his druthers. But there was no point in delaying. The old earl was in declining health, and Alec would never forgive himself if Grandfather died before he saw him again. Ten years was a long enough time to avoid the inevitable. He needed to return home and face all that awaited him, including a very particular problem that had been a millstone around his neck for ages.

A discreet tap on the library door interrupted their good-byes. Dailey, the butler, soft-footed his way into the room.

"Forgive the interruption, Captain, but you have a most insistent visitor."

Alec caught the disapproval in Dailey's voice.

"And who is this visitor, or is it a secret?" Alec prompted after a few moments of fraught silence on the butler's part.

Dailey finally pried his wrinkled old lips apart. "Mrs. William Endicott, sir. Alone."

Alec and Aden exchanged a surprised glance. Since Evelyn Whitney's marriage to Wolf, she'd become like a sister to Alec. Still, it wasn't quite the done thing for her to come calling alone. It likely meant some sort of trouble with Wolf that she wanted to discuss privately.

"You needn't worry, Dailey," Alec said. "I'm not carrying on a madcap affair with Captain Endicott's wife. Now stop looking like an outraged matron and show the lady in."

"I would never presume to make such an offensive assumption, Captain Gilbride, you may be sure," Dailey answered, making a magnificently disdainful bow.

"Excellent. And please bring us some tea," Alec added. "If you're not too scandalized by my shocking disregard for propriety."

Dailey, who'd been with the family since the time of the pharaohs, didn't bother to respond to that parting shot. It was petty, Alec knew, but twitting the old fellow occasionally was irresistible, a tendency that only showed how poorly suited he was for the life of a rich aristocrat. Alec had gotten used to the stripped down existence of a military spy, and was still having trouble adjusting to all the idiotic trappings and boring social restrictions of the British aristocracy.

Aden regarded him with arched eyebrows.

"Good Lord, you're as bad as Dailey," Alec said. "I have no idea why Evie finds it necessary to be making such a clandestine call."

"Hardly clandestine, since it's the middle of the afternoon."

"Still, it's not her usual style."

A moment later, Dailey ushered Evelyn Endicott into the room. She halted when she saw Aden, but smoothly recovered, a warm smile curving her lush mouth. Alec got a jolt, both to his brain and to his groin. The latter was an unerring barometer when it came to one person in particular.

Goddammit.

The gorgeous young woman who'd just swept into his library was no more the wife of Wolf Endicott than Alec was the King of Spain.

"Mrs. Endicott, what a pleasure to see you," Aden said with a bow.

The faux Mrs. Endicott dimpled up prettily and returned his greeting with a brief curtsey. "And you, Captain St. George, although I see I interrupted your meeting. Please forgive me."

She cast what she no doubt thought was a shy, apologetic glance at Alec. He raised an eyebrow and crossed his arms over his chest. Her brows, partly hidden by her spectacles, tilted down in a frown.

But a moment later she was directing another charming smile at Aden, who seemed completely taken in by her silly charade. Alec almost laughed out loud at the notion of the outrageous Eden Whitney pulling the wool over the eyes of England's most accomplished spy.

"No apology necessary, Mrs. Endicott," Aden said. He nodded to Alec. "I'll speak with you later."

Alec answered his cousin with a polite smile, enjoying the prospect of mocking him at a later date. But when Aden reached the door, he glanced over his shoulder, his eyebrows raised and his gaze glinting with laughter.

Clearly, the little minx hadn't fooled Aden, after all.

The woman who was fast becoming the bane of Alec's existence flashed him what she probably thought was an innocent, shy smile. It was nothing of the sort, of course. Eden Whitney exuded a mostly unconscious sensuality that could knock a man flat from twenty paces.

"I'm sure you must be surprised to see me," she said in a sweet, quiet voice.

He had to admit she got the voice right. If he hadn't been looking straight at her, he would have thought he was listening to Evie and not her diabolical twin.

"Give it up, Miss Whitney." He took her by the elbow and steered her to one of the club chairs. "You're not fooling anyone."

She gaped up at him with astonishment. "Confound it, how do you do that? I haven't been in the room for more than a minute."

It wasn't the first time Edie had switched identities with her twin, but it hadn't worked any better with him this time than it had a few months ago. There were a dozen differences between the sisters, some quite noticeable. For one, Edie carried herself with a degree of confidence and restless energy her twin lacked. She cut a swath through the *ton* like a sharpened sickle through a field of ripe wheat.

There were more subtle signs as well, like the way her clothes hugged her generous curves just a little more snuggly than her sister's. She might think she was fooling him by choosing a modestly cut carriage dress in dove gray, but Edie's sense of dash always seemed to bleed through. No cautious ponderings or sober second thoughts for Miss Eden Whitney. To her, life was a challenge and a lark, something to be enjoyed to the hilt.

"Never mind that, you daft woman," he said. "Have you no care for your reputation?"

She let out a disdainful snort. "Reputation? That's rich, coming from you. You're constantly doing outrageous things."

"I'm a man. I can get away with it. You, however, cannot."

"It's so unfair," she grumbled.

He went to sit behind his desk. When it came to Edie, he found it best to always have a large piece of furniture between them. If not, he might be tempted to shake her for acting so foolishly, or do something even stupider, like kissing her. And unless his instincts were completely off, she just might kiss him back.

Then again, she could also take his head off. Though Alec had little doubt that Edie was attracted to him, she'd made it abundantly clear that she found him thickheaded, annoying, and arrogant. On occasion that might be true, but he still didn't much like that she had so low an opinion of him.

She pushed her borrowed spectacles up her nose and studied him with irritation.

"You can take those ridiculous spectacles off while you're at it, especially since they're crooked," he said. "They make you look like you're listing sideways."

When she stuck her tongue out at him, he couldn't help but laugh. She struggled with her bad humor for a few seconds then gave him a wry smile.

"I think I'll keep them on, since it's quite a nice change to be able to see more than ten feet in front of me. Besides, I don't want to shock your snob of a butler any more than I already have. It wouldn't do for him to think I'm not

Evie, even though I have a perfectly good reason for coming to see you."

"Did you at least bring your maid with you?"

"I wanted to, but I couldn't be sure she wouldn't tell somebody. Like my mother," she finished in a gloomy voice.

"Good God, Miss Whitney, do you have any idea how much trouble we would both be in if anyone got wind of this little escapade?"

He expected her to starch up, as she usually did, but she just sighed and slumped into her chair. Behind the silver frames, her eyes were drawn and weary looking, and her pink lips were bracketed by unhappy grooves.

"I'm desperate," she said. "I had to see you before anyone else got to you first, especially Wolf."

"You can tell me all about it after Dailey brings in the tea. I believe I hear his lumbering footsteps in the hall and, as you so astutely noted, it wouldn't do for anyone to see past your little deception." Dailey's footsteps were anything but lumbering, but Alec had very good hearing, honed by years spent dodging death, French spies, and irate husbands.

"I'd rather have a brandy," she said, going back to scowling at him.

A moment later, the butler entered the room, followed by a footman carrying a loaded tea tray.

"Mrs. Endicott will pour, Dailey," Alec said. "I'll call if we need anything."

"As you wish, Captain." The butler radiated waves of disapproval.

He unbent a bit, however, when Edie flashed him a smile calibrated to penetrate the starched shirtfront of even the stuffiest domestic. He gave her a respectful bow before directing a fierce glare at the hapless footman for gawping at Edie.

The woman had a way about her—a way that usually led a man into serious trouble.

As she poured the tea, Alec rose and strolled to the whatnot tucked between a pair of bookcases. He extracted a bottle of brandy from one of the shelves, then returned to his desk and splashed a tot in each of their teacups.

Edie grimaced. "Oh, dear, I must look as dreary as I feel for you to take such pity on me."

"Not in the least, although, it must be dire if you felt compelled to come to me for help."

A rush of pink colored her cheeks, a riveting sight. He didn't think he'd ever seen her blush before. It made her look like a creamy white cake with luscious pink frosting.

Her gaze turned cool and calculating, washing away the brief impression of vulnerability. She was once more the bold young lady who sought to control everything and everyone around her. Alec liked that Edie a lot, but he had to admit he wouldn't mind seeing more of the sweet girl that sometimes peeked out from behind the dashing façade.

"You're right," she said in her usual frank manner. "Of course I'd rather not be coming to you for help. You must be positively deranged to think I'd forgotten how badly you and Wolf behaved with poor Michael Beaumont. You were terrible to him—and to me and Evie."

Now it was Alec's turn to scowl. "Are you insane, lass? We saved your precious Mr. Beaumont's backside. Without us, he would have ended up swinging from the gallows."

She perched her teacup on her knee and gave a haughty little sniff that he found rather endearing. "Things would have gone much better if you'd told Evie and me the truth."

He stared at her in disbelief. He and Wolf had been under orders from the Duke of York himself to investigate Michael Beaumont for treason. The fact that the man was

Evelyn's fiancé at the time had made the whole business sticky, but it had eventually come out right. Beaumont had been cleared, and Evelyn had ended up with Wolf. Though Beaumont hadn't been pleased about that part, it had seemed a small price to pay for his life.

"This may surprise you, Miss Whitney, but spies aren't usually in the habit of divulging the details of their mission to the people they're investigating."

"As much as I would enjoy rehashing the past with you," she said sarcastically, "I need to explain why I need your help. And not to put too fine a point on it, you need my help, too. This situation is a problem for both of us."

Now, that sounded interesting, if a tad alarming. "Please proceed."

For the first time since she'd entered the room, Edie looked uncomfortable. She took a hasty sip of the spiked tea, probably to fortify herself.

"Whatever it is, lass," he said gently, "you won't shock me. Just say it."

Her gaze met his, and she gave him a reluctant smile. "Very well. I got myself into a spot of trouble last night at Lady Charlfort's ball, and Mamma is *furious* with me." She grimaced. "My parents are convinced I need to rusticate."

Alec wasn't surprised she'd gotten herself into trouble. As far as he was concerned, she was an accident waiting to happen. But it startled him to hear that Lady Reese was unhappy with her. The woman adored her daughter and, according to Wolf, was convinced that Edie could do no wrong.

"Would I be correct in assuming this trouble involved a man?"

There was that faint wash of pink again. This time, though, Alec wasn't charmed. The idea of Edie getting into trouble with a man had him clenching a fist against his thigh.

"Who was he?" he asked sharply when she remained silent.

She seemed perplexed by his tone. "Sir Malcolm Bannister, though it really isn't any business of yours."

Now both his fists were clenched against his thighs. "Bannister? Are you mad? The man is a notorious rake."

Edie set her teacup down on his desk with a loud click. Then she crossed her arms over her impressive bosom and gave him an ironic stare. That she was silently but clearly commenting on *his* reputation as a rake did not improve Alec's mood. Yes, he liked women, but he never tampered with virgins or innocents.

"Never mind," he growled. "Just tell me exactly what happened."

"Nothing. That's what I've been trying to tell everyone."

"Then why the need for such drastic measures?"

"Well, almost nothing," she grudgingly admitted. "I'd almost escaped from him when Lady Charlfort and her witch of a mother stumbled upon us."

Alec closed his eyes, trying to ignore the fury turning his vision blood red. When he opened them, she was eyeing him like *he* was the one who'd lost touch with reality. And perhaps he had. The notion of Edie in another man's arms made him want to commit several acts of mayhem.

"Did he hurt you?" he growled.

She blinked as if surprised by the question, then waved an insouciant hand. "As if I couldn't handle a cad like Bannister. You can be sure he'll never come within ten feet of me again."

Her naïveté and reckless self-confidence bordered on criminal. Still, there was little to be gained in pursuing that point. The sooner he got the image of Edie in Bannister's lecherous embrace out of his head, the better.

"As a result of this unfortunate encounter with one of the *ton*'s most notorious rakes," he said, "you now find yourself in an awkward situation. Lady Reese is no doubt focused on the gossip."

She was obviously irritated by his characterization. "Yes, Mamma is convinced the damage to my reputation will be quite severe. It's an assessment I don't agree with, by the way."

"Imagine my surprise. And yet, your parents want you to rusticate. To Maywood Manor, I assume?" But what did any of this have to do with him?

She pressed her full lips into a grim line.

"Miss Whitney?" he prompted when she remained silent.

"Actually, Wolf suggested another alternative, something you'll find as displeasing as I do, I'm sure."

The familiar sense of premonition Alec never ignored prickled along his nerves. "Which is?"

"They want me to go to Scotland with you," she blurted out. "For the entire winter. Can you imagine? I'd probably kill myself by leaping off the nearest Highland peak. Or we'd kill each other, which is, I suppose, the likeliest scenario."

She rose from her seat, clearly agitated, then forced herself to sit back down. The air around her practically seethed with emotional disturbance.

"Well," she snapped, "don't just sit there gaping at me like the village idiot. You simply must put a stop to this immediately. You have to tell Wolf and my mother that it's entirely out of the question."

The wheels in his head—always lagging when it came to dealing with the force of nature that was Eden Whitney—ground into motion. A vague idea began to take form.

"Wolf suggested this?" he asked, playing for time.

She scowled. "Yes, the bounder. I couldn't believe he was taking Mamma's side."

"And your mother thought this was a good idea?"

She rolled her eyes. "For some demented reason she seems to like you. Or perhaps she just likes all your lovely pots of money."

Alec tried to look soulful. "You wound me, Miss Whitney."

"You have the hide of a rhinoceros. Besides, what does it matter? It's not like you're going to agree to this."

"I'm simply trying to ascertain the precise circumstances of the situation," he said. "Presumably, you could only travel with me to Scotland with an appropriate chaperone. Did that come up for discussion?"

Alec prayed it would not be Lady Reese. The idea of spending the winter with Edie's mother was enough to frighten any sane man. Perhaps it would be Wolf and Evie, although Wolf had a new assignment with the Foreign Office.

"What does it matter?" Edie exclaimed, waving her arms. The fabric of her carriage dress pulled tight over her generous breasts, something that never failed to distract him. "You don't want me in Scotland, and I have no intention of going. What in God's name would I even do there for an entire winter?"

Help me with my blasted family.

The wheels in Alec's head turned faster as he stared at her, perched on the edge of her chair and glaring at him over the top of her crooked spectacles.

Not that he could come right out and ask for Edie's help—not given how delicate and tricky his domestic problem in Scotland was turning out to be. And the dimensions of his plan were hardly more than a glimmer of an idea, so vague he could hardly articulate them. Besides, he had little hope of getting Edie to agree to anything without a great deal of work and some underhanded manipulation on his part. And for that he needed time, lots of time, with her.

It was a remarkably enticing idea, now that he thought about it.

"Well," Edie demanded, "don't you have anything to say?"

"I do," he said, giving her a roguish smile. "Hasn't anyone told you that winter is the best time to visit the Highlands?"

Chapter Three

"Are you ready, dearest?" Evelyn asked.

Edie dragged her gaze from the late evening bustle of the London streets to meet her twin's worried gaze. Guilt nagged her like a persistent toothache. Even though she was determined to bull through the gossip, she hated the impact of the whispers on her loved ones. Some of the *ton*'s worst busybodies had actually had the nerve to call at Reese House, and make their sly innuendoes. As well, Mamma's friends had confirmed how quickly the rumors were flying about town.

Mamma had naturally forbidden Edie to ride in Hyde Park or even go for a stroll with her sister through the quiet streets of Mayfair. It was immensely frustrating because Edie would have no idea how bad things were until she had firsthand knowledge.

She was about to gain that knowledge tonight at Lord and Lady Neal's ball, one of the last big events before most of the *ton* decamped to the country for the winter.

Edie flashed a bright smile at her twin. "Of course I'm ready. After all, how bad could it be?"

She ignored the derisive snort from her mother's corner of the carriage. Mamma seemed grimly prepared for battle. When she'd marched out to the carriage, Edie had almost fancied she'd heard trumpets sounding a charge.

She'd been rather surprised that her mother was even joining them. Mamma had vociferously objected, still insisting that the best course of action was for Edie to pack her bags and flee town. Fortunately, Edie had managed to convince her father to give her a chance to prove to the rest of them that things weren't as dire as they seemed. Mamma had finally capitulated on the grounds that obviously her daughter needed to see for herself "how bad things were."

That comment had sounded more like a threat than a boon, but Edie wasn't about to look a gift horse in the mouth.

Lady Neal's ball was always a squeeze, and tonight's seemed more crowded than usual. In fact, as Edie stepped down to the pavement, she noticed a large knot of guests still jostling their way into the grand Berkeley Square mansion. Mamma had insisted they arrive late to avoid a crowd in the receiving line, but they'd clearly miscalculated.

Either that or everyone had turned out to witness her public humiliation. A shiver of premonition danced along her spine.

"When do you expect William to join us?" Mamma asked Evelyn as they made their way up the steps.

"He should already be here," Evelyn replied, slipping her hand through the crook of Edie's arm. "He was to meet Captain Gilbride at White's, and then they were to come over together."

"Ah, I'm glad to hear Gilbride will be present," Mamma said, giving Edie a pointed look. "I'd like to have a little chat with him."

Edie swallowed a groan. Alec Gilbride was the last person she wanted to see after that humiliating episode in his library a few days ago. It had galled her to ask for his help in the first place, and it had infuriated her when he'd agreed to her mother's demented plans. When Edie had recovered enough to demand an explanation, he'd said that he trusted Lady Reese's judgment. If she felt her daughter needed to retreat from society, he was more than happy to offer his family's hospitality. Their discussion had then devolved into the predictable argument, and she'd finally blown up at him, calling him a complete oaf. His laugh had prompted her to storm out.

After she'd calmed down and reviewed their conversation, she still couldn't deduce why he felt obliged to help her in any way. All Edie knew was that she didn't trust him, despite the fact that he was the most handsome, most intriguing, and occasionally most charming man she'd ever met.

Edie watched her mother square her shoulders before plunging into the crowd that was milling about in the entrance hall. After handing their wraps over to a footman, she and Evelyn followed Mamma to the staircase leading up to the ballroom. And although it was too chaotic and noisy to speak to anyone, Edie didn't fail to notice the looks cast her way. Some were mildly surprised, some were openly disapproving, and several were nakedly malicious. Mamma, however, made a dignified progress through the crowd, nodding to friends and treating everyone else with magnificent disdain.

"She is rather wonderful in situations like this, isn't she?" Evelyn murmured. "I wish I had the knack for it."

Edie didn't have the knack for it either. Yet, unlike her twin, she enjoyed socializing and found it immensely fun.

Until tonight. She'd been convinced she could brazen it out, but her persistent prickles of foreboding would not go away. With each step she took up the staircase, her sense that she'd made a dreadful mistake grew stronger. She felt choked by the stuffy atmosphere, hemmed in on all sides by noisy guests, most of them reeking of snuff or alcohol or too much perfume. She could hardly draw in a breath, and for an awful moment she had trouble finding her feet. Her head swam.

"Hang on," her sister murmured, taking her elbow in a steadying grip. "The crowd's easing up ahead."

Thank God for Evelyn. They'd always known how the other was feeling and even thinking. Her sister's steadfast support at this moment made Edie realize all over again how much she missed her since her marriage to Wolf.

"There's Will," Evelyn said, her face lighting up. "He'll run interference for us and deal with anyone foolish enough to be rude."

Wolf stood at the top of the stairs. He murmured something to Mamma before she swept past, then smiled at his wife. "Hullo, love. You and Edie are both looking in prime twig. I'm a lucky man to have the privilege of escorting the two prettiest girls at the ball. Every other man will be insane with envy."

Evelyn laughed. "How silly, although I do agree that Edie looks splendid tonight." She ran a quick, assessing gaze over Edie's gown. "That color is divine on you, dear. It's perfect."

"It should be," Edie said. "Papa almost had an apoplectic fit when he got the bill."

She'd deliberately chosen her best gown tonight, a cerulean blue silk with an overskirt of gold netting. The blue brought out the color of her eyes, the gold matched her hair, and the cut framed her bosom to advantage and lengthened her short waist. It was a gown calculated to draw male attention and admiration. Edie knew she couldn't count on support from most of the females tonight, but if she could attract anything close to her usual number of swains, she'd call the evening a success. She desperately needed admirers and supporters to survive the disapproval of the *ton*.

"It was worth every shilling," Wolf said gallantly as he offered his arm to Edie.

She smiled gratefully as Evelyn took her husband's other arm.

Her brother-in-law bent down a bit from his tall height. "I have your back tonight, Edie," he murmured. "If you need any help, come find me."

She squeezed his arm. "You're a good man, Wolf Endicott. You might almost deserve my sister."

"Don't bet on it," Evelyn piped up. "I'm much too good for him, and he knows it."

Edie felt immeasurably cheered by their good-natured banter. With her twin and her brother-in-law by her side, she felt ready to brave the disapproving old biddies and anyone else.

They joined their mother in greeting their hosts. Lady Neal, a handsome woman with a sharp mind and an even sharper tongue, flicked a hostile glance over Edie. "My word, Miss Whitney, I didn't expect to see you here tonight. I was under the impression that you were recently indisposed."

Edie gave her a serene smile. "Thank you for your concern, my lady, but I'm quite recovered."

"Then I suppose we must count ourselves lucky that you could join us," Lady Neal said coldly.

"Indeed we are," Lord Neal interjected in a jovial voice. "We can never have too many pretty girls at a ball, can we, Lady Reese? And I must say that both your daughters are looking exceedingly lovely."

Lady Neal sniffed haughtily.

Mamma directed a gracious smile at her host. "Thank you, my lord. Come along, girls. We mustn't waste another moment of her ladyship's precious time." Her tone of voice made it amply clear what she thought of her hostess.

Edie gave Lord Neal a grateful smile as she passed by him. When he winked at her and then rolled his eyes at his wife, she had to bite a lip to keep from laughing. His lordship might be a bit of a roué, and he *had* pinched her bum on two occasions, but she'd never hold that against him again. It was a good sign that Lord Neal had publicly stood up to his wife—one of London's most powerful hostesses—on Edie's behalf.

"Where's Alec?" Evelyn asked Wolf as they pushed their way into the crowded ballroom. "Didn't he come with you?"

Wolf nodded. "Yes, but Lady Monteith's daughter practically dragged him onto the dance floor first thing. I imagine he'll catch up by the time we go down to supper."

Edie didn't know whether to be grateful or irritated. She dreaded running into the annoying man, but didn't relish the news that Lady Melissa was still engaged in her single-minded pursuit of Gilbride.

Not that she was jealous. Nor did she think Gilbride was keen on Melissa. He flirted with every woman who crossed his path, from the oldest grandmother to the shyest of debutantes, and Edie would never fault him for being kind to women who were often cruelly ignored by other men. What truly irritated her was the general feminine response to the man. There was barely a woman in London not ready to fling herself at Gilbride's big feet, including a goodly portion of the married ladies. And he accepted all that adulation with good-natured arrogance, as if it were the natural order of things.

Everything always fell right into Gilbride's kilted lap, whether he wanted it or not.

Wolf steered them closer to the orchestra and out of the thick of the crowd. The music made it difficult to talk though, and Edie suspected her brother-in-law had picked the spot for that very reason. She hadn't missed the nasty glances as they'd strolled along the edges of the dance floor, but if anyone had made cutting remarks, she hadn't heard them.

After murmuring to his wife, Wolf went off to fetch them something to drink. Edie could only hope that some of her swains would soon appear to keep them company. She knew there would be some deserters tonight, the ones that only flirted with her because she was in style. Several, however, she considered to be genuine friends and had little doubt they would stand by her regardless of the gossip.

Right now, though, no other guest stood closer than several feet away. It was as if someone had taken a piece of chalk and drawn a circle around her and Evelyn. Given how crowded the room was, some people practically had to step on each other's toes to keep clear of their contaminating presence.

"You'd think we were lepers," her sister huffed. "It's absolutely ridiculous."

"Never mind," Edie said. "At least we can breathe, for once." She stood on her tiptoes, peering back in the direction of the entrance. "What happened to Mamma?"

"She got waylaid by Mrs. Eglin and Lady Johnson just inside the door."

"They'll be giving her a lecture about me," Edie sighed. "Poor Mamma."

Those two women were particular friends of her mother and were both exceedingly high in the instep. As such, they would feel it well within their rights to give Mamma unsolicited advice about her daughter's scandalous behavior.

Evelyn snorted. "Don't worry about Mamma. She's as snobby as they are. Of course, she'll find it strange to be on the receiving end of a lecture instead of delivering it. I'm sure this is quite a learning experience for her."

"I only wish I wasn't the reason for that experience," Edie commented.

Her twin winced. "You're right of course. Sorry, pet."

Edie squeezed her sister's hand. "I don't blame you in the least. You've heard dozens of lectures on your behavior from Mamma over the years, and you never deserved a single one of them. It's good for her to see what it's like, for once."

Through a gap in the crowd, Wolf appeared carrying two dainty crystal cups. "Sorry, all I could snag was this watered-down punch. One would think a plague of locusts had descended on the refreshment table."

"That's not surprising, since Lady Neal is a bit of a nip-cheese," Edie said. "There's never enough to go around, especially the champagne."

Evelyn ignored the cup in her husband's hand as she peered out at the dance floor. A slight frown marked her brows.

"What is it?" Edie asked. She followed the direction of her sister's gaze, but all she saw was the usual swirl of blurred colors as the dancers circled the floor to the lively strains of the first waltz.

"Nothing," Evelyn responded brightly as she snapped her gaze back to her sister. "In fact, why don't we go down and find a table for supper right now? I'd love a glass of champagne and something to eat. As you said, there won't be any left if we wait."

The candlelight glinted off the lenses of Evelyn's spectacles, obscuring her eyes. Still, Edie didn't need to see her expression to know she was lying.

"You don't even like champagne," she said drily. "Give over, Evie. What is it you don't want me to see?"

"Nothing," Evelyn repeated before glancing at her

husband. "Will, could you find Mamma? Edie and I will meet you in the supper room."

"Too late," Wolf said in a grim voice. "The enemy approaches."

When Edie followed his gaze, she had to bite back a curse that no lady should ever think, much less know. Waltzing toward them, close enough for her to see, was the couple from hell.

Sir Malcolm Bannister, coward par excellence, was dancing with the meanest girl in London, Lady Calista Freemont, daughter of the Marquess of Corbendale. Edie and her twin had been forced to endure Calista's wretched company for two years at Miss Ardmore's Select Academy for Young Ladies. Calista and her minions had made it their special project to torment poor Evelyn. Edie, naturally, had made it her special project to torment Calista right back. Their mutual loathing had never been a problem before, since most people didn't like Calista but did like Edie.

Did being the operative word.

"Drat them both to perdition," Evelyn growled.

Edie dredged up a smile. "Evie, dear, please let me handle it. The last time you and Calista got in an argument, you dumped a plate of strawberry shortcake down the front of her gown."

"She deserved it," her twin said.

"Indeed she did, but we hardly need a scene like that tonight. Mamma would crucify us."

A moment later, Sir Malcolm swung Calista to a halt just in front of them. It was perfectly timed to match the conclusion to the music—so perfect that Edie knew Calista had planned it.

"Goodness, how surprising," Calista said, affecting a breathless laugh. "I just happened to be waltzing with Sir Malcolm when I caught sight of you, Miss Whitney, and I simply had to come over and say hello. I admire your courage in so boldly facing the censure of the *ton*. Especially after, well . . . you know."

She directed an arch look at her partner, who appeared to be expiring from death by humiliation. That Sir Malcolm was a cowardly tool for Calista's revenge was apparent. Calista might be a monster, but she was also rich and beautiful. Sir Malcolm obviously had no intention of looking a gift horse in the mouth.

Edie adopted the look of scornful amusement that never failed to irritate her nemesis. "No, Lady Calista, I'm afraid I don't know. Perhaps you might care to explain."

Sir Malcom made a horrified whimper.

Edie wondered why she'd ever wasted a moment on him. He was handsome in a polished sort of way—tall, with a nice set of shoulders and always impeccably dressed—but she'd failed to notice before the weak set to his mouth and the shifting gaze that never truly settled. In fact, he wouldn't even look at her right now, obviously ready to take to his heels and flee as if a pack of wolves was snapping at his coattails. The man was a cad, and she'd been a fool to even consider dallying with him.

The hot flush of shame staining her neck and cheeks was not because she'd kissed Sir Malcolm, but because she'd been so lacking in judgment to choose him in the first place.

Calista let out an angry titter, obviously annoyed that Edie refused to play her ugly little game. "Really, Miss Whitney, how can you be so brazen? Everyone knows you acted disgracefully. I don't know how you can stand to show your face in public, and your poor, dear mamma must be *so* humiliated."

"Oh, for God's sake," Wolf said, stepping forward to take Edie's arm and lead her away.

Edie shook him off. "You're referring, I expect, to my

alleged contretemps with Sir Malcolm. If such is the case, I have to wonder what *you're* doing in his company. Aren't you afraid your reputation will be tainted as well, Lady Calista?"

The little harpy drew in a sharp breath to level a retort, but Edie cut her off. Unlike Calista, she knew exactly where to slip in the blade.

"*Your* poor mamma," Edie said, shaking her head. "Lady Corbendale must be devastated to see you reduced to this and not even Sir Malcolm's first choice. Then again, given your inability to bring eligible suitors up to snuff, I suppose you must make do with fortune-hunters, loose fishes, and aging roués."

"Now see here," Sir Malcolm said indignantly. "I certainly hope you're not referring to me. I'm barely thirty-five years old."

Edie let out a disbelieving snort. Of all the insults she'd just leveled, that was the one that offended him the most? "Of course I'm referring to you, you bacon-brained fool."

"Edie, don't," her sister warned. "We're attracting too much attention."

Edie cast a swift, angry glance around, noting that the crowd had moved in. They were obviously relishing the prospect of a juicy spectacle, like ancient Romans waiting for a bloody mauling in the arena.

Among the group of watchers were several of Edie's devoted swains, including a few she'd come to think of as friends. The expressions on their faces, which ran from coolly amused to avidly malicious, hit her like a kick to the gut. The stifling atmosphere of the overheated ballroom closed in on her, crazily warping her perspective as her head started to spin.

Then the floor steadied beneath her, even though a red haze shimmered around the edges of her vision. In the middle of that haze was Calista's beautiful face, twisted with hatred and contempt, like a princess gone wrong in a fairy tale.

"Why, Miss Whitney," Calista said, her voice ringing with the knowledge that her time of triumph had finally arrived, "surely you know that a woman's reputation is her greatest prize. It is entirely her responsibility to safeguard it. Sir Malcolm cannot be blamed that you chose to throw yourself at him like a common trollop."

The murmur of delighted horror that rose up around them almost drowned out her sister's outraged exclamation. Evelyn hastily moved forward to confront Calista, but Edie shot out an arm to hold her back.

"We've heard enough of this nonsense," Wolf said. His commanding voice cut through the gale of scandalized comments and laughter in their vicinity, and he looked every inch the royal that he was. "Sir Malcolm, I suggest you escort your companion to the supper room. Lady Calista is beside herself, and I'm sure she could benefit from some refreshment."

"Yes, of course, of course," babbled Sir Malcolm, obviously scared witless. He took Calista by the elbow and tried to tug her away.

The idiot jerked her arm from his grasp. "Don't be a fool," she hissed at him. "I will not be run off by this lot."

"I suggest you take my husband's advice and walk away," Evelyn said sternly. "This scene does not reflect well on any of us."

No chance of that, Edie thought. The dratted girl had been waiting years for her revenge—probably since the time Edie dumped a bucket of cold water over her head at school.

"Walk away?" Calista hooted. "Your sister should have to walk away, not I." When she stretched forward, apparently preparing to deliver her coup de grâce, she looked like a viper about to strike.

"Eden Whitney is nothing but a lightskirt," Calista said in carrying tones. "She's not fit to be seen in polite company, and I intend to tell that to everyone I know. Sir Malcolm gave me *all* the details, and I assure you they're shocking in the extreme."

When Sir Malcolm let out an agonized moan, Edie rolled her eyes. He was truly a disgusting excuse for a man.

"Good heavens," Mamma exclaimed as she pushed her way through a gaggle of matrons. She scowled at her daughters. "I certainly hope you're not engaging in one of your silly arguments with Lady Calista, my dears. I will be most disappointed in all of you if such is the case."

Then her gaze landed on Sir Malcolm, changing in a blink from disapproving to downright furious. The coward cringed and took a step back.

"What is *he* doing here?" Mamma demanded.

"I haven't a clue," Edie said. "But I can assure you that he and Lady Calista were just leaving."

Edie plucked her sister's cup of punch from her hand and splashed it across Sir Malcolm's pristine white waistcoat. She saved her own cup for Calista's cream and yellow bodice. Her timing was impeccable because the colorful punch made contact just as Calista's mother sailed up to their group.

In the ensuing bedlam, Edie was almost swept off her feet. She staggered, her shoulders colliding with something that felt like a granite wall. A pair of large hands clamped onto her waist, steadying her.

She wriggled around, looking up then up again past a brawny chest and a pair of exceedingly wide shoulders. Riveting gray eyes, glittering with laughter, stared down at her.

Gilbride's teasing brogue rose above the mayhem. "Well, Miss Whitney, what say you to Scotland now?"

Chapter Four

It was going to be a very long trip north.

"It's time," Mamma announced as she marched into Edie's bedroom. "The carriages are loaded up and ready to depart. We do not want to keep the horses standing about."

Edie was fully aware of the activity around the two large travel coaches parked in front of her father's town house. For the last half hour, servants had swarmed over the conveyances like worker bees, strapping on trunks and stuffing band boxes, valises, blankets, food baskets, and a dozen other things deemed essential for the lengthy trip and a winter spent in the Highlands.

For the last half hour, Edie and Evelyn had been sitting by the window, clasping hands as they held watch. Not a single word was needed to express their grief. Edie had the oddest feeling that once the carriage passed the outskirts of the city, some invisible thread connecting them would snap, and something vital inside would die.

Evelyn rose and pulled Edie up with her. "I am always with you," her twin said fiercely. She took one of Edie's hands and pressed it over her heart. "Right here. Always here. Nothing can truly separate us."

Edie forced a smile, blinking back tears. "Not even Wolf?"

Evelyn emphatically shook her head. "Not even him."

"You are such a terrible liar. All that man has to do is snap his fingers, and you lay right down at his feet."

Evelyn let out a watery laugh. "That doesn't mean I need you any less. Besides, Will would never make me choose, and you know it."

More than anyone, Wolf understood the strength of the sisters' bond and knew their lives would always be intertwined. He'd never displayed a shred of jealousy or been anything less than supportive. Edie wondered if she would ever find a man as loving, loyal, and accepting as Wolf Endicott.

"Come along, Eden," Mamma said. "I'm sure Captain Gilbride wishes to be on his way. The sooner we start, the sooner this dreadful trip will be over."

"I'm coming," Edie sighed.

Her mother had adopted a martyred attitude ever since the debacle at Lady Neal's ball. Edie could only hope she wouldn't spend the entire trip acting like she was about to be thrown into a cage full of wild beasts.

"Last chance to turn back, Mamma," she said, only half-joking. "No need for both of us to suffer."

Her mother cast a pious gaze up to the ceiling, as if visualizing her ascension into the heavens. Edie was beginning to think that Mamma was mining the situation for every ounce of drama so as to inflict the maximum dose of maternal guilt.

Her strategy was working.

"No, Eden," she answered. "After all, I am partly responsible for this dreadful turn of events."

Edie and Evelyn exchanged startled glances.

"You are?" Edie asked.

"Yes. I allowed your father to indulge you and give you far too much freedom. Now I must accept the consequences of my accommodating nature."

"Oh, good God," Evelyn muttered.

"You're a saint, Mamma," Edie said in a dry voice. Leave it to her mother to accept responsibility in such a way that put most of the blame on poor Papa. "I don't know how you put up with horrible old me."

Cora's timely entrance prevented the impending reprimand.

"The luggage coach is ready to leave, my lady," the maid said to Mamma. "Davis is already downstairs and I just have to fetch Miss Eden's jewel box."

Davis was Mamma's dresser. She and Cora would be riding in the second coach along with the mountains of baggage.

"Very well," Mamma said. "If Captain Gilbride is agreeable, you may get underway. We'll see you tonight at the inn."

When Cora fetched the small wooden cask from Edie's dressing table, her mother frowned. "That isn't your regular box, Eden. Why are you taking so little jewelry?"

"It's Scotland, Mamma. I doubt there will be many opportunities to show off the family jewels. Besides, we'll probably end up getting robbed by a gang of highwaymen or bloodthirsty Highlanders. I don't see any point in giving them all my good things."

"It's better to have something decent to give them, so they don't kill you," Evelyn said with a rueful smile. "You know how Highlanders feel about *Sassenachs*."

"You are both being ridiculous," Mamma said. "The Highlands are all the rage these days, thanks to Mr. Scott's books and poems. Besides, the Earl of Riddick is an exceedingly rich man, so I'm certain everything will be quite fashionable."

"Just wait until they start playing the bagpipes, serving haggis and blood pudding, and wearing smelly old sheep-skins," Edie said. "And Gilbride told me they don't even wear smalls underneath the kilts. Imagine how shocking that will be on a windy day, Mamma."

Her mother glared at them, then pivoted on her heel and stalked out of the room.

"You shouldn't tease her," Evelyn said. "You'll only make things worse."

"You're one to talk. Besides, she did *not* have to come with me. I'm sure we could have found some impecunious cousin to act as chaperone."

"Mamma's convinced that she's the only one who can control you."

"And look how well that's been working out," Edie said. She took one last look around her bedroom, taking in the elegant chinoiserie wallpaper, the dainty furniture, and the four-poster bed with its luxurious bedclothes and pile of plump, soft pillows. She'd spent many hours reading and daydreaming in this room and longing for adventure. Now she was certainly embarking on an adventure, just not one she'd hoped for.

And then there was Gilbride. Edie hadn't the foggiest idea what to do about him other than to stay as far away from him as possible.

Still, she had to give him credit for his quick thinking the other night at the ball. In the midst of the pandemo-nium, Gilbride had picked her up off her feet and walked her backward out of the ballroom. Edie could still recall her shock at having his brawny body plastered along her back and the ease with which he'd carted her away.

Evelyn led her out to the hall. "I'm sorry you have to put up with Mamma without anyone else from the family to back you up."

"Don't worry. She can't stay mad at me forever."

"That's because she never got mad at you before."

"True enough. It's like wandering into a foreign country. I'll have to send you regular dispatches to ask for guidance."

"I can tell you exactly what to do right now," Evelyn said drily. "Stay out of her way."

"I can only hope Captain Gilbride's manor house is big enough for us to avoid each other."

"It's a castle, Edie. A big one."

Edie came to a halt at the top of the staircase. "How do you know?"

"I asked, silly. I believe Alec described it as an ancient stone pile at the end of a valley, complete with battlements, towers, and ghosts."

"Ugh. No doubt the three witches from *Macbeth* are in residence, too."

Evelyn laughed. "At least Will, Papa, and I will be meeting you in Edinburgh for Christmas. Won't that be fun?"

"Let's just hope Mamma and I haven't killed each other by then," Edie said, following her sister down the stairs.

They were met with the last-minute bustle of departure in the front hall. Servants milled about, and Matt huddled next to the long-case clock as if trying to blend into the background. Mamma was talking to Papa and giving last-minute instructions to the housekeeper and the butler.

"You mustn't worry," Papa was saying to his wife. "The staff and I will keep everything in fighting trim."

"You're not used to managing things without me," Mamma said in a fretful voice. "Goodness knows what will happen when I'm gone."

Edie knew exactly what would happen when they were gone. Things would continue to run as smoothly as ever, since Mamma had little to do with household management.

Evelyn would continue to keep her eye on things, as she had been for years.

Her mother let out a dramatic sigh. "My dear sir, I fear you will be quite lost without me."

Edie had to hold back a snort. If she knew her father, he was bursting with joy at the notion of six weeks or more of peace and quiet. Despite his rather pathetic attempts to look mournful, the twinkle in his eye confirmed her suspicions.

But his good cheer evaporated when Edie said her good-byes. "I'm sorry, Papa," she whispered as he folded her into a comforting embrace. "I wish I hadn't caused such a fuss."

"Well, it will pass," he said. "Take care of your mother, and be sure to write to your poor old father when you have the chance."

She readily promised she would. What else would she have to do, buried in the Highlands for this long time?

"Come on, old girl," Matt said, coming forward to take her arm. "Might as well get it over with."

"You make it sound like she's going to the gallows," Evelyn said as they followed their parents outside.

"Well, it *is* Scotland. In the winter," Edie said. "That does sound almost as bad as going to the gallows."

She clamped her lips shut when she saw Gilbride, his arms crossed over his broad chest. His gaze was full of mockery, which told her that he'd heard her comments.

"Now, what was that ye were sayin' about my beloved homeland, lassie?" he asked as he stood next to Wolf. "Surely ye can't be thinkin' it's anything but heaven on earth."

"Oh, God," she muttered. "Please, not the brogue."

He simply laughed.

Gilbride's deep, aristocratic voice normally carried only

a hint of his native land. But whenever he wished to tease someone—or trick a person into thinking he was nothing more than a big oaf from the Highlands—he affected a heavy but natural brogue. Eden found it to be an entirely irritating practice.

It didn't help that she'd often been the target of his Highland ruse. When she'd finally discovered that he was not, in fact, a dolt but a deadly and accomplished military spy, she'd been mortified to realize that he'd been playing her for a fool the entire time.

Well, she would not let the blasted man get the better of her again.

She gave him a toothy smile. "Captain Gilbride, far be it from me to criticize, but you might be surprised to learn that it's rude to eavesdrop on people's private conversations. Since, however, you have only recently returned to polite society, I feel certain you would wish me to point out any little mistakes you might make."

"Oh, Edie," her sister said, choking back a laugh.

"Goodness, Eden, that is no way to talk to our host," Mamma huffed. "Captain Gilbride is doing us the greatest of favors. I insist that you treat him with more respect."

"Have to agree with Mamma there, old girl," Matt chimed in. "Mustn't be insulting the fellow who's going to be putting up with you for the next five months."

Lovely. A family scold—just what she needed. She silently fumed at Gilbride as he regarded her with a teasing grin.

Fortunately, Papa stepped into the awkward breach. "Now, now, Edie was just funning. I'm sure the captain understands that."

"And let's not forget that Alec can be immensely irritating," Wolf added, winking at Edie. "I find that giving him a good whack in the head on a regular basis is the best way to keep him in line."

Everyone laughed except Mamma.

"You're right about that, laddie," Gilbride said, "and I'm sure Miss Whitney appreciates the advice. But I think we'd best be on our way."

That timely reminder stifled their laughter. Edie had delayed as long as possible, but now there was nothing to do but board the coach and be on her way. It was the moment she'd been dreading for days.

While her father helped his wife mount the steps, Edie turned to her sister one last time. Evelyn took her hands, her mouth drawn into a tragic line, her eyes filling with tears.

"Good-bye, love," Edie said. Her chest felt so tight she could barely draw in a breath. "Take care of yourself."

Evelyn threw her arms around her. "Write if you need me," she said in a fierce whisper. "I'll come right away, no matter what."

Edie closed her eyes and hugged back, trying to draw the comfort deep into her bones. She would never love anyone as much as she loved her twin, and saying good-bye was the hardest thing she'd ever done. Panic flared up, and she had to battle against a premonition that she might never see her sister again.

Her twin drew back a bit, her hands on Edie's shoulders. Her gaze was warm with love. "You're not to worry, pet. I promise that nothing bad will happen to either of us while we're apart."

A reluctant laugh broke from Edie's throat. "I'll happily take that promise."

Wolf gently drew them apart. "I'll take care of Evie. You may count on it."

Edie went up on her toes to kiss his cheek. "You'd better, or I'll come back and kill you, scandal or no scandal. You know how reckless Evie can be, so I'm counting on you to keep her safe."

Evelyn huffed out a little laugh. "Yes, that's me—the reckless one." She turned to Gilbride, standing by the carriage steps and looking uncharacteristically solemn. "And you take care of my sister, Alec, or I'll kill *you*." Her tone of voice made it clear she wasn't making an idle threat.

Gilbride took Evelyn's hand and bowed over it. "I pledge you my word that I will treat Lady Reese and your sister with all the care and affection I would my own family. I promise no harm will come to either of them."

His deep, serious voice had Edie tearing up again. It was, quite frankly, annoying. Just when she thought Gilbride couldn't get more irritating, the blasted man managed to sneak through her defenses again.

Wolf clapped Gilbride on the back. "Stay out of trouble, old son," he said. "I'll miss you."

As the men made their gruff good-byes, it dawned on Edie that this must be a wrenching leave-taking for them, too. Wolf and Gilbride had spent the last several years as close as brothers, comrades in the war against the French.

As Evelyn and Wolf stepped back, Gilbride took Edie's hand. "Ready, Miss Whitney?" His tone was kind, but somehow it still sounded like a challenge.

She forced a bright smile. "As ready as I'll ever be."

It was a lie, of course. She wasn't ready at all.

"That was the worst meal I have ever eaten," her mother said as they made their way back to the carriage. "I suppose it could have been worse, though. We might have had to stay overnight. Whatever was the captain thinking to choose this stop?"

"Oh, come, Mamma," Edie said, trying to be cheerful

despite the melancholy that dragged like an anchor on her spirit. "It wasn't that bad."

Her mother stopped in the middle of the yard to stare at her, oblivious to the grooms, stable boys, and assortment of vehicles and horses that crowded the forecourt of the Red Fox.

Edie shrugged. "Very well, it was awful. But it wasn't Gilbride's fault. The serving girl told me the cook broke her ankle yesterday, and the innkeeper's wife just had a baby. The poor man was obviously run off his feet."

"That's no excuse. We should have gone somewhere else."

Mamma was simply out of sorts, and Edie couldn't blame her. It had taken forever to bounce their way out of London onto the Great North Road. Gilbride's carriage was both luxurious and well-appointed, but that didn't mean the journey was comfortable or swift. Spending the next ten to fourteen days locked together in such a small space was a daunting prospect.

"And where is the captain?" Mamma scanned the busy yard with a frosty expression. Normally, her mother quite liked Gilbride, but not today. Perhaps that was because he'd abandoned them to their gloomy silence by riding alongside or ahead of the carriage on a magnificent black hunter.

Eden peered around. Although things were a bit blurry, there was no mistaking Gilbride's tall form and wide shoulders. "He's by the carriage, talking to one of his grooms."

"He barely spent two minutes with us at lunch," her mother huffed. "I did not appreciate being left alone in a public dining room with the common riff-raff."

"He did his best, Mamma, but there were no private rooms available. Besides, I'm sure he's very busy organizing the two carriages, our maids, his valet, and three armed grooms. We're not exactly traveling on the cheap."

A grumpy *hrumph* was her mother's only acknowledgment.

"Ah, ladies, here you are," Gilbride said with a smile as they came up to the carriage.

The man was ridiculously handsome—and nice when he wished to be. It made Edie feel rather gloomy, probably because she was used to men like him falling at her feet. So far, however, Gilbride seemed entirely immune to her charms.

Of course, from his point of view, she was probably little better than an aging spinster with a modest dowry and a tattered reputation. If Gilbride were looking for a wife, he'd seek someone younger, prettier, and richer.

Edie silently lectured that she shouldn't care in the least. Still, when his silver-gray gaze lingered on her, his smile warm, she couldn't repress the thrilling shiver that she felt all the way down the backs of her legs.

"Are we ready to be on our way?" Gilbride asked. "We still have a few hours of daylight left before we need to get off the road."

"Indeed we are," Mamma said as she mounted the carriage step. "The sooner we leave this dreary establishment behind, the better."

"Oh, Mamma," Edie muttered under her breath. When she wrinkled her nose in silent apology at Gilbride, he gave her a shrug and a smile. Nothing seemed to bother him, not even an irate matron. Then again, he didn't have to ride with her.

After he handed Edie up, Gilbride surprised her by stepping into the coach and taking the seat opposite.

"You're not riding?" she asked. "It's such a lovely afternoon out."

She knew she sounded wistful, but as soon as she'd seen

Gilbride mount his horse this morning, she'd thought of her beloved Castor. Edie had been forced to leave her beautiful gelding behind, despite her repeated requests to her mother to bring him.

"I would not *think* of asking the captain or his grandfather to provide for your horse or for a groom to take care of him," Mamma had firmly stated. "We are guests in his house and must not take advantage."

It seemed to Edie that throwing one little gelding into the mix would hardly make a difference. Her mother had claimed that Lord Riddick would no doubt have a suitable mount for her to ride but Edie knew that wouldn't be possible. With her bad eyesight, riding without spectacles was a tricky proposition. She'd spent months training Castor, carefully acclimating herself to the horse, and him to her. She had perfect confidence in her ability to control Castor and in his ability to respond to her needs. He was gentle, light on his feet, and uncannily attuned to his mistress. Mamma had forgotten how long it had taken Edie to train the horse, and her repeated attempts to remind her had fallen on deaf ears.

Gilbride settled in, his muscular frame taking up a good portion of the carriage. Edie tucked her feet back to give him more room, and lifted a questioning eyebrow.

"Ah, yes. My horse," Gilbride said. "My groom will take him along to the inn. I thought I'd ride with you for a while. It's a treat to have such charming ladies for company on a long trip."

Mamma made a noise that sounded suspiciously like a snort, and even Eden couldn't come up with a reasonable response to such a blatant untruth. She simply gave him a polite smile before looking out the window.

As the carriage rumbled back onto the highway, she gazed longingly at Gilbride's magnificent black stallion as it cantered past. The horse was huge, which he had to be to carry his brawny master, but he seemed to be well-trained and of gentle temperament. Perhaps at some point, when they were farther north and the traffic thinned, Gilbride might consider letting her ride him. After all, how much trouble could she get into following a carriage going no more than seven or eight miles an hour?

There was only one way to find out.

"Captain, do you ever let anyone else ride your horse?"

"Sometimes. It depends on the rider," he said, shifting to get more comfortable. Perhaps it wasn't such a good idea to have him in the coach after all, although Edie was honest enough to admit she didn't mind looking at his long, muscular legs, even if he did take up every inch of extra space.

She flashed him the smile that usually worked wonders on her male acquaintances. "I'm a very good horsewoman, so I was wondering if you might allow me to ride him at some point. Just for an hour or so, to take a break from the carriage."

And from her mother's griping.

As if on cue, Mamma scowled at her. "Really, Eden, I hardly think it proper for you to be riding on a public road behind a traveling coach. Whatever will everyone think?"

"No one will know who I am, so why does it matter?"

"That is precisely the attitude that has landed you in such serious trouble. We have enough scandals without you making a spectacle of yourself on the Great North Road."

Mentally cringing under Mamma's reprimand, Edie forced herself to look at Gilbride. His attention, however, was focused on her mother.

"I have no objection to Miss Whitney riding Darius, Lady Reese," he said. "Especially on the less traveled parts of the road. My grooms would ride with her, and she would be within sight of the carriage at all times."

The only part of Mamma that moved in response was her upper lip, and it curled with disdain. Edie had always been impressed with her mother's ability to convey so much emotion with so small a gesture. Mamma had reduced more than one family member to abject apology with that lip, alone.

Captain Gilbride was clearly not intimidated, his eyebrows lifting in a haughty tilt as he stared back. It reminded Edie that Gilbride was more than just a handsome rake cutting a good-natured swath through the *ton*. He was an accomplished soldier and spy and was both powerful and wealthy—a great deal more so than anyone in her family.

She eyed her mother to see how she would take his challenge to her authority. It took a few, charged moments, during which Gilbride's eyes narrowed to irritated slits, before Mamma backed down.

"Naturally, I will defer to your judgment as our host," her mother said, adopting a gracious tone.

Edie was hard put not to roll her eyes. Of course Mamma would defer to him. Gilbride was rich and an aristocrat, the two things she valued most.

"Well, that's settled," Edie said. She smiled at Gilbride. "Thank you, sir. Perhaps I can ride tomorrow if the weather cooperates."

"On one condition," he said.

Eden frowned. "What would that be?"

"That you wear spectacles. I can't allow you to ride my horse if you can't see what you're doing. It would be unsafe."

"Wear spectacles in public?" Mamma exclaimed, aghast. "Do you want her to look a complete antidote?"

Edie silently cursed. Her twin wore spectacles all the time and was decidedly not an antidote. But Edie disliked the blasted things almost as much as her mother hated seeing her wear them. It was one thing to do it as the occasional lark but quite another to adopt them as part of one's public persona.

"I don't need spectacles to ride a horse," she said. "I ride all the time without them."

"But that is on your own horse," Gilbride said. "One you trained. And you only ride where you are familiar with the landscape, at Maywood Manor or in Hyde Park. I cannot allow you to ride a strange horse on unfamiliar roads when your vision is impaired."

Edie was torn between irritation and surprise. Irritation for the obvious reason, and surprise because he'd discovered something about her that very few people knew. Part of her couldn't help being flattered that he cared to learn so much about her.

Wolf must have told him. She tipped up her chin. "I don't have a pair of spectacles with me. But I assure you, Captain, that I am well able to manage your horse—or any horse—without them."

He regarded her with a look of infuriating male superiority. "Possibly, but you will not be testing that theory on any of my animals."

"Are you saying that I won't be able to ride in Scotland, either, unless I wear spectacles?"

"That is exactly what I'm saying."

The notion that she would have to give up riding for at least five months was so horrifying that Edie couldn't find words to respond.

Perversely, now that Gilbride had said she couldn't ride, Mamma started arguing the opposite. She stated that any daughter of hers was more than capable of controlling a horse without making herself a spectacle. Edie was certain her mother wasn't intentionally making a pun, but that didn't stop Gilbride from laughing.

The discussion, sadly, went even further downhill from there.

Chapter Five

Alec rose from the dining table as Lady Reese came to her feet.

"If you'll excuse me, Captain," her ladyship said, "I intend to retire. I find myself quite fatigued."

"It's not even seven o'clock," Edie said, peering up at her mother. "You never go to bed this early. If you're not careful, I'll begin to think you're turning into a complete bumpkin."

Edie was squinting again, her vision obviously challenged by the shadows and the flickering light in the low-ceilinged, private dining room of the inn. Although the squint made her nose crinkle in an adorable fashion, Alec couldn't understand why the girl was so stubborn about spectacles. He thought it demented to go through life with a needless handicap, but Lady Reese had obviously convinced her fashionable daughter that spectacles would turn her into a fusty old spinster.

It was foolish, but revealed an interesting chink in Edie's relentlessly self-confident armor—one that he thought spoke more to a sense of vulnerability than to self-conceit. Despite her occasionally brash behavior, she was a sweet and kind person, surprisingly without airs or arrogance considering her popularity in the *ton*.

Since that popularity had recently been blasted to smithereens, he suspected she feared donning spectacles would make her position even more precarious. He'd done his best to convince her that safety took precedence over vanity, holding out the lure of riding his prized stallion, but Edie had held firm. Alec had a great deal of respect for the girl's ability to navigate through the world, but she was sailing into unknown territory. It was up to him to keep her safe, even if that meant saying no to her.

Naturally, given that anyone rarely said no to her, his unyielding position made for a frosty few days in the carriage, with both Edie and her mother scowling at him. But at least Edie was no longer looking like her world had come to an end. She'd been an emotional wreck the day they'd left London, and it had practically killed Alec to see her so wretched. If irritation with him cheered her up, he was happy to serve as a distraction from her woes.

Still, he'd need Edie's help once they arrived at Blairgal Castle, which meant he had to get on her good side by then. Yes, he was a manipulative bastard and his plans for her were a tad ruthless, but he was convinced that Edie needed someone to take care of her. Every moment he spent in her company told him that he was exactly the right man for the job.

Indeed, he was looking forward to taking up that role with a degree of sexual anticipation that he could barely keep under control.

"No one could ever mistake either of us for country bumpkins," her mother replied to her daughter's jesting comment. "But I do find myself with something of a headache. The roads today were very bad."

She directed a disapproving glare at Alec, as if the state of the roads were entirely his fault.

"Yes, my bottom is quite sore from all that bouncing around," Edie said.

"Eden Whitney, you will refrain from referring to body parts in polite company," her mother exclaimed. "Although I consider Captain Gilbride to be part of the family, there is no excuse for such vulgarity."

Although Alec suspected that Edie's forthright remarks had more to do with the two large glasses of wine she'd had with dinner, he refrained from comment. In fact, it was taking a mighty exercise of discipline to prevent images of Edie's naked bottom from swarming into his brain. He'd spent a good deal of time watching that portion of her anatomy as it swayed its way in and out of various coaching inns or hiked up near his face as he helped her into the carriage. Even more distracting was the bounce of her breasts whenever a wheel hit a particularly egregious pothole. Alec had found himself almost wishing for bad roads, if for no other reason than to watch Edie's lush bosom move so deliciously under the trim-fitting bodice of her spencer.

She gave her mother a sheepish smile. "Sorry, Mamma. I don't know what came over me. I suppose I'm a bit tired, as well."

"Then I suggest you retire soon, too," her mother said. "No doubt we will be making our usual early start."

Clearly, Lady Reese wasn't happy about the fact that Alec had them on the road by seven-thirty each morning. Still, the old girl gamely took on the challenge, and Edie was too good-natured to kick up a fuss about something that couldn't be helped. As far as traveling companions went, he'd had many complain far more, including fellow officers from his old regiment.

"Can I have anything fetched for you before you retire, Lady Reese?" he asked.

"No, thank you, but I would ask that you not keep Eden up to all hours. My daughter needs her sleep."

"I'm fine, Mamma," her daughter said. "In fact, I was going to ask the captain to take me for a little walk before it got too dark. I could do with some fresh air after being cooped up all day."

When Eden flashed Alec one of her most enchanting smiles, all his senses went on high alert. Trying to charm him meant she was up to something.

This should be interesting.

"I would be delighted," he said politely. There was no point in letting Edie know just how much she affected him. She was the type of girl who would take a hundred miles if you gave her so much as an inch.

Lady Reese regarded him with a thoughtful look. It wasn't the usual perusal from the average matchmaking mamma when confronted with a wealthy, single male under the age of eighty. Rather, it was a look of puzzlement, as if he were a species of animal she couldn't quite identify.

"Very well," her ladyship said, flicking a glance back to her daughter. "I'll send Cora down with your pelisse and bonnet, and she can fetch your things as well, Captain. But don't go too far afield, Eden. We don't want to set any more tongues wagging."

"No, Mamma," Edie said in a long-suffering voice. Alec couldn't blame her, since they weren't likely to stumble upon any disapproving London matrons as they strolled along the streets of a Yorkshire market town.

Lady Reese departed, and Alec sat down to finish his wine. When Edie smiled at him again, he raised a skeptical brow.

"What's wrong?" she said. "Don't you want to go for a walk? Surely you're as tired of sitting in that carriage as I am."

"With two such charming travel companions? How can you even suggest it?"

Her gaze narrowed suspiciously, but then she shrugged. "At least you get to break up the monotony by riding that blasted big horse of yours."

"Miss Whitney, why do I feel like you have an ulterior motive for asking me to escort you?"

"Perhaps because you have an innately suspicious nature?" she said. "I wasn't joking when I said that my . . . er, that I was feeling sore from all that bouncing around. If I have to sit much longer, I'm afraid I'll end up a cripple."

"Then I'd be delighted to take you for a walk. In fact, I was going to suggest it myself."

She eyed him with patent disbelief. "Really? Perhaps I'm starting to grow on you, rather like mold on an old piece of cheese?"

"You *are* looking a little green around the edges, now that you mention it. As if you'd spent too much time in a damp cellar."

"And maybe I was just joking, you idiot," she said.

He laughed at her tone but was spared the necessity of a reply by the entrance of her maid with their gear. While Cora buttoned and tied Edie into her walking attire, Alec shrugged into his coat. One of the inn's maids also came in and started clearing away the dishes from the ample and surprisingly good dinner.

"Did you enjoy your meal?" Alec asked. "The food seems rather better here than some of the other stops along the way."

"And thank God for that, or we'd both have to listen to Mamma's complaints," she said drolly. "I enjoyed it very much, thank you. In fact, I didn't need that lovely trifle at the end of the meal, but I couldn't help myself."

"You and Miss Evie always enjoyed your desserts, even as little girls," Cora said with a fond smile as she fluffed the ribbon on Edie's bonnet. "Cleaned your plates right up, you did."

"Thank you for sharing that fascinating bit of Whitney childhood lore," Edie said. "I'm sure the captain would be thrilled if you shared even more embarrassing details from my private life."

"I could tell him your childhood nickname," Cora said with a twinkle.

Edie snorted. "Go right ahead. I'll just push you off the nearest mountain when we reach the Highlands. No one will ever hear from you again."

Smiling at their banter, Alec ushered Edie down the corridor to the side door of the old coaching inn. The Angel Hotel was a busy stop along the Old North Road. Over a hundred horses were stabled behind the rambling, whitewashed building that held a large number of guest rooms and private parlors in addition to its public rooms. It was the most genteel and expensive establishment in Wetherby and was spared the comings and goings of the Royal Mail, which changed at an inn down the street.

As much as he could, Alec wished to spare Edie and her mother the discomforts of long-distance travel. They were unhappy enough without having to spend their nights on musty sheets, awakened every few minutes by a coachman's horn. Though Alec was spending a pile of blunt to finance this trip, since he'd adamantly refused Lord Reese's generous offer to pay the expenses, it would barely make a dent in his wallet. After he was buried away in the Highlands, there wouldn't be much worth spending his money on anyway.

"It's just one good laugh after another with my family, isn't it?" Edie said wryly as she took his arm and headed into the High. "But Cora doesn't mean to be disrespectful. In fact, I don't know what I would have done if she hadn't agreed to come on this trip. I've grown quite dependent on her, especially since . . ." She trailed off.

"The separation from your sister?" he finished. "It's certainly understandable."

He tucked her close, relishing the feel of her next to him. She was lush, vibrant, and full of energy. No mincing for her, like some pampered lady more concerned with elegance than exercise. Edie had a long, athletic stride that spoke of enthusiasm for physical activity and time spent outdoors. She was built for walking in the Highlands, sturdy and strong. She was not at all a die-away miss, like so many of the girls he'd met in London.

She let out a sigh. "You're very kind, but I know you must be heartily sick of us all. I'm sorry we placed such a weighty burden on you. And I am truly grateful. You didn't deserve to have me, Mamma, and our servants foisted on you for five months."

She was back to sounding anxious. Though Alec enjoyed the occasional glimpse of feminine vulnerability, he disliked it when she sounded so unsure of herself. He'd always admired Edie's confidence and assertive wit, and he hated to think that the events of the last few weeks had eroded those qualities.

He didn't answer immediately as he steered her past the inelegantly named Black Pig Tavern and dodged a small herd of cattle being driven south toward the river. He drew her to a halt in the doorway of a linen draper's shop so they were out of the flow of the still-busy High.

"Why are we stopping?" she asked. "Are you tired of me already?"

Uncharacteristically, her gaze darted away, as if she were suddenly interested in the bolts of fabric in the shop window. When he slid a finger along her jaw, tipping up her chin, she jerked a bit, her blue eyes widening. Her gaze was intent and wary, as if she were bracing for something unpleasant.

"Miss Whitney," he said, "I am honored to help you. I want you to be clear about that, and about how much I enjoy your company."

It was the simple truth.

She blinked several times and her pretty mouth rounded into a surprised oval. It looked so lush and tempting that he had to fight the urge to kiss her.

"That's rather unexpected," she said. "I always thought you found me to be a great deal of trouble."

He grinned. "I do, but you're the kind of trouble a man can get used to."

She blushed, but then her mouth curved up into a sly smile. "And what about Mamma? Do you also find her worth the trouble?"

"I wouldn't go that far," he said, as he guided her back onto the street. "Still, she's turned out to be a better traveler than I expected."

"Mamma's tough as old boots. Which is not to say that this winter won't be a challenge." She threw him an assessing glance. "I do hope your grandfather won't be put out by having strangers foisted upon him for an extended visit."

Alec was certain that his grandfather would be very put out. He'd written the earl a brief missive just before their party left London so the old fellow had no opportunity to fire back a refusal. He could only hope that his grandfather would be so happy to see him that he would overlook the two *Sassenach* women invading his stronghold.

"I'm sure it will be fine. Besides, I'm not really giving him any choice."

Her brows lifted. "That isn't very reassuring. What's he going to do—chase us off with a dirk?"

"Don't worry. I'll protect you," he said with a grin.

"It sounds very much like we *will* be a burden," she said with a grimace. "How will I ever be able to repay you?"

Alec could think of several ways, none of them appropriate topics for polite conversation.

"You could start by telling me your childhood nickname," he suggested.

When she stopped dead and stared at him, Alec had to yank her out of the way of a curricle careening toward them. She glanced around, startled, which was another indication of the perils posed by her bad eyesight. He needed to do something about that when they reached Glasgow.

When they were walking again, he prompted her. "Now, about that nickname."

"Are you really going to make me reveal such a gruesome bit of history?"

"You did say you owed me, did you not?"

She let out an exaggerated sigh, but then grinned. "Very well. It was Butterball. I was Butterball one and Evie was Butterball two."

He laughed. "Who saddled you with that?"

"My brother. Mamma was furious, but one couldn't really blame him. We were quite round when we were little, and Mamma loved dressing us in puffy dresses in shades of cream and yellow. I'm sure we greatly resembled something popped out of a butter mold."

She looked perfectly delectable now, with her blue pelisse that was buttoned snugly over her generous breasts and fell softly over her rounded hips and arse. She might have been a rotund little girl, but she'd grown into a luscious woman with a sweet face and generous curves that cried out to be shaped by a man's hands.

"I'm sure you and Evie were simply delightful."

"I'm sure we weren't. In fact, I was always getting us into one scrape after another, probably to counteract the horror of our nickname and our clothing. Sadly, poor Evie took the blame for our exploits, though."

Edie sighed, a genuine one this time. Alec figured she was thinking about her twin and how much she missed her, and he wished he could take her in his arms and cuddle her. But since they were on a public street and since she would probably slap him if she realized what he was thinking, he confined his reaction to a sympathetic silence.

She shook off the memory with a smile. "Where are we going, by the way? Mamma would not countenance gaming hells or dens of iniquity, so I suggest something a little tamer." She peered around at the tidy, gray-stoned shops lining the High. "Not that Wetherby seems to run to debauchery."

"We might find iniquitous behavior in some of the public houses, but let's confine ourselves to a sedate walk to the river. There's an old bridge and a view that might be worth looking at."

"Even Mamma couldn't object to that. In fact, I wonder how we will be able to prevent ourselves from dozing off from boredom."

"I'll do my best to keep you entertained with an agreeable flow of witticisms. As soon as I can think of any."

"Perhaps you can entertain me with your brogue," she said. "I am always vastly amused when you adopt it."

He grinned. "Vastly annoyed, more like it."

"Why do you find it necessary?" she asked, now serious. "I've never understood the purpose of it. You're clearly as well educated as the average male aristocrat—"

"—Which is to say, not very educated at all."

She flashed a quick smile. "Point taken. But I know from Evie that you are indeed educated. You speak French, Spanish, and Portuguese, besides knowing the usual Greek and Latin. Wolf also told me that you're a talented draftsman and a rather good historian. Surely your ridiculous brogue doesn't fool anyone with half a brain."

Alec couldn't repress a flare of satisfaction that she'd made a point of finding out more about him. She might pretend to be disinterested but all indications suggested otherwise.

He gave her a broad wink. "Nae, lassie, ye'll not be winkling all me secrets out of me, now will ye?"

She groaned. "Please, don't even joke. It's like someone scratching fingernails across a chalkboard."

He laughed. "You'd better get used to it, since you'll be hearing it for months."

"Surely not in that horrifically exaggerated manner?"

"You'd be amazed at how effective it can be."

"It's hard to believe. You sound so silly when you do it."

"That's the point. I play to people's assumptions and bigotries. You'd be amazed how many Englishmen—and others—that I was able to put off guard by acting like a big, Scottish oaf."

She winced, probably recalling the times she'd called him a big oaf to his face. "How ghastly of us. Although I will say that your brogue seems to have the opposite effect on the ladies."

"Aye, lassie, that it does," he said, waggling his eyebrows at her.

She let out a reluctant laugh. "Tell me, did you go to Eton?"

"No, but I did have an excellent tutor in my father. He's a noted scholar and was responsible for most of my education."

"That's both convenient and cost-effective."

"My grandfather would agree with you."

"Where did you go to university? Was it Oxford or Cambridge, or did you attend in Edinburgh?"

He glanced at her upturned face, alive with curiosity,

and wondered exactly how much to reveal to her. Since she would find out about his youthful adventures sooner or later he might as well be the one to tell her. That way he could present the information in its most favorable light.

"I never went to university," he said.

"Oh, then I suppose your father tutored you until you joined the army?"

"Not exactly."

She rolled her eyes. "Must you always be so cryptic? I do realize that you're a spy—"

"I *was* a spy."

"Was a spy," she amended. "That surely means that you no longer have to dole out information in dribs and drabs. Why are you being so deliberately obtuse?"

"I'll tell you in a minute," he said.

They were approaching the bridge, which curved out over the river like a humpbacked sea creature. It narrowed down from the road, compressing traffic, and Alec held her back until a phaeton badly driven by a young, clearly jug-bitten buck drove across in their direction. A lumbering mail coach followed, topped by several passengers. When the noise and the dust died down, he led her to the upstream side of the bridge.

They propped their elbows on the parapet and gazed at the river swirling below them. A manor house in a faded shade of yellow with an incongruously cheery red roof graced the north bank. In the meadow running along the other bank rested a herd of shaggy Highland cattle, no doubt headed south to the London markets. It was a peaceful, bucolic scene that Alec found boring as hell—probably because it reminded him of what would be awaiting him back home. As far as he was concerned, the only point of interest in the bloody town stood beside him.

"It's very pretty," Edie said. "Or at least I think it is. It's a bit hard for me to tell in the fading light. But I love the sound of the water rushing over the weir."

"Why in God's name do you insist on going through life half-blind?" Alec asked. "Do you not want to see what's going on around you?"

She flicked away his comment with an impatient hand. "I will admit that having the eyesight of a mole is occasionally inconvenient, but I have no desire to discuss the issue with you any more than I already have. Now, it's time for you to answer *my* question, is it not?"

He turned his back on the river, resting both his elbows on the parapet. She adopted the same pose.

"I didn't go to school because I ran away from home when I was sixteen," he said. "And I didn't join the army for another two years."

Her eyes popped comically wide as she stared at him. "You did what?"

"I said I ran away from home. I didn't realize you had trouble with your hearing as well as your vision."

She flapped a hand again. "There's no reason to get testy about it. Goodness, I can't imagine many boys in your position doing something so outrageous. Why did you?"

This was the tricky part. "Because my grandfather wanted me to do something I didn't want to do," Alec hedged.

She crossed her arms over her bonny chest, waiting for more. When he didn't supply it, she shook her head with exasperation. "That's it? The sum total of why you ran away from the only home you'd ever known?"

He raised his hands as if to say, *What else could there be?*

"You are so annoying," she muttered. "If you won't tell me why, perhaps you'll tell me where you ran."

"London first. From there I managed to find my way to

Naples, and then on to Greece and eventually Persia with the British Consul."

His words had Edie jerking upright. "Truly? You've been to Greece?"

"I have indeed."

"I've always wanted to go to Greece. You simply must tell me all about it." Her pretty face glowed with excitement.

Alec wanted to capture her lips in a devouring kiss, drinking in her energy and zest for life. "It was rather dusty and exceedingly hot. You'd hate it."

She wrinkled her nose at him. "I do tend to wilt in the heat. I suppose Evie told you that. But I still wish I could see Greece someday."

He smiled at her. "Perhaps you will."

He'd loved those two years, though the work had sometimes been backbreaking and the conditions primitive. For the first time in his life he'd been on his own, doing what he wanted to do and not what his grandfather wanted for him. That adventure of a lifetime had only ended when duty had called him to join the army. But where one adventure had ended, another had begun. He'd never imagined himself leading the life of a spy, but the dangers and the challenges had suited him perfectly.

"And from there you went into the army, I suppose," Edie said. "Is that where you met Wolf?"

"Yes, he and I worked together on most of our missions. Almost seven years as partners and friends." More than that—they were family, related both by blood and the unusual circumstances of their births. "Christ, I'll miss that great stupid bastard."

Then he realized what he'd just said. "Forgive my language, Miss Whitney. Feel free to box my ears."

She laid a hand on his forearm. Even through her gloves

and the layers of fabric, he swore he could feel the heat of her touch.

"I understand," she said, her eyes soft with sympathy. "Wolf is like a brother to you."

"Aye, that he is." Then he shrugged, feeling a bit uncomfortable with all this emoting. "But Wolf's on to other things now, as am I. Life goes on."

She absently pushed back a lock of hair that had strayed out from under her bonnet to tickle her cheek. He found himself missing her hand on him.

"And in all those years, you've never gone back to Scotland?" she asked.

He shook his head.

"Why not? Are you still estranged from your family?"

"No, I've seen my father several times in London over the years, and my grandfather and I write to each other regularly."

She started to look frustrated again, obviously because he was once more doling out only bits of information.

"What aren't you telling me?" she asked suspiciously. "I know you don't want to return home. Evie told me. But what exactly are you avoiding?"

Might as well get it over with.

"I'm avoiding my fiancée," he said. "Technically, Miss Whitney, I have been betrothed for the last ten years. That's why I ran away from Scotland in the first place."

Her mouth dropped open and she stared at him for what seemed an eternity. Then she snapped it shut, only to open it again a moment later. "Get out of my way, you great Scottish oaf."

She shoved past him and stomped her way back up the High.

Chapter Six

"Are you sure you're not feeling better, Mamma?" Edie asked. "After all, you've spent the last three days in bed. The physician thinks you're coming along quite splendidly."

Mamma rarely fell ill, but when she did she did so with style, taking to her bed with dramatic pronouncements and availing herself of a steady diet of medicinal cordials and powders. Edie had always suspected it was a temporary retreat from the pressures of her position as one of the premier hostesses of the *ton*. Though Lady Reese might not have the wealth and political influence of the leading doyennes, she made up for it with sheer stubborn will and a canny knack for toadying up to those who could do her the most good.

Edie knew that Mamma's ambitions were not for herself but for her children. She wanted all of them to make a better marriage than she'd had, moving up into the higher levels of the British aristocracy. Though Papa was the best and kindest of men, to Mamma he was little better than a country squire, happy to be puttering around his orchards and visiting with the tenant farmers. His lack of ambition for his family drove his wife absolutely demented.

She leaned against the carved oak bedpost and gave her mother an encouraging smile. "Dr. Grant thought you'd be well enough to travel tomorrow, since we have only one day's drive to Blairgal Castle."

Her mother glared back at her from a huge mound of pillows. "Eden, I did not ask to catch a severe cold. But that is the result of spending over a week on the road and being forced to tolerate one damp inn after another. I can only be grateful that we reached Lord Riddick's manor house before I succumbed to illness." She vigorously blew her nose into her handkerchief, as if to punctuate the statement.

Their last few days on the road had indeed been damp and cold, with a steady drizzle that had intensified the farther north they traveled. By the time they'd reached one of Lord Riddick's secondary estates in a village just outside Glasgow, Edie had been as glad as her mother to get off the road. Mamma had immediately retreated to her bed, leaving Edie with nothing to do but kick up her heels and avoid Captain Gilbride as much as possible.

That had been a challenge. She'd taken most of her meals with her mother in her lovely suite of guest rooms or retreated to her own pretty and very spacious bedroom when Mamma wished to rest. The past three days had been lethally boring, but enduring boredom was preferable to spending the rest of her life in Newgate on a murder charge. That would surely be the result if she spent time in the company of Alasdair Gilbride—the sneakiest, most frustrating man she'd ever met.

Edie flashed her mother an apologetic smile. "I know, darling, and I'm a perfect beast to nag you when you're not feeling well. Shall I fetch you another cup of tea?"

"Oh, I suppose so. And why don't you bring me one of those scones as well. I must say, the food has been quite acceptable and the staff very helpful, even though the earl isn't in residence. I can only hope Blairgal Castle is as comfortable as Breadie Manor."

"Blairgal is a very old castle, Mamma," Edie said as she took her mother's cup. "It will likely be dreary and damp and full of drafts."

"I cannot believe it. The earl is an exceedingly wealthy man. I'm sure everything will be just as it should be."

Edie cast her mother an assessing glance as she assembled a plate of treats. She recognized Mamma's expression—the one she wore when attempting to calculate the size of a man's fortune. She couldn't avoid the subject any longer, but she was so confused about her own feelings regarding Gilbride that she dreaded even discussing it.

"Mamma, I do hope you're not planning to throw me at Captain Gilbride. He's not the least bit interested in me."

"Eden, there is no need to express yourself in so vulgar a manner. I was simply remarking on Lord Riddick's superior domestic arrangements. Breadie Manor is quite a snug little seat, don't you find?"

"Nice try, Mamma," Edie said, carrying back the teacup. "But I know what you're up to. You've fired off two of your children in fairly splendid style, and now you're thinking of adding a rich Scottish earl to the family rolls."

Mamma grimaced as she took her cup. "You make me sound horridly mercenary. Is there anything wrong with wanting to see my beloved child happy and established? You're not getting any younger, my dear, and with recent events . . . well, we don't want to see you ending up on the shelf."

Edie fussed with arranging the plate on the bedside table. Her mother had never worried about her age or prospects before, but the *fatal incident* had clearly rattled her. And, in truth, it had rattled Edie, too.

"The captain is a very attractive and charming man,"

her mother added, "although he does have a rather odd sense of humor. That aside, I cannot find any objection to him. And," she said, peering at Edie over the rim of her cup, "I'm quite certain he's attracted to you."

"Trust me, Mamma, he's not."

Her mother stared at her for a few seconds before a look of foreboding came over her face. "How did you ascertain that fact? Don't tell me you tried to kiss him, or . . . or . . ."

Edie propped her hands on her hips. "Do you really think I would do anything that stupid after what just happened? Besides, I wouldn't flirt with that man if he was the last bachelor in England."

"Really, my dear, how can you be so ridiculous? Captain Gilbride is one of the most eligible men on the marriage mart. You know you find him handsome."

Edie turned her back and paced to the fireplace, the thick carpet muffling her footfalls. She stared up at the Roman motif that adorned the wall over the mantel. The painted scene was of a sleeping nymph surrounded by cherubs, framed by plaster swags and ribbons ornamented in gilt. A toga-garbed man gazed down on the sleeping nymph with a decidedly mawkish expression.

"Come here, Eden," her mother said in a determined voice.

Edie sighed, dreading yet another in a long string of humiliating conversations. Turning away from the nymph and her sentimental attendants, she trudged back.

Her mother patted the mattress. "Sit next to me, my love."

"Mamma—"

"Eden, sit."

She sat. Normally, Edie could run rings around her parents and everyone else in the Reese household, but occasionally Mamma stopped thinking about herself long enough to focus on her maternal instincts. Apparently, she was doing so right now.

"Tell me why you're upset with Captain Gilbride. And please don't pretend that you're not."

"He's betrothed, Mamma. He's been promised for ten years. Apparently ever since he left Scotland."

Her mother's eyebrows crawled up her forehead. "Where did you hear this?"

"He told me when we went for that walk after dinner the other night."

Mamma's expression grew tight, her skin seeming to stretch over her cheekbones. "I cannot believe it. I've heard nothing about this."

Edie wanted to slap herself in the head. "Mamma, did you concoct this mad scheme to spend the winter in Scotland because you thought Gilbride might wish to marry me?"

Her mother looked guilty for a moment but quickly recovered. "Of course not. William was the one who convinced your father and me that it was the best way to handle the situation. Surely you can't believe your brother-in-law would play matchmaker?"

"No, but I can believe you would."

Her mother looked down her elegant, slightly reddened nose. "I will make no apologies for the fact that I wish to see my children with partners worthy of them."

"Of course not."

Her mother was too rattled by the news to pick up Edie's sarcasm. "I don't understand why William wouldn't mention this to me and your father. I'm most displeased he didn't."

Edie shrugged, affecting an indifferent air. "It hardly matters, since I don't even like Gilbride. I know you have a soft spot for him, Mamma, or at least for his money—"

"Eden, really!"

"—But I can't imagine marrying him in a thousand years. He's a most annoying person and I'm sure we wouldn't suit."

"But—"

"He's engaged, Mamma," she said firmly. "There's nothing to be done about it."

Mamma's bottom lip thrust out like a fretful child's. Clearly, she had been cherishing ideas about Gilbride, and now they were looking at a long winter in the middle of nowhere with nothing to show for it. She could almost dredge up some sympathy for her mother's thwarted plans.

"Did he tell you why he kept his betrothal a secret?" Mamma asked. "It seems odd."

"I didn't ask him, since I didn't think it was any of my business."

Mamma let out a small snort. "Such scruples never stopped you before."

Edie flashed her a rueful grin. "I will admit that I was so annoyed by the way he told me that I stomped off in something of a huff. Honestly, how could a man hide something like that? When I think of all the girls he flirted with, and so shamelessly, too . . ." She bit her lip, annoyed that she was starting to sound jealous.

Her mother studied her for a few uncomfortable moments, then she shrugged. "Well, I suppose there's little point in thinking about it. We should simply be grateful we can avail ourselves of the Earl of Riddick's hospitality until your unfortunate contretemps with Sir Malcolm ceases to be a topic of gossip. When we return in the spring, we must hope that everything has returned to normal."

"I'm sure that will be the case, Mamma."

In the meantime, Edie would simply have to do her best to survive the winter without throttling one very irritating Scotsman. Gilbride would no doubt be married shortly after they arrived at Blairgal Castle, and the notion of being cooped up for months with him and his new wife was truly depressing.

After a light tap on the door, Mamma's dresser slipped into the room with a pitcher and glass. "Begging your pardon, your ladyship. I have some nice barley water fresh from the kitchen."

"Really, Davis, *nice* and *barley water* do not belong in the same sentence," Edie said.

"Miss Eden," Davis said, ignoring the lame attempt at humor, "you're to meet Captain Gilbride in the entrance hall in fifteen minutes. He says to be sure to dress warmly, since he'll be taking you for a drive around the estate."

Surprised, Edie practically slid off the bed. "What? I never said I would go driving with him."

"He seems to think you did," the dresser replied. "Now, her ladyship needs her rest, and you need to get your pelisse and bonnet."

Edie scowled. "Fine, I'll leave Mamma alone, but I have no intention of going anywhere with that blasted Scotsman."

"Eden, Captain Gilbride obviously wants to do something nice for you," Mamma said in a coaxing voice. "I see no harm in a little outing with him."

Edie eyed her mother's suspiciously bland expression. "What are you about, Mamma?"

"I simply think it ridiculous for you to hide yourself away like this. I'm going to take a nap, so you might as well spend a little time with our host."

"Have you forgotten that he's betrothed?"

"If so, then you have nothing to fear, do you?" her mother said as she took the glass from Davis. "The captain is a man of honor and, as you've pointed out on more than one occasion, he's practically a member of the family."

Eden propped her hands on her hips. "You're the one

who keeps pointing that out, not me. You know very well that I shouldn't be going off alone with him."

Her mother starched up. "What nonsense. There is nothing wrong with taking a little afternoon drive with your host, who is extending us a great deal of courtesy. You will go to your room and get your things, and then you will meet the captain downstairs."

"But—"

Mamma pointed an imperious finger at the door. "Go."

Edie stared at her mother in disbelief, but realized there was no point in debating the issue. When Mamma issued an order in that tone of voice, no one could change her mind. Muttering a few choice oaths under her breath, she marched out of the room and down the hall to her bedroom, where Cora was waiting. Edie silently fumed while her maid stuffed her into her pelisse and arranged her bonnet. Then she snatched up her gloves from the dressing table and stalked to the door.

"You be nice to the captain, Miss Edie," Cora said. "Don't be stomping about and scowling like an old biddy."

Edie turned and looked at her maid, who had an expression dangerously like a smirk on her face.

"You are all deranged," she said before slamming the door behind her. Edie distinctly heard the sound of laughter echoing from behind the oak panels. And she did, in fact, want to stomp down the hall, but she took a deep breath and forced herself to calm down.

As she came down the elegant cantilevered staircase, one of the doors off the entrance hall opened and Gilbride strode out. When he looked up and smiled, Edie almost missed a step. That charming smile did something peculiar to her insides, something fluttery and warm. It was an unfamiliar sensation and her mental jury had yet to rule on whether she approved of it or not.

"Good morning, Miss Whitney," he said in a friendly

voice. Much too friendly considering that the last time they'd exchanged more than two words she'd called him a great Scottish oaf. She still winced thinking about it.

His smoky gray gaze drifted over her figure, lingering with an appreciation that made her blink in surprise.

"You're looking particularly lovely today," he said as he handed her down the final step. "I count myself fortunate to have you join me this morning. It's been an age since we spent any time together."

And now he was back to teasing her, drat him. He knew very well she'd been avoiding him, and he clearly wanted her to realize that he knew. But she refused to play that game.

"Mamma hasn't been well, the poor dear. She simply wouldn't let me leave her side for a moment." She punctuated that canard with a melancholy smile meant to communicate how trying the last few days had been. With any of her suitors, it would have brought them to their knees with abject apologies.

Gilbride, however, was made of sterner stuff.

He leaned in close, towering over her, and his eyes gleamed with a wicked intent that promised things she couldn't even begin to name. Edie resisted the impulse to retreat because she never took a step back from any man. To do so would be a fatal show of weakness.

Besides, he was only pretending to flirt so as to annoy her.

"Ah, lassie, you can't fool me," he said, that seductive Scottish burr roughening his voice. It dragged across her nerves, making her shiver. "I'm not one of those manmilliners you lead around by the nose like docile geldings. I know very well you've been avoiding me."

She placed a hand on his brawny chest and gave him a shove. He stepped back, not because she could move him on her own—the man was a proverbial mountain—but because she'd obviously surprised him.

"I do not lead anybody around by the nose, and please desist using that absurd brogue. It makes you sound like an actor in a second-rate touring company performance of *Macbeth*."

He looked stunned for a second then let out a deep laugh. If the brogue made her shiver, the laugh was even worse. She almost hoped she was coming down with her mother's cold.

"Miss Whitney, if you think my brogue is heavy, I doubt you'll be able to understand anyone at Blairgal."

"That will be something to look forward to, won't it? Although I must say that so far I haven't had any trouble understanding the staff here at Breadie Manor."

He took her elbow and led her across the entrance hall to the front door, where a footman in livery sprang to open it. Even though Edie had teased her mother about the kilts and the bearskins, she'd been a tad surprised to encounter such superbly trained servants, decked out in the finest livery. They wouldn't be out of place at Carlton House.

Truthfully, she'd been rather hoping for kilts and tartans, or someone who spouted at least a few lines from *Marmion* or *The Lady of the Lake*.

They stepped out to the marble porch that fronted the house. "The staff here are mostly Lowlanders or from Glasgow," Gilbride explained. "You've yet to encounter any true Highlanders."

She glanced behind her at the Palladian-style house. It certainly didn't fit with how she'd imagined the Earl of Riddick's Scottish holdings. *Elegant* described everything about the residence, with its classic exterior lines in creamy stone. Inside, its curved walls and ceiling domes were adorned with beautiful plasterwork in pale greens and pinks, trimmed in gold. If Edie didn't miss her guess, the interior had been designed by one of the Adams Brothers, with all the taste and polished beauty for which they were renowned.

"Breadie Manor is beautiful," she said. "And very modern. Nothing like I expected from a Scottish mansion."

"I suppose you were expecting moats, turrets, and ghostly bagpipes sounding from the towers. Alas, Miss Whitney, not every manor house in Scotland is a castle. This house, for instance, was built only forty years ago."

She sighed dramatically. "How disappointing. I was so hoping for at least one bagpipe-wielding ghost. But I admit I'm enjoying chimneys that don't smoke and bedrooms that aren't drafty. Did your grandfather build it?"

"Yes," Gilbride said.

"Does he spend much time here?"

"He does have a fair bit of business in Glasgow. When he attends to it, he prefers to stay here rather than in the city, which he claims is dirty and only inhabited by packs of thieving merchants. Which, of course, doesn't stop him from doing business with those merchants," he added in a sardonic voice. "My grandfather may be old-fashioned when it comes to his views on family and the clan, but he's bloody good at running his estates and managing his investments. He's a canny Scot, if there ever was one."

"He doesn't sound nearly romantic enough for me, and I know Mamma will be cruelly disappointed. She's been imagining tableaus with Rob Roy and Robert the Bruce for days."

He laughed. "I promise you romance and gloomy castles aplenty, starting today."

Edie made a great show of peering around at the neat grounds surrounding Breadie Manor. Except for the hills she could make out in the distance, she might have been on a prosperous estate in the Hampshire or Kentish countryside.

"Really?" she said. "Are you going to conjure romance out of thin air?"

As soon as the words passed her lips, she realized her mistake. Gilbride took her hand, briefly entwining her fingers in his before settling it into the crook of his arm.

"If you give me half a chance, I certainly will," he said in his deliciously deep voice.

He's betrothed, you idiot. He's just teasing you.

Edie adopted one of her mother's tricks—an exaggerated lift of the eyebrows to signal polite incredulity. "Indeed. And are you also going to conjure a castle?"

One corner of his mouth lifted in a wry, knowing smile as he accepted her little dodge.

"As a matter of fact, I am." He urged her along the graveled drive toward the north corner of the house. "I thought at first to simply take you around the estate, but seeing as it's a sunny day—something not to be taken for granted in Scotland—I thought I would drive you to Mugdock Castle. It's not far, and the views of the fells are rather spectacular."

"Oh," she said weakly. It was one thing to go for a walk or a drive around the estate, but to go off with him on a longer outing felt much too . . . intimate.

"I don't know if I should leave Mamma that long," she said.

He drew her to a halt in the shelter of an archway that led back to the stable yard. He propped one hand on the brick wall as he gazed down at her, tall and formidably masculine, looming over her with easy assurance. She had to struggle against the sensations that weakened her knees and quickened her breath.

"Your mother is in good hands," he said in a quiet voice. "She can spare you for a few hours."

"Well . . ."

"Miss Whitney, we both know you've been avoiding me, and we both know why," he said in an uncharacteristically serious voice. "I sprang some unexpected news on you, and I apologize for my stupid and clumsy manner in doing so. You and your mother had every right to know my status, and I should have informed you of it before we left London."

Edie took refuge behind a polite manner. "Your business is your own, Captain Gilbride. You don't owe us any explanation. In fact, I don't know why you think I would even care about your status."

"You seemed to care a great deal the other night, when you called me a great Scottish oaf and stomped away from me. And you've barely uttered two words to me since."

Edie thrust her chin forward. "Perhaps I simply had nothing to say," she said in a lofty tone.

He looked incredulous. "You always have something to say, at least to me, but you've been doing your level best to freeze me out since our discussion. If you have no interest in my situation, why are you treating me like a blasted pariah?"

Her temper finally flared. "Because you've been acting like a bounder, flirting with every woman under the age of eighty while pretending you're the most eligible bachelor in London. Do you know how many girls have been standing on their heads to get your attention? You've been leading them on in the worst possible way, and now I discover that you have a fiancée!"

His eyes narrowed with irritation. "Until a short time ago, as you will recall, I was engaged in preventing a deadly conspiracy and keeping your sister from getting murdered. When would I have had time to carry on all those flirtations?"

Edie fumed. It was true that he'd been absorbed by his

spy work until recently, but that didn't excuse his behavior since the danger passed.

"And we're all grateful for your efforts, but that was weeks ago. You've had plenty of opportunity to make your situation known since then. By the way," she said, suddenly recalling a comment by her mother, "Wolf does know about your betrothal, doesn't he? I know you're both in the habit of skulking around and lying about things, but you're no longer in the Intelligence Service. You might try acting in a normal fashion for once instead of pulling the wool over everyone's eyes."

Gilbride straightened away from her. "Wolf doesn't know either."

That was a stunner. "Why would you keep something like that from your best friend?"

He studied her for a few moments before answering. "I'll explain, but first I'd like to apologize for my behavior the other night. I was an idiot, and I'm sorry."

She must have looked skeptical, because he let out a rueful laugh. "Clearly an apology isn't enough. Fortunately, I have come prepared with a gift."

Edie was beginning to feel embarrassed. The conversation was so odd she didn't know what to make of it—except for the fact that she still hated that he had a fiancée.

She flapped a careless hand. "Really, Captain, you needn't worry. As I said, your personal life is none of my business."

His firm mouth lifted into a disarming smile that teased her with an almost boyish charm. "I know, but you still deserve a present. And if it makes you feel any better, it's an exceedingly practical one."

Even as she registered another weak protest, he exacted a small object from an inside pocket. He popped open the top of a green leather case and carefully pulled out a pair of gold spectacles, finely wrought and lightweight but with an unusually ornate bridge. They had delicate earpieces and clear, sparkling lenses.

They were beautiful.

"There," he said. "You no longer have to bumble about like a blind mole."

Chapter Seven

Alec watched wrath heat up Edie's sky blue gaze.

"Really? A blind mole?" she asked. "Isn't that redundant, for one thing?"

He winced, both from his verbal blunder and her tone. Her voice was normally warm and full of laughter with an unconsciously husky note that had men slavering around her like lapdogs. She didn't screech, but referring to her as a sightless rodent had certainly altered her pitch.

She propped her gloved hands on her lovely plump hips and glared at him. "Is that how you think of me, Captain Gilbride?"

He'd been so undone by her expression when he showed her the spectacles that he'd blurted out the first idiotic thing that had come into his head. Her pretty face had lit up with an appealing combination of surprise, pleasure, and vulnerability. Perhaps because Edie was not one to show what she would call her weaker side, her look had been like a lethally honed blade to the heart.

"I believe you employed a similar term during a discussion about your eyesight only a few days ago. Surely you remember." He finished with his most charmingly rueful smile. It had never worked on her, but there was always a first time.

She huffed out an exasperated breath. "Oh, very well, but that doesn't mean I want to hear the term thrown back in my face."

"I'm an unthinking cad, and I offer you another abject apology. You couldn't possibly look anything less than delightful, spectacles or not."

She wrinkled her nose. "You are an insufferable coxcomb, but I accept your apology."

"You are all that is gracious and kind, Miss Whitney," he said in a solemn voice.

Edie let out a reluctant laugh. "I'm anything but, as is evident from the fact that I'm not jumping all over you in gratitude for such a generous gift."

Alec would certainly relish her jumping all over him. "Are you not pleased with it?" he asked, trying to banish the image of a naked Edie bouncing around in bed with him.

"It's much too generous. It wouldn't be right for me to accept."

"Nonsense. It's more of a practical matter than a gift. A necessary tool to keep you safe. If you can see correctly, then you'll be able to ride again, and drive my curricle, if you wish."

She longingly eyed the gold frames. "That would be lovely, but . . ."

"Try them on," he coaxed.

Her mouth curled up in a wry smile. "Blast you, you've discovered my weak spot."

"Which is?"

"I'm incurably vain."

He laughed. "I see, but think of it this way. You're a stranger in Scotland, so you don't have to worry about the petty censures of the *ton*. And I assure you that no one at

Blairgal Castle will care one whit. In fact, you wouldn't be the only person there to don spectacles."

"Are any of them under the age of fifty?" she asked drily.

He hesitated.

"I thought not," she said. "I know it's dreadful to be so conceited, but you have no idea how merciless people can be about a female's appearance. Most girls I know would rather fall headfirst down the stairs than risk being labeled as a dowd or a bespectacled bluestocking."

"No one would dare characterize you that way. Besides, do you think your sister looks like a dowd? Evie is a lovely girl, and Wolf has never minded her spectacles."

She frowned slightly. "No, he never has."

"So, just try them on."

She studied him for a few moments longer, as if he puzzled her, then shrugged and took the spectacles. Carefully, she settled them on the bridge of her nose. When he slid his hands under her bonnet to adjust the earpieces, brushing her soft cheeks, she blushed. He thought she looked utterly adorable, reminding him of an earnest and rather shy schoolgirl. There was an appealing vulnerability to her at that moment that Alec thoroughly appreciated.

She stared straight ahead across the stable yard, blinking several times as she waited for her vision to adapt. "Good heavens," she said with a laugh. "These are much better than Evie's pair. Where did you get them?"

He took her by the arm and directed her across to the other side of the yard where one of his grooms waited patiently with his curricle and pair. "From a specialist in Glasgow. He's been making my father's and grandfather's spectacles for years."

"Splendid. I'm now on the same footing as your elderly relations, which will thrill Mamma. I might as well say I'm in my dotage and get it over with."

Alec helped Edie into the carriage then climbed in after her. "I'll take care of your mother."

"You do seem to have her wrapped around your little finger." She didn't sound very happy about it.

He nodded to the groom to step back and then guided the pair through the archway leading out to the drive.

"I'm not sure what to make of that remark," he said once they were bowling down the drive. "Do you think your mother will object to my gift? They *were* rather expensive. Shall I send her the bill?"

"Are you mad? Of course Mamma won't object to you spending money on us. I might not approve, but she certainly won't have a problem."

He'd spent the money on *her,* not her mother. "Are you worried she'll deem them too unfashionable and forbid you to wear them?"

She shook her head. "No, she lost that battle ages ago with Evie. If I'd ever wanted to wear them, I would have."

"What worries you then?"

She took her time smoothing out an imaginary wrinkle in her glove. It was an uncharacteristic display of the fidgets.

"You do know why Mamma is so sweet on you, don't you?" she finally said. "I should think you would have figured it out by now."

Though she tossed the comment out in a careless fashion, the color staining her cheeks spoke to her discomfort.

"I expect she thinks she'll bring me up to scratch at some point this winter," he said.

He felt her slight jerk of surprise. After all, her rounded hip and thigh were pressed up against him. It was a wonder he could even concentrate with all that warm, gorgeous flesh so close at hand.

"I'm sorry," she said with a sigh. "It's rather beastly of her to impose on your hospitality on the basis of so false an assumption. I do hope you realize that I certainly didn't encourage her to come to that conclusion."

Which, as far as Alec was concerned, was unfortunate.

"Of course not," he said, "but I'm well familiar with matchmaking mammas. I've met dozens over the years."

"It's gruesome, isn't it?" she said. "And more than slightly embarrassing."

"There's no need for you to feel that way. Your mother loves you and simply wishes the best for you."

"And that would be you, I take it?"

He laughed. "Very well, that did make me sound rather like a coxcomb."

"Surely you jest," she said, exaggerating a tone of disbelief. "No one could possibly think that about you."

"You are a vixen."

"Lord knows I try," she said with an airy wave.

They passed the stone gatehouse and made the turn onto the road that led through the village and to Mugdock Castle.

"So, given your campaign of avoidance these last few days," Alec said, "I take it that your mother insisted you come out for a drive with me today. As part of her long-range plan."

Her shoulders hiked up slightly. "Yes."

"And did you tell her about . . ."

"About your mysterious fiancée?" she said.

He managed not to wince. Barely. "Yes."

"I did, and I can't say she wasn't disappointed," Edie said candidly. "Still, she insisted that I come out with you today, which was rather odd of her. She's usually such a high stickler."

She gave a little shrug and then a wiggle, as if getting comfortable. It had the opposite effect on Alec, since it pushed her thigh more closely against his. Suddenly, his breeches began to feel too tight.

"But she obviously wasn't this time," Alec said, trying to ignore his body's inconvenient reaction.

"She seems to think my reputation is safe precisely because you are betrothed." She frowned. "That doesn't make any sense since I'm not the one betrothed to you."

Ah. Clearly, Edie's mamma had not yet given up when it came to his status as a potential husband for her daughter.

It was nice to have at least one ally in the fight.

"Oh, well," Alec said. "She probably looks on me rather like family. Just think of me as a cousin or some other annoying family relation."

"No, thank you. I have plenty of those without adding you to the mix." She was silent for a few minutes, deep in thought as they trotted through the village of Milngavie and then started up the long hill to Mugdock Castle. Then she slid him a sideways glance. "May I ask you a question?"

"Anything you wish."

She let out a short laugh that held little amusement. "You may regret that."

"Let's see."

"Why have you kept your betrothal a secret from even your closest friends? Is your fiancée a madwoman, or does she squint or have a hunchback, like some character from a lurid novel?"

She tried to make a joke out of it, but Alec wasn't fooled. Edie was still upset with him for what she clearly saw as a deliberate attempt to mislead her and everyone else. And he'd better not make a botch of explaining it this time—not when he needed her help to free him of the anchor that had weighed on him for ten years.

He braced his foot against the dash, affecting a relaxed attitude. For his plan to work, he'd have to bring her along by easy degrees, not spring everything on her at once.

"The short answer would be to say that it's an arranged match. One that I never agreed to in the first place."

She'd been gazing out at the countryside—no doubt struck by how clear and vibrant everything appeared now that she could actually see—but his answer brought her head whipping around. She stared up at him, her eyes wide behind her new spectacles. "Good Lord. Do people still really do that sort of thing?"

"They do in the Highlands," he said grimly.

"Your grandfather's doing, I suppose?"

"Who else? I didn't know until I was older, but he'd been planning it from the time I was barely out of leading strings. Probably within days of Donella being born."

"Is that your betrothed's name?"

"Yes, Donella Haddon, my second cousin. I've known her all my life, since the family grew up only a few miles from Blairgal Castle. Her brother, Fergus, is now my grandfather's estate steward."

He glanced at her to gauge her reaction. She was staring straight ahead with a frown that indicated some confusion.

"You wish to ask something but are afraid of giving offense," he said.

She gave him a rueful grin. "Oh, blast, is it that obvious?"

"I've spent a great deal of time thinking about the subject, so I'm keenly aware of its many odd aspects," he said.

He was also learning to read Edie very well. Reading people was a necessary skill in the spy game. She wasn't an adversary of course, but she'd run him around in circles if he didn't stay a step ahead of her.

She gnawed on her plump lower lip, as if still struggling with a reluctance to satisfy her curiosity.

"Miss Whitney, you need not be reticent with me." He flashed her a quick grin. "You haven't held back on me before, and I wouldn't know what to do with you if you began now."

She burst into laughter. "What a wretchedly back-handed compliment that was. Very well, I'll be brutally frank."

"As I hope you always will be."

"Hmm, I doubt that. Then again, there's probably very little I could say to offend you, given your thick hide."

"You wound me, Miss Whitney. I assure you that my heart beats with all the ardent sensibility and delicacy of a poet. Lord Byron has nothing on me."

"There's nothing delicate about Byron, and you know it. Now, stop trying to distract me."

"I stand corrected. Fire away."

"Your grandfather holds one of the oldest and most distinguished titles in Scotland, correct?"

Alec kept his eyes on the narrow road that snaked up the hill leading to the castle. "Yes, it's an ancient title in both England and Scotland."

"And it's a well-endowed title from what I understand," she added.

Clearly, she—or her mother—had been asking questions about him. "Yes, although our estates aren't as extensive as some other Scottish titles. We do have a hunting lodge on Loch Venachar, but most of our principal holdings are between Loch Lomond and Loch Katrine. It's good land, and we pull a prime income in the linen trade and cattle." He threw her a sideways grin. "We distill some of the best scotch in the Highlands, too."

"How lucky for you," she said with a smile. "So, your wealthy and distinguished family holds one of the oldest titles in the land."

"Correct."

"And does your betrothed also come from such a family?"

"Hardly. If she did, my cousin wouldn't be working as an estate steward."

Her pretty features once more adopted a thoughtful frown. "That's what I thought. So I take it that Miss Haddon will not bring a large dowry to the match."

"There won't be a match, if I have anything to say about it," Alec said in a grim tone. "But to answer your question, her dowry would be negligible."

She twisted sideways in her seat to stare at him. "You truly don't want to marry Miss Haddon?"

"That I never wanted to marry Donella would surprise no one, including her. I told my grandfather that as soon as he made his plans known to me."

She shook her head. "Then why is he so set on it? It hardly seems like an advantageous match. Surely you could do much better."

She clamped her lips shut, clearly annoyed to have revealed that she thought him a good catch. When he cast her a teasing grin, she held up a hand to cut him off.

"Despite your perfectly dreadful personality," she added. "But you know what I mean. It was ridiculous how many well-dowered girls in London were panting after you."

"Ridiculous, eh?" he asked. If he didn't miss his guess, Miss Eden Whitney sounded jealous. "You don't approve of my ability to charm the fair ladies of the *ton?*"

"You are the least charming man I've ever met. But you're rich and heir to an earldom, and not *entirely* horrible to look at. So, it's no wonder you had so many girls swooning over you. That does not excuse, however, your disgraceful tendency to encourage women to dangle after you."

"I never once encouraged any woman to dangle after

me," he protested. Except for her, and it was too bad she'd always resisted his bait. "And, I repeat, I have no intention of going through with a farce of a marriage."

She waved an irritated hand. "We'll get to that in a moment. I'm still curious to know why your grandfather is so determined that you marry your cousin. Did he make some sort of deathbed promise about it?" she said sarcastically.

"Actually, he did."

"You must be joking. Who does that sort of thing anymore?"

"Highlanders do."

She didn't speak for a few moments. "It sounds barbaric, if you ask me," she finally said.

"What you don't understand is how important familial bonds are within the Scottish clans. My family is a member of Clan Graham, as is Donella's. In fact, Donella's uncle is chief of one of the oldest cadet branches in the clan. Not only did Donella's father wish her to marry me—a wish reiterated on his deathbed—her uncle also wants her wedded to the heir of the laird. As a loyal member of the clan, my grandfather chose to agree." Alec couldn't hold back a grimace. "My grandfather might be a peer of the realm and a canny businessman to boot, but when it comes to clan business he's as old-fashioned as they come. He thinks it's a grand idea to strengthen the family bonds within the clan. The old ways are the best, as he's fond of saying."

"But you're not a Graham," Edie protested. "And neither is your grandfather, since his name is Callum Frances Haddon, Seventh Earl of Riddick. And you're a Gilbride, so how can he—or you—be a member of Clan Graham?"

She *had* been doing her homework on him. It seemed Edie was more interested in him than she liked to let on.

"The Haddons are what's known as a sept family," he

said. "Those are families who have chosen to swear fealty to a particular clan. The Haddons took an oath of loyalty centuries ago to the Montrose family, which heads Clan Graham. And, of course, there have been marriages between Grahams and Haddons over the centuries. The bonds run deep."

She frowned. "I thought you said Miss Graham's uncle was the head of the clan."

"Of one of the *cadet* branches of the family, of which there are several. The head of the entire clan is James Graham, the current Duke of Montrose. In fact, Mugdock Castle, which is just on the other side of those woods"— he broke off to nod at the road ahead, which ran up to a thick stand of trees—"is the historic seat of Clan Graham. That's one of the reasons I wished you to see it."

She glanced ahead at the large hill, encircled by a moor on the lower reaches and covered by woods higher up. Mugdock sat on top, still hidden by trees and the rise of the hill.

"It's beautiful," she said, casting him a quick smile. "And I can actually see it."

"The view from the castle is even better."

She gave her head a small shake and then focused her attention back on him. "So, the duke is the head of your clan, but Miss Haddon's uncle is a branch chief, a lesser position."

He nodded. "The clans all have cadet branches, and each has its chief. For instance, there are the Montrose Grahams, the main branch, but there are also the Fintry and Claverhouse Grahams, the Menteith Grahams, and the Inchbrakie Grahams. Then there are dozens of sept families, too. Oh," he added with a wicked smile, "don't forget all the different spellings of the name Graham. All those families belong to the clan, as well."

"Good Lord. How do you keep it straight?"

"It's no more complicated than the British aristocracy. All one has to do is look through Debrett's to understand that."

"Perhaps, but let's stick with the Scots for now. You called your grandfather the laird, did you not?"

He nodded.

"If he's the laird, then why must he do what a chief from a cadet branch wants?"

"The title of laird is more about the designation of a specific estate or land. In earlier centuries, the chief of a Highland clan was called a laird, but now it refers to a member of the Scottish nobility. Not necessarily a clan chief."

"So . . . then the branch chief *can* order your grandfather around?"

"Nobody orders my grandfather around," Alec responded drily. "But Grandfather would certainly want to honor the wishes of the branch chief and show his loyalty to an important member of the clan." He shrugged. "In any case, he has always been in favor of the match for his own reasons. No one had to twist his arm."

Despite her skeptical frown, Alec had no intention of telling her why his grandfather was so adamant. It had as much to do with his deceased mother's misfortunes and his subsequent birth as it did with clan loyalty.

She tilted her head down and studied him over the rim of her glasses. He almost laughed at how perfectly the gesture mirrored her sister's. If Edie started wearing spectacles on a regular basis, no one would be able to tell the twins apart.

Except for him, and Wolf.

"And what about Miss Haddon?" Edie asked. "How does she feel about the situation?"

This was the trickiest part. "I'm not really sure."

She blinked. "How can you not be sure? When was the last time you talked to her?"

"About ten years ago."

She gaped at him. A moment later, when one of the carriage wheels hit a large rut in the road, it almost bounced her from her seat. Alec grabbed her before she went tumbling over the side of the rail.

Edie muttered a few choice words while she straightened her spectacles and then her bonnet. When she finally leveled her gaze on him again, she didn't look any less annoyed.

"Was that when your betrothal was also announced—ten years ago? You were, let me think, sixteen at the time?"

"Yes, and Donella was barely fifteen."

More muttering issued from the lady beside him.

"So, after this betrothal was announced," she said, "you did what? Simply left home?"

"Well, yes." He couldn't help thinking how ridiculous it all sounded.

"Now, after ten years away, the first thing you're going to do on your return home is try to break off the betrothal?"

He shrugged. "I suppose that sums things up."

Now she was outright glaring at him. "And you never thought to tell me or Mamma that we would be walking into the middle of a clan feud?"

Of course he'd thought about it. But if he had told them, he highly doubted they would have agreed to go north. Still, he could hardly reveal that to her.

"Clan feud? We're hardly going to be pulling out dirks and murdering each other." At least he hoped not. "Besides, I thought you said it was none of your business."

"Our very presence in your household will make it our business, you dreadful man," she exclaimed. "By the way, has no one ever told you that only the female can break off a formal engagement? It would be the height of scandal if you did it against her wishes. You would ruin the poor girl's reputation."

Dammit. The last thing Alec needed was Edie's feminine sympathy for Donella. "I have no intention of creating a scandal or ruining my cousin's good name. I'll figure out some way of managing the situation to everyone's satisfaction."

She stared at him like he was an escapee from a madhouse, then went back to muttering under her breath.

He mentally sighed. Like everything else when it came to Edie Whitney, things weren't going exactly according to plan. He needed to settle her ruffled feathers and then bring her around to supporting his plan—a plan entirely dependent on her feelings for him, one way or the other.

If he didn't, he might soon be walking down the aisle with the wrong woman.

Chapter Eight

After Gilbride's confident assessment of the mess he was in, Edie had been forced to wrestle her temper under control. Naturally, her stupid heart had leapt at the news that he didn't want to marry his intended. Still, she was gobsmacked by his insouciant assumption that he could so easily break a longstanding betrothal. From everything he'd described about his family and clan, she doubted it would be easy at all. But the mighty Captain Gilbride, favorite of the *ton,* couldn't imagine not snapping his fingers and getting what he wanted.

Well, she'd been a favorite of the *ton,* too, and look where it had gotten her.

Breaking off a betrothal was serious business. It was rarely done, and especially not by the man. And it sounded like clan loyalties added yet another layer of complexity to the mix. Unless Miss Haddon wanted out of the arrangement *and* was willing to stand up to her relatives, Edie couldn't see how Gilbride was going to manage it—not without acting like a man completely lacking in honor, which he most certainly wasn't.

All things considered, this trip was turning out to be a

disaster. Not only would she and Mamma soon be pitched into the middle of a medieval-sounding clan feud, she also had a bad feeling she would soon be witness to a Scottish wedding.

The curricle had entered a majestic wood, running under a thick cover of enormous oaks. If Edie hadn't been so absorbed by Gilbride's story, she would have been happy to enjoy the scenery. Especially since, for once, she could actually see it.

She surreptitiously touched the delicate yet sturdy frames that fit her so perfectly. Most of the men she knew would be horrified to see her tricked out like a bluestocking, but Gilbride didn't seem to mind in the least. He'd obviously spent a great deal of money on the finely wrought spectacles, and was determined she wear them. It was a truly kind gesture on his part, and since kindness had been lacking in her life as of late, it made the gift even more precious. It was a gift that didn't seem to ask for anything other than a simple *thank you* in return.

"What's she like?" Edie blurted out, suddenly needing to know.

"What's who like?" Gilbride asked rather absently.

"Miss Haddon, of course," she said.

She didn't miss how his gaze narrowed or how his mouth went flat with displeasure. She realized now that by not wearing spectacles, she'd missed so many revealing nuances of expression and manner.

"I hardly remember," he said in a clipped voice.

"But you said you'd grown up with her. Surely you remember something."

He maintained a grim silence.

"Let's start with something simple," she said. "Is she short or tall, dark or fair, slender or—"

"I take your point, Miss Whitney. As I recall, Donella is tall and slender with hair I suppose one would describe as auburn rather than red. She has green eyes, a fair complexion, and was already considered one of the prettiest girls in the county by the time I left."

That didn't sound good. One could only hope she'd grown up to be skinny. If Edie were truly lucky, maybe Miss Haddon had developed a rash of freckles to go along with her hair.

And wasn't she just a terrible old cat for hoping for such things?

"She sounds perfectly lovely," Edie said. "What's she like?"

Gilbride's attention was focused on the road and his animals. Breaking from the woods, the road curved through a lovely hillside meadow covered with bracken and heather, commingling shades of autumnal red and purple.

When he didn't answer, Edie nudged him in the ribs.

He scowled down at her. "What does it matter what she's like?"

"Since she's your intended, I assume I'll be spending a fair amount of time with her. So I want to know what I'm in for."

He said something under his breath—an oath, by the sound of it, and not one she was familiar with. She made a mental note to ask him what it meant when he was in a better mood.

"I remember that she was a very biddable girl," he finally said. "She was always rather quiet, although not necessarily shy. Just . . . quiet." His mouth edged up in a wry smile. "Although she certainly made no bones about scolding Fergus and me when we made too much noise or got into one of our many scrapes. Donella was an obedient lassie who never gave her parents or my grandfather a lick of trouble."

Eden wrinkled her nose. "She sounds . . ." She was

about to say *boring* but stopped herself just in time. "Very pleasant. Is she accomplished?"

"At least as much as I remember. She was a dab hand at reels, and she was learning all the other typical female accomplishments. Painting, music . . . she seemed to be good at it all."

Edie tried not to grind her teeth. She was good at dancing, too, but painting, drawing, and music had always bored her silly. Although she'd enjoyed studies like history, geography, and poetry, she much preferred being outdoors to sitting inside with her mother, wasting the afternoon on needlework or plucking away on the harp.

"She seems like a veritable paragon," she said, hoping she didn't sound as jealous as she felt. "Pretty, talented, sweet-natured, and obedient. In fact, she sounds like the perfect wife. Tell me again why you don't want to marry her?"

Gilbride's jaw worked, as if he was chewing on his answer. "Because she's the most boring person I've ever met."

Edie had to bite the inside of her lip to keep from laughing. His trenchant assessment cheered her up immensely.

Still, it wouldn't do to be too hopeful. After all, Gilbride had only been a boy of sixteen when he last saw his cousin. What struck him as boring back then could be quite a different story ten years later. In her experience, men said they liked strong-minded women, but the opposite was true when it came to marrying them. Just look at her parents. Her father avoided his wife as much as possible when Mamma was making her views emphatically known. Edie had little doubt that Papa would have been happier with a spouse who was less managing and certainly less opinionated.

Besides, his cousin might have matured and grown more interesting in the intervening years.

"Maybe she's changed," Edie said. "Perhaps she was just shy."

He threw her an irritated glance. "Miss Whitney, you seem intent on convincing me that I should marry my cousin. Why is that?"

Heat rose to her cheeks in a sudden rush. She supposed she did sound like she was making a case for Miss Haddon, though it would be utterly perverse. If there was one thing Edie knew for sure, it was that she didn't want Gilbride married off to anyone, at least while she was around.

She forced a laugh. "I'm just curious, that's all. As I said before, it's really none of my business."

"Good," he said through clenched teeth. "Then perhaps we can change the topic."

"Whatever you like," she said in a breezy voice.

They approached the top of the hill, allowing Edie glimpses of the castle walls beyond the stand of oaks that fronted it. Most of those trees had dropped a great deal of their leaves, creating a vibrant carpet of red and orange under the wheels of the carriage.

When they crested the hill, Mugdock Castle stood revealed in its ancient splendor, a large, crumbling curtain wall of gray stone that ringed the summit. One tower on the southwest corner looked to be intact. About four stories high, it was broader on the upper floors, giving it an odd, top-heavy look. Mugdock was certainly no fairy-tale castle, but rather a heavy, brooding structure with an almost primitive air. It made her think of ancient battles and fierce, kilted warriors who wielded dirks as they fought desperately to defend their lands from raiders or the hated English south of Hadrian's wall.

Edie loved it. "It's . . . it's so . . ."

"Ugly? Aye, lassie, that she is," Gilbride said in a heavy brogue, teasing her. "You won't be finding any handsome princes at Mugdock, although you might stumble across some howling ghoulies. Mugdock was a warriors' fortress, built to withstand attacks from other clans."

"It's amazing, like a giant brooding over the landscape. Has it always been in the Graham family?"

He cast her an odd smile, as if she'd said something to surprise him. "It changed hands once or twice in the 1600s but has remained under Graham control for most of its history."

"You mentioned that it's the official seat of the Clan Graham. Does the Duke of Montrose spend any time here?"

He snorted. "God, no. It's half-derelict, and the manor house itself isn't large. The duke and his family reside at Buchanan Castle, near Loch Lomond."

Eden frowned. "I would have thought the chief of the Buchanan clan resided at Buchanan Castle."

"Not anymore."

She threw him an exasperated glance. "Do the Scots deliberately go out of their way to make everything as confusing as possible?"

"It's part of our long-standing strategy to irritate the English. All you need to know is that we often fought each other, not just the invaders from the south, so many clan holdings passed back and forth over the centuries. The Scots are a rather fierce lot, and we don't take kindly to anyone seizing what's rightly ours."

She grimaced. "The Scots weren't always successful in that regard, were they?"

He was silent as he navigated a narrow stone gateway into an inner courtyard.

"Depending on which side your clan was on or your religious preference, no, we were not," he finally said. "Trust me when I tell you that for many a Highlander, past grievances are still fresh in their memories."

That sounded ominous. Edie decided it was time to lighten the tone.

"I do hope nobody is going to murder Mamma and me in our beds, à la Lady Macbeth. That would be a rather unpleasant way to end our trip. I don't imagine my father would be very pleased, either." She pressed a finger to her chin, as if thinking deep thoughts. "Of course, after the last few weeks perhaps he might not mind such an outcome."

He laughed. "He did seem rather pleased to see you and your mother on your way."

"Don't remind me."

"In any event, you have no need to worry about our version of Highland hospitality. My grandfather is a loyal subject of the Crown—when he's not railing against one or another of the princes, that is."

"Well, no one could blame him for that. They are a rather disgusting lot."

"You have no idea," he murmured as he brought the curricle to a halt.

Edie frowned at the strange comment. "I'm sorry. What did you say?"

"Nothing. Are you ready for a tour?"

He seemed in a rather changeable mood, which Edie supposed made sense, given that he was returning home after ten years and to a difficult family situation. She tried to remind herself that Gilbride's moods and worries were none of her business. If she had a brain in her head, she would keep a respectable distance from the intriguing captain and his entire family.

"Welcome to the official seat of Clan Graham, Miss Whitney." His gaze turned warm and teasing. "I do promise not to bore you with any more family history."

It was impossible not to smile back at him. "I quite like your family history. It's much more exciting than mine."

He was about to answer when a stable hand appeared

through a gap in an ancient-looking wall inside the main fortress, one that set off a small inner courtyard. The man doffed his cap to Gilbride and made for the horses' heads.

"That's an odd arrangement," she said as Gilbride helped her down. "A courtyard within a courtyard."

"That's the oldest part of the castle. It includes the southwest tower, which is still habitable, unlike the other towers in the ring wall."

He pointed across the larger courtyard to a small, tumble-down ruin in the corner. "That's the chapel. As you can see, there's not much left of it. And there," he said, gesturing behind her, "is the manor house. It was built in the seventeenth century after a battle destroyed most of the old living quarters."

Edie turned around to see a long and rather plain two-storied manor house tucked into the ring wall. It was composed of the same gray stone as the rest of the buildings, although it was clearly of newer construction. It was well maintained and had a rather quaint, old-fashioned air that seemed to fit the rugged nature of the castle and its surroundings.

Gilbride started her toward the house. "I'd like to let the housekeeper know we're here. Then we can wander."

Before they'd taken more than a few steps, the door in the center of the building swung open to reveal a stout, middle-aged woman in a neat gray dress, her hair covered by an equally neat white cap. She hurried across the flag-stones to meet them with a broad smile on her pleasant face. When she reached them, she dipped a low curtsey.

"Well, Mrs. Graeme," Gilbride said, "you're looking splendid. You haven't aged a day since I last saw you."

"Master, that'd be a grand story, if there ever was one," the woman said, her brogue warm and welcoming. "But it be right fine to have ye home again. Ye've been sorely missed, especially by the laird."

"And it's grand to be home," he replied. He glanced down at Edie. "This is Miss Whitney. She and her mother will be staying at Blairgal for the winter. I thought she might appreciate a tour of Mugdock."

Mrs. Graeme's gaze flashed over Edie with a quick assessment before she dipped her head respectfully. "On behalf of His Grace, the Duke of Montrose, ye're most welcome at Mugdock Castle, Miss Whitney." She looked back at Gilbride. "Will ye be wishin' to step inside for some refreshment before ye start the tour, Master?"

Gilbride glanced skyward. "I think we'll save that for later. It looks like it's clouding up, and I'd like her to see the view from the tower while the sun is shining."

Mrs. Graeme gave an enthusiastic nod. "It's a bonny view, especially of the lake and the Campsie Fells. I'm sure the young lady will enjoy it verra much."

"Then I'd say tea in about an hour," Gilbride said.

"It'll be set up in the drawing room whenever ye're ready. There are two lads in the stables and Mr. Graeme is about, so just call out if ye need anything, Master."

Gilbride gave the woman a friendly nod and then led Edie away.

"Why does she keep calling you Master?" she asked. "You're hardly a lad in knee breeches."

He waggled his eyebrows at her. "Thank God for that, eh, lassie?"

She groaned. "Please don't start in on your Highland oaf routine again. I know you must be sorely tempted now that you're home, but I beg you to refrain."

"Actually, my grandfather would murder me if he heard me playing that particular part, as would any self-respecting Scotsman."

"I'm glad to hear it. I would have to fling myself from that tower if you kept it up. *Master*." She dipped him a mocking curtsey.

"You are most definitely a vixen," he said, shaking his head. "For your information, Miss Impudent, Master is the official title of the Earl of Riddick's heir. It is the Scottish equivalent of the courtesy title of viscount that is often given to the heir of an English earldom. My full title is Captain Alasdair Hector Gilbride, Master of Riddick."

"Master Riddick," she said, rolling it on her tongue. "I like it. And if you were to marry, would your wife be the Mistress of Riddick?"

"I thought we agreed to close that rather unpleasant topic."

She grimaced. "Sorry. My lips will remain forever sealed on that subject."

"I sincerely doubt it."

"There's no need for sarcasm, Master Riddick. But I do have a question on another topic."

He slipped her hand into the crook of his arm as they strolled into the inner courtyard. Edie took a moment to appreciate the feel of his brawny muscles underneath her fingertips.

"Which is?" he asked.

"Is everyone I'm going to meet from now on called Graham?"

"No, but an alarming number of them will be."

"That will make it easier to keep everyone straight, I suppose."

"Except for the fact that there are a number of variations in spelling. The duke's housekeeper, for instance, spells her name *g-r-a-e-m-e*. And you'd best keep in mind that we're all quite touchy about what we think is the correct way to spell the name."

"Please tell me you're joking."

"Believe me, I wish I wasn't."

She affected a dramatic sigh. "You're right. It obviously

is a sinister plot against the English. How diabolical of all of you."

Edie didn't think she was imagining even more heat in Gilbride's gaze when he looked down at her.

"Oh, I think you'll find we Scots can be quite diabolical when it comes to getting what we want, Miss Whitney," he murmured in a voice so seductive that she was hard put to repress the insane impulse to snuggle against his hard, muscular frame, like a kitten seeking warmth.

And yet that would be the worst thing she could possibly do, because Edie was done with scandal, and not even charming and handsome Alasdair Gilbride had the power to entice her into another one.

Chapter Nine

Gilbride was like a male version of one of the Sirens, luring hapless females to their doom. Most of the time Edie suspected he didn't even realize he was enticing said females toward the rocks. Right now, though, she was convinced he knew exactly what he was doing because he was flirting with a lazy, sensual intent that warned her to lash herself to a metaphorical mizzenmast. *Why* he would do so was a bit of a mystery that she would solve later, once she'd had time to think it through.

He was in the middle of describing how romantic the Highlands were in autumn, painting vivid pictures of them taking long rides together through the glens—alone.

Really, enough was enough.

"Yes, that all sounds delightful, but then there are the bagpipes and the haggis and the rain and the clan feud and God knows what else," she cut in. "None of that sounds very romantic to me."

Her rude interruption appeared to make him mentally stumble. She imagined that not many girls cut Gilbride off in midflirtation, so she patted herself on the back for having the fortitude to do so.

After a moment, he flashed her a wry grin. "Are you

trying to tell me that you don't like bagpipes or haggis? I'm crushed beneath the grinding heel of your unromantic view of life, Miss Whitney."

"There's nothing romantic about haggis, and you know it. Now, stop acting like such a flirt and tell me about the castle. I want to know everything about it."

He studied her for a few seconds, that wry smile tilting up one corner of his mouth. She loved his mouth. Firm-lipped and utterly masculine, it was also generous and prone to roguish smiles that weakened a woman's knees. It was yet another temptation in a long list of temptations that made up the man. Edie could only imagine what it would feel like to have that mouth cover hers.

Idiot. Don't think about it. Despite his protestations regarding his future marital status, Gilbride was promised to another woman. Until that changed, Edie needed to keep her guard up.

"It's funny, but I never took you for a coward," he finally said.

She gaped at him for a few seconds before outrage replaced surprise. "I'll have you know, Captain Gilbride—"

"I surrender," he said, interrupting her with a laugh. "Consider me humbled before you with countless abject apologies."

She eyed him, silently fuming. But since she really wasn't sure what she'd been about to say anyway, perhaps it was best to let the matter drop.

"Am I forgiven?" he asked, trying to look as humble as he professed to be. It was an absurd attempt because Alasdair Gilbride couldn't look humble if his life depended on it.

"Oh, very well," she said. "But only because I wish to see Mugdock. If not, I'd take the curricle and leave you to walk back to Breadie Manor."

He let out a dramatic sigh as he led her past a neat set of stables, toward the main tower. "You're a coldhearted woman, Miss Whitney."

"And you are the most irritating man I've ever met. You'd better not stand too close to the edge of the tower when we get up there, or you might find yourself on the receiving end of an unfortunate accident."

He pressed a hand to his chest. "I will certainly take your advice to heart."

"I'm sure you will," she said drily.

He simply gave her a crooked grin.

They stopped at a set of stairs at the base of the imposing old tower. There didn't seem to be a door that led directly from the yard into the building.

"Is that the only way in?" she asked with some surprise.

"Yes. It looks odd, but I expect it was because the keep was easier to defend that way. Up you go now, but watch your step."

She lifted her skirts and started up the narrow steps. They were crumbled in one or two spots but otherwise in good condition. "You needn't worry, Captain. I can see perfectly."

And she could. She could see every crack in the gray stone, every spot where the edges were worn away or where a smooth piece of moss waited for a careless slip of the foot. For once, she didn't have to tread warily or depend on someone else to compensate for her wretched vision. That had always been the worst part—having to cede any ground to her weakness.

But in the end, her vanity had yielded nothing but a circle of shallow, insincere friends who'd abandoned her at the first sign of trouble.

At the top of the landing, Gilbride reached a long arm around her to open the door. He brushed up against her, his big body briefly caging her in. Feeling a little breathless, she scurried into the room, one that apparently took up the entire floor. It had a high ceiling and a large, soot-blackened fireplace. There was a massive oak table with four heavy, old-fashioned chairs, an ancient-looking settle in front of the fireplace, an iron chandelier hanging from the ceiling, and not much else. The room was dimly lit by two small windows covered in a framework of iron bars, their design obviously defensive in nature.

Slowly turning in a circle, she took in the gloomy atmosphere. The room was cool and smelled slightly of must and its thick walls blocked out all sound from the outside. It didn't take much to imagine life here in a wilder time, when marauders roamed the countryside, and clan fought clan. She'd never considered herself a particularly imaginative person, but standing in Mugdock Castle she felt the phantoms of history all around her.

Gilbride leaned against the doorframe, quietly watching her. Despite his modern dress, there was something wild or untamed about him, too, something she'd never fully noticed before in the civilized ballrooms and salons of the *ton*. With his brawny physique and confident presence, he seemed to belong in this rugged setting, one of a long line of fierce warriors who could face any challenge, defeat any enemy.

"What do you think?" he asked. "It's a relic and a rather moldly one, too. Now you can see why the duke and his family spend so little time here."

She smiled. "I think it's splendid. If I closed my eyes, I'm sure I could hear the cries of Saxon invaders, or see the witches brewing up their potions for the King of Cawdor."

"You wouldn't think it was splendid if you had to live here," he said. "You'd probably come down with a lung infection. Besides, it's not that old. Just fourteenth century."

She pointed a finger at him. "Aren't you the person who

accused me of lacking romantic imagination? I refuse to allow you to shatter my dreams with your talk of lung infection and mold. Now, what else is there to see?" She clapped her hands on a sudden thought. "Please tell me there's a dungeon."

"Only a cellar, which if memory serves is *very* moldy. It's primarily used to store furniture and other household items that no one knows what to do with. There's not a torture chamber, prison cell, or crypt anywhere in the place. Just a lot of cobwebs, spiders, and mice."

She wrinkled her nose at him. "You're determined to cast down all my hopes, aren't you? What good is a castle without a torture chamber?"

"Actually, there is something much better than a torture chamber. Come with me." He held out a hand.

Edie studied him for a moment, not trusting his seductive smile. But the enticement was too great, so she joined him, and he led her to a set of stairs tucked into the corner of the room. They were very narrow and very steep and, despite her excellent new spectacles, she slipped. From behind, Gilbride clamped his big hands on her hips to steady her.

"Watch your step, love," he murmured.

The casually uttered endearment set her heart racing. Or perhaps it was the feel of his long fingers curling around her hips, holding on to her just a fraction longer than necessary.

"Thank you," she managed to squeak out.

She finished the climb in a rush, arriving breathless on the next level. That room was a duplicate of the room below, sans furniture, so Gilbride urged her to keep going. At the top of the staircase, there was a small door that swung open to the roof. She stuck her head out, taking in the parapet that ringed the edges of the steeply peaked roof that rose from the top of the tower.

"Are you game for a look?" Gilbride asked from just below her. She felt sure he was getting quite a good view of her bottom, since it had to be almost in his face. That thought had her going hot all over, despite the sharp breeze that set her bonnet ribbons fluttering.

She scrambled onto the roof then edged away to the right, giving him room to fit his large frame through the small opening. She thought for a moment that his shoulders would get stuck, but he managed to push himself through and up onto the roof.

"I don't remember that being such a tight fit," he said.

"I imagine you were smaller the last time you were up here. Now you're practically a giant."

"Hardly that, but I was a skinny lad. Tall, but thin as a beanpole. Our cook did her best to fatten me up, but nothing ever seemed to work."

Gilbride's body held not an ounce of extra flesh, as far as Edie could tell. "Lucky you. It was quite the opposite in our house. Mamma was forever scolding Evie and me about eating too many sweets. She was terrified we'd end up as—"

"Butterballs?"

She gave him a sheepish smile.

"I assure you, Miss Whitney, there isn't anything on your frame that doesn't belong there."

That rather impudent remark was followed up by a leisurely perusal of her figure. From the appreciative look in his eyes, it seemed the compliment was sincere.

She made herself turn away from him to gaze at the view that made her almost forget that he was flirting with her again.

"It's beautiful," she gasped.

The tower was on a high point of land, looking down the hill. Straight below ran woods, meadow, and bog, the autumn colors of the fallen oak leaves, wild cranberry, and purple heather spread out in a dazzling natural carpet. To the left, shimmering in the afternoon sunlight, was a large lake.

"Are those swans?" she asked.

"They are. There have been whooper swans on Mugdock Lake for generations."

Edie leaned over the waist-high parapet, trying to get a better look. Gilbride snaked an arm around her middle to pull her back.

"Easy does it," he said. "We've kept the tower in good repair, but the stones are very old. I don't fancy explaining to your mother how I let you tumble off."

The feel of his arm around her waist left her rather breathless again, so she came back in. It startled her how much she didn't want him to let go.

"Yes, I think Mamma would be a little testy about that," she said. "Although that would certainly solve the problem of what to do with me."

He frowned. "I thought things were better between you two now. Surely your mother is not still angry with you."

She shrugged. "She's still convinced I'm ruined forever. Her words, not mine."

"That's ridiculous."

"I agree. May I see what's on the other side of the tower?"

He frowned, obviously wanting to pursue the unpleasant subject. She took the matter out of his hands by sliding past him and around the tower. Gilbride had no choice but to follow.

The view on the other side was even more spectacular and, for a few minutes, they drank in the beauty in silence.

"Those are the Campsie Fells," Gilbride finally said, gesturing toward the high ridge of hills in the distance. "From there you can get a bonny view of Glasgow in one direction and the Highlands in the other."

Edie tilted her head back to let the sun hit full on her face. The wind was bracing rather than cold, and it seemed to clear away the travails of the last few weeks. Up here, there were only the stones under her feet, the wind soughing through the trees, and the screeching of a hawk as it circled overhead. London and the *ton* were as distant as a fading memory, and for the first time in several days, she couldn't regret that she'd been driven from town. Life seemed fresher here, high above it all, offering a chance for a new beginning. If her sister had been with her, the moment would have been perfect.

Still, her current companion held more than his fair share of appeal.

Gilbride appeared lost in thought, his forearms braced on the parapet as he gazed out at the fells. From the downward pull of his mouth and the brooding cast to his brow, it seemed his thoughts were not as pleasant as hers.

"You truly didn't want to come back, did you?" she asked.

When he glanced over, meeting her gaze, she registered a slight shock at the grim expression on his handsome features. Gilbride had always struck her as the most easygoing of men, despite his dangerous career as a spy. He seemed never at a loss for words or less than completely in control. He was an insanely confident and arrogantly attractive man who swashbuckled his way through life.

But right now he didn't look like the man who always knew what he wanted and how to get it. Right now he looked unhappy.

But then something seemed to flicker in his stormcloud gaze, and the brackets around his hard mouth creased with a rogue's easy smile. She felt an odd sense of disappointment, as if he'd sounded the retreat just before something important marched over the horizon.

"I'm not jumping up and down for joy," he said. "I liked my life as it was, and I wasn't quite ready to give it up."

She turned to face him, resting her hip against the stone parapet. "Are you really telling me that you miss being shot at or dodging desperate characters who are trying to murder you?"

His smile slid into a full-out grin, one so dazzling that her breath caught in her throat. Being around Gilbride might very well resemble having a lung infection after all, since she displayed a disturbing tendency to go both breathless and lightheaded in his company.

"Not the being shot at, of course," he said. "But every day was a challenge, and I was never bored."

She envied him that. Edie might not be a terribly romantic person, but she'd often longed for escape—occasionally from the demands of her family, but mostly from the restrictions that hemmed in the life of a proper young lady. Unfortunately, she'd pushed so hard against those limits that she'd brought them crashing down around her.

"You're so lucky to have had the opportunity to travel," she said, hoping she didn't sound too wistful. "Especially to places like Persia and Greece. What were they like?"

"Greece was beautiful, especially the islands. Persia had its moments too."

"That's not much of a description. Can't you do better than that?"

He pretended to ruminate on the question. "It was hot, especially on the plains of Nineveh. Beastly hot, in fact."

She let out a snort of disgust. "How dreary of you to be so blasé about it. Did you go to Nineveh when you were a spy?"

"No, my sojourn there was before I got into that game." Now it was his turn to lean a hip against the parapet, his muscular arms crossed over his chest. He was once more his confident self, not the brooding man of a few minutes ago.

"When, exactly?" she prompted, hungry for more detail.

"When I was secretary to the British consul to Baghdad. My superior was quite the antiquarian. He was always dragging me off to one ruin or another."

"How did you end up in that position? Did your grandfather help you?"

"Of course. He was determined to keep me from getting into even deeper trouble. Since I had no intention of returning home, he begged some favors from the Foreign Office and had me put to work. It all sounded like a grand adventure to me."

"What kind of trouble had you gotten into?"

"The kind no gentleman would explain to a gently reared young lady."

"Don't be such a stick," she scoffed. "You know I don't have a shockable bone in my body."

"Regardless," he said drily, "I have no intention of sharing those particular events with you."

"You can be such an old biddy at times," she said. "Please continue with the stories you *can* tell me."

"Your wish is my command. Now, where was I? Oh, yes. Nineveh. There's not much to tell, really. It was mostly miles and miles of dusty plains, dirt mounds that all looked the same, and heaps of old bricks covered with cuneiform writing. Since no one can actually read cuneiform writing, they were rather more boring than anything else."

She gave him a jaundiced look. "May I just say that you're even less romantic than I am, which certainly doesn't square with your dashing reputation."

His gaze drifted over her face, seeming to snag on her mouth. "Oh, I can be quite romantic and dashing under the right circumstances."

She rolled her eyes. "I'm not talking about that, and you know it."

He laughed. "Yes, I do know it. And I apologize for

being such a disappointment. I will say, however, that Persepolis was entirely worth seeing. I did a number of drawings of the ruins. Perhaps you'd like to see them at some point."

Edie perked up at that. "Yes, very much."

"Then you shall. But now we'd best go down if we want to finish the tour before Mrs. Graeme serves tea."

She began to make her way back to the door but then stopped and turned to face him. There was one question she hadn't yet had the nerve to ask—the one that interested her the most. Their situations seemed alike in the sense that both of them had been forced to run in traces that didn't fit. Since he'd managed to escape his for a good long while, she found it hard to imagine how he could give up his freedom so easily. She didn't think she could, once she had a taste of it.

"What is it, Miss Whitney?"

"If you're not ready, why are you going home? I imagine not even your grandfather can force you to do what you don't want to do. Why not keep on with what you love, regardless of what your family demands?"

His eyes narrowed, as if she had annoyed him.

"Because I have a responsibility to my family, of course, especially to my grandfather. I'm neither a gadabout nor a reprobate, Miss Whitney, no matter what you might think."

His cool tone made her blink. "I never called you either of those things," she said defensively.

"No, you've called me worse—repeatedly and in public. I assure you, your opinion of me is abundantly clear."

She stared into his sardonic gaze for a few infernally long moments, then turned and started down the narrow stairs. Her cheeks burned and she wanted to kick herself for letting down her guard.

Even worse, he'd regarded her question as a genuine

insult. She'd taken a risk, hoping he wouldn't brush her off with his usual jest or practiced charm. For some ridiculous reason, she wanted to know what he truly thought about things—deep inside, where it counted.

Instead, she'd left herself wide open for yet another lesson in rejection. It shouldn't matter in the least, but she was sorry to say it did.

Repressing the impulse to flounce down the stairs, probably breaking her neck if she did, Edie descended to the main level and crossed to the stairway that led outside to the courtyard. Gilbride was a silent presence at her back, one she wished she could ignore.

She tromped down the steps and started across the small inner court toward the house. Perhaps if she pretended their nasty little exchange hadn't happened, he would go along with it. Then they could go back to teasing and insulting each other, like they did back in London. At least then she would know how to handle him.

"Hang on, lass. There's no need to go storming off," came the deep burr from behind her. Gilbride gently but firmly took her arm, halting her in her tracks.

Edie refused to look at him, keeping her gaze pinned on a water trough on the other side of the yard. She heard him sigh and then he moved around to face her, a wry expression on his features.

"I wasn't trying to insult you," she said, forcing the words out. "I'm sorry if I did."

He grimaced. "I'm the one who should be apologizing. I had no business taking my personal frustrations out on you. Please forgive me."

His apology disarmed her, but she was still unsure how to respond.

"If you'd like to beat me about the head with a nice stout stick," he offered, "I'll help you find one."

She sighed. "I'm certainly tempted, but I'd rather know why you ripped up at me like that. As you so trenchantly pointed out, you've put up with far worse before."

"I'm sure it's because you hit so close to home," Gilbride said. "I have been evading my responsibilities, as Wolf has been telling me for some time. Besides, most of your usual insults are quite entertaining. I'm not used to you being so serious. You threw me off my feed."

"I repeat, I was not trying to insult you."

He nodded. "I know."

"Next time I intend to insult you, I'll give you notice first," she said. "That way neither of us will get confused."

An errant breeze whipped through the courtyard, flipping the collar of her pelisse up to her cheek. Gilbride reached out to smooth it down, letting his hand rest against the side of her neck. "Eden Whitney, what the devil am I going to do with you?"

Her heart began to pound so hard she was sure he must feel the pulse beating beneath her skin. "If you don't know, I certainly can't tell you," she said, forcing a light tone. "Now, don't you think we should finish our tour? I'm sure Mrs. Graeme is wondering where we are."

He studied her for a few moments, then nodded. "It would be my pleasure, Miss Whitney." Slipping her hand through his arm, he led her to the outer courtyard.

Edie cast about in her head for something to say. "You must miss Wolf," she finally said.

"He's a pain in my arse, but yes. It feels odd to think I won't see him regularly anymore. Sad, too."

"That's how I feel about Evie," she said.

He pulled her a fraction closer, almost tucking her against his side. "At least we have the satisfaction of knowing that she and Wolf are happy."

"Yes, blast them. We're the ones sent into miserable exile."

"Then we must be sure to send them long, morose reports from the Highlands to make them feel as guilty as possible."

Edie laughed, and the last of her tension dissolved. "If I have to have a companion in exile, I suppose it might as well be you. Now, tell me more about Mugdock. Perhaps if I use my imagination, I can pretend I'm truly someplace exotic."

He launched into a surprisingly interesting and detailed lecture about Mugdock Castle and the family history. While he talked, they strolled around the base of the crumbling curtain wall. Edie was only half-conscious of the views, caught up in the fascinating tale of the Gallant Grahams over the centuries. Gilbride was an accomplished storyteller, and before she even realized it, they'd walked most of the way around the castle's perimeter.

"You're really quite lucky," she said as they stopped to gaze out over the lake.

He cocked an enquiring eyebrow. "How so?"

"You've had ten splendid years adventuring, and you now get to come back to all this." She swept out an arm to indicate the hills, lake, and the forest with its rustling cloak of orange and red. "Your lands, your family, your history . . . it's all so noble. It's certainly something worth coming home to."

He smiled down at her, his gaze warming with an appreciation that soothed the lingering remnants of her injured pride. "You put me to shame with your enthusiasm, Miss Whitney."

"Well, my life certainly wasn't horrible but it wasn't exciting or even particularly interesting. And now the only thing I can hope for is that the scandal attached to my name will eventually fade so I can trap some poor fellow into marrying me, despite my many faults." She wrinkled her nose at him, turning her complaint into a jest. The last thing she wanted was his pity.

He took a step closer, so close that she had to tip her head back to look at him. "Any man with a brain would consider himself lucky to call you his wife. I know I would."

His deep voice seemed to rumble through her, like a small earthquake. It rather made her knees quake, too, and she could feel herself blushing like a schoolgirl. She'd heard hundreds of fulsome compliments over the years, calculated to set a girl all atwitter. But his unvarnished statement sent her poor heart thumping even harder. Her body's response told her she stood at the edge of a precipice.

"Perhaps you can write a letter of reference for my former suitors," she said, trying to hide behind the joke. "I fear they've quite forgotten my ample charms."

When his gaze dropped to her bosom, she felt herself going from warm to hot. She'd certainly walked right into that one.

"Perhaps I'll keep you all to myself instead," he murmured in a voice that spoke of dark nights, velvet caresses, and a man's knowing hands on her body.

She pulled in a breath, staring into a wicked gaze that dragged her into a whirlpool of emotion. Unconsciously, she swayed toward him, both mind and body muddled with longing and trepidation. Gilbride started to lean down, coming closer.

Edie startled when she heard a grating, clattering sound. She glanced over the top of her spectacles at a large, blurry figure on top of the wall, and then saw large chunks of stone tumbling right at them.

Before she had a chance to cry out, Gilbride launched himself forward, wrapping his arms around her and bringing her down to the ground with him in a controlled roll.

He shielded her from the worst of the impact, but she still hit hard and it knocked the air from her lungs. Gilbride covered her body with his as large stones crashed down chillingly close to them.

And right where they'd been standing only a few seconds ago.

Chapter Ten

Home.

With each passing mile that brought them closer to Blairgal Castle, the memories rose up to meet Alec, images that both pulled him forward and urged hell-bent for leather escape in the opposite direction. The idea of home wove a tangled skein of emotions. There were equal measures of guilt and relief, a fair share of irritation, and an odd sense of yearning that never went away.

"The scenery is reminiscent of the Lake District, don't you think, Mamma?" Edie said as she gazed out the window. "It's very beautiful but not nearly as rugged as I thought it would be."

Alec forced himself to stop brooding like a daft poet, instead focusing his attention on his traveling companions. Edie and Lady Reese sat opposite, stylish in their elegant pelisses and bonnets. Bang-up to the mark, he had no doubt. In only a few minutes, they would be meeting his grandfather, the Earl of Riddick, and they were dressed to impress. They would create a stir with everyone at Blairgal Castle, but possibly not in the way they expected. Their appearance screamed *Londoner,* which certainly wouldn't endear them to his parochially Scottish grandparent.

Edie gave him a tentative smile that suggested she'd forgiven him for his spectacular string of blunders yesterday at Mugdock. After teasing her, insulting her, and then knocking her to the ground—out of necessity—he'd capped it off by bursting into laughter when she'd insisted that someone had deliberately toppled the loose rocks from the top of the curtain wall.

Though the very notion was demented, he should have been gentler with her. Not only had she had a bad scare, he'd knocked the wind out of her. The stone fall had missed them by only a few feet, which had been more luck than he deserved. But he'd been only moments away from kissing her and his brain had been addled with lust. If it hadn't been for her frightened squeak and the sudden horror in her eyes, he might not have noticed the falling rocks until it was too late.

He was damn sure no one had tried to hurt them, but he was also sure they'd only escaped death because she'd been paying more attention to their surroundings than he had.

Which only showed how deranged he'd become. He'd been blind and deaf to everything but her. She'd felt like heaven in his arms, with her soft curves and her magnificent bosom heaving against his chest. His body had instinctively reacted in an all-too-predictable manner that she obviously couldn't help but notice.

And it had gone downhill from there. Once he'd hauled her to her feet, she'd insisted he go up and uselessly search the walls for the dark-garbed man who'd knocked the rocks down on them. No amount of reasoning on his part—or denials by the Mugdock servants that any such dark-garbed man existed—could convince her otherwise that the fall had been accidental.

"Och, my dear," Mrs. Graeme had said to Edie, "those old walls have been crumbling to dust for years. I fair blame myself for not reminding the master of the dangers."

When Edie had stubbornly insisted on what she saw, Alec had made the colossal mistake of suggesting that perhaps her new spectacles had temporarily scrambled her vision. It had seemed a reasonable proposition to him at the time. After spending her entire life barely able to see twenty feet in front of her face, the change would no doubt take getting used to.

Edie had retorted that it was his brain that was scrambled. Their merry little jaunt had concluded with her giving him the silent treatment all the way back to Breadie Manor.

Alec had always found women lovely, compliant, and generally a delight to manage. Edie was certainly lovely, but she was the furthest thing from manageable.

She'd been in slightly better humor this morning, and he'd been relieved to see her wearing her spectacles. Surprisingly, Lady Reese had thanked Alec for bestowing such a thoughtful gift on her daughter, although she'd been scowling a bit when she said it. He imagined she was torn between hope that his gift signaled a continuing interest in her daughter and dismay that Edie was now, in her mamma's mind, firmly in the bluestocking category.

"Well, Mamma," Edie prompted, "you've spent quite some time in the Lake District. What do you think?"

Lady Reese cast a frowning glance out the window. "I suppose it does look rather like the Lake District, now that you mention it. How disappointing that it looks nothing like I imagined from my reading of *The Lady of the Lake*."

Edie rolled her eyes. "Mamma, that's a poem not a travel guide. I'm sure we'll have the opportunity to see a great deal of beautiful scenery once we settle in, isn't that so, Captain?"

When she gave him another encouraging smile, it occurred to Alec that she was making a special effort to draw him out. He'd been a less than an ideal traveling companion today, falling into a grim silence the closer they approached Blairgal. Edie had apparently decided to do her best to distract him.

Touched by her kindness, he smiled back at her. "This part of Scotland is a transition from the Lowlands to the Highlands. We're a bit south of Loch Katrine here, but once we reach Blairgal Castle you'll be able to see Ben Venue and some of the larger peaks in the Trossachs. Then you'll truly feel like you're in the Highlands."

Lady Reese picked up the travel guide from her lap and studied it. "Trossachs. I believe that means 'bristly country.'" She peered out the window. "It doesn't look particularly bristly to me."

"No," Edie said. "The hills look like . . . like crumpled green velvet. And those flashes of water, streams, I think, are almost like diamonds on the velvet. It truly is lovely."

"Dear me, Eden," her mother said. "You are beginning to sound like a poet yourself."

"And here I thought you weren't romantic, Miss Whitney," Alec teased.

She gave him a sheepish smile. "I'm just excited that we're finally here in the Highlands."

"I, for one, am delirious at the thought of getting out of this carriage," her mother said. "Eleven days on the road is enough to try the patience of even the holiest of saints."

Her daughter wrinkled her nose. "And no one would ever accuse us of being saints, would they, Mamma?"

"Speak for yourself, my dear," Lady Reese said in a lofty voice. "I believe I have been a paragon of civility and good humor for the entire trip."

When Edie stared open-mouthed at her mother, Alec had to stifle a laugh. "That you have, my lady. A true paragon."

"What about me?" Edie demanded.

Alec waggled his hand, as if to suggest *not so much*.

"You really are the most irritating man," she said.

"Eden, please don't be so rude to our host," her mother admonished. "I'm sure the captain was simply jesting."

Alec smiled. "I take no offense, Lady Reese. My grandfather will no doubt agree with your daughter's assessment of me."

Edie looked about to apologize to him when her mother interjected. "Oh, look, Eden. There's the castle. I must say, it looks quite splendid under the setting sun."

Edie tried to crane around her mother. "Drat, I can't see it from this angle."

"Change seats with me," Alec said.

Her eyes widened. "Don't you want to see it? You've been away a very long time."

"Believe me, I know what it looks like." He stood and, bracing his feet against the movement of the carriage, held out his hand.

Smiling, she took his hand and started to move to his vacated seat when a sudden jostling of the carriage tumbled her into him. She let out a startled *oof* and landed against his chest. Instinctively, his hands clamped around her round hips.

"Goodness, be careful," exclaimed Lady Reese. "We don't want you breaking your head before we even arrive."

"Captain, you can let go of me now." Edie sounded slightly breathless.

Alec lowered her onto the padded bench, eyeing the encouraging blush that pinked up her cheeks. There was no doubt that she did still think him a great Scottish oaf, but at least she wasn't indifferent to him. He needed more from her, of course, but perhaps he was making better progress than he thought.

She joined her mother in peering out the window. Since the image of Blairgal Castle was engraved on Alec's memory, he made no effort to catch a glimpse. Once he was home, he had the oddest feeling that he wouldn't be escaping its confines for a very long time.

"Oh, my goodness," Edie exclaimed. "It's magnificent. Look at those towers, Mamma, and it even has turrets."

"It certainly looks very old," Lady Reese said, not sounding nearly as enthusiastic as her daughter. "Quite medieval, in fact."

"It's not quite that old," Alec said, "although the original stone keep was built in the 1300s." He finally succumbed to the pull of Blairgal, and leaned around Lady Reese to gaze out the window.

They were bowling up the final rise to the front of the house, which stood on the highest point at the end of the valley. The rays of the setting sun bathed the five-story structure in a warm glow, turning it the color of old amber. Despite the guard he'd placed on his emotions, Alec felt his throat tighten.

"The color is very unusual," Eden said. "I wonder how they did it?"

"It's from the plastering process over the stone walls," Alec said. "Color is added to the lime wash to lend it that hue."

"It's splendid, and it certainly looks a proper castle," Eden said, flashing him a quick smile. "But where's the moat and drawbridge? If you tell me there's no moat, I'll be utterly devastated."

Her warmth and eagerness loosened the band of tension around his chest.

"Alas, the moat is lost in the mists of time. The tower house was built around 1670. By that time, there was no need for a fully fortified structure, with just the occasional band of outlaws wandering about. The castle was built to protect against them, not attacks from an enemy army or clan."

"Outlaws, how mundane," she said in a droll voice.

"We do have a secret passageway leading to a hidden room in the walls. It's just a priest hole, but it's haunted, so at least that's something."

"I despise ghosts," said Lady Reese. "They rarely behave in a respectable fashion, they're *always* accompanied by terrible drafts, and they insist on terrifying the servants. I don't know which of the three is worse."

"Mamma, there's no such thing as ghosts," said her daughter, obviously trying not to laugh. "I'm sure the captain is just teasing us."

"Then I wish he'd stop it, since I have no desire to encounter annoying apparitions or spend my nights freezing to death in their drafts."

Edie threw Alec a look of comical exasperation. "If you think I'm not romantic, now you know where I got it from."

"Really, Eden," her mother said, "I believe I have a perfectly acceptable degree of sensibility, and I am looking forward to our sojourn in the Highlands. I simply fail to see why that requires us to be discomforted, or inconvenienced by ghosts. Or smoking chimneys," she added as an afterthought.

"I sympathize entirely, Lady Reese," Alec said, enjoying the ridiculous conversation. "Fortunately, there's a substantial mansion house built around the base of the old towers. That was constructed around 1720, and my grandfather and his father modernized the building several times over the years. I assure you that you will have every comfort."

"There you go, Mamma, no great sacrifice will be required of you," Edie said, "beyond having to spend the winter snowbound in the Highlands with me, of course."

Lady Reese started to look anxious. "The prospect of being snowbound anywhere, much less at a remote country estate in Scotland, is quite daunting."

"I agree with you, Lady Reese," Alec said, "but my grandfather won't. He's quite touchy about that sort of thing."

Now her ladyship looked downright horrified. "Captain Gilbride, you cannot suppose I would even *think* to complain to Lord Riddick. I am determined to endure our exile with good grace, no matter how challenging it might be."

Edie sardonically regarded her mother. "Mamma, you *are* a saint. How you've managed to keep that such a secret all these years is a mystery to me."

Alec bit back a laugh, but it looked like Lady Reese was about to bite off her daughter's nose. Fortunately, they were all spared the reprimand when the carriage finally lumbered to a halt in front of the main entrance to Blairgal Castle.

Alec could no longer stave off the inevitable. He took a deep breath and smiled. "Well, ladies, are you ready?"

Edie surprised him by leaning forward to grasp his hand. She gave it a quick squeeze before letting go. "I'm sure everything's going to be just fine," she said in an earnest voice.

Perhaps, but certainly not without her help. And such help was all too dependent on what would happen in the next few minutes.

After Alec descended, he helped the ladies exit the carriage. Edie gave his hand one last squeeze as she stepped down, then she turned with a bright smile to the small crowd assembled to meet them.

To Alec, the moment felt too solemn for smiles.

His grandfather had rousted what looked like the entire staff to greet them. They had assembled in two lines extending from the wide, shallow steps at the front door. He recognized a few of them. Mrs. Alpine, the housekeeper, looked much the same, although her hair had gone fully white, and it appeared that Barclay, the senior footman, had graduated to the position of butler. Most, however, were unfamiliar, underscoring the length of time that Alec had been away.

His family stood in the center of the small crowd, and it seemed as if Alec's past rose up to meet him. Slightly in front was his grandfather, kilted and wearing the red vest of the Grahams. Beside the earl was Alec's father, graying but looking much the same, and Fergus Haddon, his cousin. They all waited for him as if suspended in time.

For a bizarre moment, Alec felt as if he'd never left home at all.

Then his grandfather moved, and the spell was broken. Alec's heart jolted as he stepped forward to meet him and realized that he was so much taller than the man who'd always seemed like a giant to him—physically and mentally. It was another shock to see his grandfather stoop-shouldered and moving slowly, using a cane. His hair was completely white and his rugged features looked drawn and deeply wrinkled.

The earl looked like an ancient oak, once strong and invincible but now withered from the passage of time. Clearly, ten years had taken their toll.

"Well, lad, you're finally home," Grandfather said in his gruff burr. "I imagine you're none too happy about that, now are you?"

"I'm very happy to see you, sir," he replied, giving a respectful bow. "And I'm pleased to see how well you look."

The old man scowled. "You needn't flatter me, laddie boy. I know I'm on my last legs, which is the only reason you've come home."

His grandfather had always been a bit fussed about his

health, ridiculous given how strong and vital he'd always been. But for the first time, Alec realized that his father's warnings about the old man were not alarmist.

"I would have come home in any event, Grandfather, now that the war is over," Alec said in a quiet voice. "And I *am* happy to see you."

His grandfather's scowl faded and his faded green eyes warmed a bit. "Your mother would have been proud to see what a braw man you've turned out to be, Alasdair."

Alec had to swallow before he could answer. "Thank you, sir."

The old man's gaze flicked past him, and his scowl returned. "Well, I suppose you'd best introduce me to those *Sassenach* standing there behind you," he grumbled.

Alec didn't bother to repress his sigh. His grandfather still liked to lay it on rather thick, and he could only hope the ladies hadn't heard. "Of course."

That hope died when he turned to see Lady Reese standing straight as a pike and looking her most forbidding. Eden's smile, however, was luminous and full of humor, emphasizing the charm and beauty that had been the downfall of her numerous suitors.

It had been Alec's downfall from almost the moment he first saw her. He was counting on that charm to work its magic on the Earl of Riddick, too.

"Sir, may I introduce Viscountess Reese and her daughter, Miss Eden Whitney. Ladies, my grandfather, the Earl of Riddick."

"Welcome to Blairgal Castle, your ladyship, Miss Whitney," his grandfather growled, making it sound like a march to the gallows.

Lady Reese dipped into a curtsey that looked precisely calibrated. "Lord Riddick, it is an honor to meet you. My daughter and I thank you for your gracious hospitality," she said in a cool, haughty tone.

The daggers were already drawn, and they hadn't even made it through the front door.

Edie stepped forward, swanning down into a low and deeply respectful curtsey, as if she were saluting the king with the graceful display. Even his crusty old grandfather seemed taken aback.

"Oh, my lord," Edie enthused as she rose, "I can't tell you how happy we are to be here. Everything is *so* magnificent, especially Blairgal Castle. Captain Gilbride has been telling us all about it, and we've been able to talk of nothing else for days. I simply cannot *believe* how lucky I am to visit a true Scottish castle, especially one so historic. I cannot *wait* to explore it."

There was no doubt Edie liked to talk, but Alec had never heard her babble with such verve. His grandfather blinked a few times, and for a horrible moment Alec thought the lass had overplayed her hand. But then the old man's wrinkled face relaxed into an expression that, on him, counted as benign.

"Well, Blairgal does have a fascinating history, and that's a fact, Miss Whitney," Grandfather said. "Once you're settled in, I'll be happy to give you a wee tour."

Edie clasped her hands together like she'd just been promised the Scottish crown jewels. Clearly, she'd deduced that one of his grandfather's few weak spots was his pride in Blairgal and the family history.

She proceeded to pepper his grandfather with questions about surfacings, plaster, and old moats, blatantly ignoring her clearly bored mother. Breathing a sigh of relief over Edie's skillful managing of his irascible grandparent, Alec finally turned to greet the man who'd been the only father he'd ever known. Walter Gilbride's gentle, scholar's face beamed with joy as he pulled Alec into a warm embrace.

"Welcome home, my son. I've been waiting for this day for a very long time."

"You're looking well, Father." Alec smiled down into Walter's eyes, twinkling behind their spectacles. "Even better than when I saw you in London six months ago."

His father waved a hand. "London air is so injurious to one's health, as is the bustle of the city. Although I was happy to make the trip on your account, I don't blame your grandfather for refusing to visit."

"His refusal to set foot in England anymore," Alec replied drily, "has nothing to do with his health, as you well know."

Walter gave a gentle grimace. "We won't speak of that now, if you please. Now, say hello to your cousin."

Fergus came forward, his expression grim and reluctant. Alec's heart sank, but he put out his hand and injected as much warmth into his voice as he could. "It's good to see you, Fergus. I hope you've been well."

His cousin had grown like a sprout and was now almost as tall as Alec. He was still on the thin side but carried himself with a cool dignity that sat well on him. He'd obviously matured into his position as estate steward and right-hand man to the Earl of Riddick. It wasn't surprising, since Fergus loved everything about Blairgal, its people, and its business. He'd never understood Alec's desire to get away because family, clan, and the estate were everything to Fergus. His cousin would no sooner run away from home than cut off his arm.

"Welcome home, Cousin," Fergus said, giving him a slight bow. "I hope you're happy to be here."

"Well, I'm happy to see you," Alec replied with a broad smile, but it seemed to have no effect on his cousin's mood. "How are your mother and Donella? Will we be seeing them tonight?"

God, he hoped not. He wasn't quite ready for that meeting.

Fergus's green gaze, so like Alec's grandfather, went glacial. "They will be coming later, after the English ladies settle in." He said "English ladies" like they were a species of poisonous snakes.

"Good God, Fergus," Alec said in a quiet voice. "Please don't tell me you're going to insist on referring to them as 'the English ladies.' That's ridiculous."

"What's ridiculous is that you brought them back with you," his cousin retorted, casting an angry look in Edie's direction. "How could you possibly insult Donella like this?"

"What effect it might have on Donella is none of your business, Cousin," Alec said. "That is between her and me."

"Anything that affects my sister affects me," Fergus snapped.

"Goodness me," Walter said in a quiet but firm voice. "We're keeping the ladies standing out here in all this wind. Please introduce us, Alasdair, and then let's go inside."

Alec throttled back his irritation. "Of course, sir. I am indeed forgetting my manners."

"You never had any in the first place," Fergus muttered.

Walter shot Fergus a warning look and stepped forward, smiling warmly at Lady Reese. Alec's father had a truly kind demeanor, and his openhearted welcome soon charmed her ladyship down from the boughs. Walter was equally warm in greeting Edie, and Alec finally began to relax. If they could get everyone inside and up to their respective rooms, they just might pull off introductions without the family skeletons exploding out of the closet.

"Lady Reese, Miss Whitney, I'd like to introduce you to

one of the most important people here at Blairgal," Walter said. "This is Mr. Fergus Haddon, Alasdair's cousin. I'm sure we'd be in a very bad spot without Fergus."

Edie dipped into a quick curtsey, giving Fergus a dazzling smile. Only a block of ice would be able to resist that smile, and Alec prayed it would exert its charm on his scowling cousin. "It's a pleasure to meet you, Mr. Haddon. I've heard so many good things about you from Captain Gilbride."

Fergus let out a derisive snort, not bothering to bow in return or make any overture. When Edie's smile faltered, Alec was hard-pressed not to take his mutton-headed cousin and stand him on his head for acting like such an ill-mannered lout.

"Now, lad," said Alec's grandfather in a coaxing voice. "Don't be shy. They may look like grand city folk, but Lady Reese and her bonny daughter are certainly no better than our fine Scottish ladies."

"Well, I don't know quite what to say to that," huffed Lady Reese.

"It's fine, Mamma, really," Edie said, her voice quivering as if she were repressing laughter.

Fergus glared at Edie but couldn't disobey a direct order from his uncle. He gave a short, choppy bow in the general direction of the ladies. "Welcome to Blairgal," he rapped out in an inhospitable voice.

"Thank you, Mr. Haddon," Edie said sweetly. "We *so* appreciate your warm welcome."

"If you'll excuse me," Fergus said to no one in particular, "I have work to do." He spun hard enough to kick up gravel from the drive and marched up the stairs into the house. One or two of the younger maids tittered, but the scowl Alec's grandfather directed their way instantly shut them up.

"What a rude young man," Lady Reese said. "I hardly know where to look."

"It wasn't that bad, Mamma," Edie said, patting her mother's arm. "Well, actually it was, but I wouldn't worry about it."

"No, you shouldn't," Alec said, finally prying his clenched jaws apart. "But I apologize on my cousin's behalf, Lady Reese. Clearly, my return home has overset him."

"And can you blame the lad?" barked Alec's grandfather. "He feels for his poor sister. God knows the lass has been slighted enough as it is."

So much for keeping the family skeletons locked out of sight.

"I understand, Grandfather, and I know how fond you are of Fergus," Alec said. "But I hardly think we need engage in private family matters in front of our guests and the servants."

The old man let out a bitter laugh. "Laddie, there isn't a man, woman, or child in this county who doesn't know exactly what you did to Donella Haddon. And what's owed to her, now that you're home," he added pointedly.

On that trenchant note, the old man thumped his way back to the house, his cane digging into the gravel and sending up sprays of dust. When he reached the top of the stairs, he turned to glare at the servants, all standing stone-faced in rigidly correct lines. "Stop your standing around like a pack of idiots and get back to work," he rapped out. "The Master of Riddick has returned home. There's nothing more to see."

The butler sprang to open the door, and Alec's grandfather disappeared into the house.

"Well, that went splendidly," said Edie.

"I have a headache," Lady Reese announced in a loud voice.

"My dear Lady Reese," Walter said regretfully. "I beg you to forgive his lordship. He suffers terribly from arthritis and spasms of the heart, which can make him rather ill-tempered at times. But let's get you out of this nasty wind, shall we? No wonder you have a headache."

Walter steered her into the house, murmuring a soothing flow of promises of tea, hot compresses, and a nice rest before dinner.

Edie studied Alec with an expression he couldn't decipher, apparently waiting to see what he would do next. He shrugged. "Welcome to the Highlands, Miss Whitney."

She rolled her eyes and took his arm to go in.

Chapter Eleven

Edie hurried down the gallery, resisting the urge to inspect the portraits lining one side of the hall. Some depicted Highland lords and ladies dressed in the colorful garb of the last century, while older paintings displayed kilted warriors in odd bonnets and auburn-haired ladies who looked almost as fierce as the men.

There was no portrait of Alasdair Gilbride. Perhaps he'd been too young to sit for one, or there had been a picture and his grandfather had taken it down. If the little welcoming scene this afternoon was any indication, the Earl of Riddick had yet to fully forgive his grandson for running away.

Then there was cousin Fergus Haddon, whose attitude had been downright hostile. Edie had been trying to charm Lord Riddick out of the grumps—and succeeding fairly well, she thought—so she hadn't caught more than a few phrases of conversation between Alasdair and his cousin. But it soon became clear that Fergus was less than thrilled with the pair of them. She hadn't yet ascertained whether his objections ran to Englishwomen in general or to Edie and her mother in particular. Whichever the case, she needed to prevent open warfare with an important member of the family. Mamma wouldn't put up with further insult and would eventually cause a scene, while Lord Riddick would surely side with his nephew and throw the English interlopers out on their backsides.

Edie certainly didn't need more scandal and bad blood. Though they were far removed from home, nasty tales of fireworks between the Earl of Riddick and Viscountess Reese would eventually find their way down to London. She and Mamma would be the butt of more jokes and more gossip, resulting in more damage to the family's good name.

That was unacceptable. Edie had every intention of restoring her reputation, no matter how gruesome or boring the process. That meant a quiet winter in Scotland and the chance for the *ton* to forget she was anything but a model of rectitude and propriety. Then she could return to London and get back to her life, eventually finding a suitable husband.

The fact that she currently had no desire to find such a husband—at least one who wasn't a brawny Scot with a tendency to call her *lass* in his gentler moments—was entirely beside the point.

She finally came to the end of the east wing, where Mamma was situated. Blairgal Castle was so big Edie practically needed a hackney coach to reach her mother's bedroom. Although her own room was in one of the older parts of the castle, it was both comfortable and surprisingly modern with elegant furnishings of the finest quality. The chimney didn't smoke, and the view was spectacular. The sun had been rapidly setting by the time Edie was shown up to her room, but there'd still been enough light to see rolling glens, dense woods, and several snow-capped peaks.

She'd gotten the distinct impression from the housekeeper that *the master* had asked for her to be placed in that magnificent room specifically because of that view. His thoughtfulness had truly touched her, although it also sounded a faint note of alarm in the back of her mind.

She tapped on her mother's door and entered.

Mamma was seated at a dressing table, examining a selection of fans displayed by her ever-patient dresser. The room, larger than Edie's, was luxuriously appointed in the Queen Anne style and well lit by candles and coal-port lamps. She couldn't help thinking again that for an old pile of stones, as Alasdair had once referred to Blairgal, it was as comfortable and elegant as one could wish for. While the hallways were drafty and cold, it was a castle after all, and one did wish for a certain degree of authenticity.

Her mother glanced up, her frown smoothing into a smile. "Ah, there you are. I was hoping you wouldn't get lost while trying to find me. In this house, one must traverse a ridiculous number of stairs and halls to go from one point to the next."

"I'm just at the other end of the gallery, Mamma," Edie said, inspecting the monumental canopy bed and the handsome tapestry that hung behind it. "If you stood outside your door and yelled at the top of your lungs, I would be bound to hear you."

"I would never indulge in such vulgar behavior, my dear. If there was any yelling to be done, I would send Davis out to do it."

Edie turned from the tapestry, a lurid depiction of a stag hunt, and stared at her mother. "Mamma, did you just make a joke?"

Her mother lifted her eyebrows. "You needn't look so surprised, Eden. I have been known to do that on occasion, have I not, Davis?"

"Not that I can remember," her dresser said. Davis was devoted to her mistress, but to say that she was a plain-spoken woman was an understatement. Edie had always found the two of them rather hilarious together, almost always unintentionally.

Mamma waved a dismissive hand. "You're from Yorkshire, Davis, an exceedingly humorless part of England. You wouldn't recognize a jest if it leapt up and bit you."

"Really, Mamma," Edie said, trying not to laugh, "that's too bad of you. Poor Davis won't know what to think."

"I'm not paid to think," Davis replied. "Now, your ladyship, stop dilly-dallying and pick out a fan. You and Miss Eden are going to be late for dinner, since a body has to walk halfway to Glasgow to reach the dining room."

"You're both exaggerating," Edie said.

"I never exaggerate, and neither does Davis," her mother said. "Davis, you pick out a suitable fan for me. I'm simply too worn out by the tumult of our arrival to make any decisions for myself. Although I suspect no one will notice such niceties," she added in a disapproving voice. "Despite the elegance of our surroundings, I was most disturbed by the rude behavior of both our host and his disagreeable nephew. I do not know how we're going to survive the winter in such uncivilized company."

Edie went to sit on a luxuriously plump velvet chaise in front of the fireplace. "I'll grant you that Mr. Haddon seemed to fly up into the boughs for no good reason. As for the earl, he was simply a bit overcome by Captain Gilbride's return home. After all, they haven't seen each other in ten years."

"Regardless, there was no reason to be so rude."

Clearly, Mamma's feathers were seriously ruffled, which meant it was up to Edie to smooth them down. "Well, Lord Riddick does suffer from arthritis and heart spasms, so I expect he wasn't feeling very well."

"I'm not surprised, given the Scottish climate and this drafty castle. Really, I don't know why his lordship doesn't reside most of the year in Glasgow or Edinburgh. Or at his town house in London, for that matter."

"Come, Mamma, you just admitted how elegant everything is. Lord Riddick obviously takes splendid care of Blairgal and has a great deal of taste."

"Well, someone does," her mother admitted grudgingly. "Perhaps Captain Gilbride's father is the civilizing influence. He seems a most genteel man."

A spare, almost frail-looking man with a sweet face and gentle manner, it seemed impossible to Edie that he could be the father of a strapping man like the captain. Father and son looked nothing alike, so she had to suppose Gilbride took after his mother's side of the family. He certainly had the commanding air of his grandfather, and the arrogance, too, although the younger man's was tempered by his roguish charm.

"Mr. Gilbride seemed very taken with you, Mamma. I'm sure you'll be great friends before the winter is over."

"I suppose one must be grateful for that."

Edie eyed the genuinely weary look on her mother's face, one that seemed to age her ten years. An odd rush of anxiety made her breathing go tight and shallow. The Lady Reese she knew was indomitable, but the trip had clearly taken its toll on her. And the only reason her mother had been forced to take the exhausting trip was because of Edie's stupid escapades.

She pushed against the sensation of guilt that threatened to choke her. "Mamma, you're not to worry one bit. I'll take care of Lord Riddick and his beastly nephew. I swear I'll have them eating out of my hand by the end of the week."

Her mother seemed to shake off the melancholic reverie. Her gaze narrowed, as if she was truly seeing Edie for the first time since she'd walked in the room.

"I'm sure you will, but not with those things on your

face." She waved a finger at Edie's nose. "Must you wear them downstairs to dinner? They make you look like a bluestocking."

Edie mentally sighed. "There's nothing wrong with that, is there?"

"Bluestockings usually end up on the shelf, Eden," her mother said in a severe voice. "You are no longer a debutante in the first blush of youth. Spectacles only make you look older than you are."

That comment knocked the air out of Edie's lungs. Her mother never criticized her looks or expressed any doubts that she would make anything less than a spectacular marriage. The fact that Mamma thought she was being helpful only made it worse.

She forced herself to rally. "Evie is a bluestocking, and look how well she did. She had not one but two eligible suitors."

In the distance, the gong of the first bell sounded. Her mother rose and picked up the fan that Davis had placed on the dressing table. "Evelyn's situation was entirely different. You cannot compare yourself to her."

Edie frowned. "We're identical twins. Of course I can compare myself to her."

Her mother let out a dramatic sigh. "Which means, I suppose, that you will insist on wearing the spectacles."

"Since Captain Gilbride went through quite a lot of trouble getting them, I don't want to offend him by not wearing them."

That, of course, did the trick.

"That is quite true, Eden. Very well, I will allow you to wear them," her mother said.

"Thank you," Edie responded drily.

There was a quiet tap on the door. Davis opened it a few inches. "It's a footman, my lady," she said, "come to show you the way down to the drawing room."

"Thank goodness," said Mamma. "I did not relish the notion of wandering around this great pile of stones by ourselves. God knows we might end up in a dungeon or even encounter a specter." She gave an exaggerated shudder. "One can imagine almost anything happening in Scotland."

"Indeed, my lady," Davis said in a doleful voice.

Edie laughed. "Her ladyship was joking, Davis." She glanced at her mother's elegant, spare features. "You were, weren't you?"

"I suppose it will depend on whether I'm awakened during the night by howling ghosts or bloodthirsty clansmen with dirks," Mamma answered with magnificent disdain. "You may ask me in the morning."

A liveried footman awaited them in the hall. He gave a respectful bow. "Captain Gilbride sends his compliments, my lady. He sent me to guide you down to the main drawing room."

Mamma flung out a dramatic arm. "Lead on, MacDuff, lead on."

The footman's eyes went wide with alarm. He backed up a few steps, then turned and scurried several feet ahead.

As he led them to the first of many staircases that seemed to crosshatch the castle, Edie squeezed her mother's arm. "I do love you, you old thing," she said. Mamma could be a trial, but no one could fault her for lacking in spirit.

"Thank you, my dear child. And I'm pleased you picked that velvet dress. The cream fabric with the gold trimming looks particularly attractive on you. We must hope it and your other attractions outweigh the spectacles, although I must commend Captain Gilbride for having the good sense to select a gold pair. Silver never suited you."

While Mamma prattled on about attractive dresses, suitable colors, and drafty hallways, Edie couldn't help thinking about the fact that her spectacles truly didn't seem to bother Gilbride. The opposite was true it appeared, since he'd almost kissed her yesterday at Mugdock Castle. That had been something of a surprise, given he'd never shown any inclination to do that until a few days ago. Even more surprising was that she'd been about to let him, which illustrated an alarming lack of common sense on her part.

But when he'd loomed over her, his gray eyes smoldering and his imposing body blocking out her view of anything but him, Edie's brain had scrambled. All she could think of was his mouth and how much she wanted to kiss it. How much she longed to be swept into his strong embrace. If not for that strange figure on the wall and the tumbling rocks, who knew what might have happened?

She remembered how stunned she'd been by the feel of Gilbride stretched on top of her, his body hard in more ways than one. Naturally, she'd gotten him off her as quickly as possible, insisting he track down the idiot who'd almost killed them. His refusal to even consider the idea that someone had deliberately thrown the rocks had led to yet another argument, which had killed any desire on her part to even think about kissing.

Which was just as it should be, she reminded herself for the hundredth time, since the blasted man was betrothed. As for the figure on the wall, she'd likely never find out who it was, so there was little point wasting her energy thinking about it.

"I suppose we'll be meeting the captain's reputed fiancée and the rest of the family tonight," her mother said, pulling Edie from her gloomy thoughts. "I do hope Miss Haddon has better manners than her brother."

Edie forced back a sigh. "There's nothing *reputed* about the engagement, and I'm sure she'll be perfectly lovely. After all, she *is* Captain Gilbride's betrothed."

Her mother gave her a quick glance. "Well, I suppose it

doesn't really matter whether we like her or not, does it? It means nothing to us."

That's what Edie had been trying to tell herself. "Correct, Mamma. It doesn't matter one bit."

Except, of course, that it did.

Alec waited for Edie and Lady Reese in the entrance hall, even though the rest of the family was already gathered in the main drawing room. The Haddons had arrived early for dinner, blast them. Donella and her mother were obviously eager to claim ownership over him as soon as possible.

At least Glenna Haddon certainly did on behalf of her daughter. When Aunt Glenna, a slight, pinch-faced woman who'd aged very little, had rushed into the drawing room where he'd been waiting with his father and grandfather, her pale blue eyes had glittered with triumph. When Alec had bent to respectfully kiss her cheek, she'd sunk her nails into his sleeve, digging in as if she had no intention of ever letting go. She'd effusively greeted him, referring to him as her son to be.

And hadn't that sent a chill skating down his spine?

Aunt Glenna had then soulfully proclaimed that Donella had barely survived the tragic separation that had sent her into a decline, all but claiming her life.

Grandfather had then gruffly ordered Glenna to stop acting like a totty-headed female, an awkward moment for everyone except Donella. She'd stood placidly silent throughout the gruesome little scene. She neither blushed at the sight of Alec, fluttered, nor looked the least bit discomposed either by his long absence or by his return.

In short, she was inscrutable as always.

Donella had always been a quiet child, her only true interests her needlework, her studies, and the religious instruction she took with the local vicar. She'd never shown any emotion for Alec other than the mild affection one expected between cousins who had nothing in common. Alec and Fergus had been the best of friends, but Donella had always seemed to regard them as nasty boys who did everything they could to raise hell and annoy their elders. As a result, he and Fergus had always given her as wide a berth as possible.

And if his cousin had spent the last ten years pining for him, as her mother insisted, Alec couldn't see any evidence of it.

There was another reason, of course, why Aunt Glenna was so hell-bent on seeing Alec marry her daughter. To his aunt, it was a case of natural justice, since Alec stood in the way of the man she considered the rightful heir to the earldom—Fergus, the next male in the family's line of descent.

Although the rumors that Alec was the bastard son of the Duke of Kent had died down over the years, he knew they'd not been forgotten here. Certainly not by Aunt Glenna, though she'd never had the nerve to come right out and say that Alec was the cuckoo in the nest, especially not in front of Walter or Grandfather. As far as Aunt Glenna was concerned, the only way that Alec—and the Earl of Riddick—could mitigate the great injustice done to Fergus was by making her daughter the wife of the next earl.

The hell of it was, Alec could see her point. He *was* the cuckoo in the nest. And although the Haddons lived a genteel life in a tidy little manor house at the other end of the valley, they'd never been rich. If not for Alec, Fergus would now be heir to a wealthy earldom, and Donella would be a prize catch on the marriage mart. Instead, Fergus had to work for his uncle, and Donella had to make do with a modest dowry.

But if Donella became the future Countess of Riddick, the family's fortunes would of course significantly change for the better.

He scowled up at the old heraldic banners that hung over the stone-fronted fireplace of the entrance hall. Big enough to hold an ox, the deep hearth hosted a blaze that roared against the chill of the November eve. This hall, with its suits of armor and ancient weaponry hung on the walls, spoke to his family's history, one of conflict, drama, and complicated relationships.

At the sound of footsteps on the spiral staircase in the antechamber at the end of the hall, Alec turned to see Lady Reese and her daughter. The meeting between Edie and Donella was not one he was looking forward to. He'd made some progress in softening up Edie these last few days, or at least he thought he had. But meeting his fiancée in the flesh might prompt in the lovely Miss Whitney some unfortunate display of female loyalty. He'd hoped to be much further along in his campaign of courtship and prayed that he wouldn't lose further ground tonight.

One of the junior footmen led Lady Reese and Edie in. The viscountess was looking both imposing and elegant in a stylish gown of wine-red silk, but Edie took his breath away. For a few seconds, he stood and stared like a dumbstruck fool.

She wore a velvet dress trimmed with gold lace and spangles that lovingly shaped her ample curves and imparted a creamy glow to her perfect complexion. The plush fabric combined with her equally plush body put him in mind of a kitten, one he would like very much to stroke. Her thick hair was piled into a high, artfully disheveled fall, with streams of gleaming gold falling down the back of her neck. Her big, blue eyes gazed back at him from behind the spectacles that he was still inordinately pleased to see her wearing. Her full mouth curved up in a smile that sent a bolt of heat right to his groin.

She was bonny, all right, and the cheeky lass knew it, too.

Lady Reese swanned forward, and Alec mentally shook his stunned brain back into action. "Good evening, my lady, Miss Whitney," he said with a bow. "Allow me to say that you both look exceedingly lovely."

Lady Reese snapped open her fan and gave him a gracious smile. "Thank you, Captain Gilbride. You cut quite the figure tonight, as well." She waved a vague hand at his body. "That's a very authentic looking outfit."

"It's called a kilt, Mamma," Edie said in a sardonic voice. "Don't you remember Captain Gilbride's dress regimentals for the Black Watch? Although tonight I do believe he's wearing a costume more closely associated with his clan." Her gaze dropped somewhere below his waist. "Sporran and all," she finished in a low purr.

Kitten my arse.

She was a she-devil who knew exactly the effect she had on him. It took a stern mental command to quell that part of him twitching beneath his kilt.

"This is a splendid hall," Edie said, switching from notorious flirt to enthusiastic guest in an instant. "And really quite cozy given how imposing it is. Are we to meet the rest of your family here?"

"No, my family is gathered in the drawing room."

She let out a dramatic sigh. "What a shame. This room is so splendidly medieval I feel like I've stepped back in time. One almost expects a band of howling warriors to come crashing through the door at any moment."

"Not to worry, Miss Whitney," Alec said. "Our drawing room is feudal enough to satisfy even the most bloodthirsty of souls."

"Dear me, that sounds positively dreadful," Lady Reese said.

"*Au contraire,* Mamma," Edie said in a droll voice, "it sounds most exciting. I suspect it will be the perfect setting for meeting Captain Gilbride's family."

Alec could only hope she didn't realize how prescient her comment was. "Shall we go in, ladies? The family is waiting."

After he escorted them through the door of the drawing room, Edie and her mother stopped dead in their tracks, their eyes widening in comically identical expressions as they took in the decor.

He couldn't blame them. After all, it wasn't every day that one walked into a room that bristled with dozens of mounted stag heads, their racks reaching up in neat rows to the ceiling. For good measure, there was a gigantic stuffed eagle, wings spread and mounted over the fireplace in a symbolic reference to the Graham heraldic crest, which featured an eagle dismembering a hapless stork. Under the visual onslaught of dead wildlife, it was difficult to even notice the elegant and quite modern furniture or the expensive Axminster carpet that graced the polished floorboards.

"My goodness," Lady Reese said in a weak voice.

"You certainly weren't exaggerating the bloodthirsty part," Edie said with something of a snicker. Then her gaze latched onto his family, and she went stiff as a fencepost.

The men were lined up in front of the fireplace, his grandfather and Fergus eyeing the new arrivals with scowls even more forbidding than this afternoon's display. While Walter had a smile on his kind face, it looked thin and strained, as if he'd been arguing with the others while Alec was out of the room.

As for Donella, his cousin was inspecting Edie with a surprised lift to her elegant brows, as if she didn't know quite what to make of her. With his aunt, however, there was no mystery, since the glare she directed at Edie and Lady Reese was positively murderous.

Edie slid him a sideways, mocking glance. "Tell me something, Captain Gilbride," she murmured. "How do you think Mamma and I will look on the wall with the rest of the trophies?"

Chapter Twelve

Edie had only been half-joking about ending up with her head mounted on the wall of the splendidly barbaric drawing room. Fortunately, no one besides Alec and Mamma had heard the comment. It was a good thing, because Lord Riddick and his relations, with the exception of Mr. Gilbride, still seemed more inclined to murder their English guests than welcome them into their midst.

By the time they moved into dinner, she'd deduced the primary reason for their resentment—Mrs. Haddon, Fergus, and possibly Lord Riddick all saw her as a threat to Donella. Since she'd only just arrived at Blairgal she certainly hadn't had time to leave that sort of impression, but she supposed it might seem suspicious for the prodigal son to return home after a long absence escorted by a single young lady and her mother. Given the sometimes cutthroat tactics employed by the girls of the *ton* and their matchmaking mammas—and she presumed those tactics applied in Scotland, as well—it was a reasonable assessment to make.

Interestingly enough, Donella wasn't nearly as outraged as her relations. Oddly, she spoke to Edie with more warmth than she did to her erstwhile fiancé. True, they hadn't seen each other in ten years, but Alec was a devastatingly handsome and charming man who could make most any woman tumble into his lap.

Donella, however, seemed to suffer no such inclination.

After a mercifully short interval in the drawing room, Lord Riddick had overcome his dislike long enough to observe appropriate decorum. He'd escorted Edie's mother into the family dining room, which to Mamma's evident relief had contained no animal heads, only elegant green wallpaper and burgundy velvet drapes drawn against the chilly Highland night. Fine crystal, silver, and china gleamed in the light of a vast number of candles, and the parade of dishes that graced the table would have rivaled any meal served in the best houses of the *ton*.

By all rights it should have been a delightful evening, especially after so many long days on the road. Unfortunately, it was shaping up to be anything but.

Well, when it came to strained domestic relations Edie would put her family up with the best of them. While Alec might find his relatives a challenge, as far as she was concerned he'd gotten off lightly. Girls didn't have the luxury of running off on adventures or to dashing military careers. They had to stay home and learn to manage their parents and siblings, and hope they would eventually find a husband they could stand to look at day in and day out.

Edie stole a glance at her host, who was glaring at no one in particular while grimly eating his soup. She'd concluded that Lord Riddick's fractious mood resulted mostly from poor health and badly unsettled nerves. His lordship reminded her of her maternal grandfather—gruff and prone to barking at people, but underneath a kind and generous man. The earl simply liked to get his own way, which made him no different than the average aristocratic male.

Edie had no doubt she'd be able to make her way past his prickly façade in short order.

The rest of the family was another story. Mrs. Haddon could barely bother to be polite. She'd even made a few digs about Edie's spectacles and delivered several veiled insults about English people in general. She'd behaved as badly as one could imagine—except to her prospective son-in-law, who seemed to welcome her attentions as much as he'd welcome a rash on his backside.

Fergus Haddon, stuck next to Edie at the dinner table, had done his best to ignore her. Three times she'd tried to strike up a conversation but had been rewarded with nothing but blighting comments. The idea of dumping the contents of her soup bowl over his head was remarkably tempting.

Clearly, it was going to be war, with Alec as the spoils.

As for the third member of the Haddon family, Edie found Donella rather fascinating. She appeared completely uninterested in capturing her fiancé's attention. Although she replied to Alec's queries or comments in a thoughtful, soft-spoken manner, one would never have guessed they were engaged.

And unlike the rest of her family, Donella was a paragon of elegant decorum. She was also a beauty—tall and willowy, with gorgeous auburn hair that looked like it never frizzed. She had stunning green eyes and a pale complexion that mimicked the finest of ivories. Edie had been seized with the most dreadful pang of jealousy when she'd first set eyes on Miss Haddon, and it had taken a great deal of effort to wrestle it under control. That particular emotion had always struck her as a foolish waste of time, and she'd yet to meet a man worth the expenditure of energy.

Until now, unfortunately, thanks to blasted Alec Gilbride.

Edie smiled at the footman who was removing her

plate from the first course. She almost felt like striking up a conversation with him, since he had to be an improvement on her current dinner companions. With Fergus on one side and Mrs. Haddon on the other, she might as well be in Outer Mongolia.

"Tell me, Miss Whitney, are you finding everything at Blairgal quite to your satisfaction?" asked a deep, masculine voice that jerked her from her ruminations. "I do hope your bedroom is as comfortable as you could wish it to be."

It took her a moment to register that Alec was speaking to her from across the table, and in a tone of voice that made the innocent question sound a bit like an innuendo. She blinked at him, taking in the gleam in his eyes and the smile that curled his lips. She'd seen that particular smile more than once over the last few days, and she thought she knew what it meant.

Would he actually flirt with her in front of his family *and* his betrothed?

Out of the corner of her eye, she could see Mrs. Haddon staring at her nephew with a look of mute horror. She then slowly turned her Medusa-like gaze on Edie, as if threatening to turn her into stone if she dared respond to so shocking a breach of etiquette.

Strictly speaking, Mrs. Haddon's reaction was overblown, given the small size of their group. Still, Mamma would expect Edie to observe the established rules, regardless of the informality of the occasion, and not engage in conversation across the dinner table. What she *should* do is give Alec a vaguely disapproving frown and an even more vague reply, and then keep her attention firmly on her plate.

But with the evil eye of Mrs. Haddon upon her and Fergus fuming away on her other side, Edie couldn't bring herself to listen to her better angels. After all, if there was one thing she could never resist, it was a challenge.

"My bedroom is perfectly delightful," she said. "Thank you for asking, Captain."

"You'll be sure to let me know if you need anything," he replied. "Anything."

Edie arched an eyebrow at his darkly seductive tone. Good Lord, it was a family dinner, after all. "I will be sure to do that," she replied politely.

Mrs. Haddon let out a dramatic gasp. "Well, I never," she huffed. "Such indelicate manners are not to be borne."

The dreary woman was glaring right at her, not her nephew. Anyone with eyes could see that he was the one indulging in flirtatious behavior over the creamed onions, not Edie.

And why was he acting so outrageously in the first place, and with Miss Haddon sitting right next to him? Not that his betrothed seemed to mind. She glanced first at Alec and then at her mother before accepting a spoonful of turkey with dressing from the footman.

"Mamma, there's no need to work yourself up over nothing," Miss Haddon said. "Alasdair was simply being polite to one of Uncle's guests."

At the head of the table, Lord Riddick suddenly decided to pay attention to the conversation. "Alasdair, what the devil are you talking about that has upset your aunt? This isn't London, you know. I'll not be welcoming any of your smart town ways to my dinner table."

Alec's eyes narrowed on his grandfather. Edie intervened before he could further inflame the situation.

"Captain Gilbride was simply making sure I was comfortable," she said, smiling down the table at the old man. "He wanted to know if I needed anything."

The earl's bushy white eyebrows climbed up his forehead. "If you need anything, lassie, you'll take that to the housekeeper or butler. You'll not be asking my grandson to be jumping like an English jackanapes to indulge your every whim."

Before she could even think how to respond to that startling rejoinder, her mother leapt into the fray. "My daughter is never self-indulgent, Lord Riddick. One cannot find a more biddable or sweet-natured girl anywhere in England. Or Scotland, for that matter, I'm sure."

That was humbug, naturally, but Edie appreciated her mother's loyalty.

"That's not what I heard," Fergus said in a nasty tone. "Quite the opposite."

That froze everyone at the table for a good five seconds.

"And what do you mean by that, laddie?" Alec asked.

His voice had gone low, his brogue dark around the edges. Edie had to repress a shiver. She'd heard that tone in his voice on a few occasions, and it never boded well. Not that she needed the reappearance of his brogue to tell her that. The frigid glare he directed at Fergus was ample evidence of his sudden shift in mood.

"I'm sure Fergus meant nothing by it," Walter Gilbride said in a genial but firm voice. "It was just a silly, offhand remark, wasn't it, my boy?"

Edie turned to fix Fergus with the cold, practiced stare that had reduced many an impertinent fellow to jabbering apology.

Fergus blushed a dull red and tugged a nervous finger at his cravat, rumpling its precise folds. "Ah, I . . . I don't know what I meant," he stammered, looking at Mr. Gilbride. "I think I was simply muttering to myself."

"I thought as much," Mr. Gilbride said cheerfully. "No harm done. Now, Miss Whitney, I'm pleased to hear that you're comfortable." He smiled across the table at Mamma. "And I trust everything is just as you like it, Lady Reese?

I believe his lordship put you in the Green Room. I've always thought it quite the loveliest bedroom in the castle."

"Thank you, sir," Mamma said in a gracious tone, clearly quite taken with Mr. Gilbride. "I am exceedingly comfortable."

"Splendid. I'm hoping you'll allow me the honor of giving you and your daughter a tour of Blairgal tomorrow." Alec's father gave a self-deprecating chuckle. "I don't like to boast, but I believe I have a better knowledge of the castle's history than anyone in the family, even though I am a mere in-law."

Lord Riddick, apparently restored to a better humor, let out a gruff laugh. "Mere in-law? Walter is the grandnephew of a duke and one of the finest scholars in Scotland. Nobody knows the history of Blairgal and the clan better than he does. A tour of the castle with him will be quite a history lesson for a pair of pampered English ladies."

Edie saw rather than heard Mr. Gilbride's sigh. She couldn't fail to hear, however, Mrs. Haddon's malicious titter at the earl's ill-mannered remark. Mamma was annoyed again, but Edie could only be grateful that Lord Riddick hadn't trotted out the *Sassenach* label, too.

"You're welcome to take Lady Reese on a tour if you like, Father," Alec said. "But I already promised to take Miss Whitney around the castle myself." When his gaze jumped to her, going dark and smoldering, Edie had to resist the urge to fan herself.

"Especially the dungeons," he added in a voice as smooth as sin. "You do remember asking me to show you the dungeons, don't you, Miss Whitney?"

That voice suggested there were other things besides the dungeons he wanted to show her—things generally not mentioned in polite company. Only by a supreme effort of will did Edie manage to keep her mouth from dropping open. Alec was deliberately flirting with her, blast him.

She was no prude, but his behavior this evening could only be characterized as provocative, especially since he was sitting right next to his betrothed.

Predictably, Fergus looked ready to kill Alec, his fork and knife clutched in his hands like weapons. "Alasdair, I've warned you not to insult my—"

"Miss Whitney, I've been meaning to ask you a question," his sister interjected in a loud voice. "Have you ever been to the Lady Chapel in Westminster Abbey?"

The bizarre but timely question cut Fergus off at the knees and brought the conversation sliding to a halt. Edie mentally scrambled to formulate an answer. "Ah, yes, I believe so," she hedged. There were so many chapels and crypts tucked away in corners of the Abbey that it was difficult to remember exactly what they were called or where they were.

"I'm wondering if you recall seeing the tomb of Mary, Queen of Scotland," Donella said with an encouraging smile. "I understand it's very beautiful."

Edie couldn't remember one royal tomb from the next, but she did appreciate the woman's attempt to deflect impending mayhem.

"Yes, it's very imposing and beautiful," she said, casting about in her mind for details. "If memory serves, there's even a Scottish lion at her feet."

For the next few minutes, she babbled on about marble canopies, double aisles, Gothic vaults, flying buttresses, and any other detail she could extract about the Abbey from her increasingly frazzled brain. All through her demented lecture, Donella regarded her gravely, occasionally nodding her head, while everyone else at the table looked either confused or annoyed.

Except for Alec, confound him, who studied her with growing amusement. By the time Edie finally ran out of ideas—and breath—she felt as ready to kill him as Fergus had a few moments ago.

"Thank you, Miss Whitney," Donella said in a solemn tone. "That was extremely interesting and informative."

"It was indeed," Alec added with a teasing grin. "In fact, you are a veritable fount of architectural information, Miss Whitney. I've never thought of you as the scholarly sort."

"I should certainly hope not," Mamma exclaimed. "Although I suppose one might be tempted to think so, given that she is wearing the spectacles you were so kind to bestow upon her. But I assure you that Eden is no blue-stocking."

"Thank you, Mamma," Edie said with a sigh.

Mrs. Haddon peered at her. "My nephew gave you that pair of spectacles? Why would he do that?"

Lord Riddick barked from the other end of the table. "What the devil do you mean buying presents for an unattached young miss? Have you no sense of propriety, boy? A gentleman doesn't go around giving gifts to other women when he's engaged."

Edie had to resist the urge to drop her head into her hands and groan. She thought she'd steered them away from this particularly touchy topic, but her mother's ill-timed remarks and Alec's persistent attempts to flirt with her—which she rather thought was an attempt to annoy his relatives—had laid waste to her good work.

Every person in the room was acting deranged—except, ironically, for Alec's fiancée.

"I got them for her because she's as blind as a bat," Alec said in a blighting voice to his grandfather. "And since she will insist on riding and other outdoor activities, I thought it best to take defensive measures before she kills herself or one of us."

"How considerate of you," Edie said. "For your information, I'm quite skilled at any number of outdoor activities, with or without spectacles. For instance, I'm quite a dab hand with pistols. Perhaps you'd allow me to use you as target practice. I could put an apple on your head and pretend I was William Tell."

Alec had been scowling at his grandfather, but her comment brought his focus back to her. He looked startled for a few seconds then broke into a grin.

"I'm loath to correct a lady, but William Tell was an archer," he replied. "He used a crossbow to be exact. Have you ever used a crossbow?"

"No, but I'm adept with a regular bow. I might, however, make an exception in your case and decide to miss. Although I suppose it would be best not to wear my spectacles in that case, so as to avoid a charge of murder." She gave him her sweetest smile, even though she felt like sticking out her tongue. "Of course, my defense could always argue that it was justifiable homicide."

Donella laughed, although she tried to cover it up with a cough.

"Goodness, Donella," exclaimed her mother. "Please do not encourage such foolish raillery. And it's very unseemly to laugh at one's fiancé in polite company. I insist you apologize to Alasdair right this second."

Edie could barely keep herself from gaping at the confounded woman. As far as she was concerned, Lord Riddick and his family were the least polite people she'd ever met.

When Donella flushed a dull red, Edie's heart went out to her. She hadn't expected to like Alec's fiancée. And although it was too soon to make that assessment, the young woman had treated Edie with friendliness and respect, unlike the rest of her family.

"Of course, Mamma," Donella replied in a flat tone. "Forgive me, Alasdair. I didn't mean to offend you."

Alec gave the girl a truly kind smile. "Lass, you didn't offend me, and you don't owe me any apologies. I'm happy to see you laugh."

His cousin gave him a shy but sweet smile in return, as if basking in the genuine warmth of his regard. Edie barely managed to repress the surge of jealousy that tried to bore a hole right through her chest.

"Now, that is what I want to see," Lord Riddick said. "You and your cousin have been apart for too long, Alasdair. You simply need a little time to get to know each other again."

"I hope not too long, my dear Riddick," Mrs. Haddon said. "After all, we *do* have a wedding to plan. Before Christmas, if possible. If we wait too long, the weather will turn severe, and it will be harder for the clan to gather."

"Aye, you're right about that," replied his lordship. "The clan will certainly wish to gather for the union between the Master of Riddick and the finest flower of Clan Graham." He directed a broad smile down the table at his niece. "We've all been looking forward to this for a long time, lass. I promise we'll give you and Alasdair the grandest wedding you've ever seen."

Busy wrestling down the unpleasant emotions evoked by that announcement, Edie almost missed the change that came over Donella. The life seemed to drain out of the girl, leaving her pale and still.

"Thank you, Uncle," she replied in a colorless voice. "But I don't think we need to discuss this in front of our guests."

Walter Gilbride finally stirred. He cast an anxious glance at his son, whose face had gone almost as stone-like as his cousin's. "Of course not. There's plenty of time to make plans. No need to settle everything the first night home, now is there?"

Mrs. Haddon let out another of her annoying and artificial laughs. "I disagree, Walter. We cannot begin planning soon enough." She shot Edie a glance full of malicious triumph. "And, Miss Whitney, what a piece of luck for you and your mother. You will be able to attend the wedding of my daughter, the niece of the branch chief, to the Master of Riddick. Weddings are always so enjoyable, and Highland weddings are a particular treat."

Eden forced down her anger at the woman's rudeness. She flicked a quick glance at Alec, whose gaze had gone narrow and frigid as he stared at his aunt.

But when he looked at Edie, she saw something else in his stormy gaze. It was a silent plea, a look so compelling that it seemed to reach across the table and grab her by the throat. And she finally understood that he was asking for help.

The idiot. Why in blazes hadn't he come right out and asked her ages ago? It was a question she'd have to defer until later.

Right now, she had no choice but to ignore his plea, since Mrs. Haddon had backed her neatly into a corner. Right now, Edie couldn't help him any more than she'd been able to help herself a few weeks ago, after she'd pitched herself headfirst into scandal.

She turned and gave the wretched woman her most charming smile. "Indeed, ma'am. After all, who doesn't love a good wedding?"

Chapter Thirteen

Edie's mother was ensconced in bed with a huge pile of pillows supporting her back and her portable writing desk on her lap. It was almost eleven o'clock in the morning, but she didn't appear ready to venture forth from her bedroom anytime soon.

"Mamma, are you sure you don't want a tour of the castle?" Edie asked. "I'm sure Mr. Gilbride would be more than happy to give us one."

Her mother looked up over the half spectacles she wore only when attending to her correspondence. "Mr. Gilbride is a very kind and genteel man, but I prefer not to have to interact with the family any sooner than I must, after that gruesome excuse for a dinner party last night."

Edie leaned against one of the scrolled posts at the foot of the enormous bed. "I'm sorry, Mamma. If not for my idiotic behavior in London, we wouldn't find ourselves in this mess. It's not fair that you have to spend the entire winter with a band of lunatics."

When Mamma studied her in silence for a few moments, Edie had to resist the urge to shuffle her feet. She'd been managing her mother since she was a child, and rather deftly, too. It was disconcerting to know that, for once, her mother was managing her.

"What's done is done, Eden," Mamma finally replied. "Besides, there is no sacrifice I am not willing to make on behalf of my children."

Because there was no way Edie could respond truthfully to that comment, she settled for what she hoped was an appropriately grateful expression.

"Thank heavens I am such an attentive parent," her mother added, "since I could not tolerate the idea of you having to bear the company of Lord Riddick's insufferable family without the support of your mamma."

Edie wrinkled her nose. "They're not all bad. Mr. Gilbride is a lovely gentleman, and I'm sure I can bring his lordship around soon enough. And you know you're very fond of Captain Gilbride. You've said on more than one occasion that he's almost like family."

"That was before I met his *real* family. I do hope the captain has the good sense not to be forced into marriage with that dreary Miss Haddon. What a tragic mistake that would be."

Edie felt her throat go tight. She'd lain awake for hours trying to sort through the complicated obligations and relationships of Alec's family. Unfortunately, she kept returning to the fact that he was well and truly betrothed, and it was highly unlikely that he would be able to free himself from that long-standing commitment. Alec might be reckless, but she knew he would never wish to dishonor his cousin or his family, no matter his personal feelings.

That depressing conclusion had kept her awake until the wee hours of the morning.

But she'd also reached another conclusion—that he'd been up to something last night with his obvious attempts to flirt with her. Edie fully intended to tackle him on the subject as soon as she got her wayward emotions under control. She had no desire to make a fool of herself by revealing how easily he could obliterate her common sense just by casting her one of his famous smoldering gazes.

More than one suitor over the years had accused her of lacking a tender heart, simply because she wasn't stupid enough to succumb to empty flattery. Perhaps she *had* developed a bit of a varnish over her heart these last few years, but it was a necessary and practical defense. That Alec had penetrated that coating was beyond a doubt.

"I don't think he has a choice in the matter," Edie said, determined once more to be that practical person. "Surely you can see that he must honor his commitment to Miss Haddon. And from what I observed last night, his family certainly expects him to do so."

Her mother gave her a patently condescending smile. "We'll see, my dear."

"Mamma," Edie said in a warning voice.

"Run along now, Eden." Her mother made a shooing motion. "I promised your father a letter on our arrival to Blairgal, and I have several other notes I must write as well."

When Mamma decided a conversation was over, it was generally over. Besides, Edie didn't really feel up to the task of talking her mother out of foolish hopes when it came to Alec.

"Are you still here, Eden?" Mamma asked without looking up from her lap desk.

"All right, I'm going," she grumbled in reply.

She turned on her heel and marched out to the long gallery, where she came to a halt, wondering what to do next. Although she wasn't yet ready to see Alec, Edie wasn't inclined to talk to anyone else either. What she truly needed was fresh air and a visit to the stables to see if she could find a suitable horse. Right now the castle made her feel caged in. A walk in the brisk Highland air—or a ride across the pretty glens she'd seen on their arrival yesterday—would no doubt do wonders in clearing her muddled brain and helping her think.

When she turned to go back to her room to change, she had to repress a startled shriek. Alec stood only a few feet away, his arms crossed over his brawny chest, a shoulder propping him against the wall. He'd clearly been waiting for her, and that made her heart thud even harder against her ribs.

"What in heaven's name are you doing, skulking about in the hall?" she demanded.

He let out a low, rumbling laugh. "I never skulk. It's undignified."

"You were a spy, remember? Of course you skulk."

He shrugged. For a moment, she stood transfixed by the sight of his broad, beautiful shoulders moving under the fine wool of his coat.

"And if I was skulking, lass, I should think the reason obvious. I've been waiting for you." His silky voice was expressly designed to ruffle the nerves of any woman not halfway to the grave. "I thought we would go on that tour of the castle I mentioned last night."

Irritation feathered its way into her brain. Was he really going to pretend that his behavior last night—or his family's—was in any way acceptable? He must either think her dicked in the nob or one of the silly society misses who trailed after him.

Edie might be halfway to falling in love with him, but she had no intention of giving Captain Alasdair Gilbride the upper hand.

"And did ye now, laddie?" she retorted as she propped her hands on her hips. "I would have thought ye had other things to do—like spending time with yer fiancée."

He winced as he pushed away from the wall. "I suppose I deserved that," he said ruefully.

"You certainly did, and a great deal more besides," she said.

"I need to speak with you," he said bluntly.

He'd dropped the charming rogue routine, at least for the moment, but Edie didn't know if she was quite ready to discuss what she thought they were going to discuss.

"About?" she hedged.

He looked slightly annoyed. "It would appear I owe you an explanation for my behavior last night."

"Really? I thought you owed me an apology."

He stared blankly at her for a few seconds before breaking into a grin that charmed her all the way to the bone. "As bad as that, was it?"

"You know it was," she scoffed.

He started to answer then clamped his mouth shut as he looked past her. Edie glanced over her shoulder to see a housemaid reach the top of the stairs, her arms loaded with freshly pressed linens.

With a slight flush to her cheeks the girl hurried by them, murmuring an apology in a soft Highland accent. Alec smiled back at her, and Edie couldn't help but notice the interest in the maid's eye and the way she dimpled at him. In fact, she even darted a look back, slowing down to inspect him from the rear. The back view was just as nice as the front view, so Edie couldn't blame the girl for wanting to look, but she narrowed her gaze nonetheless. The maid took the hint and scurried down the hall to disappear into one of the bedrooms.

"Why are you scowling at the maid?" Alec asked.

Sometimes Edie wondered if he had any idea of his effect on women. "I'm not scowling at her. I'm scowling at you."

"I don't see why, since I just apologized."

"You most certainly did not."

"If I didn't, it was because I have no intention of

groveling in the hallway in front of half the staff," he said, taking her arm. "We need some privacy to talk properly."

When he started to tow her in the direction of her room, she raised a protest. "First, you needn't manhandle me. Second, if you think I'm going to allow you to haul me off to some secluded corner for a tête-à-tête, you must be mad. I have no desire to court scandal with you, Captain Gilbride."

He propelled her past her room and down a corridor that seemed to lead to another wing. "That's rich, coming from you. As far as I can tell, scandal is your middle name."

Edie wrenched her arm away, pivoted on her heel, and started to stalk back to her room. He let out a rather salty curse and came after her.

"Edie, please stop."

She almost stumbled to hear him use her nickname, but she forced herself to ignore him. A moment later a large hand clamped down on her shoulder, bringing her to a halt.

Fuming, she stared straight ahead, refusing to look at him. She was afraid he might see how deeply his words had wounded her.

"I'm sorry," he said. "I don't know why I said that."

"Perhaps because you're an idiot?" she replied in a tight voice.

Edie let him gently turn her to face him. She had to steel herself against the wry, charming smile that curled up the corners of his strong mouth. When he smiled like that, she could practically feel her heart drop out of her chest and commence flopping around at his feet.

"I believe the correct term is *great Scottish oaf,*" he said. "And I certainly am one for saying something so foolish and undeserved. Please accept my apology." His expression seemed utterly sincere.

Edie sighed. "Unfortunately, it's not entirely undeserved. I accept your apology, but you still owe me another."

"I do, but I'd still like to speak with you privately. What I have to tell you is of a rather delicate nature."

That set her heart pounding again, but she forced herself to be sensible. "I meant what I said about not wanting to cause a scandal. I can't afford to do that sort of thing again."

"I have no intention of putting you in any sort of compromising or indelicate position." Alec glanced out one of the windows that lined the side of the corridor. "I suppose we could go for a walk around the grounds, but it looks like there'll be rain within the next few minutes."

Edie stared wistfully at the view, an extensive garden of hedges and flowerbeds at the base of a large terrace that was edged by a lawn that eventually gave way to rolling glens. She could just make out a stream flashing in the distance. Beyond that, dark peaks rose up to a glowering sky. "Oh, drat. I was so hoping to get a ride in this morning. It was completely sunny only a half hour ago."

"Welcome to the Highlands. If you wait another half hour, it'll likely start snowing."

She couldn't help laughing at the annoyed tone to his voice. "How ever does one plan for outdoor excursions in Scotland?"

"One can't," he said, taking her arm again. "You simply dress warmly and hope you bloody well don't get soaked or freeze to death." He started to walk her down the corridor.

"Now where are you going?"

"Don't worry. If anyone sees us, we can tell them I'm taking you on that tour I promised you."

"I thought that was mostly a ruse to annoy your relatives. One I'd say succeeded quite admirably."

He flashed her a grin. "It did, didn't it? But you're wrong

to think that I don't want to spend time with you, Edie. I very much do."

The breathless sensation that so often overcame her while in his company returned. "You're very free with my given name, all of the sudden. Don't you think you're being a trifle impertinent?"

He grinned down at her. "Oh, I do hope so."

Edie had some hopes of her own, but she knew it best not to express them—or even think of them.

While he led her through what seemed an endless number of corridors, he talked about the castle's architecture and its ancient history. She found herself becoming fascinated.

Blairgal Castle was enormous, with three imposing towers, several wings, and a center block that comprised the most modern part of the house. Amazingly enough, the entire structure seemed to be both in use and well maintained, which spoke to the wealth and management of the estate and title. Edie had never been impressed with either grandiosity or luxury, but she was impressed with Blairgal. Its history and beauty had been lovingly preserved, and she could certainly understand the earl's pride in the Riddick family's ancestral home.

Even more interesting was Alec's deep knowledge of Blairgal's history and his reluctant pride. He was pointing out a particularly fine example of a feudal carving at the top of one tower's staircase when she interrupted him.

"Why did you run away?" she asked. "Did you hate it so much back then?"

He glanced at her, clearly startled. "I never hated it."

She frowned. "Then why run? And why stay away for ten years?" She suspected the basics, of course, but she wanted to hear his reasoning.

He stared up at the old carving, as if the answer to her question was contained in the smooth, polished stone.

Then he gave a slight shrug and flashed another of his rogue's smiles.

"Don't you think it's time you called me Alasdair? Or Alec? After all, as your mamma has pointed out on more than one occasion, we're practically family."

"We're nothing of the sort, and you know it. Now, stop avoiding my question."

He crossed his arms over his chest and planted his feet in an oh-so-masculine stance. "I'll tell you the entire story if you call me Alasdair."

"There's no point in trying to be masterful with me," she said. "It won't work." That probably wasn't true, but there was no need for her to acknowledge it.

He casually took a step closer. She had to resist the impulse to step back.

"Really?" he asked. It was amazing what he managed to suggest with that one simple word.

"Yes, really."

When he took another step forward, Edie did move back. And when the satisfaction in his gaze flared into something darker—and hotter—she flapped a hand at him.

"Oh, all right, you beast," she said. "I'll call you Alec, but only when we're by ourselves."

He rewarded her with a smile that seemed to light up the gloomy corners of both the corridor and her heart.

"And I do hope we'll be spending quite a bit of time alone together," he said.

She shook her head. "You are such a wretched flirt."

"Me?" He adopted a wounded look. "I'm the soul of rectitude."

"The soul of ridiculousness, perhaps."

Laughing, he directed her down the spiral stone staircase, keeping a firm hand on her arm as he carefully guided her down the narrow steps. His touch felt protective—even possessive—and Edie had to wrestle down an instinctive rush of pleasure.

They came out in a long, tight passage that she suspected was in the oldest part of the castle. If she stood in the center, she could have flattened her hands against both walls. And yet almost every square inch of those walls was covered with antique tapestries and gilt-framed portraits that were clearly centuries old. Cool gray stone lay under her feet, and the carved wooden ceiling was crosshatched with beams that had turned smooth and dark with age. Deep window alcoves ran along one side, the space between them covered with more huge tapestries.

Edie felt like she'd stepped back in time to feudal Scotland.

Carefully, she touched one of the tapestries, which depicted a scene of battle. Despite the obvious age of the piece, the colors were still vibrant and the handiwork exceptional.

"What a splendid corridor," she said. "It's like living history."

"It connects the two oldest towers. The tapestries are part of a set that were woven here at Blairgal and are considered some of the family's greatest treasures."

"I can see why your grandfather is so proud of the place," she said, smiling up at him.

"You must be sure to tell him how wonderful it is, repeatedly. And ask him as many questions about its history as you can."

"Yes, I had deduced that was the best way past his crusty exterior."

He let out a quiet sigh. "He wasn't always that way. Well, yes he was, but he's gotten worse. I think he's in a lot of pain."

She grimaced. "I'm sorry to hear that."

He waved her to a window alcove that was fitted with

a snug padded bench. It overlooked an inner courtyard with carved stone benches, several large urns and pots for flowers, and a pretty ornamental pond. It would be a lovely retreat in the summer.

Edie sat and arranged her skirts, then looked up at him. He towered over her, but his attention wasn't on her. Rather, he stared out the window. She fancied that he didn't see the courtyard as it appeared now, but as how it had appeared long ago, perhaps when he was a child.

"My mother loved to sit in that courtyard, by all accounts," he said. "She would spread a blanket on the grass on warm summer days and read for hours."

"Do you remember her?" Edie asked softly.

His focus pulled back to her. "Not really. I was only two when she died of a fever. That's when my grandfather truly started to change, my father said. He was devastated by her death."

"Of course, she was his only child," she said. "But at least he had you."

That knocked the somber look off his face. "Yes, a little hellion. Apparently, I was getting into trouble from the moment I took my first steps."

"That clearly hasn't changed."

He propped a shoulder against one wall of the alcove, getting comfortable. He was so ridiculously handsome—and so close to her—that it took all her will not to give him sheep eyes like a foolish girl.

"I'd ask you to sit," Edie said, "but this bench is too small."

"I'm willing to try squeezing in," he said, waggling his eyebrows in a silly fashion.

"That would be most improper." She glanced around his big body down the hall. "I take it this is your solution for privacy while maintaining the proprieties."

He nodded. "This hall is normally deserted at any given

time of the day, but it's still quite public. We should be fine here if anyone stumbles upon us."

"Very well," Edie said. She pinned a stern expression on her face. "You may commence with the apology."

He smiled. "I've forgotten what I was supposed to be apologizing about."

"Then let me remind you," she said tartly. "You were making a concerted effort to flirt with me in front of your betrothed. I presume the purpose was to get some sort of rise out of her or to make her jealous, for reasons I haven't figured out yet."

Alec jerked himself up straight. "Bloody hell. It wasn't to make her jealous, I can tell you that," he said, his brogue coming out.

"Then perhaps you can enlighten me as to what you *were* doing, because I have the feeling you were using me to do it. I must say that I don't very much appreciate that fact, Captain Gilbride."

"I thought you were going to call me Alec."

"I am not in the mood for personal intimacies. I'm quite irritated with you."

And hurt. He'd all but admitted that he was using her.

He sighed. "I'm sorry, Edie. I didn't think you'd mind engaging in a mild flirtation with me. After all, you have legions of suitors in London, and you never seemed to mind keeping all of them dangling after you."

She stared up at him. "You did not just say that."

"Why? What did I say?" he asked, looking puzzled.

She had to bite back an oath. God save her from thick-headed Scotsmen. "You just accused me of being a flirt."

He looked startled. "No, I didn't. I implied that you *like* to flirt. There's a difference, you know."

She eyed him in disbelief. "I suppose I should ask you to explain that difference, but you would just confuse us both. What I really want to know is why you were flirting with me in the first place, and doing it in such an outrageous fashion in front of your entire family and your betrothed. And," she said, starting to get wound up again, "did you really think I was going to flirt back with you in those circumstances?"

He winced slightly. "I suppose I hadn't really thought that far ahead."

She shook her head in disgust. "And you call yourself a spy. I can only imagine the fixes you got yourself into if last night is any indication of your talents."

"I never had to deal with a fiancée on any of my missions," he said. "Only Frenchmen trying to kill me."

"I suspect that almost everyone at the table wanted to kill you last night." Edie paused, remembering the different reactions she'd seen. "Except for Miss Haddon. She didn't seem to mind at all."

He crossed his arms over his chest, waiting quietly while she thought it through. And piece by piece it was finally becoming clear. "Oh, good God," Edie exclaimed. "You're trying to make her angry enough to break off your engagement, is that it?"

He smiled at her, as if she'd just done something splendid. "I was hoping I wouldn't have to spell it out for you. It is rather an awkward situation, you must admit."

"Awkward, indelicate, and insanely stupid," she said, coming to her feet.

Edie was so furious she could barely see straight. She was tempted to box his ears, but she'd probably damage her hand on his thick skull. She settled for jabbing her finger at his chest instead.

"How dare you manipulate me like that?" she raged. "And how dare you treat your fiancée in so shabby a fashion? What in God's name must she think of me? Of all the stupid . . ."

She tried to push past him, blinking her eyes against a

sudden rush of tears. After everything she'd gone through, this was the final humiliation. And the fact that it had come from him, the only man for whom she'd ever developed real feelings, made her want to hide in the nearest dark corner.

He stepped in front of her. She tried to slip past him, but he was just too blasted big. Clenching her teeth, she refused to look at him as she tried to will away the tears.

"Edie, let me explain," he said. "I swear it's not as bad as it sounds."

His hands came up to her shoulders. Then one slipped behind, gently cradling her neck. The other moved to her chin, nudging it up and forcing her to look at him. His handsome face, looking as unhappy as she felt, swam at the edges, blurred by tears.

"Ah, lass," he said in a low rumble. "Please don't cry. You'll kill me if you cry." When his fingers stroked along the edge of her jaw, it made her shiver.

"I'd like to kill you," she whispered. Her throat was thick and tight. "Alec, how could you?"

His mouth pulled taut and a muscle twitched in his hard jaw, as if he were clenching his teeth. The hand at the back of her neck moved up, his fingers digging through her hair in a gentle grip. She couldn't escape if she tried.

And when his gaze went dark and smoky, she didn't want to.

"Because," he rasped, "I'm a great Scottish oaf."

And then his mouth came down on hers in a kiss that knocked her heart straight into her ribs.

Chapter Fourteen

For a few horrible seconds, the most exasperating woman Alec had ever known stood as rigid as a post in his arms, her lips firmly closed against him and his clumsy attempts at apology. He was no doubt making things worse by kissing her but couldn't seem to help himself. The pain on Edie's sweet face and the shine of tears behind her spectacles had ripped through his heart like a mortar shell. She'd started a riot in a society ballroom and still come out strong, for Christ's sake, and yet he'd managed to wound her. Those tears had told him just how much.

Oaf was too kind a word, for him.

He was half-expecting a knee to the bollocks when she breathed out a funny little whimper that vibrated softly against his lips. Hands that had been balled into fists and pushing against his chest suddenly relaxed. Her fingers opened, trembling as they grasped the fabric of his coat.

And, miracle of miracles, her mouth finally softened. A moment later, she was kissing him back with an eagerness that almost took him out at the knees.

He cradled her head, his fingers tunneling through her silky hair as he adjusted the fit. His other hand slid to her waist, holding her gently against him as he began to explore the lush promise of her mouth. Teasing, he slicked his tongue across her lips, tasting honey and cinnamon, an intoxicating, perfect mix. Every nerve and muscle in his body silently urged him forward, straining to further plumb her luscious depths.

When Edie hesitated for a fraction of a second, Alec's heart stuttered with dismay. But then her hands slipped up to his shoulders and she slowly parted her lips. He surged in, taking too much too fast, but she didn't retreat. Instead, she tangled her tongue with his, going up on her tiptoes to meet him.

He was finally getting her measure. Edie had enough charm and confidence to launch a thousand ships. But innocence lurked behind that bold façade, as did an entirely unexpected vulnerability. Her kiss was eager, open, and without artifice. It was all Edie, wild and sweet, giving as good as she got with a heady promise of more to come.

He had every intention of taking her all the way down that road.

She let out an engaging little moan and snuggled closer, brushing her full breasts against his waistcoat. Sensation bolted through him, driving what felt like every ounce of blood down to his cock. Instinctively, he slipped his hand to her delightfully round bottom—good God, the woman was a lovely handful—and nudged her into him, flush against his erection. Then he picked her up and took a step forward, trapping her between his body and the passage wall.

Edie froze in his arms. Alec went still as well, suddenly all too aware that he was preparing to make love to a virginal spinster—in a corridor, against a wall, in broad daylight.

Jesus.

Then she came to life in his arms, and not in a good

way. She jerked her head away and a funny little growl issued from her lips.

"Get off of me," she hissed, trying to struggle her way out of his embrace. "Are you deliberately trying to destroy my reputation?"

Alec mentally sighed. He almost wished someone would catch them, since it would make things a damn sight easier for both of them, although she had yet to realize it. But now that a small portion of his blood was finally heading back to his brain, he realized what an idiot he was. If he had any hope of winning Edie over, this certainly wasn't the way to go about it.

She was worse than a nest full of French spies when it came to playing havoc with his plans. It was time to get the situation—and her—under control.

"Do I have to kick you in the shins to make you let me go?" Her cheeks were pink and her eyes shot daggers at him. But her full mouth was rosy and damp from his kisses, and her breasts heaved against her trim bodice. She looked so damn tempting that it took every ounce of his discipline not to carry her off to the nearest empty bedroom and have his way with her.

That was the most enticing image to come into his brain in a very, very long time.

No, ever.

"Stop wriggling about like a worm on the end of a hook," he growled.

"I cannot believe you just called me a worm," she snapped, wriggling harder as she tried to escape.

"Oh, for Christ's sake." He wrapped his hands around her waist and picked her straight up off her feet. She squeaked out a startled protest, but he simply plopped her back on the padded window bench and braced himself in front of her to prevent her from bolting.

Her eyes flashed from behind her spectacles, promising

all sorts of retribution, but her lenses had gone partly foggy.

"Can you even see?" he asked.

"Confound it." She whipped off her spectacles and rubbed them on her sleeve before jamming them back on her nose.

Her gaze said quite clearly that she would like to rend him, limb from limb.

"You needn't look at me like I'm some sort of ogre," Alec said, "or like I'm going to ravish you right here in the hallway. I promise you, I'm not."

She stared at him a moment longer, then looked down pointedly at the fall of his breeches. "Really? You could have fooled me," she said.

Alec had to bite back a disbelieving laugh. Only Edie would have the nerve to comment on the state of a man's equipment at a time like this.

"I sincerely hope you're not in the habit of making that sort of comment to other men of your acquaintance," he said. "It's not exactly the most appropriate thing one could say under the circumstances."

She crossed her arms over her chest. "Of course I'm not! But in your case, one could hardly fail to miss it . . . that."

Her words, coupled with her reluctantly fascinated gaze, had the predictable effect. Repressing a sigh, he turned his back to her and adjusted himself.

He heard a slight, choking sound from behind him. Glancing over his shoulder, he lifted an ironic eyebrow. "Is something wrong, Miss Whitney?"

Even though her cheeks were now bright red, she still managed to meet his gaze with a defiant one of her own. He had to give her credit—Edie never backed down from anything.

"Nothing at all," she responded sarcastically. "Except for the fact that you're the rudest man I've ever met."

"I doubt that," he said drily, turning around.

She eyed him for several seconds, still fuming, before letting out an exasperated sigh. "You're right, which I suppose doesn't say much for the company I keep. Or, should I say, the company I *used* to keep."

He propped a shoulder against the wall of the alcove, settling back in. "I wouldn't disagree with that assessment. I've always wondered why you hung about with that pack of idiots who call themselves your suitors."

"They might be idiots, but at least they're not lummoxes." Her insult held little heat. She sighed again, and this one held more than a measure of melancholy. "Not that I actually have anymore suitors."

He hated the brooding expression that had come over her face. Melancholy did not sit well on Eden Whitney, especially when only moments ago she'd gone up like fire in his arms. Her sudden shift in mood made Alec want to throttle every man who'd treated her like anything other than the splendid girl she was. Edie was wasted on the *ton,* and every second he passed in her company convinced him that she was exactly what he was looking for. What he needed.

"You're well rid of them," he said. "Especially when you have a great lummox like me sniffing around your pretty ankles. I'm much more fun than that feeble-minded lot. You should stick to me from now on."

She peered up at him in disbelief. "Have you forgotten something?"

"I don't think so."

"How about Donella Haddon? She's your betrothed."

"Not for long, I hope."

"You are such a dreadful rake," she said. "I don't know how you can bear to live with yourself."

"If by *rake* you mean I like women, you're correct. But I've never seduced an innocent . . ." He paused for a moment when she gaped at him but then forged ahead.

"I've never seduced an innocent or an unwilling woman, or manipulated one for ulterior motives."

"I cannot believe you have the nerve to say that to me," she exclaimed.

"Until now," he amended. "You're my first."

"You, sir, are shameless. May I remind you that you manipulated people for a living? You and Wolf ruthlessly did that to Evie and me just a few months ago, or had you forgotten? As far as I'm concerned, manipulation is your middle name."

He flicked that away with a casual hand. "That's different. I was protecting king and country. One uses the tools at one's disposal when forced to save the day."

She looked awestruck, and not in a flattering way. "Alasdair Gilbride, you are the most—"

He cut her off by crouching down before her and taking her hands. "I know. I'm arrogant and immensely irritating, and you have every reason to be thoroughly annoyed with me. But despite my nefarious and underhanded dealings—"

"And clumsy," she interrupted. "You forgot clumsy."

When he smiled at her, she bit her lower lip, suddenly looking rather shy. On her, it was absolutely adorable.

"That, too," he said. "But despite my many faults, there is something that you should know."

"What?" she whispered, gazing at him as if he were a cypher she needed to crack. Right now, she didn't look like the sophisticated miss who'd spent years leading the men of the *ton* in a merry dance. She looked like an earnest girl stumbling headlong into her first romance.

He leaned in to brush a quick kiss across her lips. "That I've never wanted a woman like I want you, Eden Whitney. And I intend to have you."

She blinked with surprise. Then her eyes narrowed suspiciously. "What, exactly, do you mean by that?"

"I'm not offering you a carte blanche, if that's what you're thinking."

She jerked upright, almost toppling backward into the window frame. "Are you asking me to marry you?" she asked.

"I thought I'd try courting you first," he said.

After all, despite the enthusiasm of their recent kiss, Alec had no real idea how Edie felt about him. He knew she was very fond of her life in London, and there was every indication she intended to flee back south as quickly as his carriage—and the restoration of her reputation—would allow. Spending a good part of her life in the Highlands would not be how she envisioned her future.

She stared at him a few moments longer, looking utterly perplexed. Then she gave a funny little shake, as if she were a spaniel coming in from the rain. Her head tilted back and the mocking gleam in her eye signaled the return of the self-confident girl who'd swaggered through London's ballrooms.

"As much as I enjoy having a big, strong man worshiping at my feet," she said, "you'd better stand up before you get a crick in your back. You're much too big for me to lug all the way back to your room if you hurt yourself."

"I'd much rather carry you back to your bedroom," he said as he came to his feet.

She let out an exasperated sigh. "Aside from the fact that your comments are entirely inappropriate, must I continually remind you that you are engaged to be married?"

"Believe me, I haven't forgotten for one moment."

She flung her arms out, almost hitting the sides of the window alcove. "Then why do you keep flirting with me?"

He winced. "No need to yell, lass."

"There is every need, since it's apparently the only way to penetrate your thick skull," she said. "Now, before we were sidetracked by . . . by . . ."

"The kissing?" He was a brute to tease her, but it was so much fun. Edie challenged him in a way no other woman ever had. She would make even the most staid, rule-bound life worth living.

"Yes, before that you were about to explain your deranged plan to trick Miss Haddon into breaking your betrothal. I'd like to continue that discussion without any such further distraction."

He adopted an appropriately contrite look. "I promise to behave. Now, what would you like to know?"

"For one thing, why don't you want to marry Miss Haddon? She seems like a perfectly lovely young woman to me—beautiful, gracious, and well mannered, and with all the usual accomplishments one expects. Just the sort of wife the average, thickheaded aristocrat should want by his side, I would think."

Conventional, in other words, which was one of the reasons why Alec didn't want to marry Donella. Fortunately, from the tone of her voice and the sour look on her face, he suspected Edie didn't want him to marry Donella either. "I won't deny that she's a bonny lass," he said in a musing tone.

She reached out and whacked him on the arm. "Stop teasing me and just answer the question."

He grinned. "No need to pummel me, sweetheart. Aside from the fact that we don't love each other, we're entirely unsuited. I have no doubt we would bore each other to death, if we didn't murder each other first."

The tense set to her shoulders seemed to ease as she digested his comment. "I see. But you grew up with her, so I assumed you were close."

Alec frowned. "I'm fond of her in the way one is generally fond of one's relations, but we've never been close. Fergus and I were the best of friends when we were lads, but Donella was never particularly interested in us or what we did. She was always reading or doing whatever else girls did at home all day. When she wasn't off at the kirk, that is, taking lessons or helping the minister's wife tend to the poor."

Edie's eyebrows rose. "Is she very religious?"

"Pious as a nun, at least she was back then."

"Did you never write to her when you were away to find out what she thought about everything?"

He grimaced. "God, no. That would have only compounded the problem."

"How so?"

Alec shifted, trying to get comfortable against the cool stone at his back. Clearly, Edie wanted a full explanation, and he supposed it was time to give it to her. Well, most of it, anyway. There were a few facts he couldn't yet share with her—not until he was more certain that she felt about him the way he now realized he felt about her.

"I'm sure you've deduced that I ran away mainly because of Donella and that bloody engagement. I'd known since I was a lad that my grandfather and her father had planned for us to marry, but I'd never taken it seriously." He gave her a rueful smile. "What boy of thirteen even thinks of that sort of thing?"

She wrinkled her nose. "Girls have to start thinking about making a good marriage at a ridiculously early age. If we don't snag a husband by the time we're twenty, we're practically on the shelf."

"You didn't seem in the slightest hurry."

"I never had to worry about it until recently, but let's not get into that now. Please continue."

Alec had never met a woman less in danger of becoming an ape leader. He thought about disabusing her of any such notion but decided he'd best leave that for later when he could do it properly.

"As I said, Donella's father and my grandfather had, as

I subsequently found out, been planning our wedding almost from the day Donella was born. In that desire they were supported—and still are—by Angus Graham, who is branch chief and Aunt Glenna's brother. The Grahams are also related to us through my maternal grandmother. Angus Graham's father was my grandmother's brother."

She took a few seconds to work the relationships through in her head, then nodded. "Obviously both sides of the family feel strongly about this, which isn't necessarily unusual. Parents are always trying to manage their children into advantageous matches. After all, they don't call it *the marriage mart* for nothing." She frowned. "But this is what I don't understand. If you don't want to go through with it, why would your family try to force you? It's not a matter of money or land, is it?"

"True, it's nothing like that. Donella's dowry would be quite small. It's all about the clan."

"I'm not entirely sure what you mean. I understand the clan is important, but . . ." She trailed off, her skepticism evident.

"Clan and family mean everything to a Scotsman—and to Scotswomen. For centuries in the Highlands, we fought for land and power, and many times simply fought to survive. Sometimes those battles were with other clans, and sometimes with the English. Our strength depended on clan loyalty, both among the direct members and the sept families. Marriage was an important way to strengthen those loyalties and increase our power."

"That I can understand, but we are living in the nineteenth century. There's no need for that sort of thing anymore. Scotland is as much a part of England as, well, England is."

It wasn't really, but there was no easy way to make her see that. For Scotsmen, their identity and loyalty to the traditional ways was bred in the bone.

"Tell that to my grandfather," he simply said.

She raised her eyebrows. "Have *you* told your grandfather that?"

"Of course I have. Do you think I'm a complete dimwit?" he asked, exasperated.

Edie flapped a hand. "All right, I apologize. I suppose I can understand it, given that he's from an older and more traditional generation. And it certainly makes sense from Mrs. Haddon's point of view, since you're heir to a wealthy estate."

"And the future laird. Aunt Glenna is very big on that sort of thing."

"Well, I can't blame her for that. Mothers always want their daughters to marry up," she said. "Still, it's not right for either your grandfather or Mrs. Haddon to pressure you to marry against your will. It's positively medieval."

He couldn't hold back a cynical snort. "My grandfather defines the word *medieval* when it comes to telling his family how to live their lives, especially me."

"Which, I'm sure, didn't include working for the Foreign Office or becoming a spy for Wellington."

"Grandfather didn't even want me going away to university. A year a two at Edinburgh, perhaps, but certainly not Oxford or Cambridge."

"Why ever not?"

"Let's just say he didn't want me coming under any more English influences than were necessary." Not that he could entirely blame his grandfather—not after what had happened to Alec's mother that one Season she'd spent in London with a husband who, by Walter's own account, was a loving but inattentive mate. She'd fallen under the influence of one particular Englishman—a bloody prince, as it turned out—and he had left her in an exceedingly compromised position.

That, however, was not something he wanted to share with Edie just yet.

She shook her head. "He is rather strident on the subject of Englishmen, as are Mrs. Haddon and Fergus."

He grimaced. "I'm sorry. I wish he was less so."

She waved an airy hand. "Please, the average society doyenne is much worse. And it's not as if I have the most biddable temper in the world, either." She flashed him an enchantingly self-deprecating grin. "After all, I have been known to be a tad rude to certain members of the opposite sex now and again."

He assumed a shocked expression. "I cannot believe it."

When she laughed, Alec had to resist the urge to haul her into his arms again. She had the most enticing laugh he'd ever heard—low, husky, and laced with a natural sensuality.

"Although I must say," he added, "you managed my family quite well last night, all things considered. You put Fergus entirely off his feed."

"That's because I'm the real master manipulator," she said cheerfully. "Now, please tell me the rest of this sordid tale. When did you decide to run away from the family hearth and home?"

He loved the fact that she didn't pretend to be something she wasn't.

"My grandfather and I had already been fighting over his refusal to let me leave Scotland for university. Walter did his best to persuade the old fellow to send me to Oxford but met with little success."

Edie gave him a faint smile. "You certainly seemed in a hurry to escape the Highlands."

"I loved the Highlands and I loved Blairgal. When I was a child, they were my entire world. But when I realized that my grandfather had no intention of letting me leave—at least not for very long—it started to feel like a prison. I began to think that if I didn't escape, I would end up in a madhouse."

He paused, and then let out a rueful laugh. "I know that must sound ridiculous, given all the advantages I had. I can only say that I was a headstrong, foolish boy who had read one too many tales of adventure."

"I completely understand. Imagine what it's like for girls. We're never allowed to do anything exciting, much less travel abroad. And the sooner we leg-shackle ourselves to an eligible suitor, the better."

"So, imagine my horror when Grandfather announced my betrothal to Donella at a clan gathering to celebrate my sixteenth birthday." Alec still remembered the fight they'd had on the eve of the announcement. Though he'd never raised his voice to the earl before, he hadn't backed down and the vicious argument had only ended when Grandfather threatened to lock him in his room for a week.

"If you can believe it," he said, "he and my uncle only told Donella about their decision an hour before the announcement was made."

Edie looked horrified. "That's awful. What did your poor cousin have to say about it?"

"She acted rather martyred about the whole thing but told me it was our duty to obey. I tried to get her to fight back, to no avail. As I mentioned," he added drily, "she's always been a very obedient girl."

"That does sound dreadfully insipid of her, though she was quite young at the time."

They'd both been young, but Alec had still managed to stand up to his grandfather. And he couldn't imagine Edie allowing herself to be forced into a similar situation, no matter how young she was.

"She was fifteen and I was sixteen. We were to be married when I turned eighteen."

"That's appalling. I can't blame you for running away, even though it must have been a blow to your family."

"It was, but I had to do it. The announcement of the betrothal was the last straw." He let out a ghost of a laugh. "Sometimes I still can't believe I pulled it off."

Her lips quirked up in a wry smile. "Boys that age usually have more bottom than brains, as my father always said."

"I certainly did," Alec said. "And I wouldn't have blamed my grandfather for leaving me to my own devices. But he made sure I was looked after instead of leaving me to be murdered in some backwater London slum."

"It's very clear that he loves you, despite his gruff manner," she said softly.

Alec sighed. "Yes, he does. He also has a ridiculous amount of pride. I'm sure he couldn't bear the idea of his heir living like a pauper on the streets."

"He's not the only one in the family with a fair measure of pride," she said. "One might even call it arrogance."

"You wound me, Miss Whitney, you surely do."

"I doubt it." She took in a deep breath. "And now we've come to the crux of the matter. You've finally returned, and your family expects you to take up where you left off."

"Sadly true, as my grandfather made amply clear right after the war ended. I was to return home immediately, marry my cousin, and assume my rightful position as Master of Riddick. No more running around Europe like a frippery fellow."

Her eyes widened. "Your grandfather does know what you were doing there, doesn't he?"

"Yes, but he wasn't overly impressed. Not that he didn't see Napoleon as a threat," he hastily added when she blinked with shock. "He feared something would happen to me, and he didn't want me to put myself in harm's way."

"I can understand that," she said.

Alec understood it too, especially in light of his

mother's early, tragic death. But once the war started, Alec had known what his duty was. To abandon that duty for the safety of the Highlands would have made him a coward. Of course, there'd also been a fair measure of selfishness in that decision, too. He hadn't been ready to return home and had partly used his duty to the Union as an excuse.

"What are you going to do now?" she asked.

"About what?" he asked absently, still half-lost in the past.

She rolled her eyes. "About your betrothal."

"I'm trying to break it off, of course. In the only way I know how."

"By convincing your fiancée that you're an unrepentant rake? That's a splendid plan."

"You're the one who pointed out that only the female can honorably break it off," he countered.

He wouldn't, even if he could. He would never shame Donella, and that made him feel rather desperate, as if the old stone walls off Blairgal were falling in on him.

"Well, I certainly didn't expect you to use me as the vehicle for your ridiculous plan," she retorted.

"I'm sorry, but I did the only thing that made sense under the circumstances," he said, grimacing. "I couldn't just give the poor girl the old heave-ho, could I? As you rightly pointed out, it would besmirch everyone's honor. Publicly flirting with you seemed like a plan that might work, since I know Donella doesn't exactly worship the ground I walk on. I was hoping she'd be so disgusted with my behavior that she'd give *me* the heave-ho."

When Edie cast her gaze up, as if looking for heavenly intervention, he couldn't hold back a flare of irritation. "What else would you expect me to do?"

"I would expect you to first ask me for my help."

He lifted an ironic brow. "And would you have willingly assisted me?"

She hesitated, then let out an exasperated sigh. "Of course not."

"I rest my case."

She eyed him with distaste. "I suppose it never occurred to you that I would be offended by your stupid plan."

That had been an error of monumental proportions on his part. He realized now that her flirtations had all been good-natured and more innocent than they might appear to the casual observer. She treated all the men who trailed after her with the same offhanded, friendly demeanor. If they pursued her, it was because she was such a damned enticing woman, exuding an outrageous but entirely natural sensuality that any red-blooded man would find hard to resist.

But until that one serious error with Sir Malcolm Bannister—an unworthy bastard whom Alec intended to deal with the next time he was in London—she'd always kept to the right side of propriety. Some might think her behavior fast, but Edie was simply high-spirited, strong-willed, and much too curious for her own good. She chafed against the restrictions that society imposed upon young women, and Alec could certainly understand that.

Well, he had the solution to her problem. The more he thought about it, the more he realized what a splendid wife she would make—what a splendid countess. Edie needed a challenge, and Alec knew he would be a challenge to any sane woman. And a large, thriving household and estate, with all its duties, would provide abundant opportunities for her to exercise her energy and brainpower to good effect.

As for an outlet for her other physical energies, Alec was more than ready to allow her to exercise those on him in any way she chose.

But first they needed to sort out the business with Donella.

"I'm sorry that I offended you," he said. "I was a complete idiot."

"We can at least agree upon that point," she said. "Did it never occur to you that your plan might backfire on you? That flirting with me might simply make Miss Haddon more determined to have you?"

"No, and she wasn't determined, as I'm sure you noticed."

She looked thoughtful. "Yes, and it does seem rather odd."

He cocked an eyebrow. "Why odd?"

"If you can't figure that out, I'm not going to explain it to you."

"Oh, right." He grinned. "It's because I'm so irresistible."

"So irritating, more like it." She peered at him over the top of her spectacles. "Are you sure your cousin isn't in love with you?"

"Positive."

"Then why are you so sure that she wants to marry you? She certainly didn't seem keen to discuss the plans for the impending happy event, did she?"

"Most definitely not."

Edie shook her head with exasperation. "Then why are you so certain?"

"Because my grandfather told me that she still wants to."

"And you haven't actually asked Miss Haddon herself?"

The incredulous tone in her voice made him feel rather defensive. "Why the devil would I need to do that? I already had my answer."

"From your grandfather, you birdwit. You have to talk to *her,* and you have to do it alone. If she doesn't wish to marry you, then you can join forces and stand up to your relations together."

Knowing Donella, and knowing that she'd spent the last

ten years hearing all the reasons why she should marry him, he didn't think that very likely. But he supposed he didn't have a choice, since Edie clearly thought his plan was the silliest thing she'd ever heard.

She'd gone back to looking more thoughtful than annoyed. She opened her lips, pressed them shut, and then opened them again. "Are you quite sure you don't want to marry Miss Haddon?" She managed an offhand manner, but Alec heard the uncertain note in her voice.

"Actually, I think I'd rather marry you."

Her eyebrows shot up, and it took a few moments for her to answer. "That's not exactly a ringing endorsement, Captain Gilbride. I can only assume this impulse is a recent discovery, deriving more from circumstance than emotion."

"No, it isn't recent," he responded quietly. "I've been thinking about it for some weeks now."

She blinked at him several times, looking completely off-balance. "Oh, that's . . . that's nice," she stuttered. "I think."

He reached down a hand to cup her determined little chin. "You think?"

Her eyes went soft and warm, and her lips parted slightly. Heat gathered in Alec's chest before starting to make its way down to his groin. He bent to kiss her, but she jerked back, batting his hand away.

"It's complicated, Alasdair Gilbride. You're *engaged*."

"That complication will be resolved shortly. I promise."

She put a hand to her forehead. "You're a menace."

He grabbed her by the elbows, lifting her into his arms. She gasped with outrage—not very convincingly, he thought—and braced her hands against his chest.

"I'd like to be a menace to you," he murmured, ducking down to feather a kiss across her lush lips. When she quivered in his arms, he couldn't hold back a low laugh. "Think of all the fun we could have if you married me."

For a moment, she leaned into him, her mouth ripe and perfect for kisses. Then, those lips clamped shut against him and she gave him a shove.

"We are not having this conversation until you talk to your cousin," she said. "You need to find out how she truly feels about you."

He let out an exaggerated sigh. "Fine. If that's what it takes, I'll do it."

Alec had already decided to talk to Donella. As Edie had pointed out, it was the right thing to do and, at this point, the smartest.

He gave his future wife a seductive smile as he tried to reel her in again. "You drive a hard bargain, lass. Now, how about sealing our deal with a kiss?"

Edie gasped again, this time sounding genuinely annoyed. "I haven't agreed to anything, you big Scottish oaf. Now get out of my way."

She shoved past him and marched down the hall, disappearing down the stone staircase in an outraged swirl of skirts.

With a sigh, Alec sank down onto the bench, pondering the question of just when he'd lost his touch with women.

Chapter Fifteen

Alec forced himself to smile at the boy who hurried out from the stables to take his horse. "Give Darius a good rubdown," he said, handing over the reins. "We had a bruising ride back from Haddon House."

"Aye, Master," said the boy. "I'll take bonny care of him."

"Captain or sir will do, lad. You needn't call me Master."

The boy eyed him uncertainly. "Whatever ye say, Ma—, sir."

Edie was right. That proper title was positively feudal, and the sooner he could break the servants of using it, the better.

Alec headed out of the stable yard toward the front of the castle. His mood was black after his disastrous talk with Donella, and even a long ride along the river hadn't made him feel any better. The Highlands were as beautiful as he remembered, but right now they still felt like a prison. Along with the beauty and the privilege came obligation, and his cousin's answer had told him just how much of a burden that obligation was about to become.

Edie had been convinced that being honest with Donella was the best way to achieve his goal of breaking the engagement, but such hadn't been the case. It now began to look like his admittedly devious plan would have had a better chance at success than honesty. It was a sad comment on his entire family, starting with himself. Clearly, they were all as barmy as dogs howling at the moon.

He stopped to gaze out over the long valley with its wild glens and its glimpse of mountain peaks. He could admit that some part of him had missed those spectacular sights when he was away, but he hadn't missed the future that apparently now awaited him as laird of the castle and all he surveyed.

A future that would include Donella Haddon, not Eden Whitney, as Lady of Riddick.

Donella didn't love him, and she'd made it abundantly clear. But she'd also confirmed that she had every intention of honoring their betrothal. When he'd tried to explain all the reasons why she shouldn't, she'd cut him off.

"It was my father's fondest wish," she'd said in a flat, chilling tone. "I promised him on his deathbed that I would honor it."

Alec didn't usually find himself at a loss for words, but a deathbed vow was a bit daunting. He'd contemplated telling Donella that he had feelings for another woman but suspected his cousin already knew that and wouldn't truly care.

Donella had also gone on to say that she had an obligation to serve as an obedient daughter of the clan. While that was downright silly as far as Alec was concerned, she didn't see it that way. She then proclaimed that she'd spent the last ten years preparing to be Countess of Riddick, and that she gratefully accepted both the burden and the privilege of the role. Before Alec could even think of a rational reply to that horrifying statement, Donella had risen, dropped him a graceful curtsey, and glided from the room.

She'd rolled him up, leaving him no other choice but to stalk out, mount his horse, and ride like a madman in a futile effort to shake off his anger with his family, Clan Graham, the bloody Highlands, and life in general.

Blowing out an exasperated breath, he spun on his boot heel and marched up the steps of the castle to the wide double doors. Because the November afternoon had grown warm and fine after the morning's cold rain, the doors had been left open to the fresh air. A footman waited in the hall, giving him a deferential nod as he took Alec's coat and hat.

"When ye have a moment, his lordship wishes to see ye in the library, Master," the footman said.

Alec's teeth clenched, but he managed not to snap the poor fellow's head off. His first order of business—after he figured a way out of his current mess—would be to have a word with Blairgal's butler about the appropriate manner of addressing him.

He headed toward the stairs on the other side of the cavernous entrance hall. Before he reached it, he heard a quick tread on the staircase, and a moment later Fergus appeared carrying a stack of ledgers. His cousin looked abstracted and slightly worried, but when he saw Alec his thin, handsome features slid into a scowl.

Christ.

No doubt he was about to receive another lecture. That would be the third of the day, given that Edie and Donella had already had a go at him.

"The laird wishes to speak with you," Fergus said in a cold voice. "In his library."

No deferential treatment from his cousin, that was for sure. Fergus didn't give a damn that Alec was Master of Riddick, probably because he was next in line to hold that title and would, in fact, someday be laird if anything happened to Alec.

Would have *been* Master if Alec had died in the war or, indeed, never been born at all.

Alec arched his eyebrows in polite enquiry. "And do you have any idea what he wants to talk to me about?"

Fergus's green eyes took on a decidedly glacial cast. "I think you know very well what he wishes to discuss."

"My betrothal to your sister, no doubt. As I also have no doubt you were discussing it with him."

When his cousin glared back, Alec crossed his arms over his chest and stared down at him. He was several inches taller than Fergus, and right now he didn't mind using his height to his advantage.

"I'll thank you to mind your own business, Fergus. This matter is between Donella and myself."

"She's my sister, Alasdair," his cousin flashed back. "It's my duty to protect her and the family's good name. And I'll do whatever is necessary to do that."

"Good God," Alec exclaimed. "She's my family, too. Do you really think I want to hurt her?"

"I don't know what you're capable of. You've been away so long that I hardly recognize you anymore," Fergus said in a harsh voice.

Alec forced himself not to respond in kind. After all, his cousin was simply trying to do his duty, as he saw fit. "Lad, you've spent all of three hours in my company since I've been back. Besides, I hardly think I've changed all that much. You certainly haven't."

As far as he could tell, his family was fairly well stuck in time, with the same ideas about how life—especially his life—should play out.

Fergus let out a disbelieving scoff. "Not changed? You must be joking. For all intents and purposes, you might as well be English."

"Ah, the ultimate insult. I'll let you in on a secret, lad. The English put their breeches on one leg at a time, just like the rest of us."

His cousin's eyes flared wide with anger. "Have you

forgotten what they did to us less than a century ago? What is still happening in some of the other counties, especially up north? They're clearing the crofters and the farmers out, Alasdair. Throwing them off the land that supported them for centuries. That's what the English have done and are still doing to us."

Alec had the impulse to bash his head against the stone surround of the fireplace. It would certainly hurt less than this conversation, which served no purpose but to dredge up old grievances.

"Fergus, I haven't forgotten one bit of our history, I assure you. How could I, since it's been pounded into my head since the day I was born? But don't blame the clearing of the lands entirely on the English. There are fine Scottish lords and ladies doing that now, too."

"That's hardly the point—"

"I agree," Alec said, interrupting him. "In fact, I don't have a bloody clue why we're even discussing this."

Fergus was practically vibrating with fury. "We're discussing it because you seem to have forgotten both where you came from and your responsibilities, especially to my sister and your family name."

"I wish I could forget them," Alec couldn't help muttering. Really, though, he just wished he could find a way to address them without making a wreck of his life and possibly Edie's and Donella's, too.

His cousin fell silent for a few moments as he struggled to master his temper.

Alec sighed. "Fergus, I don't want to fight with you."

"I don't care what you want. The only thing I care about is whether you intend to honor your obligation to my sister."

"Have any of you actually bothered to ask your sister what she'd like if she had only half a choice? She relishes the idea of our marriage as little as I do, although she's reluctant to say it."

Fergus blinked and took a step back, clearly thrown by the question. Alec couldn't help but shake his head. Clearly, no one in his idiotic family had ever discussed the issue with her—at least not in a way that truly took into account her feelings.

Not that he could really complain, since he'd done the same thing until Edie straightened him out.

"That's ridiculous," Fergus said. "Of course she wants to marry you. She's spent most of her life preparing to be Countess of Riddick."

That was almost exactly how Donella had put it, confirming his suspicion that the family had continued to drum the foolish belief into her head during Alec's years away. It was now so firmly established as gospel that no one seemed even capable of reconsidering it, much less rejecting it.

"Fergus, your sister doesn't love me," Alec said gently. "I'm not sure she even likes me very much. Don't you want to see her with someone who will make her happy?"

His cousin waved an impatient hand. "Not love you? That's stupid. What does that even mean? This is about the family and about what Donella is owed. What she deserves. And what she deserves is to be Lady of Riddick."

Alec's involuntary snort had Fergus thrusting his chin up in the air.

"It's Donella's rightful place," his cousin practically snarled. "You can't deny her that."

Alec struggled to hold on to the frayed ends of his temper. "I don't think this is really about denying Donella her rightful place, is it? It's about denying *you* your rightful place. Without me standing in your way, you'd be Master of Riddick right now. I think that's what truly sticks in your craw, not this dredged up insult to your sister's honor."

Fergus sucked in a sharp breath, taking another step back. His fists were still clenched, but he'd gone white, making his hair look like a blaze of red around his face.

Alec mentally cursed. "Fergus, lad, I'm sorry—"

"Don't bother, Alasdair," he replied in a bitter voice, half-turning away. He gazed up at the family coat of arms over the fireplace for a few moments.

"You know, I never doubted you," Fergus said, "not once. You were the laird's grandson and the rightful heir to Riddick." He laughed, and the sound was low and grating, as if it had been wrenched from his throat. "You were my hero when we were growing up, and I wanted to be just like you, fool that I was. But then you abandoned all of us, just not Donella. Do you have any idea what that did to your grandfather? You were all he had left, and you fairly broke his heart."

His cousin's pain seemed to punch a hole straight through to Alec's own heart. Rationally, he'd always known his actions had caused anguish, but he'd had the luxury of distance to insulate himself against its effects.

"He had you, lad," he said past a tight throat. "I know how much that meant to him—still means to him."

Fergus gave an angry jerk of the head. "All that matters is that you keep your promise to all of us and marry my sister."

Alec shook his head. "We were children. Besides, you know very well that *I* never made such a promise to Donella. My grandfather and your father made that commitment, one I never agreed to."

Fergus stared at him with disbelief. "You're really going to say no, aren't you? It's because of Miss Whitney, isn't it?"

Alec chose not to answer, simply returning his cousin's glare with a steadfast gaze.

Fergus went red, rage chasing away his pale, anguished expression. "Unbelievable. You would pick that English—"

"Stop, Fergus," Alec barked. "You will not say a word against Miss Whitney. In fact, you will not say another word on this subject, to me or to my grandfather. Do you understand?"

Alec might not feel entirely comfortable in his role as rightful heir, but he knew how to command. His years in the military had taught him that. Hell, and he *was* the son of a royal duke.

Fergus looked genuinely startled but then recovered. He clutched the ledgers to his chest with one arm and pointed an index finger at Alec's nose. "You do the right thing by my sister, Alasdair. You owe her that. You owe *me* that."

Exasperated but unwilling to argue anymore, Alec simply shook his head.

Fergus stared at him, and his gaze was filled with something that looked too close to hate. "If you dare to humiliate my sister, Alasdair, I'll kill you. I swear I'll kill you."

And on that trenchant note, he turned on his heel and stalked back the way he'd come.

Alec had been forced to strangle his temper under control before heading to his grandfather's library. He and the earl would likely come to verbal blows soon enough, but he wouldn't be the one to start it.

He closed the door behind him, pausing for a moment to take in what had once been his favorite room at Blairgal. The current library was only twenty-five years old, having been built as a grand addition to the east wing. It held one of the best private collections in Scotland in its bookcases, with leather-bound volumes lining the walls. Alec had spent a great deal of time in this room, both with his grandfather and with Walter, and by himself. Stepping into the library now was almost like stepping back into his childhood.

His grandfather, ensconced at his desk in front of the fireplace at the far end of the room, glanced up.

"About time you showed up, lad," he said in his gruff tone. "I've been waiting all afternoon for you to grace us with your presence."

Alec took one of the red and gold velvet chairs in front of the desk and settled into it. "With such a gracious welcome awaiting me, perhaps you can imagine why I took my time."

His grandfather's craggy features cracked a smile. "I'll thank you to watch your lip, you young jackanapes." He nodded in the direction of a mahogany sideboard that held an assortment of crystal decanters and glasses. "Fetch us a dram of whiskey while I finish off this letter. Try that decanter at the end. It's a single cask from our distillery, just tapped this month."

Alec strolled over to the sideboard and splashed out a dram for each of them. After placing a glass on the desk for his grandfather, he settled back in his chair and held up the crystal tumbler to the sunlight that streamed in through a set of windows overlooking the valley. Shards of amber glinted from the glass, glowing with a clear, warm tint. He closed his eyes and took a sip. He could taste the peat and the fresh Highland air, and the cold, clear water of the loch.

"It's a grand one, isn't it?"

Alec heard the pride in his grandfather's voice. He opened his eyes and smiled. "I've never tasted anything better."

"And you won't."

"And which distillery did this come from?" Alec asked sardonically. "The legal or illegal one?"

Given the heavy taxes imposed by the Crown on whiskey distilleries, illegal operations outnumbered legal ones by a factor of ten to one. While Blairgal operated one of the legal ones in Scotland, Alec was well aware that a few illicit operations dotted the estate grounds as well.

His grandfather grinned. "I'll leave you to figure that one out by yourself."

He sanded and folded his letter, slipping it into a leather file. Then he settled back in his chair, giving Alec an assessing look.

Here we go.

"You visited Donella this afternoon, I hear," Grandfather said. "I hope you came to some decisions."

A mouse couldn't wander across Blairgal grounds without the old man knowing about it. "I take it you're referring to my impending nuptials—nuptials I never agreed to, as you know."

His grandfather began to scowl. "I agreed to them on your behalf."

"That's not acceptable, sir, and you know it," he replied calmly. "I will not be forced into this, nor will I allow Donella to be forced into a marriage that doesn't suit her."

His grandfather slammed down his glass, slopping whiskey onto his blotter. "And did Donella turn you down? Did she break the vow she made to her father on his deathbed?"

"For God's sake, Grandfather, she was barely seventeen when Uncle Angus died. Neither of you had the right to put that kind of pressure on the poor lass, regardless of the circumstances."

"Angus was dying," his grandfather snapped. "He wanted to know that his daughter would be taken care of."

"Donella will never want for anything, as you well

know," Alec ground out. "She doesn't need to marry against her will to secure her future."

"I repeat—did she refuse to marry you this afternoon?"

Alec narrowed his gaze on the old curmudgeon. "I have no doubt you already know she didn't."

Not that Donella's answer would be a surprise to anyone at this point. After all, his family had had ten years to convince her that marriage to him was not only to her advantage, it was her bloody duty.

His grandfather gave a satisfied grunt. "I thought not."

Alec tried another tack. "Grandfather, she doesn't want to marry me. You know it, I know it, hell, everyone knows it."

The old man frowned. "Of course she wants to marry you. You're the future laird."

"That's not a good enough reason."

"It's a bonny reason."

Now it was Alec's turn to glare. "The hell it is. Donella and I barely know each other. Christ, I don't think the girl even likes me."

"Don't be ridiculous." His grandfather waved a hand at him. "Just look at you. You're a braw man and a war hero, too. I'm sure you had a string of girls trailing behind you in London, all wanting to get their hands into your trews and your wallet."

For a few seconds, Alec was struck dumb by his grandfather's earthy comment. The old fellow had always been a devout member of the kirk, rather more the hellfire and brimstone type than not. He couldn't recall him ever making a rude jest.

"Besides," his grandfather continued, "you and Donella will have plenty of time to get to know each other once you're married."

Alec leaned forward, directing his most intimidating stare at his grandfather. But the old fellow looked supremely unaffected. "I have no intention of marrying Donella, sir.

And if you lot would just leave her alone, I'm sure I could make her see sense. I am quite certain my cousin has no great desire to be my wife."

"She has a great desire to be Countess of Riddick," the old man said bluntly.

Alec forced himself to pull back and think about his grandfather's claim. It didn't take long. "Aunt Glenna is for her, but left to her own devices, Donella wouldn't care one way or another."

"Can you blame your poor aunt?" his grandfather snapped. "Of course she wants her daughter to be countess. It's only right and fair, given what's been denied her family."

Alec froze. His grandfather grimaced, then began to look uncomfortable at the slip.

"So, it really is about that," Alec said, shaking his head. "All the talk about clan and family loyalty—that's bollocks. It's really about Fergus, isn't it?"

And about how, in a just world, Fergus would be the heir to Riddick. Yes, Alec's mother had been married to Walter Gilbride when she'd conceived her only child, but their marriage had been strained for months before Lady Fiona's short-lived affair with the Duke of Kent. Only the unstinting loyalty to Fiona and her baby on the part of Walter and her father had been able to reduce the rumors to a dull rumble.

The Earl of Riddick had always been clear that Alec was his legitimate heir, the only child of a beloved daughter whose name he safeguarded with fierce devotion. Nor had Alec ever heard his stepfather breathe an unkind or disloyal word about his wife, even though she'd so foolishly betrayed him.

But as far as Alec was concerned, that simply proved his point about Donella. From everything he'd ever heard, Walter and his mother had been a terribly mismatched pair.

He was a serious scholar, years older than the vivacious, beautiful, and spoiled young miss who'd become his wife. It had been an all-too-predictable recipe for disaster.

Unfortunately, his grandfather was too pigheaded to see that.

"But that's just it, lad," the old man said in an earnest voice. "It is all about clan and family loyalty, and what we owe to each other. What we owe to both the Haddon and Graham names." He paused, as if collecting himself. "And, yes, it's what we owe Fergus. It's what *you* owe him."

A monumental frustration pushed Alec up from his chair. This was exactly why he hadn't wanted to come back. All these damn half secrets and obligations were crushing them all.

He pressed his palms onto the desk, leaning toward his grandfather. "I'd happily give up the bloody title to Fergus. We all know he'd make a much better earl than I would, anyway. Just say the word and I'll do it."

It would be a legal nightmare to end all legal nightmares and the biggest scandal of the decade. But it would be worth it if he could break free of Blairgal, the title, and all the burdens that came with it.

His grandfather sucked in a horrified gasp and fell back into his chair. "Don't say that, Alasdair. Don't ever say that. You'd destroy this family—Graham and Haddon, every one of us. Our names, our clan, dragged through the mud. Your mother's name dragged through the mud, and poor Walter, the most loyal man in Scotland, made a cuckold before the entire world."

He raised a thin, frail hand to his face, now bleached white and looking as old as death. Even from across the massive desk, Alec could see that his grandfather's frame was shaking like a dried oak leaf in the wind. Too late he remembered that the old man had a weak heart and suffered from spasms that might one day kill him.

How could you forget that, you bloody fool? It's the reason you came home in the first place.

"Alasdair, do you really hate us that much? Do you really hate *me* that much?" his grandfather asked in a trembling voice, looking alarmingly close to tears.

Alec was shocked as hell, because the old man had always been the strongest person he'd ever known. He came to his feet, speaking in a soothing voice. "Of course not, Grandfather. Don't worry, it'll be fine. I promise that everything will be fine."

But would it? Without a sudden and miraculous intervention, it seemed as if Alec's fate was all but sealed.

Chapter Sixteen

"I never thought I'd see the day when I labeled my favorite child a coward," Mamma said. "Really, Eden, I expected better of you."

Edie spun around on the stool at her dressing table and stared at her mother with disbelief. "Good God, Mamma, what do you expect me to do? Trap the poor man in a compromising position?"

The thought had actually crossed her mind, she was sorry to say, along with an equally strong desire to murder Alec bloody Gilbride.

"And do you really want me to cause yet another scandal?" Edie added. "My improper behavior is the reason we're here in this blasted castle in the first place."

This conversation was exactly the reason she'd been avoiding everyone for the last few days. Ever since Lord Riddick announced that Angus Graham, branch chief and uncle of Donella, would be attending a formal dinner this evening to celebrate the impending nuptials of Alec and his cousin. His lordship had casually dropped that information on the rest of them when they'd gathered before dinner two nights ago.

It had caught Edie entirely unaware, but apparently not Alec. He'd been staring right at her, stony-faced when his grandfather gave them the news. Alec had blown out a harsh breath but made no attempt to contradict his lordship. Not that he'd had much chance, given the fact that Mrs. Haddon and the rest of the family had launched into a round of congratulations so effusive that it made Edie's teeth ache.

She and Mamma, of course, had been forced to join in, one of the most gruesome experiences of her life. The only person who wasn't at their festive little gathering was the bride. Apparently Donella was home with a headache, probably from *all the excitement,* as her mother had crowed. Alec looked like he had a headache, too, but for different reasons. He'd seemed deeply unhappy in fact, and had grimaced when Edie had wished him and Donella well. That had been a terrible moment, and Edie hadn't known whether to slap him, throw an epic tantrum, or burst into tears and run from the room.

She couldn't even be furious with him for not trying to warn her, because he had. He'd waited outside her room again, trying to catch her before she went down, but he'd barely gotten two words out of his mouth when Mamma had interrupted them. Although Edie had sensed that Alec's talk with Donella hadn't gone well, she'd still been knocked off her pins to know the end result.

Since the banns were to be read in the local kirk on Sunday, in three weeks' time Alec and Donella would be married. That meant Edie and her mother would have to make a prompt escape from Blairgal. She could only hope that tonight's formal dinner, with the entire family and selected guests in attendance, would be one of the last meals she and Mamma ate under this roof.

With any luck, they would be on their way to Yorkshire in two days, at the latest. As far as Edie was concerned, spending the winter with Great-Aunt Eugenia was infinitely preferable to seeing Alec escort his beautiful Scottish bride to the joyous celebration that would follow the wedding of the Master of Riddick to the pride of Clan Graham.

Edie's mother, however, was clearly not yet ready to give up the fight.

Magnificently attired in an emerald silk gown that wouldn't have looked out of place in the ballrooms of the *ton,* Mamma sailed over to the chaise and gracefully sat. "Of course I'm not expecting you to put yourself in a compromising position. Although that particular strategy did work out rather well in your sister's case," she said thoughtfully. "And the circumstances *were* similar."

"They weren't the least bit similar. Michael Beaumont and Evie weren't engaged when she and Wolf were discovered in, er, well, you know," Edie said, windmilling a hand.

Mamma's brows went up. "Of course I remember. I'm the one who discovered them."

"Technically, it was Michael who discovered them, but let's not quibble. Besides, I can't really believe you would seriously suggest such a thing. There's no guarantee that it would work, and if it didn't then I would end up with an even worse reputation."

Her mother let out a dramatic sigh. "I suppose you're right, but that doesn't mean you can't have a serious chat with Captain Gilbride and find out what he really thinks. If he truly doesn't want to go through with it, there must be a solution to this exceedingly ridiculous situation."

Edie turned back to the mirror, blindly reaching for her garnet ear bobs. "There isn't, Mamma. Trust me on that. Besides, I already informed the captain that there's nothing to be done, so there's no point in talking about it any further."

"When did you do that?" her mother demanded.

Edie tried to insert a bob, but her hands were shaking too badly. Mentally cursing, she put it down. "This afternoon, when I happened to run into him."

Actually, he'd run her to ground outside the library, where she'd gone to pour her heart out to her sister in a ridiculously self-pitying and sentimental missive that she'd eventually tossed into the fire. She'd been stalking out of the library when she ran right into Alec, who'd been searching for her. He'd made it perfectly clear that he was annoyed with her for avoiding him when they obviously had *a great deal to talk about.*

Steeling herself against the pain lurking in his stormy gray gaze, she'd asked if there were any new developments in the situation with Donella. When he'd hesitated, obviously thinking of some way to placate her, she'd tersely told him that she refused to engage in any more private discussions with him since matters remained unchanged. She'd then turned on her heel and marched off, forcing herself to ignore his exasperated demand that she come back.

He'd made no attempt to come after her, and that was just as well. After all, what was there to say that wouldn't make them both feel worse? Alec would fulfill his obligations to his betrothed and his family and would eventually make his peace with it. In fact, she had little doubt he would soon find himself satisfied with the bride chosen for him. Donella was beautiful, kind, and intelligent, and she obviously understood what the role of Countess of Riddick entailed. It was ridiculous to ever think Edie and Alec could have made a go of it in the first place. They were like chalk and cheese, and had been from the moment they met.

At least that's what she'd told herself when she'd hurried away, desperate to hide the tears that trickled from beneath the beautiful pair of spectacles Alec had given her. Spectacles that now sat in their pretty green case on her dressing room table. Edie might someday be able to wear them again, but not now. Not tonight, when she felt like her heart was being sundered in two. Tonight, she actually preferred not to see what was going on around her.

She took a deep breath and told herself to stop acting like a tragedy queen. She picked up her ear bobs and smoothly inserted one and then the other. Then she turned around to face her mother. "It's over, Mamma. In fact, it never really got started, so there's no need to make such a fuss."

Her mother's eyebrows ticked up. "I never make a fuss, Eden, as you well know. I will not, however, stand aside and do nothing while my daughter's happiness is at stake."

Edie tried to laugh it off. "That's rather dramatic, don't you think?"

Her mother tilted her head, inspecting her with the canny expression that Edie was beginning to find distinctly unnerving.

"Eden, my dear," she said in a quiet voice, "you've been out on the marriage mart for almost seven years, and not once have I seen you give even a corner of your heart to a man. But you have to Gilbride, and quite decidedly."

Edie felt her chest constrict. "I haven't, Mamma, I assure you."

Her mother rose in a graceful rustle of silk. "Of course you have, child. You're in love with him."

Even though Edie was seated, the floor seemed to drop out from beneath her. Or perhaps it felt more like a bandage had just been ripped off a wound. "That's . . . that's ridiculous," she said. It was an unconvincing protest.

"And he's more than halfway in love with you," Mamma said. "It certainly wouldn't take much on your part to bring him the rest of the way. Then the captain will be motivated enough to convince Miss Haddon that they simply won't suit."

Edie stared at her mother's complacent smile, dumbstruck that she could be so naïve.

"And I would be perfectly happy to speak to Lord Riddick on your behalf," Mamma added with an insouciance that bordered on the unbelievable.

"Mamma, no," Edie gasped, jumping to her feet. "You cannot speak to the earl about this. He'll be furious."

Her mother's chin went up in an arrogant tilt. "The earl's anger cannot be allowed to stand as an impediment to my daughter's happiness. It's time someone talked some sense into that man. If Captain Gilbride won't do it, then I must take that duty upon myself."

Edie groped for words. Clearly, she'd failed to take into account just how firmly Mamma had set her heart on her daughter marrying the heir to a rich earldom.

As for her mother's assertion that Edie was in love with Alec, well, she refused to think about that right now. It didn't make one bit of difference, and it hurt too much to even contemplate. What truly mattered right now was preventing Mamma from speaking with Lord Riddick. The two could barely stand to be in the same room as it was, and broaching this topic right before the formal betrothal dinner would surely result in verbal explosions that would blow all the roofs off Blairgal Castle.

"All right, Mamma, you win," Edie blurted out. "I'll find Captain Gilbride right now and speak with him."

Her mother rewarded her with a dazzling smile. "Splendid, my dear. I believe I overheard the captain ask his father to meet him in the library before the guests arrived."

Overheard? Eavesdropped, more likely, which only showed how determined her mother was to manipulate events in Edie's favor.

"I'll try the library, then," she said. "Why don't you get your things and go down to the drawing room. I'll meet you there after I've talked to Alec."

Her mother came over and gave her an airy kiss. "Good luck, my dear, not that you'll need it. You look perfectly lovely in that dress. And I'm *so* glad to see you've decided not to wear your spectacles tonight. Why, the captain won't have a hope of resisting you."

On that appalling note, her mother glided out of the room. Edie grabbed her spectacles and shoved them onto her nose, then snatched up her gloves and fan and stalked to the door. With every step, she mentally cursed her mother, Lord Riddick, Alec, and everyone else she could think of.

Events were careening out of control, and it was up to her to rein them back in.

"I know you're ambivalent about this decision, Alasdair, but I'm sure it will be fine if you give it some time," Walter said with an encouraging smile. "Donella is a lovely girl, and she'll make you a fine countess. You've made everyone very happy with this decision."

Alec pinched the space between his eyebrows, right where a headache had been lurking for the last two days. The conversation was not going the way he'd wanted, as usual. "I think we all know that the decision was made over my objections."

He turned from Walter and stalked over to the window overlooking the valley. The landscape, bleached under the light of a huge moon, looked otherworldly and eerily beautiful. He could imagine the fairy folk coming down from the slopes of Ben Venue or up from the depths of the forests to dance in the glens. Too bad the wee bastards couldn't make a visit to Blairgal and cart his entire bloody family back to their hidden kingdom beneath the hills—preferably for several centuries.

He heard his stepfather's soft footfall approach. "Alasdair, I know this isn't what you want, at least right—"

"It's not something I want, ever," Alec growled.

"You don't know that," Walter said in a firm voice. "You're not giving Donella a chance. You're not giving your family a chance."

Alec tried to scowl, but it was hard with Walter, who stood there so patiently and with such a worried look on his thin, lined face. His stepfather wasn't getting any younger either, and not for the first time did Alec realize how much Walter and his grandfather needed him. Yes, Fergus had been there to help, but it wasn't the same. The responsibilities of Blairgal and its estates were burdensome. His grandfather had carried that burden for most of his lifetime, and Walter had done his best to support him. But they were both wearing down, that much was clear.

Alec wasn't even sure how much time on earth his grandfather had left, given the poor state of his health, and that dragged him down with a fair measure of guilt. He'd stayed away for ten long years, and his family had not held him back. Now, they needed him, so how could he turn his back on them?

But what he couldn't understand was why he had to turn his back on Edie.

"Of course I'm giving you a chance," he said. "I came home, did I not?"

Walter gave him a sad smile. "Not willingly, I think."

Alec shrugged. "If I'd wanted to stay away, I would have."

"It seems to me that you want to make this choice entirely on your own terms." Walter's voice held a hint of disapproval.

"I fail to see what's wrong with that," Alec said, not

hiding his exasperation. "Nor do I believe that my terms, as you call them, are unwarranted."

Walter's eyes went wide. "Alasdair, you're proposing to renege on a long-standing commitment of honor. How can that be anything less than acceptable?"

He repressed the urge to snap back, because Walter had the best of intentions. But the family's willful blindness on this issue would soon drive him crazy.

"Father, the family is trying to force Donella and me into a loveless marriage, and that's hardly in either of our best interests."

Walter tut-tutted the notion. "Hardly that, Alec. You and Donella were always very fond of each other—"

"No, we weren't," Alec bluntly interjected.

"You were always fond of each other," his stepfather repeated with determination, "and you simply need time for those feelings of affection to resurface."

"Donella doesn't even like me," Alec protested. "She used to call me a godless heathen when we were young."

Walter smiled. "I'm sure she wouldn't call you that now, Alasdair. You've grown into a fine young man. Your cousin sees that as well, I'm sure. She's simply a little shy about expressing it."

"She doesn't want to marry me," he replied through clenched teeth.

"Has she told you that?"

"Of course not. She's afraid to."

Walter frowned. "Why?"

"Because she bloody well doesn't want to disappoint her family, that's why. It was that damned deathbed promise. You know how religious she is. Christ, it's like she took some sort of sacred vow."

"Alasdair, there is no need to employ that sort of language," his stepfather replied in an austere voice. "And a deathbed vow is a very serious business."

"Father, she was little more than a child at the time, and she was grieving over the impending death of her parent. It was badly done."

"Alasdair, if I truly believed your cousin didn't want this marriage, I would be the first to support you," Walter said earnestly. "But I feel certain that she does. As I said, she's simply feeling a little shy because you've been parted for so long. Despite what her mother says, there's no need to rush right into marriage. If you want to take some time to court the lass, I will certainly support you on that count."

"Tell me something. Have you ever asked Donella specifically if she wants to marry me?"

"Of course I have."

That gave Alec pause. "And what did she say?" he asked.

"That she was looking forward to becoming Countess of Riddick."

That was a bit daunting, but not insurmountable. "I'm not entirely surprised by that, since she's been raised to believe she *is* the rightful countess. That, however, does not mean she wants to marry me, per se. The opposite would seem to be true, in fact, if her behavior is any indication. It's simply that she can't get one without the other."

His stepfather let out a gentle scoff. "That makes no sense."

"Aunt Glenna has been banging the notion into Donella's head for over ten years. What else is the poor girl supposed to think?"

Not to mention the fact that his cousin was so blasted obedient that it would never occur to her to stand up to the wishes of her family.

His stepfather shook his head, his sad expression making Alec feel rather like a worm. "I'm loath to say this, Alasdair, but I'm quite disappointed in your reaction to this situation. Donella doesn't deserve this shabby sort of treatment from you. None of us do."

And didn't that feel like a rusty blade to the gut? Alec wasn't used to giving up. Not until there was a pistol pointed right at his head, and usually not even then. But things were beginning to feel more than a bit desperate.

"Father, you know as well as I do that mismatched marriages can be a disaster, do you not?" He knew Walter hated talking about his fraught marriage to Alec's mother, but what choice did he have at this point but to pull out the big guns?

His stepfather let out a heavy sigh, but he surprised Alec by giving him a gentle smile. He turned and walked over to the fireplace, stopping to gaze up at the enormous portrait of Alec's mother that dominated that end of the room. "Come join me, lad," he said.

Alec trudged over to join him, and they gazed up at the slender, dark-haired girl who smiled down at them. The artist had skillfully captured his mother's beauty and charm. A smile played about her lips and her silvery-gray gaze gleamed with mischief and a zest for life. She'd been barely twenty then, just prior to her first trip to London. That trip was when she'd thrown caution and her marriage vows to the wind, engaging in her brief, tempestuous affair with a royal.

Walter smiled up at his wife. "I loved her, from the first moment I set eyes on her."

"I know you did. I also know you weren't happy." Alec lifted a hand to his mother's image. "Even then, when this portrait was painted, you were already fighting."

Walter let out a gentle sigh. "Yes, although that was certainly more my fault than hers. She was so young and unused to having to take another person's feelings into consideration. It was very hard on her to deal with a husband who was older and something of an old stick."

Alec bit back the words he wanted to say—that his mother was selfish. He'd never truly known her and didn't have the right to make that judgment. But there were other judgments he could make.

"She didn't love you, did she?" he asked, hating that he had to ask the question.

Walter glanced at him. "No, she did not, as you well know. She married me to please your grandfather."

"And look how well that turned out."

His stepfather turned to face him. "I think *you* turned out very well," he said in a dry voice. "I have no regrets, Alasdair, either about my marriage or having the privilege of raising you as my son. Besides, your mother was very young when we married, and we barely knew each other. Such is not the case with you and Donella. You won't make the same mistakes we did."

"I'd like the chance not to make those same mistakes in the first place."

His stepfather's eyes narrowed behind his spectacles. He was starting to look annoyed, and when Walter got annoyed he got stubborn. For all that he was a gentle scholar, he was also the grandson of a duke and a son of the Highlands. And he could be as bloody pigheaded as any Scot Alec had ever met.

"Alasdair, you are missing the point," Walter said.

"Which is?"

"That, despite your mother's mistake, we stayed loyal to her. Your grandfather and I never gave up loving her. And after you were born, she never gave up loving *you* till the day she died." His stepfather took a step forward and rested a firm hand on his shoulder. "We all remained loyal to you."

And there it was, the knife that slid all the way in and lodged itself in his heart. Because Walter was right—they had all remained loyal to Alec and to each other. His grandfather and father could have turned their backs on Lady Fiona, but they never did. They'd cherished her, as they did her son. Instead of treating him as a shameful thing to be hidden away, they'd loved and protected him against all the ugly whispers and rumors. That had made it possible for him to have a life of privilege and wealth.

True, he'd not asked for it, or the burdens that came with it, but that hardly mattered. His grandfather, Walter, Fergus, even Glenna and Donella—they'd all made sacrifices for him. They'd all remained loyal to him.

How could he possibly not do the same?

With a sense of defeat that dragged at his bones, Alec subsided into a chair in front of his grandfather's desk. He stared at the portrait of his mother, cursing her for the mistake that had been passed down through two generations and would be for at least one more.

His stepfather sat beside him. "I know you have feelings for Miss Whitney, Alasdair, and that you worry for her."

Alec jerked his head up. "Feelings? Aye, I have." Christ, he was in love with the lass, and had known it for weeks. He simply hadn't wanted to admit it to himself, given the fix he was in. But he could no longer deny it.

Walter grimaced. "I understand, but I urge you not to worry unduly about Miss Whitney. She's a lovely, charming girl who will no doubt find herself a good husband. One who will be well-suited to her vivacious character."

Maybe, but Alec was quite sure that he'd happily murder that man if given half the chance.

"I do think it's for the best," Walter said, starting to look anxious again. "I don't really think Miss Whitney would find life in the Highlands quite suited to her. London seems more her style."

That notion made Alec scowl. He thought Edie would do perfectly well in Scotland. There wasn't a challenge she couldn't seize and conquer.

But it didn't matter. Walter and his father were right—

Alec owed his family a debt of loyalty, and that family included both Donella and Fergus.

Besides, it appeared that Edie shared that view. Only yesterday, she'd walked away from him, refusing to even listen. He'd only let her go because he'd needed more time to come up with a workable plan.

But finally, after ten years, he'd truly run out of time.

"All right, Father, I understand," he said. "You needn't keep beating me over the head. My skull isn't that thick. And if it makes you feel any better, Miss Whitney shares your opinion."

Walter let out a tiny sigh of relief. "Thank you for telling me that, my boy. I think—"

A quick knock interrupted them, and a moment later the door opened. Edie slipped in, pausing for a moment when she saw them. Then he saw her shoulders go back and her chin go up with that stubborn determination he'd come to love.

"I'm sorry to interrupt you, Mr. Gilbride, but I was hoping I could have a moment to speak with the captain."

They rose as she came forward, marching with a firm tread that made it clear she wouldn't take no for an answer. Walter shot Alec a worried glance but managed to dredge up a smile. "Of course, Miss Whitney. I'll see you both in the drawing room shortly."

He sent Alec a glance that clearly said *be careful*, and then made his way out.

Edie stood quietly, waiting for Walter to close the door behind him.

Alec took those few moments to let his gaze travel over her pretty face—that little chin still up in a stubborn tilt—and her lush body, in its soft, sky blue silk that clung to her lovely curves. It almost hurt to look at Edie, knowing that she could never be his. And if he didn't miss his guess, she was feeling the same. Her mouth was pulled in a tight, unhappy line, and her gaze behind her spectacles looked drawn and slightly haggard. It took a mighty exertion of will not to pull her into his arms and kiss away all the sadness he saw on her face.

"Yes, Edie?" he asked, prompting her when she didn't speak.

She sucked in a breath, as if for courage. "I've come to say good-bye, Captain Gilbride. Mamma and I will be leaving for Yorkshire tomorrow."

Chapter Seventeen

Her announcement took Alec like a punch to the gut. He couldn't seem to absorb the shock in any way that made sense or made it feel right.

Because it didn't feel right. It felt terribly, monumentally wrong.

When he didn't respond, she started to look annoyed.

"Well, don't you have anything to say?" she asked, her voice tinged with asperity.

"What do you want me to say? That I'm happy you're running away?"

Just when he and Edie had both arrived at the point where they'd decided to take the honorable course of action, Alec realized he couldn't let her go. Despite everything he and Walter had just talked about, he refused to believe there wasn't a sensible way out of this mess. He'd escaped from a Spanish prison, for God's sake, so it beggared belief that he couldn't find his way out of a marriage neither party wanted.

Edie threw her hands up in exasperation. "I'm not running away. I'm doing the only sensible thing, under the circumstances."

He crossed his arms over his chest and lifted a mocking eyebrow. "I never took you for a coward, lass."

She eyed him with distaste, a distinct improvement on her tragic expression of only a few moments ago. Edie's annoyance with him was a small price to pay if it chased away the haunted look from her gorgeous eyes.

"You and my mother," she said, shaking her head. "No wonder you both get along so well—you're equally deranged."

Now, that was interesting. Clearly Lady Reese was counseling her daughter not to give up the fight. His spirit lifted at the notion that he had one ally in the house.

"What does your dear mamma have to do with anything?" he asked, pushing for more information.

She made a funny little grimace and turned partly away from him, staring at the portrait of his mother. "She's threatening to go to Lord Riddick and explain exactly why you should be marrying me, not your cousin."

That gave Alec a nasty little jolt. As much as he appreciated Lady Reese's support, that would not be a helpful intervention.

Edie glanced back at him. "I'm sure we can both imagine how well that conversation would turn out."

Probably with Edie and her mother out on their arses on the gravel drive, Alec reckoned.

"Yes, that doesn't seem like the right play at the moment," he said, "but I fail to see what that has to do with you turning tail."

She faced him straight on, hands propped on hips and a full scowl on her pretty face. "Because I've got to get my mother out of here, you stupid man. Mamma and your grandfather will surely come to verbal blows, if nothing else. In fact, we'll be lucky if they don't start bashing each other over the head with some of the medieval weaponry that hangs from every wall in this ridiculous castle. The wisest course of action is for us to leave first thing tomorrow morning. If you'll be so kind as to lend us your carriage as far as Glasgow, we can then make our own travel arrangements."

Alec scowled right back at her. "You'll do no such thing, you daft girl. Do you really think I'd allow you and your mother to make that trip by yourselves?"

"I don't see how it's any of your business," she replied with a haughty sniff.

"Because I promised your father that I would take care of you," he said through clenched teeth. "Trust me, Edie, when it's time for you to return to London, I'll take you myself."

And if he had anything to say about it, it would be a good long time before that happened. Now that she stood before him, so determined to go, he knew for certain that he could never let her escape. If he did, she'd be lost to him forever.

"And when will that be?" she asked. "Before or after your wedding?"

She tried for sarcasm, but her voice quavered at the end. Abruptly, she paced to the window and she stared out into the night.

He shook his head in self-disgust. He was handling this all wrong. Edie had a way of knocking him about the head until he couldn't think straight.

And he desperately needed to think his way out of this mess, for both their sakes.

He followed in her steps and stood just behind her. The rigid, proud set to her shoulders made his heart contract. Everything in him cried out to pull her into his arms and comfort her. She'd probably give him a good whack if he tried, so he settled for gently resting his hands on her shoulders. She jerked a bit when he touched her but then went still. But her entire body seemed to vibrate with tension under his fingertips.

"I've not given up yet, love," he said in a quiet voice. "If you can just give me a few more days—"

"No, I can't," she blurted out in a gruff little voice. "It's simply not possible."

She was a stubborn little thing, but Alec could be stubborn, too. "Why not? Don't you trust me to figure this out?"

He wished she would turn around so he could properly see her face, not have to make do with her wavering image in the window glass. Her mouth was pulled down in a tragic tilt, but her gaze was obscured by the flickering candlelight off the double reflection of her spectacle lenses and the dark mirror of the windowpane.

"There's nothing to figure out, Alec. Can't you see that? You're doing the only thing possible and the honorable thing. I respect you for that, I truly do. But I cannot stay here and watch you . . ."

Her voice trailed off, and he heard her swallow, as if forcing down tears. Christ, she was killing him. And every word she uttered made it all the more impossible for him to let her go.

He cupped her partially bare shoulders, all too aware of the soft, satiny skin under his fingertips. Gently, he forced her to turn and face him.

"You won't have to, I promise," he whispered.

Now he could see her eyes, and gazing into them was like falling into an evening sky that glittered on the edge of nightfall. And for a moment, he saw a fragile hope gleam through them like a comet.

But then hope faded, leaving a somber determination in its place. Alec's heart sank when she shook her head.

"You can't make that promise." She stared earnestly up at him. "It would be a terrible scandal if you broke your engagement."

He had to fight the impulse to tighten his grip on her. Edie belonged to him, dammit. Why the hell couldn't everyone—including her—see that?

"And for me, too," she added. "I will not bring more scandal down on my family—on myself."

"It won't make a damn bit of difference, because you'll be married to me."

She peered up at him for a few seconds, looking rather lost. Then she straightened under his hands, and her gaze grew calm and resolute. He thought back to the first time he'd met her, when she'd been so daring and flirtatious, never seeming to take anything seriously. But she was so much more than that charming, vivacious girl who led men around at the end of a string. She had both heart and character—more than any woman he'd ever met.

"You need to let me go, Alec," she said in a quiet voice.

"Edie," he started, hearing the desperate tone that infused his voice.

"If you respect me, you'll respect my wishes."

And what could he hope to say to that? Alec forced himself to pry his hands loose, even though it felt like an offense against nature to let her go. When she took a step back, her warmth seemed to drain from him, leaving him cold and still inside.

She tried to dredge up a cheery little smile that was nothing less than a travesty. "Well, we'll be leaving first thing, so I'll say my good-byes now. I suppose I won't be seeing you for a l . . . long time . . ."

Then she finally broke. Tears welled up in her eyes, and her mouth started to tremble. She whirled around, as if preparing to flee. Alec couldn't stop himself. He reached out and snaked his arms around her waist, pulling her tight against his chest.

"Don't cry, lass, please don't cry," he begged as he cradled her close. "I'll think of something, I promise."

She let out a waterlogged, slightly hysterical laugh. "You can't, you big oaf."

Then she turned in a luscious flurry of soft curves and whispering silk to face him. She wrapped her arms around his neck and went up onto her toes.

"And I bloody well don't give a damn," she said with a little growl.

Then she pulled his head down and plastered her mouth to his.

She'd clearly lost her mind, but right now Edie didn't care. Not when she'd suddenly realized she'd probably never see Alec again. Soon he would be a married man with a lovely Highland wife and, soon enough, lovely little Highland children who would no doubt look just like him. It was a horrible image of the future, and it had brought her mentally to her knees.

As had the look on Alec's face when she'd started to say good-bye. Devastation was not an expression that sat comfortably on Alasdair Gilbride. It had wrenched her heart into her throat and the tears into her eyes, and her only thought had been escape.

But when his strong arms went around her, she'd realized escape was no longer possible. He would never be hers, but she wanted him to know that she would always love him.

She would always belong to him.

Edie tunneled her fingers into his thick hair, kissing him with all the desperation in her heart, with all the years of loneliness that would soon be facing her. She needed this moment, this kiss, to steel herself against what she faced tomorrow.

Alec's arms tightened around her, pulling her against his rock-hard chest. One big hand slipped down to her hip, nudging her close. When she felt the ridge of his erection press against her belly, she gasped. He took delicious advantage, slipping his tongue inside and taking her in a hot, open-mouthed kiss.

She moaned at the delicious slide of tongues, and everything in her body seemed to go soft at once. Trembling, she clutched at him. Her legs lost all ability to keep her upright, and she swayed in his embrace.

Without breaking the kiss, he dipped a bit, sweeping an arm behind her knees and then lifting her high, cradling her against his chest. Edie jerked back, staring at him through some sort of mist.

Drat. Her spectacles had fogged. She peered at him over the top of her frames, taking in the hot, determined gleam in his eyes. "Alec, what are you doing?"

"I'm picking you up. What does it look like?" he said as he strode across the room to a chaise near a set of bookcases.

She couldn't seem to make her brain function properly. "Why?"

"Because you were about to fall down, and we don't want that happening, do we?" He lowered himself onto the plush, wine-red velvet chaise, bringing her with him to tumble across his lap.

Edie scrambled to right herself, but Alec kept a firm hold. She let out an undignified squeak when she felt his erection against her bottom. Given how thin the fabric of her gown and chemise was, she certainly felt a lot more of him than she would have expected.

Even more startling was her body's response. She wanted to wriggle against him in a demented attempt to soothe the sensations coalescing between her thighs. And if she gave in to that mad impulse, she might as well lay herself out flat, offering herself to him on a platter.

"Don't be ridiculous," she said in a breathless voice. "I would never do anything that stupid."

"Mm, you on the floor isn't such a bad thought," he said, ignoring her objection. One big hand curled around her thigh. "Especially if I'm there with you. Even better, on top of you."

That image lodged in her brain and refused to depart. She was trying to manage a more appropriate response to the situation—like demanding that he let her go—when he tipped her chin up and began to nibble along her jaw. It made her shiver, stirring up her need for him—a need she'd been trying to repress for weeks.

Sadly, she wasn't doing a very good job of it. All she could seem to do was tip her head back to give him better access to her throat.

You idiot. Get control of yourself.

"Alec, I don't think this is a very good idea," she managed in a thin voice.

"You started it," he replied between nibbles.

"Yes, I know, but . . ."

But whatever she'd been about to say was wiped from her brain when his hand slid up her stomach to her breast. When he cradled it and then gently thumbed the tight nipple that had immodestly thrust against her bodice, sensation stormed through her. She turned her head to meet his mouth again, her defenses crumbling under the hot onslaught of his lips and tongue.

Just for one more minute longer. Then I'll stop.

Before that minute arrived, a confused jumble of noises penetrated her brain. It soon resolved into footsteps and then loud—very loud—voices close by.

Her eyes popped wide at the same moment that Alec

pulled back from the kiss. Edie stared up into Fergus Haddon's furious green gaze. He was tipped at the strangest angle, looking down at her with a sideways slant, and seemed obscured around the edges. It wasn't until Alec brought her upright that she realized she'd been all but lying flat across his lap, with him bent over her as he kissed her into stupidity.

Oh, and her dratted spectacles had partly fogged again.

"You bastard," Fergus snarled at Alec. "I will kill you for this."

The man's face was almost as red as his hair, and his hands were balled into fists. Edie felt quite certain that if Alec hadn't been holding her in his lap, Fergus would have already commenced the killing.

"You'll do nothing of the sort," Alec said sharply as he held Edie close, half-turned into his chest. "You'll wait until Miss Whitney and my father have left the room, and then we'll talk."

His father?

She peered around Fergus to see Mr. Gilbride standing back a few feet, looking highly disturbed as he shook his head. She followed the path of his gaze down to her thighs, which were exposed, thanks to the fact that her dress and chemise had rucked up around them.

"Good God," she yelped, struggling to get free. "Alec, let me up."

"Yes, let her up, so I can get at you," Fergus said through clenched teeth.

"Edie, sit still for a moment," Alec ordered. "You're not arranged correctly."

Holding her so tightly wasn't helping matters in that respect.

By this time, Mr. Gilbride had covered his face with one hand and Fergus had taken another threatening step closer.

"Don't take another step, Fergus," Alec said in a harsh voice. "I'm warning you."

Edie tried to wriggle free again. "If you two are going to start pummeling each other, I'd rather not be in the middle of it." She shoved against Alec's shoulder without the slightest effect. "Let me go!"

"I'm trying to preserve your modesty, you daft woman," Alec growled as he attempted to wrestle her skirts down over her legs. "Hold still."

Her modesty? That had flown out the window several minutes ago, when she'd been insane enough to kiss him.

"What is going on in here? Where is my son?" came a shrill voice, followed by a hasty clatter of heels.

Mrs. Haddon heaved into view on the other side of Alec's father. She let out a penetrating shriek as she clutched at poor Mr. Gilbride's arm. "Alasdair, what are you doing? Why are you with that whore?"

"Right, that tears it," Alec said.

He stood up, bringing Edie with him. He set her carefully on her feet but kept her behind him, protecting her. But she didn't need protection—she needed to get out of there. Her skirts were twisted around her legs and she'd just discovered her bodice had gone entirely askew, exposing the lace trim of her stays.

Repressing a curse, she turned her back, struggling to straighten herself out while the various members of the Haddon family started yelling at each other.

Another feminine voice cut through the chaos. "Mamma, what's going on? Why are you screaming—"

The sudden silence that followed that interruption felt louder than the previous bedlam. Her heart sinking—it should be hitting bedrock by now—Edie slowly turned to meet Donella's wide-eyed gaze. The young woman was stone-faced and deadly pale as she took in the scene, her gaze ultimately snagging on Edie's still suspicious-looking bodice, rumpled skirts, and no-doubt lopsided coiffure.

Edie went hot with shame. "It's not what it looks like. Really. Nothing happened."

No one with a modicum of intelligence could believe that. But if they all pretended to believe it, she and Alec might still escape with their hides intact. Yes, it was all very embarrassing, but if everyone agreed to ignore this little incident, Alec might be able to salvage his honor and Edie her reputation.

"Are you insane?" Fergus thundered. "It's exactly what it looks like, you . . . you *Sassenach*. You were seducing my cousin. Not that he seemed to be making an attempt to stop you."

"So much for taking the sensible way out." Alec glanced at Edie, one corner of his mouth edging up in a wry smile. "It was a valiant try though, lass, I'll give you that."

She gaped back at him. How could he even smile—much less joke—at a time like this?

"She's a whore," Mrs. Haddon snarled, apparently recovered from her hysterics and pointing her finger straight at Edie's chest. "And we should treat her like one."

"Aunt Glenna, I realize you've had a shock and I'm sorry for that," Alec said in a low, quiet voice that still held a clear warning. "But I'll not countenance that sort of address."

His aunt's face pulled into a harsh grimace. "How could you do this to my daughter? How could you bring your English lightskirt—"

"Not another word, Mamma," Donella cut in. "I will deal with this situation."

Mrs. Haddon turned on her daughter. "How can you bear—"

Donella flashed up a hand. "Not another word," she said in an icy tone.

Surprisingly, her mother clamped her lips shut, although she shot Edie a look that was pure hatred.

Donella flicked another cool glance over Edie, then she

calmly regarded her betrothed. Edie stole a look at Alec out of the corner of her eye. He was standing steadfast under his cousin's gaze, but the color was high on his cheekbones, likely from both anger and embarrassment. They'd both been unforgivably impulsive, but Edie knew he would never have wished to humiliate Donella so thoroughly.

"Alasdair, this is exactly what it appears to be, is it not?" Donella asked.

He grimaced slightly, then nodded. "Aye, it is."

Donella gazed at him for a few moments longer, unnervingly cool and collected. Then she gave a brisk nod. "Thank you for being truthful, Alasdair. I entirely release you from your vows to me. You are free to do as you wish."

Then she turned on her heel and walked to the door, leaving them all slack-jawed.

Not for long, though, since Mrs. Haddon started shrieking again. Most of it was incoherent, but Edie couldn't fail to miss the words *English* and *whore*.

For the third time, a voice cut through the commotion. Edie's mother's voice.

"Cease that ungodly noise *immediately*," Mamma rapped out as she stalked up to them. "You will bring every servant in this household down on our heads. Not to mention Lord Riddick."

That threat froze them all into near silence, even Mrs. Haddon. Weeping, she subsided against Mr. Gilbride, who supported her by the arm and made little clucking noises, as if trying to soothe a fractious baby.

Fergus recovered first. "I can assure you, Lady Reese, that my uncle will hear all about this from me. Lord Riddick needs to know just how disgracefully his grandson has behaved himself."

"And I'm sure he will, Mr. Haddon," Mamma answered in her most aristocratically condescending voice. "But in the appropriate manner and from the appropriate person, which would be Captain Gilbride, not you."

"How dare you tell us how to conduct our business?" Fergus responded hotly. "You and your daughter, coming up here and ruining everything."

As insults went, that one was exceedingly mild, especially considering some of the other terms that had been bandied about only a few minutes ago.

"I believe that Lord Riddick has a bad heart, does he not?" Edie's mother asked.

"That is true, Lady Reese," Mr. Gilbride said anxiously. "I'm very worried about him."

"As am I," said Mamma. "Which is why Captain Gilbride and I will discuss the situation with him."

"And what am I supposed to do?" Fergus asked. "Just sit around while you and your light—"

A low growl from Alec had Fergus stumbling over the word, but he managed to recover. "Sit around while you and your daughter cut my sister out of her rightful position in this household?"

Mamma's imperious gaze flashed over to Edie. It was the first time her mother had looked at her since she'd entered the room. "I assure you, Mr. Haddon, I will deal with my daughter in good time. The best thing you can do right now is to escort your mother and sister home and wait to hear from his lordship. There is nothing more you can do tonight."

"Lady Reese, we have guests about to arrive," Mr. Gilbride said. "How do we explain this?"

"We will explain that Mrs. Haddon was suddenly taken quite ill, and that her children insisted on returning home with her."

Given that the woman in question was now leaning heavily against Mr. Gilbride, moaning as if in extremis, it was certainly an excuse that had merit.

"Yes, that makes sense," Mr. Gilbride said with a relieved smile. He looked at Fergus. "Come, lad. Help me get your mother to the carriage, and then we'll find your sister."

Fergus went to take his mother's other arm, but not before he glared at Alec. "This isn't over, Cousin. I promise you."

Alec let out a weary sigh that tore at Edie's heart. This was all her fault. If she'd only had the brains—and the courage—to leave the room when she should have, none of this would have happened. Now she'd blown up Alec's relationship with his family, not to mention possibly putting his grandfather's health at risk.

Well done, Edie, and it took you less than a week.

If only Evelyn had been here to keep her straight. Then again, her twin had found herself in a similar situation not that long ago. It would appear that Edie was following in her sister's footsteps, which was rather mind-boggling.

"Yes, I'll speak with you later, Fergus," Alec said.

As Mr. Gilbride and Fergus carted Mrs. Haddon out of the room, Mamma turned and ran a practiced eye over Edie's gown. She let out a *tsk,* then expertly rearranged Edie's bodice and flicked her skirts into some semblance of order.

"You're respectable enough to get back upstairs," Mamma said, "but you'll have to change your dress and have Cora fix your hair. And you'll need to be quick about it."

Her mother's attitude was coolly practical, but Edie didn't miss the irate glimmer in her eye. "Mamma, I'm so dreadfully sorry," she said. "I don't know what came over me."

Her mother cast a glance at Alec, who looked both slightly disheveled and outrageously handsome in his kilt and formal jacket. "I believe I know exactly what came over you," she said in a severe voice.

Alec winced. "Lady Reese, this is all my fault—"

"I very much doubt that," Mamma interrupted ruthlessly. "But I have neither the time nor the desire to listen to feeble excuses. Not another word from either of you until I speak to Lord Riddick. Tonight will be difficult, but I believe I can manage to get us through it without too much gossip—if his lordship will cooperate."

"Good luck with that," Alec muttered under his breath.

As if on cue, the old earl stomped into the library. "What the devil is going on? Glenna is in hysterics, Donella has called for their carriage, and Fergus wouldn't even speak to me."

He came to a halt in the center of the room, his gaze going wide as he took in the little group clustered before the chaise.

"Ah, Lord Riddick, there you are," Mamma said calmly as she glided forward to meet him. "I'm afraid you and I need to have a little chat."

Chapter Eighteen

"Mamma, hasn't it occurred to you that it's just as bad to force Alec to marry me as it would be to Donella?" Edie asked, exasperated.

Her mother batted the objection away with an imperious wave. "It's a completely different situation, my dear. Captain Gilbride does not want to marry Donella Haddon. He *does* want to marry you. Now get in bed, and let me tuck you in."

Edie could feel her eyes bug out at that suggestion. Mamma hadn't tucked her into bed since, well . . . never. She glanced at Cora, who tried to hide a smirk while she bustled around the bedroom putting away various items of strewn apparel.

Her mother waved her into bed with a shooing motion. "Eden, to bed, now."

"Oh, all right." Edie climbed up onto the high mattress. "But I'll never fall asleep—not with everything so unsettled."

"Then you can sit up and read for a while," Mamma said. "But I assure you that nothing is unsettled except for some of the financial details. I just spent another half hour with his lordship discussing what must be done next. I'll need to consult with your papa about the settlements, of course, but I'll be sending him a letter by first post to-morrow."

Edie didn't even want to think about her father's response to yet another scandal. "The thing is, Mamma," she said, halfheartedly tugging the coverlet up around her waist. "I'm not entirely sure that Alec *does* think it's a good idea to marry me."

Her mother's elegant eyebrows crawled up her forehead. "I don't mean to quibble, my dear, but he seemed fairly enthusiastic in the library just before dinner."

Edie's cheeks started to burn at the memory. "As I tried to tell you, we were just saying good-bye."

"Most people simply shake hands and leave it at that."

"Yes, well, we did get a bit carried away, but we'd already decided that honor demanded that he marry Donella. I think we'd both made our peace with that."

"Clearly not, but in any event it doesn't matter," her mother said. "Miss Haddon released the captain from his vow. And I assure you that Gilbride does want to marry you. He raised not a single objection when we discussed the situation with his grandfather."

"And who raised the issue first? You or Alec?"

"I did, naturally. The poor captain had already been forced to explain why Miss Haddon no longer wished to marry him, and that provoked a rather unfortunate reaction from his grandfather."

"I can imagine," Edie said with a sigh. Lord Riddick had refused to look at her for the rest of the evening. "And that's just my point, Mamma. This is a dreadful situation, and forcing everyone's hand is simply going to make everything worse."

"Eden, didn't Alasdair already tell you that he wished to marry you and not his cousin? I quite got the impression that he had."

Edie thought back to her conversation with Alec, that

afternoon when he'd first kissed her. "He said he rather thought he might want to marry me instead, which is not exactly a ringing endorsement."

"Pish," said Mamma. "I'm sure he was stating the matter in a delicate fashion, given the difficulties of his situation at the time."

Edie almost laughed. There was nothing delicate about Alec Gilbride.

Her mother studied her for a few moments. "My dear child, I've never known you to back down from a fight before. Don't you wish to marry the captain?"

"That's not the point, Mamma. I'm afraid Alec doesn't know his own mind. He might think he's fond of me, but it could have more to do with the fact that he doesn't want to marry Donella. You have to admit that this is all rather convenient."

Mamma looked puzzled. "It's not like you to be so uncertain about yourself, Eden. It's most disconcerting."

"Imagine how I feel," Edie said with a sigh.

It wasn't like her at all, and that's what was bothering her. Because as much as she wanted to marry Alec, and she would no longer deny that, she wasn't sure that he did know what he truly wanted. Until only a few weeks ago they'd barely been able to tolerate each other's company. Yes, Edie had always felt a ridiculously strong pull toward him, but that hadn't stopped them from fighting like cats and dogs. The truce between them was very new and too fragile a base on which to build a life together.

"I'm just not sure that he loves me, Mamma. Besides, we haven't even had a chance to talk about all this. You sent me out of the room when you and Alec talked to Lord Riddick, and then he and I barely had a chance to exchange two words for the rest of the night."

In fact, after she'd changed, she'd had to cool her heels in one of the private family drawing rooms for half an hour while Mamma and Alec talked to Lord Riddick. A harassed-looking Mr. Gilbride had finally arrived to escort her to the main drawing room where the guests were assembled before dinner. Mr. Graham, the branch chief, had been puzzled by Donella's absence, and all the guests had surely sensed the awkward, if not downright hostile, atmosphere at the party. Mr. Gilbride and Mamma had done their best to steer the conversation away from any talk of the supposed impending marriage, but it had been one of the most gruesome social encounters Edie had ever attended.

Even worse, she'd been seated at the opposite end of the table from Alec, who, like his grandfather, had spent most of the night glowering. The few times he'd glanced at Edie, it was with so somber an expression that she felt sick. She'd spent most of dinner convincing herself that Alec had concluded that he wanted to marry her as little as he wanted to marry Donella.

"Well, as I suggested earlier, my dear, you must convince him that his feelings for you are very strong indeed," her mother said. "After tonight's little incident, I doubt you'll have any trouble with that."

Edie didn't know whether to laugh or tear her hair out. "Mamma, that's an appalling attitude."

"Nonsense." She leaned over and kissed Edie on the forehead. "Now, go to sleep. You can have a nice little chat with Alasdair tomorrow. When you do, I'm sure you'll find out that everything's just fine."

"From your point of view, anyway," Edie said drily. "If I didn't know better, I'd think you planned it all to work out this way."

"One might say the same of you, my dear," her mother said, tapping her cheek.

"Touché," Edie muttered.

"Stop fretting and go to sleep."

"Yes, Mamma."

Edie waited until the door was closed, and her mother's footsteps faded. Then she slid out of bed and groped around for her slippers.

"I suppose you'll be wanting this," Cora said in a resigned voice, holding up her dressing gown.

"Do you mean to say I don't have to argue with you over this?" Edie asked as she pulled on the wrapper.

"Would you actually listen to me?"

"I'm afraid not."

"Then I'll save my breath to cool my porridge. Just be sure you don't get caught."

"I never get caught, Cora."

"Tell that to Captain Gilbride—and Sir Malcolm Bannister," Cora said.

Edie winced at the reminder. "I have to speak with him tonight before everything spins completely out of control. By tomorrow it might be too late to put a stop to any sort of announcement."

"He'd be barmy not to want to marry you, Miss Edie. Just be careful and don't stay too long. Oh, and take a candle so you can see where you're going."

Cora's vote of confidence made Edie's throat go tight with emotion, so she simply gave her maid a grateful smile before slipping out to the hall. She paused there and listened but heard only an echoing silence. Picking up her skirts, she ghosted down the hall toward the east wing where Alec had his set of rooms. It took a good ten minutes of traversing stairways and corridors to reach them, as well as ducking into an alcove to avoid being spotted by his valet. Edie blew out her candle and hid behind the marble bust that inhabited the alcove, heart pounding, until the man passed by without seeing her.

She waited a few more minutes and then crept out. The darkened hallway was empty, so she took the last few yards at a dash. She paused for a moment outside Alec's door, her nerve almost failing. But there was no point in standing around like a ninny, so she tapped once then opened the door and slipped into the room.

The large room was drenched in shadows, the only light cast by the flickering flames of a fire. Edie blinked, waiting for her vision to adjust, then peered about to get her bearings. Hesitantly, she took a few steps forward.

"I was wondering when you'd finally show up," rumbled a masculine voice.

She spun around. Alec strolled toward her, obviously coming from a connecting room, rubbing his damp head with a towel. He was naked from the waist up, and below he wore only his kilt. His big feet were bare and made not a sound on the carpeted floor. For such a large man, he had the disconcerting ability to move without making a sound.

"Stop sneaking up on me like that," she hissed, pressing her hand over her pounding heart.

"I told you, I never sneak," he said, looming close. A slow, sensual smile curled up the edges of his hard mouth.

Edie gazed up at him and had to swallow twice before she could answer. "And I told you—"

He cut her off by pulling her into his arms, lifting her right off her feet. She barely had time to let out a squawk before his mouth descended on hers in a kiss that felt like a branding. Heat flushed her body at the feel of his muscular, naked chest plastered against her. She clutched at his shoulders, helpless to do anything but let him kiss her into stupidity.

After a minute or so, about the time one of his hands moved from her waist to clamp on her bottom, Edie's brain started to function. Forcing herself to break free of his kiss, she pushed against his shoulders in a pathetic effort to inject some space between them. He let her move back a few inches, but her breasts still rubbed against him, sending sparks sizzling through her body. And those sparks erupted into fireworks when he let her slide slowly down to the floor, every inch of her dragging over him on the way down.

His wicked grin told her how much he had enjoyed that slow slide to the floor.

"Good God," she managed to get out. "You are a menace, Alasdair Gilbride."

He laughed, a dark rumbling that she felt in those parts a lady never referred to in polite company—or any company, for that matter.

"You're the one who came barging in here. How else did you expect me to react?" he said.

"Perhaps wishing me a good evening would have been more appropriate?"

He settled his hands on her hips, keeping her close. "Isn't that what I just did?"

It was almost impossible to resist his smile, but she had to try—at least until they'd had a chance to talk.

"I take it you were expecting me," she said.

He affected a large yawn. "Yes, but I almost gave up on you and went to bed."

She gave him a shove. "You are *so* irritating."

He laughed and dipped down to kiss her on the nose before letting her go. "I know, but you'll put up with it because you love me."

The fizzy feeling inside her subsided.

"What's wrong?" he asked.

"We need to talk."

He steered her toward a comfortable-looking sofa by the fireplace, but she pulled away and sat on a low chair instead, with her hands folded in her lap and feet tucked under her skirts. Sitting straight-backed, she tried to look as serious as possible.

Alec planted his feet wide and crossed his arms over his

brawny chest. She took a moment to take it in—the carved muscles, lovingly highlighted in the glow of the fire, the dark hair that dusted his chest and then arrowed down to the kilt slung low on his hips. She had the impulse to fan herself—or rip off her clothes and throw herself into his arms. But that was the impulse that had gotten them into this mess in the first place.

His gaze traveled over her, then he shook his head. "You are the furthest thing from prim and proper I've ever seen, Eden Whitney, so don't even try to adopt that particular persona."

She opened her eyes wide. "I find that hard to believe, given your history with women. Besides, I'm wearing a cap and a dressing gown that covers a great deal more than the average evening gown. And spectacles, in case you haven't noticed. I must look a perfect antidote."

"Then perhaps you should take them off. Along with your dressing gown and everything underneath."

When he reached for the tie of her gown, she slapped his hands away. "You're not touching anything until we talk."

He grinned at her again. "But I can touch after we talk. Splendid, then. Let's get right to it."

She sighed. "Alec, I'm serious."

"All right, love, we'll talk."

His casual, intimate endearment made her chest ache, and she had to repress the urge to rub right over her heart. Instead, she simply watched in silence while he built up the fire and then sat on the sofa across from her. He braced his forearms on his powerful thighs and raised an eyebrow.

"What do you want to talk about?" he asked.

She gaped at him. "You have to ask?"

When he shrugged, the glorious movement of his shoulders distracted her.

"I admit there's quite a lot," he said.

She forced herself to focus on his face. "Let's start with your grandfather."

That chased the last remnants of good humor from his face. "Must we?"

"I take it he wasn't very happy with the unexpected turn of events."

"That's putting it mildly. For a few moments, I was afraid the old fellow would fall into an apoplectic fit."

Edie's stomach cramped with guilt. "Alec, I'm so sorry. Is he all right?"

"Sweetheart, he's fine," he said with a reassuring smile. "I must say that your mother handled him beautifully."

"What did she do?"

"She made him sit down and put his head between his knees for a few minutes. Then she all but forced a snifter of brandy down his throat. That did the trick."

"Mamma can be very masterful," Edie said, almost tempted to laugh.

"And thank God for that. She explained exactly why it was a fool's errand to try to force me to marry Donella, since it was obvious that my cousin didn't want to marry me. Lady Reese then told my grandfather in no uncertain terms why you were the best candidate to fill the post." He grinned at her. "If you ever doubted your mother's affection, I can assure you that she holds you in the highest regard. According to your dear mamma, you are the greatest prize on the marriage mart, pursued by thousands, and I should bow down and kiss your feet with gratitude that you've deigned to consider my suit."

Edie shook her head. "How utterly mortifying. How did his lordship react?"

"Believe it or not, it fired him up in my defense. He launched into a catalogue of my many attributes, and why *you* should be thanking your lucky stars that you have the opportunity to wed the next Laird of Riddick. All of which is true, of course," he added with a sly grin.

"It sounds rather like an auction at Tattersall's," she said. "Then what happened?"

"They agreed it was in everyone's best interest to proceed quickly and quietly before too much gossip could spread. My grandfather will speak to Fergus and Aunt Glenna tomorrow, and then to Angus Graham, the branch chief. Obviously, none of them will be happy, but since Donella was the one to break the engagement, there's really nothing more to be said."

"And are you absolutely certain that your cousin doesn't want to go through with your engagement?" Edie asked, anxiety burbling up. "Perhaps she was simply reacting to the moment. She might think differently once she calms down."

Alec leaned forward, intent. "Trust me when I tell you that Donella is happy for the out. It relieves her of any responsibility in the situation and effectively negates the need to feel guilty about breaking that ridiculous deathbed vow. Which only goes to show that my original plan was the right one all along."

Edie huffed at him. "I cannot believe you just said that."

His eyebrows lifted in a sardonic tilt. "Well, nothing else seemed to do the trick, did it?"

Since she actually couldn't refute his appalling logic, she decided to ignore it. "Alec, are you going to speak to Miss Haddon? Truly, we both owe her an apology."

"I'll see her tomorrow and explain everything."

"Perhaps I should go with you."

"That's not a good idea. Donella wouldn't mind, but my aunt might try to murder us both."

Edie sighed and rubbed her temples. "What a mess. I am truly sorry about all of this, Alec. I'm afraid I've made things very difficult for you with your family."

"They'll get over it," he said, once more shrugging those magnificent shoulders. "I have no doubt that Lady Reese will continue to manage my grandfather into compliance, and my father mostly just wants me to be happy. As for the others, it's not as if they actually have a choice."

Edie's heart sank. Despite what he said, tonight's events had caused a great deal of distress within his family and possibly even an irreparable breach. That breach would likely grow rather than heal, if she did marry Alec.

She forced herself to say what needed to be said. "But *you* have a choice."

He sat up straight, a slight frown marking his brows. "I don't follow."

"You don't have to marry me. You're free now. There's absolutely no need to trap yourself in another commitment, especially not one that was forced upon you."

His dark gaze narrowed with irritation. "No one is forcing anything on me."

"Really? Circumstances suggest otherwise. But I will not be party to that, Alec. I will not force you to marry me, regardless of what my mother says. All you have to do is say the word, and I'll simply maintain that I refused to marry you."

Even if it would kill her to do it.

After a fraught silence, Alec slowly rose and took a step forward, his entire presence radiating masculine ire. "Edie, do you have any idea what it would do to your reputation if I let that happen? Christ, woman, it would be completely destroyed!"

She lifted her chin to glare up at him. "It wouldn't be the first time, and you needn't try to intimidate me, either. It won't work."

He shook his head. "Edie, we are getting married, and that's the end of it."

His pigheaded, ridiculously male attitude drove her to

her feet. "I will not allow you to be forced into marrying me, Alasdair Gilbride. You may think you owe it to me, but I assure you that you don't."

His fierce glower suddenly lifted. "You sweet, daft girl. Do you really think I'm being forced into this?"

"Well, aren't you?" She firmly repressed the mad impulse to burst into tears.

He made a scoffing noise, then reached out to pluck the spectacles from her nose. "And you call *me* the idiot," he murmured as he set them on the mantelpiece.

"What are you doing?" she asked, her nerves jumping.

"Showing you how much I want to marry you."

He swept her into his arms.

Chapter Nineteen

Edie's heart did a little gallop as Alec swept her up, a natural response to both his strength and the feel of his naked torso against her. He was obviously taking her to his bed—an enormous, lavishly carved oak bedstead that looked decades old. From the smoldering look in his gaze, it seemed he was planning more than just a few chaste kisses.

He carefully sat her on the edge of the mattress, and before Edie could even catch her breath, he'd stripped off her cap and tossed it over his shoulder. Then he went down on one knee to remove her slippers.

She nervously cleared her throat. "You seem to be taking quite a lot for granted, Captain Gilbride."

When he paused to look up at her, one big hand wrapped around her ankle, Edie forced herself to lift an eyebrow. His response was a smile that managed to be both utterly charming and odiously smug.

"Am I indeed, Miss Whitney?" he said. "I thought the opposite was true."

When he ran a hand up her calf to rest behind her knee,

she couldn't help but shiver. No man had ever touched her so intimately, and it felt . . . wonderful.

"After all," he added, "it was you who accosted me—in my own bedroom, no less."

"To talk, not to . . ." She windmilled an arm, not sure how to categorize what she thought was about to happen.

"Make love?"

"Yes, that," she said, feeling like a naïve idiot.

He studied her with a thoughtful air while he stroked her leg, as if to soothe her. Then he sat back on his heels and crossed his arms across his chest. "Edie, my love, what is it you want right now? In this moment?"

She shrugged. "I suppose I wanted to know if you're happy with the notion of marrying me."

"I believe I was in the process of answering that question. Or, rather, showing you." He flashed her a rueful smile. "I'd very much like to get on with that, but I won't force you to do anything you're not comfortable with."

"You have to admit that this isn't what one would call an average courtship. We do seem to be rushing things, don't you think?"

He nodded. "I'll grant that it's been anything but normal, but trust me when I tell you that I've been waiting for this moment for a very long time."

"But that's just it—we haven't known each other for very long, have we?"

"Sometimes it feels like we've known each other forever," he said drily.

Edie let out a reluctant laugh. "You brute, that's my point. For weeks and weeks, we could barely stand to be in the same room together, and—" She broke off when both hands slipped under her nightgown, caressing their way up to the sensitive skin behind her knees.

Alec came up on his knees, moving in close. His calloused

fingertips drew light circles on her skin, teasing down her calf then drifting back up.

"I don't think that's true." His voice was a dark, thrilling rumble. "In fact, I think we were all too aware of each other and not quite sure how to respond." His lips curled into a wicked grin. "Correction—I knew exactly how to respond."

She shook her head, although she couldn't help but smile back at him. "You're incorrigible."

"I know." He leaned in and planted his arms on the mattress, caging her in. He ducked his head a bit, so he could look her directly in the eye. "I also know how much I want you, in my bed and my life. Be assured, love, I've known that for quite some time."

Her jumpy insides started to settle. She gently rested her hands on his shoulders, allowing herself to enjoy the feel of his warm, bare skin under her fingertips.

"That's . . . that's nice," she whispered. It was silly how shy she felt. She'd never been shy with him before, but, after all, they were sitting about half-naked. She supposed she might be forgiven a few maidenly blushes.

"Of course, I wasn't sure how you felt about me," he said in a musing tone. "For some weeks I was convinced that you loathed me."

"Well, you did go out of your way to irritate me, so that's really your fault."

He laughed. "I suppose that's fair. I was an idiot, but I truly wasn't sure how to deal with you, especially after all the nonsense with that bloody conspiracy and Evie and Wolf. I was afraid you'd never forgive me for deceiving you."

She began stroking his shoulders, much as he stroked the backs of her legs. "Actually, I forgave you right away," she confessed. "I just couldn't admit it."

"Why not?"

"You knocked me completely off-balance. No one had ever done that before."

He gave her a quizzical smile. "You certainly hide it well. Why didn't you give me a hint?"

"Because you never gave *me* a hint that you were the slightest bit interested. In fact, you seemed to take a great deal of pleasure in teasing me and acting the opposite of what one expects from a suitor or beau."

"Well, there was that business with Donella and my blasted betrothal," he said. "I must admit it cramped my style. Still, you gave me very little encouragement."

"You may have noticed that I rarely encouraged any of my suitors," she said. "A girl does have her pride, after all. Or, at least, she should."

Alec leaned in even closer to nuzzle a delicious kiss across her lips. Edie's brain started to go fuzzy around the edges.

"Well, my proud, beautiful lass," he said in a husky voice as he released her mouth, "now that we've ascertained that I do, in fact, wish to marry you, perhaps you can tell me how to proceed. Do you stay, or do you go? Or, as I asked before, what do you want right now?"

Edie stared into his silvery-gray eyes, gleaming with tenderness. The potent desire she saw there, too, made her heart race and her muscles go weak with longing. But now that they'd hammered out the bare essentials, she should take herself off to her bedroom like a sane, respectable woman.

But she didn't feel very respectable, not while he looked at her like that.

As for her sanity, she'd pitched that out the window some time ago, when she decided to get involved with him in the first place. Edie still had no idea if Alec loved her the way she loved him, but she knew he wanted her.

He was right—it wasn't the regular way of things. In

fact, it was outrageous. Edie hadn't been feeling very outrageous of late, dogged by unfamiliar anxiety and doubt about an uncertain future. Their situation was still not entirely settled, and the idea of taking this final step made her as nervous as a cat in a storm.

But she also knew one thing beyond doubt.

"I want to be with you," she whispered, leaning forward to rest her forehead on his. "Now."

He blew out a relieved breath. "Good God, you don't know how happy I am to hear that. If you had decided to go back to your room, I fear I would have been forced to immerse myself in a very cold tub of water. Or go outside and throw myself into the closest stream."

Edie choked out a laugh. "That sounds most unpleasant. Why ever would you need to do that?"

He sat back on his heels again and pointedly stared down at his lap. Edie's gaze followed. When she took in the way he tented the fabric of his kilt, she didn't know whether to laugh again or blush.

She settled on blushing, if for no other reason than Alec's impressive erection, even swathed in fabric, hardly seemed like a laughing matter. Exciting, yes—amusing, most definitely not.

He came to his feet with smooth, masculine grace. That naturally brought his erection to her eye level as it bobbed beneath the wool of his kilt. Edie's fingers twitched with the impulse to take it in her hands, but she decided that such boldness might be a bit much for her, starting out.

"Let's get the rest of your nightgear off, shall we?" he said. His voice had dropped to a husky rumble that flickered like fire along her nerves. "I can barely see you under all that ridiculous flannel."

"Mamma's idea," Edie said as he began to deftly unbutton and untie her wrapper. "She was convinced we'd freeze to death unless we were bundled in multiple layers. Just be happy I'm not wearing a greatcoat on top of it."

Alec slipped the wrapper from her arms and wriggled it out from under her bottom. Edie pushed up a bit on her hands to help him.

"The Highlands aren't exactly the outer reaches of Mongolia, you know," he said.

"Tell that to my mother."

"Well, *you* must be sure to tell Lady Reese that I intend to keep her daughter very warm at night from now on."

She opened her eyes at him. "Good Lord, I have no intention of telling her any such thing."

He chuckled as he draped her wrapper over the end of the bed. "Yes, that's probably wise. Although I must admit that you look quite fetching, even garbed in flannel."

Edie smiled. Her nightgown might be flannel, but it was also a soft, fine weave trimmed lavishly with lace and silk ribbons. "One can still be warm and fashionable, you know."

"I'd rather you be warm and naked," he said, reaching for her.

He cupped one of her breasts, then thumbed the nipple, which was already starting to bead up. When he caught it between two fingers and gently squeezed, she breathed out a moan. His caress caused a delicious sensation deep in her belly and between her thighs.

"Christ, that's lovely," he murmured. Her nipple poked stiffly against the soft fabric of her gown. "I can't wait to get my mouth on you, lass."

"Um, thank you," Edie said, trying not to squirm with embarrassment—and excitement.

Alec seemed to be in the mood to take his time, bringing both hands up to stroke and play. Or perhaps he was giving her time to get used to the odd situation, which she appreciated. But the movement of his hands, the way he cupped her, or tweaked her stiff nipples or stroked the sensitive underside of her breasts, fueled a rising impatience. Edie could hardly sit still.

When he pushed her nightgown up to her thighs and spread her legs wide, stepping between them, she couldn't hold back a squeak. But then his hands came to her breasts again to resume their enticing, tormenting play. When he tugged on both nipples at once, gently rolling them between thumbs and forefingers, Edie groaned and let her head fall back. It was the most delicious sensation, making them ache and burn at the same time.

And now she understood his earlier comment, because she wanted his mouth on her, too, soothing the stiff points with his tongue.

"Alec," she said, sounding breathy as she collapsed back on her elbows. Honestly, it was a miracle she could stay upright at all, and he'd barely started to touch her.

He followed her over, bracing his fists on either side of her shoulders. His gaze bored into her, hot and avid, and her nerves flickered with anticipation.

"Do you like that, sweet?" he asked in a gravelly voice. "Do you want more?"

"Yes, please," she whispered back.

She reached up and curled a hand around his neck, bringing him down for a kiss. He answered eagerly, surging between her lips with a bold sweep of his tongue. Edie opened her mouth, tasting him in a gorgeous, wet slide. When she sucked on his tongue, he growled into her mouth and gave her lower lip a little nip. She jerked beneath him, and her sheath grew soft and damp as a gentle ache started to build between her thighs.

For a long, wonderful stream of moments, Alec took her mouth in leisurely, possessive kisses. He didn't rush, tasting her with deep strokes and little bites soothed by deeper kisses. It was everything she'd dreamed kissing could be.

Hot and provocative, wet and deep, skating just on the edge of control. It was earthy and lustful, but also intense and beautiful in a way her mind groped to explain—as if every particle of Alec's being was focused on giving her as much pleasure as possible.

It felt like he gave rather than took, and it was so different from any kiss she'd ever experienced.

Unbidden, the image of Sir Malcolm Bannister and his slobbering ways sprang into mind. Edie spluttered out a laugh.

Alec pulled back with a jerk. "Edie, what the hell are you laughing at?"

The slightly aggrieved look on his face made her giggle again. "It's not you, I promise," she said. "I just thought of something funny."

His eyes narrowed, an intriguing combination of masculine ire and lust. It made her feel quite wicked. "What?" he demanded.

"I was thinking how well you kiss. You're not at all like a mastiff slobbering all over me, which is exactly what Sir—"

Alec groaned and let his head drop. "I swear, I'm going to kill Bannister the next time I see him."

Then his head came up, his gaze fierce and deliciously possessive. Edie practically wriggled with delight. "You're not jealous, are you?"

"I am madly jealous of any man touching you besides me," he growled.

This time she did wriggle. "That's splendid. I must try to make you jealous more often."

He pulled her upright. "And for that, Miss Impudence, you deserve to be punished."

That sounded rather fun. "Really? How?"

"First, I'm going to get this bloody thing off you, and then I'm going to have my wicked way with you."

And so quickly that he left her gasping, Alec had whipped her nightgown from her body, leaving her completely exposed. His gaze flamed as he took a step back, getting a better view.

Edie sat perched on the edge of the mattress, unsure what to do with herself and quite certain that she was blushing a fiery red from head to toe. It wasn't every day that one sat entirely naked in front of a man, even if it was the man one intended to marry. It took a great deal of courage not to scurry as quickly as possible beneath the bedclothes.

Her hand was, in fact, reaching to pull back the coverlet, but the look on his face stopped her. His high cheekbones had flushed under his tan, and his eyes had gone wide. His chest rose and fell on one, deep breath, and he placed a hand over his heart.

"Christ, lass," he said in a low, almost reverent voice. "You'll be the death of me. But I can't think of a better way to go."

It seemed an odd, if nice, thing to say. And even though she couldn't help feeling shy, she had to admit she liked the way he looked at her.

Her courage bolstered by his admiring gaze, she leaned back on her hands. That brought her breasts nicely up and showcased her nipples, now stiff and flushed. Alec's dark gaze went as hot as pitch.

"Well," she teased in a husky voice, "aren't you going to punish me?"

He let out a laugh that sounded more like a groan, then stepped forward. Placing his hands on the inside of her thighs, he pushed her open. Edie's heart practically jammed up into her throat, but she held still, letting him look his fill.

"You're the most gorgeous thing I've ever seen," he rumbled as he pushed her a little bit wider. Good Lord, he could see every intimate detail. "So sweet and pink. So pretty."

He gently combed his fingers through her fluff. "And your gold curls. I can't wait to be deep inside you, love, with those curls tickling against my skin."

Edie's mouth went dry. She had to lick her lips before she could speak. "Are you going to do that now?"

His gaze came up to her face, his expression so avid that she felt more than a niggling of doubt about what would happen next.

"Not yet. I have to get you ready, first."

"What does that entail?"

"I'll show you." He swooped down and pressed her flat against the bed, with her lower legs dangling off the mattress. He took her hands and placed them to the side of her head, encircling her wrists in a gentle but unbreakable grip.

She was completely at his mercy, laid flat and vulnerable, with his hips wedged between her spread thighs. The wool of his kilt gently abraded her skin and brushed against her most sensitive parts, making them twitch with sensation. She'd never felt anything like it before, not even from her own tentative, secret explorations. It was absolutely delicious.

His wicked smile shot fiery sparks along her nerves.

Still, she wouldn't let him get the best of her. "Now what?" she asked, trying to sound pert rather than breathless.

"This," he rumbled. He started at her throat, nipping and licking his way along the underside of her jaw. Shivers raced along her skin, and she couldn't help jerking against his hold.

"That's it, love," he said in a rasping voice as he nuzzled the hollow at the base of her throat. "Move as much as you want. But know that I won't let you go. You're completely under my control."

That sounded both terribly naughty and terribly exciting, and Edie couldn't help shifting beneath him. That brought her breasts in contact with the coarse hair that dusted his brawny chest, and she let out a gasp. Her nipples, stiff as beads, dragged against him, making her arch up even closer in a desperate attempt to soothe the pleasurable ache.

Alec groaned his approval as he flexed his hips. The fabric of his kilt rasped against her exposed, tender flesh. It both irritated and stimulated, and it fed her growing need, driving her to move.

Edie fought his hold. She couldn't get close enough, squirming hard to try to assuage the ache in her breasts.

Alec slid down a few inches, kissing and licking his way across the rise of her chest. For a few, torturous minutes, he circled her nipples with his tongue, teasing her as he skillfully built up the restless throb of wanting in her veins.

"Alec," she finally panted, "I need you to do something."

What she needed was his mouth and tongue on her breasts—and all over her body. But it seemed rather shocking to voice so forward a request, especially during their first time together.

She did, though, squirm a little for emphasis.

"Oh, my pleasure, love," he whispered.

Then, his mouth found her nipple. He dragged his tongue over the stiff point, then sucked her in. Edie let out a startled cry. Good God, it felt so delicious that she almost could imagine she'd died and gone to heaven.

He finally let go of her wrist and brought his hand down to her other breast. As he licked and tongued her, driving her wild, his other hand played. Her breasts quivered under his lavish attentions. While he sucked on her, he cupped and squeezed her other breast, lightly flicking her nipple. When she couldn't take it a second longer, he switched, bringing the sweep of his tongue to soothe the luscious ache.

Instinctively, she hooked her ankles around the backs of his thighs. With a low growl, he brought his pelvis flush to her mound, gently flexing his hips and pushing into the aching bud of her sex. The rasp of his erection through the wool of his kilt made her burn and go soft and slick.

Alec sucked her hard into his mouth at the same time as he pushed against her. Sensation jolted her, and tiny contractions started to ripple out from deep inside. Edie gripped his shoulders and jerked against him, letting out a startled cry.

He eased back with a last tender lick. Then he straightened up to stare down at her, even though he kept one hand curled possessively around her breast.

"Christ," he said, his voice low and harsh. "You're so goddamn beautiful. Look at yourself, sweet. Look at us."

She blinked, startled by his profanity, but she glanced down to take in her body, lying sprawled beneath him. Her thighs were spread wide around him, her golden nest of curls tangled and gleaming with her own moisture. Her breasts quivered from her uneven breathing, and the nipples were wet points, flushed red from his attentions. She looked entirely wanton.

But it was the sight of Alec that made her heart pound—all sensual brawn and ready to ravish her. His gaze was hot, narrow, and devouring. But his touch was so loving as he stroked her breasts that it brought tears to her eyes and a trembling smile to her lips.

"I need to be inside you, Edie," he whispered. He sounded almost tortured, and she could feel a slight tremble in his hands.

She slid her hands to his forearms, caressing him. "I need that, too."

He let out a fractured breath. When he started to unfasten his belt, she pushed herself up on her elbows and started to sit up.

"No need to move, love," Alec said.

She subsided with a frown. "Shouldn't we get in bed before we, er, you know."

He flashed a grin as he took off his belt and began to unwind the kilt. "I'm enjoying you like this. I can see everything. Besides, it might be a little easier for you in this position, at least for the first time."

"Well, you're the expert," she said. "I leave myself in your capable hands."

Edie rather thought it was a good thing that one of them knew what to do, because she was starting to get nervous again, despite the fact that she wanted him as much as he wanted her. And when he finished unwrapping the length of plaid, finally exposing himself, it was a jolt—a big jolt, almost as big as Alec himself. His erection, thrusting up long and thick from its nest of dark hair, was impressive, to say the least.

And just a wee bit terrifying.

Her face must have shown her trepidation, because he swooped down to kiss her. She wrapped her arms around his neck, taking comfort in his strength and warmth.

He nuzzled her lips. "It'll be fine, I promise. I'll make sure you're ready."

She gave him a tremulous smile. "I trust you, Alasdair Gilbride."

And she did, down to the marrow of her bones. Finally, they would be together, with no more obstacles standing between them.

He nudged her thighs a fraction wider, and then his hands drifted to the damp nest of curls that concealed her.

Gently, so gently, he parted her inner folds and began stroking, slicking his fingertips through her moisture. He circled and played, rubbing her with a soft but steady pressure that coaxed forth a lovely throbbing sensation in the tight knot of her sex.

Edie's fingers curled into the bedclothes beneath her. Her gaze latched onto Alec, so large and masterful as he loomed over her. She couldn't even begin to find the words to describe how she felt, what she thought. She only knew that she loved him, and that every instinct urged surrender to that love and to him.

And then she was nothing but sensation and a tight spiral of need. He slid his hands through her inner folds and dipped inside, gently scissoring her open. It burned but also ached, and her need grew. She felt open and ready for him, desperate to be filled.

With a light touch, he flicked his thumb over her tight bud as he buried two fingers inside her. Edie moaned and arched her back, clenching around him. Everything inside seemed to contract and then strain toward release.

"Aye, lass, you're ready." Alec's burr was low and thick.

He leaned over, propping one hand by her shoulder. "Look at me, love. Just keep looking at me."

Edie reached up to curl her hands around his neck. She smiled, too moved to say anything. He nudged her, and the broad head of his erection penetrated. She felt her eyes go wide at the burn as he leaned in.

Good heavens, he felt enormous. She sucked in a breath and held it. Alec let out a groan and closed his eyes. He nudged again, sinking in a bit more, then held himself still.

Edie glanced down, unable to help herself. And despite her trepidation and the stinging she felt, her stomach clenched. The sight of Alec standing between her spread legs was so intimate that it brought tears to her eyes.

"Edie, love, am I hurting you?" he asked in a tight voice.

She glanced up. His eyes were open and his features looked almost grim. Perspiration glazed his skin. She shook her head and managed a smile, finding it difficult to speak.

Gently, he smoothed her messy hair from her forehead. "Then why are you crying, sweet lass?"

She reached up to plant a kiss on his chin. "Because I'm so happy. I still can't believe it all worked out."

He unleashed a smile that was both smoldering and full of tenderness. It burrowed deep into her heart and took up permanent residence.

"I couldn't let you go, Edie," he said. "I can never let you go."

Since the burn between her legs had started to fade, replaced by an altogether nicer sensation, she gave him a saucy smile. "Well, now that you have me, what do you intend to do about it?"

Nothing could have prepared her for the greedy, demanding kiss that left her breathless and shaking when he finally pulled back. "I'm going to make love to you," he growled.

He started to move again, slowly pressing forward. With soft commands, he urged her to wrap her legs around his hips, opening her up. Slowly, he parted her, forging all the way. He left her breathless.

"All right?" he murmured.

She nodded. It was better than all right—it was *him*. And it got even better when he started slowly rocking, pulling out just a bit more each time he withdrew. Then pushing forward, a little deeper. He was so thick, and her passage felt tight and slick as it clung to him. His ragged moan vibrated through her, reflecting her own rising pleasure.

"God, you feel so good," he rasped out.

Suddenly, he cupped a hand beneath her bottom and tilted her up as he rocked into her. Edie gasped. It was the perfect angle, bringing the peak of her sensitive sex into contact with his pelvis with each thrust. Tiny spasms rippled through her passage.

He moved faster now, short thrusts that sent sparks shooting through her body. Her breath coming in sobs, Edie clutched at his shoulders. His body, his heat, and his scent surrounded her, overwhelming her senses.

Overwhelming her heart.

She clung to him, staring into his eyes as he drove her closer and closer to climax. His gaze glittered and his features were pulled into a taut, almost fierce expression. She arched up, desperately reaching for release as it shimmered just beyond her reach. Then Alec pulled up her leg, opening her wide as he thrust into her. He flexed one more time, nudging hard against her, and release blasted through her like a storm.

Crying, she curled up and pressed herself against his chest, vibrating with the force of her climax. Alec wrapped her in a muscular hold, cradling her against him. A moment later he bit out a curse as his body found its pleasure, and his arms tightened around her until she could barely breathe.

But Edie didn't care. She wanted him to hold her forever and never let her go.

Chapter Twenty

Something tickled Edie's nose, and a low rumbling vibrated through her body.

"Wake up, sweetheart. I need to get you back to your room."

"Don't want to," she mumbled, refusing to open her eyes. She snuggled in closer to the warmth that surrounded her, breathing out a sigh of satisfaction as she started to drift off.

Then her sleep-dazed brain registered the source of the warmth—a hard, naked body. She dragged open her eyelids and tried to focus. It was still dark. Her mind was fuzzy and she was sated with an enormous sense of well-being, both urging her to slip back into slumber.

Alec tickled her nose again. "You can sleep more in your room. Right now we've got to get up."

She turned her face into his chest and wriggled a bit, getting even more comfortable. That seemed to make the body embracing her go even harder, and Alec muttered something under his breath.

"It's still dark," she said, closing her eyes. "No one will be up for ages."

"*I'm* most decidedly up, and that's going to be quite the problem if I don't get you back to your room."

Since she had no idea what he was talking about, she ignored his comment and snuggled in closer. Never had she felt so warm, so safe, or so happy, and she had no inclination to move.

Alec's chest rose and fell under her cheek as he huffed out a laugh. But when he lifted her off him, Edie voiced an incoherent protest that unfortunately failed to stop him from sliding out from under her.

"Hush, silly girl," he said as he pulled the covers up to her shoulders. "Just stay there while I get dressed, then I'll help you."

She cracked open an eyelid. The view was so enticing that she opened the other eyelid as well.

Alec stood next to the bed—entirely naked, entirely delectable, and thoroughly aroused.

"Goodness, you are up," she said, eyeing his impressive erection. "Does that happen every morning?"

He smiled. "Yes, as a matter of fact it does."

She let out a happy sigh and turned on her side, hugging his pillow. "That's something to look forward to."

He laughed, then bent to press a quick kiss to her cheek. "You, Miss Whitney, are thoroughly incorrigible."

"I know. Aren't you glad?"

"Indeed I am."

She drifted back into a lovely doze as he moved quietly about the room. When he roused her again a few minutes later, he was fully dressed. She sat up with a yawn. "What time is it?"

"Time for you to get back to your room," he said as he fetched her nightgown.

She sat on the side of the bed and let him dress her. Despite the fact that she was half-asleep, it was a thoroughly enjoyable experience. It was accompanied by several luscious kisses and a few intimate caresses as he wrestled the voluminous amount of fabric over her body. He helped her with her slippers, then lifted her down to the floor and retrieved her dressing gown.

"Don't forget my cap," she said around a large yawn.

"I hope you don't intend to wear so much gear to bed after we're married," he said as he carefully placed her spectacles on her nose.

"Just think how much fun you'll have getting me out of it," she said, smiling up at him.

When he smiled back at her, she thought her heart just might burst open for joy. Any doubts she might have had about their marriage had been dispelled by their mutual passion. Edie hadn't yet worked up the nerve to ask Alec if he loved her, but she had no doubt that he wanted her in his bed and in his life. Though they might not be exactly where they needed to be, it was a good start to a future life together.

She squeaked a bit when he lifted her into his arms. "What are you doing?"

"I'm carrying my future bride to her room," he said, settling her against his chest.

"That's very decent of you, but I'm perfectly capable of walking."

"I like carrying you," he said, juggling her a bit as he opened the door. "Especially when you're half-dressed like this."

"It's an awfully long way back to my room," she said as she draped her arms around his neck. "I'm not exactly a lightweight, you know. I don't want you hurting yourself."

He scoffed. "You're absolutely perfect. Besides, I don't want you to be cold in these drafty halls."

She happily subsided into his warm, powerful embrace. As he traversed the corridors and stairways of Blairgal,

Edie closed her eyes again, drifting in a delicious haze. She rubbed her cheek against his starched neckcloth—

Her eyes flew open and her head came up off his chest. She leaned back a bit, inspecting him in the dim light of the breaking dawn that filtered through the long windows on one side of the hall.

Alec glanced down at her. "What's wrong?"

"You're dressed." Right down to waistcoat and sturdy wool tailcoat, buckskin breeches, and riding boots. "Where are you going?"

He hesitated just enough to tell her something was wrong.

"I'm going riding," he said in a clipped tone.

"At this hour of the morning?" she asked incredulously. "Are you insane?"

"It'll be lighter by the time I get down to the stables."

"Not that much lighter. Tell me truthfully what you're doing."

He shook his head. "Hush, Edie. Someone will hear us."

She fumed silently until he got her back to her room. As soon as he set her on her feet, she grabbed the front of his coat. "Alec, I am not letting you leave this room until you tell me where you're going."

"Edie, I don't have time for this," he growled. "I'll explain everything when I see you at breakfast."

She took in his expression, now shuttered. The answer blazed into her mind and she couldn't hold back a horrified gasp. "You're going to meet Fergus, aren't you? You're going to fight a duel."

He rolled his eyes, then covered her hands with his. "Don't be ridiculous. I would—"

"Don't lie to me. Not about this. Did he challenge you to a duel?"

When he rolled his lips together, refusing to answer, she

dug her fingers into his coat, as if by clutching on to him she could keep him safe.

"You can't do it, Alec. It's insane, and it's not necessary. You said Donella never wanted to marry you, so why go through with something so dangerous?" Her voice had gone high and screechy, but she didn't care.

"Hush, love," he soothed, steering her over to her bed. "I'm just going to talk to him, I promise. I won't hurt him."

He hoisted her up and plopped her on the bed, but she still managed to keep hold of him.

"I'm not worried about him, you stupid man. I'm worried about you. I'll die if anything happens to you." Her heart was beating so hard she could barely get the words out.

He dropped a quick kiss on her lips. "Sweet, nothing is going to happen to me." He cracked a sly grin. "I'm a very good shot."

She let go of his coat, only to haul back and whack him on the arm. "That's not funny."

He immediately looked contrite. "I'm sorry. I swear, Edie, I'm not going to fight him, no matter what he might want. But I do need to speak with him, somewhere quiet and out of the way. If I don't, he'll just come roaring up to the house and cause all sorts of trouble. And that would simply contribute to the gossip."

"I don't care about the gossip," she said desperately.

"Well, I do. I won't see you and Donella further smeared by this. Fergus is angry and hurt, but he's no fool. I'll be able to make him see sense once we have a chance to talk."

Edie very much doubted that. Fergus had too many reasons to want to kill Alec, starting with the fact that he was next in line to inherit.

The image of those rocks tumbling down upon them at Mugdock Castle rose in her mind. She thought about bringing up that incident but knew he would simply dismiss it as the result of her over-active imagination.

"Is someone going with you? Do you have a second?" she asked, starting to feel truly panicky.

"Of course not." He was working to pry her other hand loose from his coat. "We don't need anyone else knowing about this."

Lovely. Fergus could shoot Alec in cold blood and no one would be any the wiser. A perfect way to dispose of the man who'd supposedly besmirched his sister's honor *and* knocked him back in the line of inheritance.

"You need to speak with your grandfather," she said. He'd finally pried her hands loose and was now holding them down in her lap. "He'll talk sense into Fergus."

"Trust me, he won't. He's more likely to pitch a fit, which won't do his heart any good."

"Alec—"

He cut off her desperate plea by swooping in to give her a searing kiss. It lasted only a few seconds, but it was so thorough and abandoned that he left her gasping for breath.

"Go back to sleep," he said, straightening. "I'll be back before you know it."

Before she could respond to that idiocy, he strode out of the room.

Cursing, Edie slid off the bed, landing on legs that still quivered from both fear and the force of his kiss. She started to stalk after him when the door to her dressing room flew open. Cora rushed out, mostly dressed but with her nightcap still on her head.

"Miss, what's happening?"

"Captain Gilbride is going off to fight a duel and I've got to stop him."

Cora's eyes went wide as dinner plates. "How?"

"I don't know yet. But I need you to go down to the stables and try to find out where he's going. Can you please do that?"

Cora hurried up to her and straightened Edie's cap. "I can. And you go wake up Lady Reese. She'll know what to do."

Edie blinked. She'd thought to wake up Lord Riddick first, but Mamma would no doubt be able to manage the old man much better than she could.

She dragged Cora out to the hall. "I'll meet you in the stables or back here."

The maid scurried off toward the back of the wing, while Edie picked up her skirts and flew down the hall to her mother's room. She barged in, not bothering to knock.

"Mamma, wake up!"

Her mother bolted up. Her large, lace-covered cap slid to the side, letting her braid escape. "Eden? What's wrong?"

"Alec's gone off to fight a duel with Fergus." Edie rushed over to the chair in front of the dressing table and snatched up her mother's wrapper.

"Didn't you try to stop him?" Mamma's voice had gone high enough to shatter glass.

"Of course I did. But he's just like every other bloody man I've ever met—he doesn't listen."

Her mother rose from her bed, looking as outraged as an avenging fury. If there was one thing she abhorred, it was rising before mid-morning.

She took the robe and pushed her arms into the sleeves. "I have had quite enough of this nonsense, Eden. It really must stop."

"I couldn't agree more, Mamma. And that means we've got to get Lord Riddick on our side."

"I'm well aware of that, my dear," her mother said as she shoved her feet in her dainty slippers. She stormed for the door, the wide skirts of her robe flaring out behind her like a cape. "And I'm going to tell him exactly what I think about how poorly he manages his domestic affairs. This clan nonsense has to end."

Edie, quite a bit shorter, had to scurry to keep up with her mother's long-legged stride as she headed down the corridor to Lord Riddick's chambers.

"Mamma," she said, "he feels very strongly about his family's traditions. You'll simply annoy him if you say that."

Her mother threw her an irate glance. "Good, because then he'll know exactly how I feel."

A minute later, they rounded the corner into the adjoining wing, where his lordship's rooms were located. Her mother marched up to the door and rapped on it loudly. "Lord Riddick, wake up," she called out. "It's Lady Reese. I need to speak with you."

"Well, if that didn't give the poor man a heart attack, nothing will," Edie muttered.

"We don't have time to waste, Eden." She rapped again. "Lord Riddick—"

The door flew open and a slight, dark-haired man—presumably the earl's valet—stood gaping at them. "Lady . . . Lady Reese," he stuttered.

"Out of my way," Mamma commanded. She pushed past the poor fellow, who looked ready to faint. Edie grimaced an apology and followed her in.

They found themselves in an enormous bedroom decorated in a style that Edie could only describe as Heroic Highlander. There was quite a lot of plaid and yet more weapons, along with a huge and ancient four-poster bed hung with, yes, more plaid. Sitting in the bed, Lord Riddick looked furious and terribly aristocratic, despite the fact that he too was still in his nightgear and cap.

"What the hell are you doing, you daft *Sassenachs?*" he thundered.

"Trying to save your grandson." Mamma stormed up to the bed, not the least bit embarrassed. "He and your benighted nephew have snuck off to fight a duel."

His lordship was struggling to free himself from his bedclothes, but her announcement gave him pause. His gaze flicked to Edie. "Is that true?"

Edie nodded. "Yes, but Alec said he wouldn't fight him. He said he wanted to try and talk some sense into Fergus."

Her mother snorted. "I have seen precious little of that commodity in this household."

"I'll thank you not to insult my family. Besides, *your* family is hardly blameless in this matter," Lord Riddick growled.

"Oh, for God's sake," Edie exclaimed. "Stop arguing and do something. They're going to kill each other."

The earl started to look stubborn. "I doubt it. Besides, there's nothing I can do about it. It's a matter of honor, one Fergus has every right to demand."

Edie wanted to slap him. "You doubt it? Do you really want to see your grandson dead in a pool of blood? Or your nephew?"

He glared at her. "It won't come to that, you noddy. They'll just fire their shots in the air, or knock each other about for a while. It's best we leave them alone to sort it out for themselves like gentlemen."

Mamma planted her hands on her hips. "Have you been paying attention to your nephew, sir? He's been staring daggers at Captain Gilbride and spewing vague threats ever since we arrived. You should be stopping this stupidity, not encouraging it."

The old earl looked ready to spit fire. "I wouldn't expect a blasted woman to understand an affair of honor."

He grabbed his robe from the valet, who'd been standing by his bed making odd bleating noises.

Mamma drew herself to her full height, towering over the stoop-shouldered earl in righteous wrath. "I am so sick of men and their damned honor. To *hell* with your honor, I say."

Edie gaped at her mother. She'd never once heard Mamma utter an oath.

"Your grandson survived eight years of war, including that carnage at Waterloo, and you truly intend to let him throw his life away over this?" her mother raged. "Let me tell you about honor, sir. My daughter's honor is in ruins, as is Miss Haddon's. And I'll tell you whose fault that is. It's yours and Miss Haddon's family's for forcing two young people into a marriage that neither wanted. And instead of acting like rational human beings, you're now all rushing about like characters from some demented Shakespearean tragedy. Well, I won't have it. If you won't do something to save your grandson and nephew, I will."

She glared at the earl, who seemed stunned. Mamma then snorted in disgust, turned on her heel, and sailed out of the room. Edie ran after her, catching up in the hall.

"That was the most splendid thing I've ever heard, Mamma," she said, jogging to keep up. "But what do we do now?"

"We follow those ridiculous young men and stop them. Go to your room, put on your boots and pelisse, and come fetch me. We don't have time to waste getting properly dressed."

If not for her terror that something might happen to Alec, Edie would be enjoying herself. Her mother's conduct in the midst of this crisis was both an eye-opener and entertaining.

Edie raced down the corridor to her room, throwing open the door and pelting inside. "Cora, are you back?"

She rummaged around in the tallboy in the corner and unearthed her riding boots. "Cora," she yelled again.

"Here I am," the maid answered, hurrying in from the hall.

Edie sat on the floor to pull on her boots. "Did you go to the stables?"

"The captain didn't go there," Cora said, coming over to help her.

Edie's heart clenched. "Do you know where he went?"

Her maid grinned. "I was running to the stables when I saw the captain cross the courtyard toward the back of the castle, so I followed him. He went to a sort of meadow right below the main garden. Then he sat down on a bench, looking ready for a bit of a wait."

Edie had walked out to that meadow just yesterday, seeking solitude. It was close to the house but still private. "Waiting for that blasted Fergus, no doubt. Cora, go find my pelisse."

"Miss, ain't you going to get dressed?" Cora said, sounding shocked.

"There's no time to lose. Mamma's waiting."

Muttering that everyone had gone barmy, the maid fetched Edie's pelisse. Edie snatched it from her and took off at a run, shoving her arms into the thick wool garment as she went. She burst into her mother's room to find her parent garbed in boots, pelisse, and what was obviously the first bonnet that had come to hand—an elaborate confection with purple feathers and a large satin bow. In combination with her nightshift, it was the most ludicrous outfit one could imagine.

Davis, hovering close by, was fully dressed and looking mortally offended that she had to send her mistress out looking like an escapee from a madhouse.

This would be quite the story for Edie to tell her

grandchildren—if their future grandfather managed to survive the morning.

"Do you know where to look for them?" Mamma asked as they headed into the hall with Cora and Davis bringing up the rear.

"I do," Edie said. "It'll be faster if we cut through the old part of the castle."

She thanked God that she'd spent the last few days exploring Blairgal, when she'd been trying to avoid Alec and his family. She knew exactly where she was going and the fastest way to get there.

After taking two separate staircases and three corridors, they emerged into the gardens. The sun was finally coming over the horizon. A layer of frost coated the lawn and the shrubs, and grass crackled under their feet as they raced between rows of clipped shrubbery. Once, Mamma started to slip, but Edie and Davis managed to catch her and keep her from falling on her backside.

"Eden, I will be having a very stern talk with Alasdair once this is over," Mamma said as she yanked her bonnet back into place. "I have never in my life experienced anything so outrageous as the conduct of this family."

"You're more than welcome to do so, Mamma, after I've boxed his ears." Edie pointed ahead to a break in the rustic stone wall that surrounded the gardens. "There are the steps down to the meadow."

They hurried down the steps only to come to an abrupt halt at the bottom, almost piling up on each other. Edie heard her mother utter a salty curse as she grabbed Davis to steady herself.

Alec and Fergus were standing at opposite ends of the small meadow, pistols in hand. Alec had his pressed down along the side of his leg, while Fergus was raising his.

"Stop," shrieked Edie at the top of her lungs.

Fergus whipped around, so startled that he yanked his

gun to point it right at the group of women clustered at the bottom of the steps.

"Fergus, put the gun down," Alec shouted, already on the move toward Edie and her mother.

Edie dashed out to meet him. "You put that damn thing down too." Before he could say a word, she threw herself against his chest and wrapped her arms around his neck.

"What the hell are you doing here?" he growled, his free arm going around her waist. "I told you to wait in your room."

"I'm saving your life." She slid her hands down to grab the lapels of his coat. "Not that you deserve it, you stubborn man."

He did a quick scan of her outfit, his brows lifting with surprise. Then he looked at her mother—who was stalking over to confront Fergus—and let out a choked laugh. "Good God, you're both still in your nightclothes. Have you lost your minds?"

"There wasn't exactly time to change," Edie retorted. "What with the need to stop you and Fergus from murdering each other."

"I had no intention of hurting him, as you know."

"And what were your cousin's intentions, may I ask? They didn't look to be particularly friendly when we arrived."

Alec hesitated before answering. "I'm not quite sure. I don't think he is either, although he did insist that we go through with this absurd exercise."

Edie shook him by the lapels. "Absurd and deadly. Alec, this must stop. It's immoral *and* illegal."

"I agree, but right now it looks like we have to stop your mother from murdering Fergus."

She glanced over her shoulder to see her mother waving a finger in Fergus's face as she berated him. He was obviously trying to defend himself, but Mamma was having none of it.

"Oh, no." Edie wriggled out from Alec's embrace and dashed over to her mother.

"Mamma, it's fine," she said, resting a hand on her mother's arm. "We stopped it."

"You stopped nothing," Fergus exclaimed, his face beet-red. "If you think this is the end of it, you are as insane as my cousin. Besides, it's none of your business. Just go away and leave us alone, you bloody Englishwoman."

Edie had spent the last half hour trying to keep her temper—and hysterics—under control, but no longer. She stepped forward and jabbed a finger right under the young man's nose. "It is my business, you nitwit. Whether you like it or not, I'm probably going to marry your cousin—"

"Probably?" Alec interjected in an annoyed tone.

Edie ignored him. "And that, Mr. Haddon, will make me your cousin and therefore someone you're going to have to learn to live with. So the sooner you start doing that, the better—for you, for your mother, and especially for Donella."

Fergus had been starting to look rather abashed, but the mention of his sister's name set him off again.

"Don't you dare talk to me about what's best for Donella. I'm doing this to protect her," he yelled.

"And how will either killing Alec or getting yourself killed protect your sister?" Edie snapped. "That's insane logic."

"What do you expect, Eden?" her mother interjected in a toplofty tone. "The captain's entire family belongs in an asylum, as far as I can ascertain. Perhaps madness is a particular affliction running in the Haddon and Graham lineages."

Edie thought she heard a snicker from Alec. She ignored him again, glaring at her mother. "That is not helpful, Mamma."

"And I'll bloody well not stand here and be insulted by the likes of you," Fergus exclaimed.

He was still looking mad as fire, but Edie thought some of the starch had gone out of him.

"No one truly intends to insult you, Mr. Haddon," Edie said in a firm voice. "But you must stop acting in this irrational fashion. It won't solve any of our problems."

Fergus glared past her at Alec. "Why did you have to bring them back with you? Everything would have been fine if you'd come home by yourself." Then he swiped an arm across his eyes and half-turned away, as if he didn't want them to see his emotion.

Alec placed his hands on Edie's shoulders and moved her aside. "No, lad," he said in a gentle voice. "It never would have been right for your sister and me."

"You didn't even give it a chance," Fergus said, waving his arms about.

Which meant he was waving his pistol about, too.

"Put that weapon down," Mamma snapped, stepping in front of him. "Davis, come stand next to me. Eden, you and Cora block Captain Gilbride. They will have to shoot through us to proceed with this idiotic duel, and I feel sure they will not dare to do so."

Davis let out a weary sigh and trudged over to stand by her mistress. Edie was certain that Fergus had no intention of shooting anyone at this point, but followed her mother's instructions as well.

"Edie, that's really not necessary," Alec said, clearly torn between frustration and laughter.

Cora reluctantly sidled up beside her. "Now what?" she said in a loud stage whisper.

"I have no idea," Edie whispered back.

They stood frozen in a ridiculous tableau until a roar had them all spinning around. Lord Riddick stomped toward them, leaning heavily on Mr. Gilbride's arm.

"Put those pistols down this instant," thundered the earl.

Alec shook his head. "Lovely. That's all we needed to make this a complete farce," he said. "Now what, indeed?"

"No need to worry, Captain Gilbride," Edie's mother said as she plucked the pistol from Fergus's hand. "I know *exactly* what to do."

Chapter Twenty-One

Edie sat on a chaise in the impressive entrance hall of Blairgal, chewing on the edge of a now-ragged nail. She glanced yet again at the Louis XVI clock on the mantel, silently cursing the fact that the minute hand seemed frozen. Without a doubt, the last hour had been the slowest of her entire life.

"Eden, stop chewing on your nail," her mother ordered from her chair on the other side of the enormous fireplace.

"Yes, Mamma," she absently replied. Though her mother had reprimanded her in front of her reputed fiancé and his family, she was too rattled by the events of the last twenty-four hours and too worried about what might happen next to care.

Alec wrapped his fingers around her wrist and pulled her hand into his lap. "There's no cause for anxiety, sweetheart. Your mother knows exactly what she's doing."

She cut him a skeptical glance. "Are you sure about that?"

"Aye. Just wait and see."

Edie let out a heavy sigh as she curled her fingers around his and waited for the rest of the Haddon family to appear. After Lord Riddick's arrival in the meadow, he and Mamma had spent several tense minutes in whispered conversation. The earl had then ordered Fergus to fetch his sister and mother and bring them to the castle. Then everyone would assemble in the grand entrance hall—scene of many an important family meeting over the centuries, according to Alec—to discuss the issue of the broken engagement.

"What's going on?" Edie had asked her mother as they trooped back to the castle. "Why did his lordship send for Miss Haddon and her mother?"

"Lord Riddick and I agreed it was necessary to hear from Miss Haddon," her mother had said. "The final say regarding this ridiculous situation should be hers. If she still wishes to marry Alasdair, I think we must abide by that decision."

"What?" Edie had yelped, sliding to a halt on the slippery grass.

Her mother had urged her along, practically dragging her through the garden to the back of the castle. "It's the only way anyone in this dreadful family will accept your marriage to Alasdair. Miss Haddon must state once and for all that she has no desire to marry him, without any duress. Once that declaration is made, the way will be clear for you."

That had struck Edie as the worst plan she'd ever heard. Donella might very well have reviewed her stance since last night and decided she wanted to marry Alec after all. And since Mamma had apparently promised Lord Riddick that Edie would honor Donella's decision, her fate now rested in the hands of a woman she'd thoroughly humiliated.

When she'd raised that objection, her mother had simply marched Edie back to her room and ordered her to get dressed. She'd managed that in record time and had then flown down to the hall to see if she could buttonhole Alec before everyone else arrived. He had yet to even make her a formal offer of marriage, and the decision had once more been taken out of their hands.

Unfortunately, Alec, his father, and his grandfather were already ensconced in the entrance hall, sitting in front of a roaring fire in the massive hearth. Alec had greeted her with a loving smile that had made Edie want to cry, escorting her to the chaise and then sitting next to her. When he'd put an arm around her, tucking her against him, Lord Riddick had grumped and Mr. Gilbride had *tsked,* but Alec had ignored them. Mamma had arrived a few minutes later, looking calm, imperious, and elegant. They'd all settled down to drink coffee and wait in uncomfortable silence.

Edie felt like she had ants crawling under her skin and her insides churned, although that might well be the result of nervously downing two cups of coffee on an empty stomach.

When the footman opened the front doors at the far end of the hall, the Haddons entered. They handed over their coats and hats before making their way to join them.

"Courage, sweet," Alec murmured in her ear. "Everything will be just fine."

She glanced up at him, wanting to roll her eyes. How could he be so blasted self-confident when their fate hung in the balance?

But from the wild-eyed look on Mrs. Haddon's face and the long-suffering one on Donella's, everything was decidedly *not* fine. Edie's stomach cramped on the horrible thought that Fergus and Mrs. Haddon had talked Donella round to their way of thinking once more.

"Ladies, thank you for coming," Lord Riddick said in a gruff voice. "Please take a seat."

Alec stood and took Donella's hand, giving her a friendly smile. His cousin looked anxiously up at him, but she visibly relaxed when he murmured something in a low voice as he escorted her to one of the seats gathered around the enormous fireplace. That was hardly reassuring, and the fact that they looked so comfortable—and splendid—together made Edie's stomach clench even more.

The feeling was exacerbated when Alec didn't return to sit with her, instead moving to stand next to his grandfather's chair. It was a silent but clear signal of respect, and Edie certainly took it to mean that Alec would stand by the decisions made today.

They were barely seated when Mrs. Haddon launched into an aggrieved rant.

"Really, sir," she said in a high-pitched voice to the earl. "Can we not have one family discussion without these outsiders taking part?" She directed a hate-filled glance at Edie. "My poor daughter shouldn't have to sit in the same room with that—"

"That'll be enough, Glenna," the earl interrupted in a stern tone. "Lady Reese and her daughter are my guests. Given the present circumstances, Miss Whitney has every right to be here."

Edie appreciated the earl's intervention. He might be gruff and old-fashioned, but she was convinced he was a fair-minded man. In fact, he was beginning to grow on her, and she only hoped she'd get the chance to know him better.

Mrs. Haddon practically quivered with outrage. "I never thought to see the day when you would choose strangers over your own family, Callum. I wonder what my brother will have to say about that."

"At the moment, I don't care," the earl replied in blighting tones. "What I care about is clearing up this blasted mess, so I'll thank you to hold your tongue."

In the face of so comprehensive a set-down, Mrs. Haddon had no choice but to fume in silence.

"Thank you, Glenna," said Mr. Gilbride, jumping in to

smooth things over, as usual. "I know how distressing this is for everyone." He switched his attention to Donella. "Now, my dear, I think Fergus must have explained the, er, dust-up we had here this morning. I hope you are not too unsettled."

Donella, who was sitting with her hands primly folded in her lap, frowned. "Not nearly as unsettling as it would have been if my foolish male relations had gotten around to shooting each other."

Mr. Gilbride looked taken aback by that response, as was everyone else.

In the startled silence, Donella turned and smiled at Edie. "Miss Whitney, I must thank you and your mother for intervening in so prompt a fashion. We are all grateful. Or, at least, we should be." When she threw a significant glance toward her brother, Fergus had the grace to look embarrassed.

"You're welcome," Edie said, blinking. Gratitude from her rival was the last thing she'd been expecting.

"We all share your relief, my dear," said Mr. Gilbride. "But I'm sure we're all aware that the matter which precipitated the unfortunate meeting is yet to be fully resolved."

"It most certainly is," Mrs. Haddon said in a strident voice. "The only honorable recourse is for Alasdair to honor his long-standing commitment to my daughter."

Edie's mother let out a ladylike snort, which brought Mrs. Haddon's Medusa-like gaze swinging around to her. Mamma simply gave her a bland smile, perfectly conveying the message that she found the other woman a dead bore.

"I've made it very clear that I have no wish to marry Alasdair, nor is it necessary for him to feel any sense of obligation toward me," Donella said in a cool voice. Her glaze flickered over to Edie before returning to rest on Lord Riddick. "It's quite obvious that he has feelings for

Miss Whitney. I had not, in fact, realized how deep his attachment was to her, which was an error in judgment on my part. And although I deplore the manner in which he communicated the depths of that attachment last night, I do not resent him for feeling it."

Every muscle in Edie's body went slack with relief. She darted a look at Alec, who gave his cousin a rueful smile.

"I never meant to embarrass you, Donella," he said. "I'm sorry you had to find out that way."

She gave a ladylike shrug. "Perhaps it was the only way to get through to everyone, myself included."

Alec cut Edie a sly glance as if to say, *see?* If she hadn't been so relieved, she would have been immensely irritated that his underhanded plan had apparently been the right course of action after all.

Fergus leaned forward in his chair, staring earnestly at his sister. "Are you sure this is what you want, lass? You've spent years getting ready to be Countess of Riddick."

Donella smiled at her brother, genuine warmth lighting up her beautiful face. Not for the first time, Edie wondered why Alec hadn't fallen in love with her years ago.

"Only because no one gave me any other choice," Donella said frankly. "I suppose I believed it was for the best, as you all seemed to think. But I never really wanted to be Countess, and I certainly never wanted to marry Alasdair."

"Thank you," Alec said in a wry voice.

Mrs. Haddon had been sitting rather stonelike through the exchange, but she responded to her daughter's words by letting out a loud moan and dropping her face into her hands.

"Then why in all that is holy didn't you tell me that ages ago, Niece?" the earl demanded in an aggrieved tone. "You would have saved us all a great deal of trouble."

Donella regarded him with a slight arching of her elegant

brows. "Because I thought it my duty to honor my father's wishes. And your wishes as well, Uncle. Besides, I did express my reservations on at least one occasion."

"You did?" Alec asked, clearly surprised.

Donella shrugged. "I tried to, but Uncle Callum dismissed them. He said I was simply suffering from maidenly nerves."

"Your mother told me that any anxiety you might express on this issue was simply maidenly nerves," the earl said, sounding defensive. "How was I supposed to know any different?"

Mrs. Haddon's head popped up. "And that *is* all it was," she spat out. "If Alasdair hadn't brought that . . . that woman back with him, everything would have been fine."

"No, Mamma," Donella said. "I'm glad Alasdair brought Miss Whitney home with him. Now we've both been spared a marriage neither of us wanted."

"Good Lord, what a mess," sighed Mr. Gilbride. "I apologize for my role in causing you any unhappiness, my dear. I truly thought you wanted this."

Donella smiled at him. "It's not anyone's fault but my own. Although I did not wish for this marriage, I knew what it meant to the clan and especially to my dear papa. I didn't want to disappoint him."

Edie's mother gave Donella an approving nod. "Such feelings are entirely to your credit, Miss Haddon. Deathbed vows are not to be taken lightly. In your case, however, such a vow would have caused a great deal of harm."

"What do you know of deathbed vows?" snarled Mrs. Haddon, half-rising from her chair.

"Please, Mamma," Donella implored. "I believe Lady Reese is correct. As much as I revered my father and cherish his memory, it was wrong of him to ask me to make such a vow, especially since it went against my own wishes as a good Christian."

The expression on Mrs. Haddon's face suggested she was about to embark on another rant—or fall into an apoplectic fit.

"Which brings us to another point, Donella," Mr. Gilbride hastily intervened. "There will be some degree of gossip resulting from this turn of events. The earl, of course, will do what he can to mitigate it, as will your good uncle I have no doubt. But you must be prepared for some unpleasantness, I'm afraid." He glanced at Alec. "We all must."

Donella nodded. "I understand, but I don't expect to be around to hear much of it."

Lord Riddick frowned. "Why not?"

His niece flashed him a smile that was almost blinding in its radiance. "Because, dear Uncle Callum, I will soon be taking my vows as a postulant with the Sisters of the Holy Cross at their abbey in St. Andrew's."

Fergus gaped at her, clearly flummoxed. "You mean you want to become a . . ." he trailed off, as if he couldn't even say the word.

Donella nodded. "Yes. I'm going to become a nun."

For the third time in twenty-four hours, pandemonium ensued.

"We're not even Catholic," Alec said. "No wonder Aunt Glenna fell into hysterics."

"From what I've seen, she's always falling into hysterics," Edie replied.

He couldn't help laughing—at all of it, including his cousin's stunning announcement. For the first time in months, he felt free and truly happy, thanks to the bonny lass who rode by his side.

Edie looked dashing and entirely at ease in her trim-fitting habit as she handled her spirited mare. And since she was wearing her spectacles, he had no fear she'd come to any harm. For such a dab thing, Edie was a bruising rider, guiding her horse with competence as well as the zest for life that was so much a part of her.

That included a zest for lovemaking, if last night's foray into that arena was any indication. Edie had been fairly nervous starting out, but Alec had managed to settle her nerves in a manner extremely pleasing for both of them.

They now had a future together, thanks to Donella's courage in finally fighting for the life she wanted instead of the one everyone else had chosen for her. It had been heavy going for a while, but Alec was confident that he and Edie had surmounted all major obstacles to their union.

Well, that wasn't quite accurate. Two possible problems still remained, which he intended to address today. That was why he'd taken Edie riding. They could speak frankly, without the possibility of interruption. She would no doubt have many questions and probably at least a few doubts. He needed privacy, and he needed time to make the proper explanations.

"Aunt Glenna was always prone to nervous excitement," he explained. "But she seems to have gotten a great deal worse since I last saw her. No wonder Donella wants to enter a convent. I would, too, if it was the only way to escape from her mother."

Edie laughed. "You'd make a terrible nun. And I'm sure they'd never be able to find a habit big enough to fit you."

He grinned as he reined in his horse. Since the path had grown narrow down by the stream, he let Edie go before him. Once they cleared the path and entered an open glen, he moved Darius up and joined her.

"So none of you had any idea that Donella wanted to be a nun?" she asked.

He shook his head. "I mentioned to you that she was always very religious, but we had no sense that she wanted to convert, much less bury herself away in a convent. Still, even Grandfather can see how much she wants it, so I think he'll eventually give Donella his blessing. And I'm sure that Father and I can talk him into making a substantial contribution to the order when she joins."

Edie cast him a worried glance. "I do hope all the commotion hasn't been too much of a strain on Lord Riddick. By the time everything finally calmed down, I thought he was looking very tired indeed."

"He was, but he's holding up much better than I thought."

"I'm sure it's because he's genuinely happy that you're home, despite the fact that you've stirred up so much trouble."

He snorted. "That's the pot calling the kettle black. You've been nothing but a pain in my arse since the moment we met."

She flashed him a cheeky grin. "And you wouldn't have it any other way."

"Very true, but it does take some getting used to, at least for the others."

Her smile faded. "I don't think Fergus has any intention of getting used to me. He was still livid when your grandfather instructed him to take his mother and sister home. I thought you two were going to come to blows again."

It had gotten rather ugly for a few minutes, with Aunt Glenna alternating between sobbing hysterically and berating everyone and Fergus yelling that Alec's betrayal was forcing his sister to slink away in shame to a convent. "Yes, it did get a tad medieval there for a few minutes, didn't it? I rather thought the lad was going to pull one of the old dirks off the wall and run me through."

Edie shuddered. "That's an awful thought."

"Love, I'm joking."

"Well, don't. I'm just grateful that Donella was able to intervene in so effective a fashion."

Yes, his cousin was turning into something of a revelation. She'd shouted Fergus down, and then given her screaming mother a good shake. Unfortunately, that hadn't really worked, so Lady Reese had tossed a glass of water into Aunt Glenna's face.

That had cut off the hysterics in mid-shriek. Alec was beginning to like his future mother-in-law a great deal more than he ever thought he would.

"Still," Edie continued, looking perturbed, "Fergus is clearly furious with you."

Alec waved it off. "He'll get over it."

"I'm not so sure about that."

He wasn't either, but he didn't want her to worry. Fergus was his problem, not hers.

"Let's not talk about it," he said. "It's a beautiful afternoon, we're together, and I'm going to marry you, not my cousin. We should enjoy our moment of victory, at least until the next crisis strikes."

She slid him a sideways glance—a sly, sensual one that sent heat rushing to his groin. He shifted, barely stifling a laugh at how quickly his body responded to her.

"Is that so, Captain?" she said in a light tone. "I do not believe I have yet received a formal proposal."

"That's very true, Miss Whitney, and I have every intention of redressing that grievous error in just a little bit."

She dipped her head, looking at him from under the brim of her jaunty riding hat. "And why the wait?"

"I want you to see something first. And there are a few other things we need to clear up."

She sighed. "Confound it. I knew it was too good to be true. Now what?"

He hesitated. "Nothing too serious, but I do need to ask you a question."

"Then just spit it out," she said. "After everything we've been through, surely it can't be that bad."

"I hope not. It's just that I know you're not very keen on the Highlands, or Scotland, for that matter. And while we'll certainly be able to spend part of the year in London and Edinburgh, I do need to spend the bulk of my time here at Blairgal. Especially now that Grandfather's health is poor. I trust that won't make you too unhappy."

Part of him steeled himself for her answer—that she intended to spend most of the year in London or at her family's estate in Hampshire, whether he could accompany her or not. He'd take her any way he could get her, but he dreaded the thought of having a fashionable marriage where husband and wife rarely crossed paths. He'd fought too hard to win her, and he wanted Edie with him as much as possible.

"Good Lord, Alec. Where in God's name did you get the inane idea that I don't like the Highlands?" she demanded.

He was so surprised he dropped his hands, and Darius broke into a canter. He reined him quickly in so Edie could catch up. "I got it from you," he said. "From all those cutting remarks about Scottish oafs, and all the jokes about the Highlands and my demented family."

She winced. "Surely to God you didn't take all that seriously."

When he raised his eyebrows, she flapped a hand at him. "All right. From now on, don't listen to me."

"I'll remember that the next time you scold me," he said drily.

"Except for when I'm scolding you. And besides, I never called your family demented. That was Mamma."

"I concede the point. But seriously, Edie—"

"Seriously, Alasdair Gilbride," she cut in. "I think Scotland is beautiful, at least what little I've seen of it. And I'm very eager to learn more about your family and the history of Blairgal. Even the clan, now that I'm going to be part of it. I might act like a featherbrain on occasion, but I was rather good at history, and I'm looking forward to learning more about yours."

He scoffed. "You are anything but a featherbrain, love. But are you sure you won't be missing your sister too much? I know what that relationship means to you."

She gave him a misty sort of smile. "And you're a dear to think of it. I miss Evie dreadfully, but she and Wolf will be spending a great deal of time on the Continent now that he's been assigned to the Foreign Office. We'll simply have to schedule our visits to London to coincide with theirs. And they can also visit Blairgal—I'm sure they'd love it."

"You truly don't mind spending most of the year at Blairgal?" he said, still skeptical.

"It's a *castle*, Alec! A beautiful, big castle. And you're rich. Honestly, most of the girls in London would kill to be in my shoes." Then she laughed. "I only wish I could see the look on their faces when they find out I'm going to marry you. Especially that dreary Calista Freemont."

"Ah, so that was your evil plan. Use me to restore your shattered reputation and lord it over your former friends."

"If it wasn't my plan, it should have been. It's an awfully good one, don't you think?"

He laughed, loving the curve of her lush mouth and the humor in her beautiful eyes. She would no doubt lead him in a merry dance for the rest of his days, and he couldn't wait.

"Yes, love, I do."

"Splendid. Now, is there anything else?"

He nodded. This was the last hurdle to clear before they were home free. "Yes, just one more thing. It's about Fergus, partly, and why my family was so insistent I marry Donella."

Her eyebrows ticked up over the rim of her spectacles. "There's more to it than clan and family loyalty?"

He nodded.

She looked thoughtful. "I suppose that makes sense. It did strike me as rather strange that they were all so insistent on it. Family honor and loyalty is one thing, but it seemed exaggcrated."

"Under normal circumstances, I would agree with you. But it's more complicated than it appears."

"And it concerns Fergus?" She flashed him a grin. "Is he the rightful heir to Blairgal Castle and all its estates, and are you an evil interloper who somehow managed to have him cast aside and deprived of his true place in the world?"

He let out a ghost of a laugh. Even though she was clearly joking, she'd hit it bang on the mark without even trying. "Yes, actually, I am."

Her smile turned to one of puzzlement. "You are . . . what? An evil interloper? I don't understand."

He shook his head. "Not evil, but some might think me an interloper. Some, in fact, *do* think that."

Her smile faded completely. "What are you talking about, Alec?"

He took the plunge. "You said once that Wolf and I were very close, almost like brothers. Well, you're not far off. Wolf is my first cousin, through our fathers."

When she drew her mare to a halt, he was forced to do the same. She stared at him then shook her head, clearly not understanding.

"Walter Gilbride is not my true father," Alec said. "I'm the natural-born son of the Duke of Kent."

Chapter Twenty-Two

"That certainly explains a lot," Edie said, after Alec had briefly outlined his complicated family history. It was so fascinating and surprising that she barely noticed their horses were presently meandering through a lovely stand of yew trees that lined the narrow road. "It was never really about Donella, was it? It was about Fergus."

Alec nodded. "Yes, and in a way I can't blame them, at least Aunt Glenna and Fergus. I think my grandfather simply feels guilty about it, especially since Fergus has been such a great support to him."

Edie was silent for a few seconds as she tried to sort it out in her head. Alec's stunning announcement had left her speechless, and her lack of response clearly unnerved him.

"It's a lot to take in," he said, still looking worried. "And you're sure it doesn't bother you?"

"That you're the by-blow of a prince? Or that some members of your family think you're the cuckoo in the nest?"

He let out a startled chuckle. "Both, I suppose. By the way, I suggest you refrain from using those terms when talking to your dear mamma about this."

She shook her head. "Don't worry about Mamma. After

the last few weeks, I'm convinced she can manage just about anything. Besides, she already has one son-in-law who's the illegitimate son of a prince. What's one more?" She couldn't help laughing at how ridiculous that sounded. "Good Lord, what are the odds?"

While Wolf was fairly close to his father, the Duke of York, Lord Riddick had objected to Alec forming a relationship with his natural father. Under the circumstances—the illicit seduction of a young, innocent woman who'd been married for only a few years—Edie didn't blame him at all.

"Astronomical, I would imagine," Alec replied. "Are you sure you don't want me to explain it to her? I don't want her fussing at you."

Evelyn had told her some weeks ago that Alec was a *soft touch,* which Edie had found hard to believe. But these last few weeks had shown her just how gentle he was underneath his brash exterior, as well as protective of anyone under his care or responsibility.

"Trust me, she won't," she said. "I am completely redeemed in her eyes, thanks to you. Funny how snagging a rich, titled husband will do that."

His eyes gleamed with amusement. "I'm happy to be of service."

Oh, Edie could think of all sorts of ways he could be of service, especially in the bedroom. She supposed it illustrated a true lack of modesty on her part, but after their intimate encounter last night, her wedding day couldn't come soon enough.

When the laughter faded from his expression, she cocked an enquiring eyebrow. "What's wrong?"

"It's Fergus. I'm afraid he might not make it easy on you, at least at first. I'm not quite sure how Grandfather will handle things, either."

"I'll handle Fergus. As for your grandfather, don't you think he'll want you to be happy?"

He hesitated just a fraction too long. "Of course. But he's very close to Fergus. My cousin held things together while I was gone, and that's something that neither I nor my grandfather will ever forget."

He gazed straight ahead, looking rather grim. "I owe Fergus a debt of gratitude that can never be repaid."

Edie mentally sighed. The puzzle pieces were finally falling into place, and she didn't much like the image they presented. But she held her tongue, because at that moment they broke free of the woods.

A gracious old house rose before them. It was painted in a warm shade of yellow, with brick bays and a turreted roof. A small archway divided two neat wings, leading into a cobbled courtyard. In the center of the yard and just before the front door was a pretty stone fountain empty of water and looking a little worse for wear. But the yard was tidy and there was a general air of neatness about the place. Edie saw pretty lace curtains in the windows and smoke wafting up from the chimneys.

"And what's this?" she asked as they clattered to a halt in the yard.

Alec swung down from his horse and came around to help her dismount. "It's an old hunting lodge. When I was a boy, it used to get quite a lot of use, especially when guests were in residence. No one really uses it anymore, but Grandfather has kept it up."

When he lifted her down, Edie couldn't help feeling a little thrill at his easy yet commanding strength.

"It seems rather unusual to have a hunting lodge so close to the main house," she said once she'd gotten on her feet.

"According to Walter, my great-grandfather built it to give himself and his friends a little privacy."

"Because God knows you couldn't find any of that at Blairgal," she said. "What with only a few hundred rooms at your disposal."

He waggled his eyebrows. "Not for what that particular earl had in mind. He was a well-known rake and reprobate with a bit of a dragon for a wife. This is where he stashed some of his lady-birds from Glasgow."

"Then how splendidly convenient it must have been for him."

He laughed and moved to tie the horses to the hitching post when the door to the house opened and an elderly man in a neat white shirt and leather apron hurried out to meet them.

"Mr. Monroe, it's good to see you," Alec said. "I hope we're not inconveniencing you by dropping in unexpectedly."

The old man bobbed up and down like a turkey, his wrinkled face wreathed in smiles. "Nay, Master. Ye are always welcome in yer own house, God love ye."

Alec drew her forward. "Edie, this is Mr. Monroe. He and his grandson keep the hunting lodge in fine trim. Mr. Monroe, this is Miss Whitney."

The old man bowed again but shot her a close look from under his eyebrows. Edie had no doubt that he'd already heard rumors about the unusual events up at the castle. But his manner was friendly.

"Ye're most welcome, miss. If ye give me a few minutes, I'll be bringing some tea. I'll just be fetching Heckie and having him take care of the animals."

"Tea won't be necessary, Mr. Monroe," Alec said. "I'm giving Miss Whitney a short tour and then we'll be on our way."

"As ye say, Master."

Alec led her into the entrance hall, a warm, wood-paneled space with a lovely old oak staircase. They strolled through the rooms on the ground floor—which included a spacious drawing room with a small, attached study, and a dining room, all decorated in the Queen Anne style. Some of the furnishings and the carpets were a bit faded, but on the whole it was a very pretty house with a comfortable, almost homey atmosphere. After spending several days in the grand but somewhat overwhelming Blairgal Castle, Edie appreciated the intimate feel of the lodge.

"I want to show you the bedrooms," Alec said, guiding her to the stairs. He rested a hand low on her back, just above the curve of her bottom. She loved the warm, possessive feel of it, and smiled over her shoulder at him.

"I do hope you don't have an ulterior motive in mind, Captain Gilbride," she said. "I'm very easily shocked, you know."

His gray gaze went smoky and dark with intent. "I would like very much to shock you, Miss Whitney. Repeatedly."

The tone in his voice made her stomach deliciously clench and her knees go a bit shaky. She forced her mind away from the naughty images that had popped into her head.

"I'm very happy you brought me to see the lodge," she said to distract herself. "But was there any particular reason you wished me to see it?"

He guided her down a hall and opened a door, gesturing her into a bedroom with large bay windows and a gorgeous bed with a carved, rosewood canopy. Edie walked to the windows and gazed out at the expansive view of the Highlands. When Alec came up behind her and rested his hands on her hips, she had to resist the urge to snuggle back into him. After all, she *was* trying to behave.

"I thought we might have this place spruced up and redecorated," he said. "However you'd like it."

She turned in his arms, resting her hands on his chest.

"That might be rather fun, but why? Do you intend us to do a lot of hunting and shooting?"

He shook his head. "I thought it might be nice if *we* had a little privacy from the rest of the family. A place of our own, as it is here." His gaze had gone serious again. "Things could be a bit challenging at Blairgal for a while. A little distance might not be amiss."

Touched, she went up on tiptoe and kissed his chin. "You're worrying about Fergus and your grandfather again, aren't you? You really needn't, you know. I can handle them."

"I know you can, but you shouldn't have to."

Edie narrowed her eyes at him. Alec adopted what he no doubt thought was an innocent expression, but she wasn't fooled. "It's not just about me, is it? *You* don't want to deal with them, either."

He looked like he was going to deny it but then relented. "All right, guilty as charged. But truly, Edie, I think it would be best if Fergus and I weren't tripping all over each other every blasted day. For all our sakes."

She couldn't help recalling her mother's words a few days ago, when she'd challenged Edie to fight for what she wanted. "Alasdair Gilbride, I never thought of you as a coward, but perhaps I have to revisit that notion."

His eyebrows shot up. "What the hell is that supposed to mean?" Then he scowled. "Do you think I'm afraid of Fergus? I would have thought this morning's pistols-at-dawn farce should have made that amply clear."

"Of course you're not afraid of him. But I think you feel guilty about Fergus, just like everyone else in your blasted family. It's ridiculous."

He grimaced. "Well, of course we all feel guilty."

"Why?"

He rolled his eyes. "As you so delicately put it only a

short time ago, I *am* the cuckoo in the nest. Fergus, by all rights, should be the heir to Riddick."

Edie whacked him on the arm. "That's the most ridiculous thing I've ever heard."

"Ouch," he said dramatically. "Madam, have you ever considered a pugilistic career?"

"I'm being serious," she said severely.

"So am I," he said, sounding a bit snappish. "The truth is, Fergus and his family have every right to resent me. If I had married Donella and she had become countess, there would have been at least an element of justice done for them."

She forced herself to remain calm. "And are you having second thoughts about that?"

He looked horrified. "What? No, of course not, you goose." He pulled her back into his arms. "Never think that, Edie. You're the best thing that's ever happened to me, I swear."

Because she'd freed him from an obligation he'd been fighting for years? Was that the true basis of his affection for her? It was a daunting thought, which she decided to put aside for the moment until she had a chance to think it through a bit more.

She rested her cheek against his brocaded waistcoat, letting him cradle her for a few seconds longer. Then she disengaged herself from his embrace.

"As I understand it," she said, "Scottish titles can be inherited through the female line, correct?"

He nodded.

"Then your mother was, in fact, the heiress apparent to the earldom."

"She was, but—"

"And you are your mother's only child, are you not?"

He began to look annoyed. "Obviously."

"And she was married when you were born?"

"Yes," he gritted out.

"Then I fail to see the problem."

"It's not that simple, and you know it," he growled.

"In the eyes of the law it is." When he started to object again, she held up a hand. "Alec, you were born to a woman who was married to a man who clearly and proudly claims you as his son. There is no problem, whether you wish to see that or not."

He shook his head. "You sound just like my grandfather."

"Then I am in good company."

Breathing out a heavy sigh, he wandered over to the bed and sat on the mattress. She followed him. Her heart ached a bit at the brooding expression on his face. Never had she met a kinder or more worthy man, but on some level he didn't see it in himself. His past made so much sense now—why he'd run away and stayed away, seeking a life of adventure and danger. Not only was he running away from the life he deserved, he'd been trying to prove himself worthy of that life in the first place.

She reached out a hand and stroked his sleek, close-cropped hair. He pulled her hand over and pressed a kiss into her palm.

"You do deserve this, you know," she said. "All of it."

"So does Fergus," he said, shrugging.

"Why?"

"Because, unlike me, he's actually earned it," he said, sounding a bit impatient. "He's the one who stayed, helping my grandfather and learning how to run the place. He's the one who found solutions to problems and helped the place grow and continue to prosper. Fergus has earned the respect of everyone at Blairgal, and he'd have made a damn good earl if things had been different."

"Perhaps, but you'll be a better one."

He scoffed. "How the hell do you know that?"

She grabbed him by his coat and shook. "Because I

know *you,* you great Scottish oaf. You are strong, smart, and brave. You can do whatever you set your mind to. I'm sure everyone respects Fergus, but you're a leader. You've been leading men for years, and protecting the weak and innocent from those who would harm them. All that sounds like the perfect recipe for an earl to me."

"I was just a soldier, Edie. A spy. I fail to see how that qualifies me to run this great, bloody earldom. Quite the opposite, in fact."

"Well, you'll have your grandfather to help you learn, and I'm sure Fergus will eventually come around. You don't have any plans to fire him, do you?"

"Of course not!"

"Then what is the problem?"

"Edie, you have no idea—"

She jabbed him in the chest. "Now, you listen to me. It's time for you to stop running away. You've been doing it for quite long enough. It's also time you stopped wishing that life was different and started accepting responsibility for who you are—Alasdair Gilbride, formerly of the Black Watch, now Master of Riddick. You were not only born into that title thanks to your mother, you've earned it. And everyone knows it, too, including Fergus, I'll wager." She jabbed him in the chest once more for emphasis. "Stop moping about and start doing what you were born to do. Your grandfather will help you, I'll help you, and Fergus will help you, too."

Halfway through her lecture, his mouth had started to curve up. "I see. You're very wise and masterful, all of a sudden. When did you figure this all out?"

"About the same time I figured out that I needed to accept responsibility for my own actions. I've not been particularly good about that, either, and it's time I was. Besides, it's not like we have a choice. It's that or run off together to the Orient, which really isn't a very good plan when one thinks it through."

His slow smile turned into a full-on grin. He wrapped both hands around her waist and then slid them up to rest just below her breasts.

"I believe you're correct, Miss Whitney, and that means you're about to take responsibility for your actions right this minute."

He stood and turned in one swift movement, then lifted her up high and tossed her onto the bed. She fell back in an inelegant sprawl, her skirts twisting up around her knees and her hat flying off her head.

"What are you doing?" she squawked.

"Getting ready to make love to you," Alec said with a seductive smile.

Edie struggled to a sitting position. "You must be joking."

He stripped off his coat and dropped it on the floor. "Does it look like I'm joking?" he asked, casting a significant look down to the area below his waist.

Her cheeks flushed as she took in the obvious erection pushing against the fall of his breeches. Choking out a horrified laugh, she tried to flip down her skirts to cover her legs. Alec thwarted her attempts to preserve her modesty by batting her hands away and then pulling her skirts above her knees.

"Alasdair Gilbride, I will not make love to you in a strange house in the middle of the day," she protested as he plucked off her spectacles and laid them carefully on the small table beside the bed.

"Why not?" He crawled onto the mattress, making her scramble over to give him room.

"Why not?" she echoed, doing her best to sound scandalized.

Of course, she was scandalized, but her body clearly approved of his mad idea. Her heart raced with anticipation, and she was mortified to realize she was already growing soft and damp between her thighs. She was also having difficulty formulating an argument that held any conviction.

"Well, ah, because it's not respectable," she spluttered as he settled onto his side, propped up on one elbow as he faced her. "We're not even married."

He began unbuttoning her bodice. "But we will be soon. Besides, I think that particular defense went out the window last night."

"I suppose that's true," she said, feeling a tad breathless. And no wonder, since he'd just slid his hand inside her clothing. "But certainly the other reasons apply. It's broad daylight, and we're in a strange house."

Alec flashed her another wicked grin as he began tugging at her stays. "It's not a strange house at all, not to me. Besides, daylight is the best time to make love, because then I can see this." He gave another tug, and the top of her breasts popped up above her stays, exposing her nipples.

Edie let out a whimper when he rubbed his palm across one nipple, which made it tighten into a stiff point. She had to resist the urge to press her thighs together to assuage the ache already building deep inside.

"Now that," Alec said as he gently squeezed her nipple between forefinger and thumb, "is one of the prettiest sights I've ever seen."

Stifling a moan, Edie made one last attempt to make him see reason. "But what if Mr. Monroe hears us? Whatever will he think?"

He shrugged, clearly only half-listening as he played with her breasts. "What difference does it make whether he hears us or not?"

"Alasdair Gilbride!"

His hand stilled on her breast, and his gaze came up to meet hers. He gave her a rueful grimace. "I'm obviously a sex-starved brute, aren't I? But I can't seem to help myself, not when it comes to you."

He leaned down and gave her a long, slow kiss that had her collapsing onto the pillows. Her toes curled inside her boots.

"But you make everything better, Edie," he murmured, pulling back to look at her. His gaze was hot and yet infinitely tender. "And when I'm with you, my life—everything I'm expected to be—finally makes sense." He let out a ghost of a laugh. "It's a miracle, if you ask me, given how bloody confused I've been. But when we're together like this, with no one and nothing else between us, it's just . . . perfect."

That was exactly how she'd felt last night when he'd told her he truly wanted to marry her. Alec wasn't prone to wearing his heart on his sleeve, but he'd shared a great deal with her today. He'd made himself vulnerable, trusting her with his deepest secrets. It was the most precious gift anyone had ever given her and not one she took lightly.

He bent down again and kissed her on the tip of her nose. "I need you more than I've ever needed anything in my life. Let me make love to you, Edie Whitney. Right here, right now."

And how could she possibly say no, since she wanted the same thing?

She wound her arms around his neck. "Well, the lodge appears to be very soundly built, so I suppose Mr. Monroe won't hear anything, if we're quiet."

He huffed out a laugh as he reached a hand down to her skirts. "Oh, the walls are quite thick, I assure you. And don't forget that I was a spy. I can be very quiet when the occasion calls for it."

Then, so suddenly that it robbed her of breath, he swept the skirts of her habit up above her hips, exposing her mound and nest of curls. When he cupped her sex, she jerked against the pillows.

"Spread your legs, love," he crooned in a low, gravelly voice. "I want to see all of you."

She swallowed then looked down at herself, sprawled so wantonly on the bed. "But I still have my boots on," she said inanely.

He let out a wicked laugh as he gently urged her thighs open. "And your garters and stockings, too. All that's missing is the whip."

She narrowed her eyes. "What does that mean?"

"I'll explain another time. Right now, I have something else in mind."

"And that is?"

He came up on his knees and straddled her. "This," he said, yanking her stays down another inch.

Then he dipped down and sucked a nipple into his mouth. Edie let out a moan, grabbing his shoulders as he teased the rigid bead. She shivered, fighting for air as he lavished attention on her breasts. All too soon he pulled back, and she had to stifle a protest.

But a moment later she was biting back a startled exclamation as he slid down her body and settled between her thighs, his broad shoulders pushing her wide.

She came up on her elbows to stare at him. "Alec, what are you about?"

He glanced up, and the avaricious gleam in his eyes made her heart flutter.

"I'm going to taste you, love," he said as his fingers brushed through her curls. His voice had dropped to a growl. "And I swear you're going to enjoy it."

She frowned. He couldn't possibly mean what she thought—

He swept his tongue right over her sex. She let out a startled cry and grabbed at his shoulders. "Alec!"

"Hush, love," he murmured. She could hear the laugh in his voice. "You don't want Mr. Monroe to hear, do you?"

"No, but—"

"Then just lie back and enjoy it."

He didn't give her much choice, since he spread her wide and dipped back down again, licking between her soft folds. She arched off the bed, sensation storming through her body. The vision of Alec between her legs, his mouth playing over her most intimate parts, was so forbidden and erotic that she had to fight to keep from climaxing almost immediately.

But she did fight it. Because even though it was the most shocking experience of her life, it made her body come alive in a way she'd never thought possible.

With devastating skill, Alec drove her toward her peak as he greedily feasted on her. Spasms began deep inside her womb and rippled outward in lovely, lush waves. When he sucked on her tight bud, Edie practically shot off the bed. She curled forward and dug her fingers into his shoulders, every muscle in her body starting to tremble, her lips clamped shut against the scream that threatened to break from her throat.

With a swiftness that startled her, Alec pulled away, leaving her poised on the knife's edge.

"Why are you stopping?" She winced at the screechy tone to her voice.

On his knees, Alec tugged at the fall of his breeches. His rugged features were taut, his cheekbones glazed with color. His gaze skated upward, lingering on her mound, her breasts, before catching on her face.

"Because I want to be inside you when you come," he rasped.

His erection sprang free, huge and flushed. Edie's heart thumped against her breastbone. He was a big man in every way, powerful and intimidating. Even though she'd taken all of him in last night, she still experienced a moment's trepidation. But that didn't stop her from wanting him with a need that made her tremble.

She expected him to spread her legs wide and position himself between them. Instead, he came down beside her, his weight dipping the mattress. She rolled against him.

"Come here, my love," he said, reaching for her.

Before she could say a word, Alec lifted her and set her astride his hips. He tugged her skirts free and bunched them up around her waist. Her sex, hot and slick, rode the length of his erection. She had to fight the urge to rock against him and bring herself to completion. He wanted to be inside her when she climaxed, and she wanted that too.

Still, it felt rather awkward, sitting on top of him, so indecently exposed. It was thrilling, but she couldn't help blushing in spite of herself.

And wondering what to do next.

Alec curled his hands around her breasts. "Hmm," he purred. "Now I have you exactly where I want you."

She wrinkled her nose at him. "I don't mean to sound like a complete ignoramus, but what do you want me to do now?"

He let out a husky laugh. "That's the fun of it, sweetheart. Trying out new things."

When he thumbed her nipples, she let out a gasp. Well, two could play at that game.

Edie began to move, rocking against his thick erection. When Alec hissed in a breath, she smiled. It felt so wonderful that she could imagine doing it for hours—except for the fact that she was already building to a climax again.

"God, you're so wet," Alec groaned.

A gorgeous throb pulsed through her passage, taking her to the edge. "Now," she begged. "Please."

His hands clamped on her hips. "Up on your knees, love," he murmured.

He guided her into position, the broad head of his erection nudging between her folds to penetrate her opening. To his whispered encouragement, she sank down, his thick length forging into her in an endless, glorious slide. He filled her completely, reaching so deeply inside that she couldn't tell where he ended and she began.

She loved it. She loved *him*.

Never taking his gaze from her face, Alec began to move, his powerful body thrusting up, rocking into her. She found the rhythm and began moving with him. His thickness rubbed against her with delicious friction, building her passion. Edie felt herself swelling around him, going softer, wetter, and incredibly slick as he stroked into her. She rocked faster and faster, desperate to find her release.

Suddenly, he tilted her forward, bringing her pelvis flush against him as he thrust. Edie cried out as her climax rolled over her. She rose up on her knees, trembling with the force of it. Alec followed her up, hips pumping, his hands wrapped around her waist and pressing her down as she contracted around him.

Then he let out a ragged groan of release. She felt the rush of his warmth inside and slid down onto his chest, boneless and utterly sated. Alec wrapped his arms around her, holding her close in his powerful embrace.

Her stays were digging into her ribs, her skirts were bunched uncomfortably around her waist, and she could feel her foot starting to cramp. Edie didn't care, because it was the perfect moment. She felt safe and cherished, and happier than she'd ever been.

In Alec's arms, she could believe that nothing bad could ever happen to her again.

For a few minutes, he simply stroked her with gentle

hands. Then he finally stirred. "Well, that was great fun," he said, his voice a low rumble. "But I suppose we'd best get up before Monroe comes looking for us."

That notion jerked Edie out of her lovely daze, especially since she was sprawled on top of Alec with her skirts around her waist and her bottom immodestly on display.

"Good God," she said, pushing herself up on her elbows. "I cannot believe I let you talk me into this."

He let out a regretful sigh as she wriggled off him. "Strictly speaking, I don't believe I had to talk you into anything."

"Which only goes to show that I'm as bad as you are," she said as she scurried to a large mirror hung opposite the bed. She almost let out a shriek when she saw how thoroughly disheveled she looked.

"And thank God for that, my sweet," Alec said as he set himself to rights.

It took Edie a few minutes longer to appear presentable again, although her coiffure was a total loss. She stuffed as many of her tangled locks as she could under her riding hat and then went to straighten the bedclothes.

"You don't have to do that, love," Alec said. "Monroe will take care of it."

Edie cast him a horrified glance. "If you think I'm going to let that dignified old man know what we were doing up here, you're quite mad."

Alec chuckled. "I'm sure he already knows. I'm also quite sure he doesn't blame me in the least."

"Splendid," she said sarcastically. "Let's be sure to ask him on the way out."

He simply grinned at her and took her by the hand to lead her downstairs. Edie had to admit that part of her was embarrassed that she'd so readily succumbed to Alec's indecent seduction, but the rest of her—mind and body—seemed to be fizzing with happiness, as if someone had uncorked a bottle of champagne inside her chest.

A few days ago she'd been convinced that the only thing life held for her was a dreary procession of days that stretched into years, a life where she would dwindle into an unhappy woman living on the edges of society. Now she faced the joyous prospect of marriage to the man she loved and a life that would be both privileged and interesting. Edie couldn't believe how lucky she was, and she intended to spend the rest of her days showing Alec and his family that she deserved their affection and, she hoped, their trust.

Mr. Monroe met them in the entrance hall with a twinkle in his eye and a knowing smile that showed a few gaps in his teeth. When Alec gave her a roguish, I-told-you-so grin, she rolled her eyes but couldn't help smiling back.

"Heckie has the horses out front, Master. All rested and watered for the ride back to the castle."

In the courtyard, a tall, freckle-faced lad of about sixteen stood with the horses. He greeted Alec and Edie with shy respect, opening up a bit when Alec asked him questions about the state of the stables behind the house.

"We hope to see ye and the Master again soon, mistress," Mr. Monroe said when Edie wished him good-bye. "It's grand having the young laird back, and that's the truth. He's grown up to be a braw figure of a man, and we're all right proud of him."

Edie slid Alec a look, hoping he'd heard the old man's enthusiasm. By the smile lifting the corners of his mouth as he spoke to Heckie it appeared he had.

"Thank you, Mr. Monroe," she said. "I'm sure we'll be visiting again very soon."

"And perhaps ye'll be able to stay and have some tea next time, eh?" he said with a twinkle.

She choked on a laugh but simply nodded as Alec came to help her mount. Then he swung up on Darius and brought him alongside Edie's mare.

"We'll have to hurry a bit," he said, "if we're too—"

Stucco from the wall behind them exploded in a puff of dust. Almost simultaneously, Edie heard a muffled crack, and then Alec launched himself off his horse and ran to her. The movement startled her mare, and Edie fought to get her under control.

"Edie, get down," Alec snapped as he reached for her.

She slid into his arms just as more stucco exploded only a few inches away from their heads. Her horse reared, startled by the commotion, but Alec had already dragged her clear. He pulled her off to the side of the yard and shoved her down into the shelter of the thick wall to the left of the archway. Then he ducked low and raced back to grab Darius's bridle and pull him away from the arch.

"Heckie, goddammit, let her go," he yelled at the boy, who was tying to bring the mare under control.

Mr. Monroe grabbed his grandson by the collar and yanked him to the other side of the archway, where they hunkered down against the wall. The mare danced around the courtyard, her hooves clattering on the cobblestones. When she settled, she walked over to join the big stallion, and a fraught quiet descended on the courtyard.

Edie winced as she pushed herself up on her knees. She'd gone down hard on her hip when Alec shoved her to the ground but was otherwise unharmed.

With a trembling hand, she pushed her hat up from her eyes. "I don't suppose I imagined that, did I?"

Alec looked at her, and the fury she saw in his cold gray gaze blew through her like a winter storm.

"No, you didn't. Someone just tried to shoot us."

Chapter Twenty-Three

"I refuse to believe it," Lord Riddick said in a distressed tone. "I'll grant you that Fergus was angry, but he'd never try to hurt Alasdair. It's not in his nature."

Edie stared across the big desk at the earl, dumbstruck by his assertion. Mamma, however, had no trouble finding her tongue.

"That is the most patently ridiculous thing I've ever heard, my lord," she said in a stern tone. "We were all witness to the ugly scene in your garden this morning. If not for my timely intervention, the captain might well be lying in a coffin at this very moment."

"Mamma, that's a bit much," Edie protested, casting a worried eye at the earl. Alec's grandfather was looking decidedly frail at the moment despite his irate demeanor. Edie was mad as fire herself, but it wouldn't help matters if Lord Riddick succumbed to a heart spasm. "Besides, I don't think Mr. Haddon really intended to shoot Alec. At least not then."

When the earl glared at her, Edie winced. "Well, someone shot at us at the lodge, I'm sorry to say. He almost hit us, too."

They'd made that clear to their respective relatives a few minutes ago, when Alec had tersely outlined the afternoon's events.

"I understand from my daughter that Mr. Haddon has made several threats against your grandson," Mamma said. "That, combined with this morning's aborted duel, certainly points to him."

Walter Gilbride, who was seated next to Mamma in front of the earl's desk, stirred uneasily. He glanced over his shoulder at Alec, who was standing halfway down the length of the library, his back to them as he stared out the window. Edie wanted to drag him away from the glass, convinced he was making himself a target.

Instead, she hovered between Lord Riddick's desk and the window, ready to throw herself on Alec and shield him if need be. It was a ridiculous notion, of course, since it would be well nigh impossible for someone to take a shot without Alec spotting him first. That particular section of the gardens consisted of only low bushes and shrubs with no real hiding places. The garden then ended in a wall overlooking a steep drop into a ravine along the north side of the castle.

Back at the lodge, Alec had made a terrible fuss about *her* safety. When he'd finally let her up off the stones in the yard, he'd run his hands over her body, ascertaining for himself that she was unhurt. She hadn't missed the slight trembling in his fingers as they'd brushed over her. He'd then mashed her against him, growling out a torrent of oaths that were both hair-raising and fascinating in their specificity.

After about ten minutes, they'd finally ventured out from their hiding place. All seemed quiet, and Alec had dashed upstairs to one of the rooms fronting the house. After Mr. Monroe unearthed an ancient-looking spyglass, they'd scanned the meadows and woods in front of the house for any sign of their shooter.

Fortunately or unfortunately, depending on one's point of view, there wasn't anything suspicious to see. Heckie had volunteered that he'd seen a rider in the distance while Edie and Alec were upstairs earlier. The rider had been heading toward the lodge when the boy last saw him, but since no one had subsequently appeared, Heckie hadn't thought twice about it.

In light of subsequent events, however, it had seemed likely that the rider was, in fact, their shooter.

After about half an hour, Alec had decided that it was safe to venture back to Blairgal. He'd wanted to leave Edie in the safety of the lodge until he returned with an armed escort to retrieve her, but she'd strenuously objected. She was quite convinced that no one was trying to kill her, which clearly meant Alec was the target. If anyone needed an escort it was him.

That had led to a rather fierce argument until Edie reminded him of the odd incident at Mugdock Castle when the stones had come tumbling down, nearly killing them. He'd grown silent for a minute or so, as if that thought hadn't occurred to him. But it had been the first thing Edie had thought about, once she'd picked herself up from the stones of the courtyard.

Alec had again ordered her to stay behind until he could return with an escort. But when Edie said she would simply wait till he was out of sight and follow him, he had grudgingly relented. Mr. Monroe and Heckie had insisted on going with them to serve as backup, and Alec had agreed. After they'd armed themselves with pistols—the lodge had quite a lot of them, which didn't surprise her—they set out. Alec had placed Edie astride on a regular saddle, and they had thundered back to Blairgal in record time, riding fast and low over their horses' necks in order to present as small a target as possible. She'd counted it as one of the most unpleasant half hours of her life.

She didn't think she'd ever seen as welcome a sight as Blairgal Castle when it rose up before them at the end of the valley.

After Alec had hurried her indoors, they'd gone to look for his grandfather. As it happened, Lord Riddick was in his library with Mamma and Mr. Gilbride discussing marriage settlements. That discussion had gone out the window when Alec, followed by Edie, burst into the library demanding Fergus's whereabouts.

The subsequent discussion had not been pleasant.

Mr. Gilbride peered at his son with concern. "Alasdair, is that true?" he asked. "Did Fergus make threats against you?"

"Yes, he did." Alec didn't bother to turn around. "He said he would kill me if I didn't marry Donella."

Mr. Gilbride scrunched up his face. "Oh, dear. That's not good."

"I would say that is something of an understatement," Mamma said sardonically.

Edie cast a worried glance at Alec's back and then another at Lord Riddick, who was looking decidedly whey-faced. She hurried over to a sideboard and poured out a healthy splash of what she assumed was brandy into a crystal tumbler.

"Here, your lordship," she said, bringing it back to him. "This might help a bit."

The old man gave her a wan smile. "Thank you, lass."

So far, the earl didn't seem to be holding her responsible for any of his family's current troubles, and he had been just as aghast as Mamma and Mr. Gilbride that she'd been put in danger. In fact, after his initial defense of Fergus, the wind seemed to have gone out of his sails. No one could blame him, given that his nephew had probably just tried to kill his grandson.

"That is a splendid idea, Eden," Mamma said, rising. "Mr. Gilbride, can I get you a drink as well?"

"I'll have the whiskey," Alec's father said in a distracted voice. "It's the one on the end."

While Mamma fetched the drinks, Edie went to fetch Alec.

"No one knows what to do," she murmured as she slipped her hand into his. "You've got to manage this, especially for your grandfather's sake."

His profile looked carved from granite. "I know." Then he glanced down at her, and a little warmth crept into his bleak gaze. "Thank you, love."

She cocked her head. "For what?"

"For being here." He paused. "For loving me."

Her heart jolted. She hadn't yet worked up the courage to confess her love to him, nor had he said the words, either. But she heard the question in the statement and knew what he needed to hear.

"I do love you," she said. "I'll always love you."

He drew her close, dropping a kiss on the top of her head, then led her back to the desk.

"Grandfather, where is Fergus now?" he asked.

The old man's gaze was utterly weary. "In Glasgow on business. It made sense to send him off for the day. I thought it might cool him down."

"Anyone else go with him?"

Lord Riddick winced. "No. He rode."

Alec breathed a curse under his breath.

"I believe he went to run some errands and speak to our lawyers, is that not correct?" asked Mr. Gilbride.

"Aye, that's right," Lord Riddick replied.

"Grandfather, why don't you write down exactly which

errands you sent him on," Alec said. "I'll dispatch two of the grooms to track him down and bring him back home."

"That's assuming he went in the first place," Edie's mother said. "But even if Mr. Haddon isn't the culprit, somebody is. Which means there could still be a murderer lurking about the castle." She shuddered. "And people think London is dangerous."

Edie refrained from pointing out that her other daughter had been kidnapped and almost murdered in London just a few months ago.

"That is exactly why everyone is staying inside until further orders," Alec said in a voice that brooked no opposition.

Lord Riddick nodded. "And I think we should post footmen and grooms at all the entrances, just in case."

"Excellent idea, sir," Alec said. "I would also suggest that the ladies not wander too much inside the house. We'll post guards on the doors, but there are simply too many ways to get into the castle unseen. The ladies should stick to their bedrooms or to the main family rooms until we get this sorted out."

Edie rolled her eyes. "We're not the ones in danger, you are. You're the one who shouldn't go wandering about."

Alec scoffed. "I can take care of myself."

Edie only resisted the impulse to throttle him because someone else was already trying to do something similar. "Alasdair Gilbride, I swear I will drag you upstairs and tie you to your bed if I have to. And lock the door to your room."

He flashed her a dazzling grin. "Promise?"

She gaped at him for a moment, and then decided she'd changed her mind. She *would* throttle him.

"Really, Captain," Mamma said in a dry voice. "This is hardly the time for that sort of jest."

"What the devil are you all talking about?" snapped Lord Riddick. "It sounds like a lot of blither to me."

"Yes, well, no need to worry," Mr. Gilbride hastily interjected, looking rather red-faced. "I'm sure Alec can take care of himself."

Edie still had doubts about that, but Alec clearly wasn't going to listen. She just had to trust that his skills as a soldier and spy would keep him safe until the villain was run to ground.

Besides, she had every intention of sticking as close to him as possible. Perhaps she'd look for a working pistol among the battery of armaments on various walls throughout the castle. It didn't hurt to be prepared for the worst.

"I've got to speak with the butler, the housekeeper, and the head groomsman, and get some grooms off to Glasgow," Alec said. "Grandfather, if you could work on that list of errands, I'll send someone up to fetch it in a few minutes."

Lord Riddick nodded and reached for his pen. He was looking better, which Edie suspected was due to the fact that Alec had given him something to do.

Mr. Gilbride came to his feet. "How can I help, my boy?"

Alec rested an affectionate hand on his father's shoulder. "You can escort the ladies up to their rooms for me."

"I'm not hiding out in my room," Edie protested.

"Well, I am," said Mamma. "I have no aversion to stopping foolish duels, but I simply refuse to confront a cold-blooded murderer. I intend to lock myself in and have Davis stand guard at the door."

"Oh, I can't wait to hear what Davis will have to say about that," Edie said. "Are you also going to ask her to fling herself in front of any bullets?"

"There is no need for sarcasm, Eden," Mamma said in a frosty voice.

"I think it's a splendid idea for you to retire upstairs,"

Alec said, trying to hide a grin. "Perhaps you can keep Edie with you."

"Mamma and I will probably come to blows if we're locked up together," Edie said, "which would defeat your intention to keep us safe. I'll wait in the family drawing room for news, if you don't mind. I have a number of letters to write, anyway. That should keep me occupied until you do what you have to do."

He looked like he was going to object to that eminently sane plan, until his father stepped in.

"I'll sit with Miss Whitney after I escort Lady Reese to her room," said Mr. Gilbride. He smiled at Edie. "It will give me a chance to spend a little time with my future daughter-in-law. Get to know her better."

"I should like that very much," Edie said, smiling back.

Alec still wasn't looking happy. "Very well, but Edie is not to leave unless you escort her personally back to her room, or I come to fetch her."

"You're the one who needs the escort," Edie retorted.

"Children, please don't argue," said Mr. Gilbride. "Lady Reese, may I take your arm?"

Mamma let out a dramatic sigh. "You certainly may. I feel another one of my headaches coming on and wish to retire immediately."

Edie shook her head at her mother's dramatics, especially since she'd never suffered headaches until coming to Scotland. Then again, it was turning out to be a very aggravating day.

Alec took Edie's arm and started her toward the door. "Come along, you. I want you safely out of the way and out of trouble."

She narrowed her eyes at him. "As I have said repeatedly, I am not the one in trouble."

"Trouble is your middle name."

Naturally, she objected to that, and they engaged in a

vigorous little debate on the way to the drawing room. Most of the argumentation came from her, since Alec simply marched her along, only deigning to speak a few times. And when he did, it was more or less to tell her to stop acting like a nitwit.

"I am not a nitwit," she exclaimed when he hauled her into the drawing room. "I'm worried about you, you great Scottish oaf." She stared up into his rugged face and cool gray eyes, and her throat suddenly went tight. "If anything happened to you, I would just die."

The determined set to his jaw softened, and he brought his hands up to cradle her cheeks. "Love, nothing is going to happen to me. I'm used to dealing with this sort of thing, as you recall."

She rested her palms on his hands. "Promise?"

"Promise."

He leaned in, briefly nuzzled her mouth, and then brushed his bristled cheek against hers. She let out a sigh of regret when he pulled back.

"After I dispatch the men to Glasgow," he said, "I'll go down to the kitchen and talk to the rest of the servants. I want to know if they've seen or heard anything suspicious in the last few days. I'll come for you as soon as I'm finished."

Edie clutched at his coat, not wanting to let him go. She'd never thought of herself as a die-away miss, but she couldn't help feeling that something awful would happen if she let him out of her sight.

"And you promise you won't leave the house?" she asked anxiously.

"Just to go to the stables. Now, stop worrying and write your letters. I'll be back as soon as I can."

She reluctantly let him go. She heard him talk to the footman stationed outside the door, and then his quick steps sounded down the hallway, fading away. A hush fell over the room, broken only by the crackle of the fire and the tick of the long-case clock.

Sighing, she headed to the writing desk in the corner and sat down to pen a missive to her sister. She hadn't written to Evelyn in several days, which made her let out an odd little laugh. Leaving London, Edie had been terrified of life without her twin, fearing she'd be a wreck without Evelyn's support. Instead, life had grown more interesting—if occasionally alarming—and more worthwhile with each passing day.

As she wrote to her twin about all the events of the past few days and her hopes that the rest of the family could travel to Blairgal as soon as possible, the footman stepped into the room. He explained that Mr. Gilbride had been called to assist Lord Riddick but would come sit with her as soon as he could. Edie nodded absently and went back to her letter.

Sometime later, as she was finishing her missive, the door opened again. When the footman ushered Mrs. Haddon into the room, Edie almost groaned out loud. She managed to swallow it and rise to her feet, pinning a smile on her face.

"How do you do, ma'am?" she said as the pinch-faced woman swept into the room. "Mr. Gilbride is expected shortly. Would you like me to send for him?"

Mrs. Haddon's lips lifted in a slight sneer. "No, my business is with you, Miss Whitney." She turned and glared at the footman. "You may go. And see to it that we're not disturbed."

The footman, one of the junior ones, cast an uncertain glance at Edie.

"Would you like some tea, Mrs. Haddon?" she asked.

"I hope I will not be staying long enough to drink it."

Edie let her eyebrows lift in silent commentary on the woman's rudeness before nodding a friendly dismissal to the footman. He bowed and walked to the door but turned before closing it after him.

"Just call out if ye need anything, miss," he said.

Edie smiled, taking heart at the unofficial vote of confidence. Clearly, she wasn't the only person at Blairgal who didn't like Mrs. Haddon. "I will. Thank you."

"Would you care to sit, ma'am?" Edie asked after they were alone.

Mrs. Haddon's sneer grew more pronounced. "Already putting on airs, I see. You clearly fancy yourself mistress of Blairgal already."

"I fancy myself a polite person, Mrs. Haddon," Edie replied. "Since, however, we seemed to have dispensed with the pleasantries, perhaps you can tell me what you'd like to speak to me about."

Whatever it was, Edie intended to say as little as possible. She doubted that there'd been time for rumors to spread about the shooting at the lodge. And whether Fergus was the culprit or not, it was neither Edie's responsibility nor right to inform his mother of their suspicions.

"I wish to know if you intend to carry through with your scheme to supplant my daughter from her rightful position in this family," the woman said in a voice that vibrated with emotion.

Edie hesitated, eyeing her almost manic expression. Mrs. Haddon was certainly prone to hysterics, but now she seemed on the verge of coming unhinged. That wasn't entirely surprising, given that her son had tried to shoot her nephew in a duel, and her daughter had decided to enter a nunnery.

"Mrs. Haddon, I don't wish to supplant anyone," she said. "Your daughter is clearly an intelligent woman who knows her own mind, and it seems that she made up that mind this morning."

"Because you forced her to," the other woman spat out.

"You preyed on my poor nephew and seduced him. What other choice could Donella make to preserve her dignity and reputation?" She let out an angry sob and clutched her large reticule to her waist. "My darling daughter burying herself in a convent for the rest of her life, when she should have been Countess of Riddick. I cannot bear it."

Edie let out a sigh. "Mrs. Haddon, I truly am sorry that this has caused you pain, but I assure you that I never seduced your nephew. His decisions are entirely his own, and I believe he's made it clear for quite some time that he didn't wish to marry your daughter. Nor, it would appear, did she ever wish to marry him."

"What choice did Alasdair have once you lifted your skirts to him?" Mrs. Haddon said contemptuously. "And now an English slut will be walking the halls of Blairgal Castle, lording it over the rest of us. It is not to be borne, I tell you."

Definitely unhinged.

Edie wrestled to hold on to her temper. "Mrs. Haddon, I see little point in discussing this any further with you. If you wish to wait here for Mr. Gilbride, I will gladly leave, since you obviously find my presence distressing."

"I find your presence disgusting."

Edie clamped down on a scathing retort and started for the door. Mrs. Haddon stepped in her path, blocking her.

Sighing, Edie crossed her arms over her chest. "Yes?"

Mrs. Haddon glared at her, her face dead white except for two blazing red patches on her cheekbones. Her green eyes glittered with hatred. "I want you to answer my question. Are you really going to marry Alasdair?"

Edie debated whether she should answer or not, given the woman's emotional state. But it was time to stop feeling guilty about how things had turned out. Aside from the fact that Donella had never wanted to marry Alec in the first place, Edie had not seduced him. In fact, she'd done everything she could to push him away until that fatal moment when she'd succumbed to him.

"He has asked me to marry him, and I have said yes."

Mrs. Haddon seemed to freeze into the proverbial pillar of salt. Although she was staring straight at her, Edie got the distinct impression she was seeing something else.

"Ma'am, why don't you sit down?" Edie said in a gentle voice. "I'll fetch Mr. Gilbride and have some tea sent up."

The woman blinked a few times and then sucked in a harsh breath. Her gaze focused on Edie with a cold fury that seemed almost inhuman.

"No, Miss Whitney," she said in a calm voice. "You'll stay right there and not move or make a sound until I tell you to."

Edie huffed out an exasperated breath. "Mrs. Haddon, I fail to see the point in any further discussion. Now, if you'll excuse me—"

Her words caught in her throat when Mrs. Haddon extracted a pistol from her reticule. And not one of those charming but inaccurate little guns that ladies sometimes carried. No, this was a large, lethal looking weapon, and it reminded Edie of the one Fergus had almost fired at Alec this morning.

"You're not going anywhere," the older woman said in that ghastly calm voice. "Except to hell."

Chapter Twenty-Four

Edie had to struggle to get her brain to kick into action. "Don't tell me you're the one who fired on us at the hunting lodge," she finally said on a gasp.

Mrs. Haddon let out a chuckle that Edie could only describe as evil incarnate with a good dollop of madness stirred in. "My mind is not disordered, you foolish woman. I do not ride around the countryside trying to shoot people."

"Then who did?" she cautiously asked. "Was it Fergus?" Her heart sank at the idea that both Mrs. Haddon *and* Fergus were plotting to kill Alec. One murderer in the family was bad enough.

"Certainly not," Mrs. Haddon said, "although I suppose you all think so. Fortunately, Fergus is in Glasgow today and will not be held accountable for any of this."

Edie couldn't keep her eyes from bugging out. "He tried to kill Alec in a duel this morning, or had you forgotten?"

The woman's brows pulled down with irritation. "I always knew he wouldn't have the nerve to go through with it. My poor Fergus is a sweet, gentle boy. He would never be able to kill Alasdair, no matter how much he might want to."

From what she had seen this morning, Edie suspected

Mrs. Haddon was probably correct. Which left one, big unanswered question. "Then who did shoot at us today?"

"Shoot at Alasdair," Mrs. Haddon corrected. "Not both of you. The man who did so is in my employ. He was a groom at Blairgal but was let go some months ago. There was quite a bit of bad blood and resentment over the incident, especially toward Lord Riddick. That made Ewan perfect for my purposes."

"Was it him at Mugdock Castle, too? When the section of the wall came down on us?"

Mrs. Haddon's mouth thinned with displeasure. "Ewan was trying to make it look like an accident, which was exceedingly foolish of him. He had a clear shot from the top of the wall, and yet he failed to take it. I am most disappointed in him."

Even though Edie had broken out in a cold sweat and her knees were threatening to knock, she almost let out a startled laugh. "Yes, I suppose you are. But how did this Ewan find us in the first place?"

Mrs. Haddon shrugged, although the pistol barely wavered from where it pointed at Edie's chest. "I knew Alasdair would stop for a few days at Breadie Manor. I had found Ewan some weeks ago in Glasgow and set him to watching the manor until you arrived. He had his instructions to take advantage of the first opportunity to kill my nephew."

Edie pressed her fingertips to her temples, trying to think—and praying desperately that Mr. Gilbride would come into the room. But not Alec. Anyone but Alec since the deranged woman would likely shoot him immediately.

"I don't understand," she said. "If you wanted Alec to marry your daughter, why did you try to kill him before he even arrived at Blairgal?"

Mrs. Haddon's eyebrows went up, as if to suggest that Edie was an idiot. "Do you think I didn't know my daughter had no real desire to marry him? She is the light of my life. I know her every thought."

That clearly wasn't true, given that Mrs. Haddon had been caught off-guard by Donella's decision to enter a convent.

"Besides, why would I want my innocent child to marry that faithless whoreson?" Mrs. Haddon continued. "Like mother like son, I always said, not that Lord Riddick would ever hear a word against his precious Fiona. If I could arrange for Alasdair to be killed before he returned to Blairgal, Donella would be released of her obligation to marry him. And Fergus would take his place as the right-ful heir."

"But he did return," Edie said. "And your daughter did decide to honor her vow to marry him."

"Yes. My dear daughter wished to honor her sacred vow to her papa. Nor was there ever any doubt that she would make a splendid Mistress of Riddick." She gave Edie a cold smile. "But there was no reason to think I wouldn't have had the opportunity at some point to get rid of Alasdair, which I concluded had certain additional advan-tages. My daughter would have been a wealthy widow *and* have the title. With a large dowry and her beauty, she could have then made an even more illustrious marriage. And Fergus would still inherit the earldom."

Edie had to swallow several times to keep her stomach from crawling into her throat. "You're insane," she said in a hoarse voice.

Mrs. Haddon shrugged. "I do what is necessary to protect my children."

Edie tried not to feel desperate. But where *was* every-one? "Your children will be destroyed when they find out their mother is a murderer."

Mrs. Haddon laughed as she switched her pistol to her other hand. "Why would they find out?"

Edie gaped at her. "Because you're going to shoot me?"

"Only if I have to."

Well, that made no sense. "If you just talk to your daughter—"

Mrs. Haddon took another step forward, waving the pistol in a menacing fashion. "I'm through talking, Miss Whitney. Now, turn around and go out those doors."

For a second, Edie thought about crying out for the footman, but the bloody woman was too close. She had no doubt Mrs. Haddon could fire a shot and hit her square in the chest before the footman could even get into the room.

She spun on her heel and walked to the French doors leading out to the terrace. Her legs felt weak and her head was swimming a bit, so she sucked in a few slow breaths to steady herself. Outside, she might be able to get some distance from the woman, or find something to throw at her.

Or perhaps someone would glance out one of the upstairs windows and see what was happening.

That thought gave her a welcome spurt of courage. Calmly, she opened the doors and walked out onto the terrace. She crossed to the steps that led into the garden and started down.

"Stop right there," Mrs. Haddon ordered.

Edie slowly turned to face her. As she did, she cast a quick glance up at the windows that overlooked this part of the garden, but the setting sun reflecting on them turned the panes of glass opaque.

The older woman came out, close enough to not miss if she fired but far enough away to keep Edie from taking a chance at knocking the weapon from her hand.

"All right, now turn around and walk slowly to the wall overlooking the ravine," Mrs. Haddon said.

Edie turned and walked across the grass, the skin between her shoulder blades prickling as if anticipating the shot. This part of the garden was narrow and private, enclosed on three sides by high walls that set it off from the rest of the castle grounds. The fourth side, demarcated by a rough, low wall, looked out over a steep ravine. The only entrance or exit was across the terrace into the drawing room or over the wall into the ravine.

Edie began to get a very bad feeling about what was going to happen next.

"Climb up onto the wall," Mrs. Haddon said from behind her.

As slowly as she could, Edie climbed onto the stone barrier. She cast a quick glance into the ravine and had to once more order her stomach back down her throat. The steep, rocky slope pitched straight down to a fast-running stream. She might survive a fall down that slope, but the odds weren't good. And even if she did survive, she'd probably break every bone in her body.

She turned to face her tormenter, carefully picking her way around on the slippery stone. "Mrs. Haddon, why are you doing this? Even if I'm out of the way, Alec is not going to marry your daughter."

Mrs. Haddon's lips lifted in that ugly sneer that Edie knew she'd never forget, no matter how long or how short her life.

"Alasdair will no doubt be quite distraught when your body is found broken at the bottom of the ravine," the older woman said. "Donella is an exceedingly kind girl and will want to comfort him. Nature will then take its course."

Edie wiped her damp palms against the sides of her skirts, trying for any argument that might buy her time. "What if I promise not to marry Alec?" she asked desperately. "I'll get my mother, and we'll leave right away."

Mrs. Haddon laughed. "Do you really think I'm that stupid?"

Edie clenched her fists. "You won't get away with this. Alec will figure it out."

The woman shrugged. "Perhaps, but what does it matter? You'll still be gone."

"You will ruin your children's life, Mrs. Haddon. They would not wish you to do this."

Rage flared in the woman's gaze as she took a step closer. "You know nothing about my children."

Edie lifted her chin, even though tears were stinging her eyes at the thought of what her death would do to her twin and to the rest of her family.

To Alec.

But she simply couldn't back down before this evil woman, no matter what happened. "Alec will never marry Donella. You can be sure of that."

Mrs. Haddon tilted her head and gave her a queer sort of smile. "We'll see."

"But—"

"There's only one thing left for you to do, Miss Whitney. And that's jump."

Alec headed for the stairs that would bring him up to the drawing room. There he hoped to find Edie and his father safely staying put. He'd spoken with the senior staff about security arrangements for the castle and also questioned them about anything they might have seen out of the ordinary.

The only interesting tidbit of information concerned a former disgruntled employee his grandfather had let go some months back. One of Blairgal's footmen swore he saw him riding near the estate grounds two days ago. That would merit further investigation, but right now he needed to focus on finding Fergus and keeping Edie safe. Edie had been with Alec both times an attempt had been made on his life, and he had no intention of taking any chances with her safety.

That meant he would have to keep watch on her every damned second, since Edie wouldn't think twice about putting herself in danger to protect him. While that terrified him, it also touched him deeply—as had her admission that she loved him. Hearing her say it out loud had dissolved much of the icy feeling in his gut every time he thought about Fergus.

As he reached the bottom of the stairs, he heard the door to the entrance hall open and a scurry of footsteps behind him. He turned to see Donella, garbed in a riding habit and her hair whipped into a tangle under her hat. She rushed toward him across the stone floor.

"Alasdair, have you seen my mother?"

"No, but I haven't been upstairs in over an hour. Did you expect her to come visiting this afternoon?"

She shook her head, looking anxious. "No. After we got home this morning, she took to her bed. She was quite distraught, so I gave her a few drops of laudanum to help her sleep. But when I checked on her later, she was gone. Her maid and I looked all over the house, but we couldn't find her."

He frowned. "Perhaps she went for a walk, or into the village."

She shook her head. "No one saw her leave, including her maid. Mamma always takes the carriage, but it's still in the stables. One of the horses is missing, though."

Alec repressed a mental sigh. On top of everything else, it now looked like he would have to track down his aunt. Still, it wouldn't do for Donella to be anxious. "I'm sure she's fine, but I'll send some of the grooms out to look for her."

Donella grabbed his arm. "Alasdair, I'm very worried. She said some dreadful things this morning after we left."

"About me?"

She grimaced. "Yes, partly, but more about Miss Whitney. It rather frightened me, if you must know the truth."

Alec didn't like the sound of that. "Edie and my father are upstairs in the drawing room. Why don't I take you up to sit with them?"

They'd just reached the main floor when they heard footsteps clattering down the stairs from the rooms above. A moment later, Lady Reese appeared, running flat out.

"Captain Gilbride," she gasped. "It's Eden. She's in trouble."

His heart jolted hard against his ribs. "Where is she?"

"In the garden, off the main drawing room. That deranged woman is pointing a gun at her."

Donella let out a huge gasp. "Mamma!" She pelted off down the hall toward the drawing room.

Alec cursed and raced after her. "Wait, Donella. Don't go rushing in there."

He caught up and grabbed her just as she reached the door to the drawing room. One of the junior footmen stood in front of it, his startled gaze bouncing back and forth between Donella and Alec.

"Who's in there with Miss Whitney?" Alec snapped out, holding on to Donella.

"Just Mrs. Haddon, sir," he answered. "She arrived a few minutes ago. She asked that they not be disturbed."

Christ. He didn't have time to fetch a pistol. He looked at the footman. "Find Barclay, and tell him to give you a loaded pistol. And hurry."

The young man nodded and took off at a dead run.

"You two stay here," Alec said to Lady Reese and Donella.

"I'm coming with you," Donella said firmly.

"No—"

"She'll listen to me, Alasdair. She won't listen to you."

He grimaced, knowing she was right. "Fine, but stay behind me." He glanced at Lady Reese, who was looking as white as a ghost but also fiercely determined. "But *you* stay."

She scoffed. "Don't be ridiculous, and stop wasting time."

Mentally cursing all the stubborn women in his life, Alec led the way into the room. The French doors were open, so he quickly crossed through and stepped out onto the terrace.

And felt his heart plummet down to the stones beneath his feet. Aunt Glenna had Edie up on the low wall that looked over the ravine, a gun pointed right at her chest. Edie apparently had no intention of going quietly, because she seemed to be arguing with her captor.

When Donella tried to launch herself past him, Alec managed to catch her just in time. "Easy," he whispered. "We don't want to startle her. Just call out to her, as calmly as you can."

His cousin gave a jerky nod, then cleared her throat. "Mother," she called in a steady voice, "it's Donella. Please step away from there before someone gets hurt."

Aunt Glenna stiffened, but didn't move from her stance. Edie's gaze flashed across the garden to meet Alec's. Her hand went to her chest, and some of the tension seemed to go out of her shoulders. She gave him a shaky, heartbreaking smile, then her attention flicked back to Glenna.

"Mamma, please turn around," Donella said, taking a step forward. "I need to speak with you."

Her mother backed a few feet away from Edie, well clear of her reach but still close enough to pull off an accurate shot, and then half-turned to look at her daughter. Both Donella and Lady Reese gasped, and Alec couldn't blame them. Aunt Glenna's face was pulled into a rictus of hatred, her eyes blazing with fury. He'd always known that his aunt was emotionally erratic. Now he realized she was insane.

Unfortunately, the hand that held the gun on Edie was rock-steady.

"Go back inside, my love," Aunt Glenna called. She gave her daughter a ghastly parody of a smile. "I'll be along as soon as I finish this."

"Mamma, please put the gun down," Donella pleaded. "I beg you not to hurt Miss Whitney."

"Oh, but she has to die, my love. How else can you marry Alasdair?"

Lady Reese stepped forward. "If you dare touch my daughter, I'll kill you."

Aunt Glenna laughed. "Not if I kill you first. After I dispose of your whore of a daughter."

Lady Reese tried to stalk past Alec, but he hauled her back. "You're not helping," he said through clenched teeth.

"Mamma, please stay where you are," Edie said. "Everything will be fine."

She edged along the wall, clearly trying to get out of the direct line of fire. Aunt Glenna whipped back around to her, holding the gun level.

"Don't move," she barked out.

Edie froze.

"Aunt Glenna," Alec said, slowly walking across the terrace to force his aunt's attention away from Edie and onto him. "You need to know that I will not marry Donella under any circumstances. Even if you go through with this mad scheme, I won't do it."

He walked down the steps to the lawn, moving close enough to his aunt to force her attention almost fully onto him. When Edie started moving again, inching to get behind Glenna, he had to bite back a curse. He flicked her a warning glance that said *stay still*.

Naturally, she ignored him.

"Nothing you do will compel me to marry Donella," Alec said, staring straight into his aunt's mad gaze. "Nothing."

Donella came up behind him. "And I won't marry Alasdair in any case, Mamma. So, please put the gun down, I beg you."

"But, darling," her mother said, "don't you want to be Countess of Riddick? You know you do."

"No, Mamma," she said. "I *never* wanted that. You and Papa did, so I went along with it. But I never wanted to marry Alasdair, and you know it."

Her mother's face seemed to twist in on itself in a bizarre contortion. Then it smoothed out into an oddly benign smile. "Very well, my dear, then you shan't."

She swung the pistol around and pointed it at Alec. "I'd rather kill you anyway. It's what I always wanted. Then Fergus will be the laird, as he should have been in the first place."

"That's right," Alec said, taking another step forward. "I'm the problem. I've always been the problem."

Edie glared at him as she inched along the wall. He glared back, shaking his head.

"Mamma, you can't," Donella choked out. "You'll hang for murder."

Aunt Glenna shrugged. "It'll be worth it to see my boy take his rightful place. That's all I ever wanted for him. For both of you."

Suddenly, Edie launched herself off the wall at Aunt Glenna. But she was too far away to reach her before the pistol discharged. The bullet grazed the sleeve of Alec's greatcoat, but he ignored it and charged across the lawn.

Edie was now on top of his aunt, struggling to keep her down on the ground. Alec plucked the pistol from Aunt

Glenna's hand and tossed it behind him, then grabbed Edie by the back of her dress and hauled her up and into his arms. Aunt Glenna rolled to her side, her eyes going wide as she stared across the garden.

"Donella," she screamed. She staggered to her feet and lurched over to her daughter, lying on the ground.

Alec's heart caught in his throat, as Edie let out a horrified gasp. They raced back across the lawn to join the small group huddled at the base of the terrace steps.

Lady Reese was on her knees beside Donella, trying to stanch the blood that seeped from the girl's arm with a kerchief. Aunt Glenna crouched next to her daughter, rocking back and forth as she wailed. When Alec and Edie approached, she glared at them, her eyes blazing with hatred.

"I'll kill you for this, Alasdair," she spat out. "You and your whore both." She started to scrabble up.

Lady Reese reached over and clamped a hand on Glenna's shoulder. "You'll do nothing of the sort," she said. Then she hauled back and delivered a bruising uppercut to Glenna's chin. His aunt's eyes rolled back and, with a whimper, she collapsed in a heap onto the lawn.

Her ladyship grimaced and shook out her hand, then glanced up at Alec and Edie, both staring at her, mouths agape.

"Good riddance," muttered Lady Reese. Then she went back to pressing her kerchief on Donella's wound.

Choking out a startled laugh of relief, Alec pulled Edie into his arms. "I never knew your mother was a boxer," he said.

Her only reply was a watery giggle as she burrowed into his arms.

"You daft woman," he said as he held her in a fierce embrace. "You could have been killed." His brain told him that she was safe, but it would take his heart some minutes to catch up.

"I didn't have a choice," she said in a muffled voice. "You *would* have been killed."

He cradled her against him, reluctant to let go. But a moment later, she pulled out of his arms and crouched down to help her mother.

Alec hunkered down beside them. "How bad is it?"

"It's only a graze," her ladyship said. "But she must have knocked her head when she fell. Ah, in fact, I believe she's starting to come around."

Alec breathed out a sigh of relief. "Thank God."

A moment later, his father rushed out, followed by the footman and Barclay. The butler clutched a pistol.

"Alasdair, what's going on?" Walter cried. He skidded to a halt at the edge of the terrace, his eyes going wide as he took in the gruesome little scene. "Is . . . is Glenna dead?"

"No, unfortunately," said Lady Reese in a severe voice.

"Mamma, really," Edie said. "You mustn't say things like that."

"She tried to shoot you, Eden. Have you forgotten that already?"

Edie grimaced. "Well, I suppose you're right."

Alec glanced up at his father, who seemed too thunderstruck to move or speak. "Any word about Fergus?"

Walter shook his head.

"Fergus had nothing to do with this," Edie said. "Mrs. Haddon planned it all out herself and hired someone to come after you. The duel was just an ugly coincidence."

The band around Alec's chest loosened another notch. "You can explain the rest to me later. Right now we've got to take care of Donella and lock my aunt away until we decide what to do with her."

He stood up and began issuing orders to the small crowd of servants now gathering on the terrace, including sending for the surgeon. Aunt Glenna was carried away and Donella was taken up to one of the spare bedrooms, accompanied by Edie and her mother and the housekeeper. The chaotic scene quickly settled down, leaving Alec to explain what little he knew about the situation to his father as they went back into the drawing room.

Walter let out a heavy sigh as he sank onto one of the settees. "Well, it's dreadful, of course, but I'm relieved to hear that Fergus isn't involved."

"Yes, but I'm not looking forward to explaining to him that his mother has gone barking mad." Alec shook his head. "I don't know if he'll ever forgive me for all the harm I've done to him and his family."

Walter's brows lifted in surprise. "Alasdair, you are not responsible for this tragedy. Glenna has always been emotionally unstable, but clearly more than any of us knew."

"True, but Fergus still blames me for Donella. I should never have let things get so out of hand. If I hadn't been such a coward, I would have come home long ago and dealt with it."

"My boy, the last thing you are is a coward," his father said in gentle reproof. "As for the situation with Donella, neither you nor she can be held to blame for that. Your elders must take on that responsibility. Not one of us truly listened to what you both were trying to tell us."

Alec grimaced. "True, but—"

Walter held up a hand. "No buts. It's time for you to stop feeling guilty about everything, my son. It is entirely unnecessary."

Alec gave him a wry smile. "Edie said the same thing."

"Then she is a very sensible girl."

"So you really don't mind that I'm going to marry her?"

"Alasdair, I want you to be happy, as does your grandfather. And Miss Whitney seems like a truly splendid girl. I'm sure she'll make you a fine wife." Walter smiled.

"Better than Donella, I suspect, since Miss Whitney will no doubt bring you to heel whenever it's necessary."

Alec snorted. "Aye, there's no doubt about that. Speaking of Grandfather, what blessed piece of luck kept him from landing in the middle of all this?"

"After that distressing meeting in the library, I convinced him to go for a nap. I am supremely grateful that his rooms do not overlook this part of the gardens, because such a shocking sight would have been extremely deleterious to his health."

Alec sighed. "Well, I'd better go explain what happened before he hears it from one of the servants."

His father rose. "I'll do that. Why don't you stay here and . . . ah, here she is now."

Alec turned as the door opened and Edie came into the room. He went to meet her. "How are you, love?"

She slipped into his arms. "I'm fine, all things considered. It's not every day that one faces a murder attempt at the hands of a madwoman." She glanced past him toward Walter and winced. "Oh, dear. Forgive me, sir. That was an exceedingly indelicate thing for me to say about one of your relations."

"Also exceedingly accurate," Walter said. "How is poor Donella?"

"The surgeon dressed her wound and gave her a dose of sleeping powders to help her settle. He said she can return to Haddon House in a day or two."

Walter shook his head. "The poor lass. I cannot imagine what she must be feeling. And what will we do with Glenna?"

Alec clasped his shoulder. "We'll figure it all out together, Father. As a family."

His father blinked several times, then smiled. "Dear me, you cannot imagine how happy it makes me to hear you say that. Well, I'm off to speak with your grandfather. I suppose I'll see you at dinner."

After the door closed behind him, Edie sighed and laid her head against Alec's chest. "It seems odd to be speaking of dinner, after all this. How utterly dull and normal to sit down to lamb and peas."

"Dull and normal sounds rather splendid at the moment. Although perhaps we should bring our pistols to the table, just in case."

She laughed. "I can't wait to write to Evie and tell her everything that's happened. Now she's not the only one who sneered in the face of death and lived to tell about it."

Alec hugged her close. "Christ, don't even joke about it. It was the worst moment of my life when I saw you up on that bloody wall. I thought I was going to lose you."

She leaned back in his arms, staring earnestly up at him. "I felt the same about you. I wanted to shake you for putting yourself in harm's way like that."

He cradled her sweet face between his hands. "I would do it a thousand times over if it meant saving you. Never doubt that."

Her gaze went soft and misty behind her spectacles, and her lips trembled just a bit. "Then I suppose that means you must love me," she said, gently mocking his earlier words in the library.

Still, he heard the faint, questioning note in her voice. It suddenly occurred to him that he had yet to tell her how he truly felt about her. What a fool he was.

He leaned down and pressed a soft kiss to her lips. "Lass, I adore you—more than life itself. I've adored you from the moment I first saw you."

She laughed. "Now *that* is a lie. I remember that moment as if it happened yesterday. You thought I was the most dreadfully rude person you'd ever met."

"True, but also the most adorable. And the prettiest."

When she scoffed, he walked over to the door, turning the key in the lock. She tilted her head to study him, one corner of her mouth kicking up in a questioning smile.

"What are you doing?" she asked.

When he swept her up in his arms, she let out an endearing little squeak. "I'll just have to show you what I mean," he said as he carried her to a very large, very plush chaise in the corner of the room.

A slow, sensual smile curled up the corners of her mouth. He felt the power of it race through his body, straight to his groin.

"Now who's being the masterful one?" she said.

"I am Master of Riddick, after all. It's my job."

She grinned. "How could I have forgotten that?"

"Don't worry, I'll be happy to remind you frequently."

And settling her onto the chaise, Alec took his time doing exactly that.

Epilogue

December
Blairgal Castle

"That was a splendid wedding ceremony," Evelyn said as she fussed with the ribbons in Edie's hair. "I loved the way you and Alec were piped around the castle grounds with all the Grahams and the entire village following behind."

"It was fun, wasn't it?" Edie said, gazing at her twin's reflection in the mirror. "Even though it was rather cold and blustery. I'm certain my nose turned as red as a beet."

"Don't worry," her twin said in a droll voice. "I'm quite sure Alec was looking down the front of your bodice, not at your nose."

"Evelyn Endicott, you will refrain from making vulgar remarks to your sister," their mother said. "You're a married lady now."

Evelyn widened her eyes at Mamma, who was seated in a comfortably padded chair in the small but luxurious retiring room down the hall from Blairgal's ballroom. They'd repaired there after the wedding ceremony to lay aside their wraps and freshen up before the festivities began in earnest.

"Mamma, that makes no sense," Evelyn said. "If we can't make that sort of joke after we're married, when can we?"

Surprisingly enough, their mother seemed to ponder the question as she sipped her whiskey. Mamma had grown rather fond of whiskey over the last several weeks, ending most evenings sitting with Lord Riddick in the drawing room indulging in a *wee dram,* as the earl called it. It was one of the only times those two weren't arguing over something, although Edie suspected they both rather enjoyed twitting each other.

"I suppose it's acceptable to make a naughty jest or two when alone with one's husband," Mamma admitted. "In fact, your father and I have been known to indulge on occasion. Why, just the other night, shortly after your dear Papa arrived here at Blairgal for the wedding—"

"Mamma, I think we'd better join our guests," Edie said, hastily breaking in. "Alec and I are expected to lead the first reel."

"Oh, yes, I suppose so," her mother said.

As Mamma tossed back her whiskey, Evelyn threw Edie a wide-eyed, laughing glance. Their mother rarely let down her hair, so Edie was sure that her twin was finding Mamma's behavior something of a revelation. In truth, their sojourn in the Highlands had been almost as good for her mother as it had been for Edie. Mamma had been growing rather bored with life in London, Edie suspected, and their time in Scotland had been anything but.

"There, pet," Evelyn said. "Your hair looks perfect, as do you."

Edie gave her reflection a critical once-over. "My nose

still looks rather red. Do you think I should send Cora for some powder?"

"I'm sure all our noses are red," said Mamma. "December in the Highlands is certainly not for the fainthearted. Why we all had to march around in the middle of a snowstorm is beyond me."

"Mamma, there were only a few flurries," Edie said. "Besides, it's tradition for the clan and the villagers to accompany the bride and the groom from the kirk to the festivities."

"I wish those dreadful shrieking bagpipes were not part of that tradition," her mother replied. "I don't see how anyone could avoid a headache after listening to that din."

"Better not let Lord Riddick hear you say that. You know what he's like about the old clan traditions," Edie said as she came to her feet.

"Well, I like the traditions," Evelyn said, fluffing out the back of Edie's wide skirts. "I found it especially moving when his lordship pinned that lovely tartan sash over your gown. I think almost everyone in the kirk got teary-eyed, even the men."

"The Scots do tend to get rather sentimental about such things," Mamma said. "But I have to admit the tartan looks quite nice with your gown."

"And the clan badge is simply gorgeous," Evelyn said.

Edie ran a hand over the wide sash, made of the finest wool in the colors of Clan Graham. It draped over her shoulder across the front of her gown, secured with the clan badge, a silver brooch. When the earl had pinned it on right after she and Alec had taken their vows, it was one of the most emotional moments of the entire ceremony for Edie. She'd felt truly a member of her new family and clan. When Alec had bent down to whisper that the beautiful old pin had belonged to his mother, she'd slipped her hand into his, blinking away tears.

"My gown does look splendid, doesn't it?" Edie said, inspecting her cream-colored silk dress. It was an old-fashioned design, modeled on Lady Fiona's wedding gown, with wide skirts and a low cut, crystal-trimmed bodice. It was the perfect canvas for the colors and badge of Clan Graham, and she'd loved it from the moment she'd put it on.

From the look in Alec's eyes when she'd joined him at the altar, he'd liked it too. And she had no doubt he'd like getting her out of it even more.

Her twin reached over and took her hand. "You look incredibly beautiful, Edie. Will and I are just so happy for you and Alec." Her eyes were rather misty-looking behind her spectacles, but then she flashed a grin. "Will had been predicting this for weeks, you know. He said you'd fallen head over heels for each other, but that you just hadn't quite figured it out yet."

"I wish he'd told us," Edie said in a dry voice. "It would have saved us a great deal of fuss and bother."

"Well, it's all turned out for the best," Mamma said. "Despite the trouble with that dreary Haddon family."

Edie sighed. "Mamma, we've been over this a dozen times. Donella has been nothing but kind and supportive, and Fergus has been as nice as can be expected under the circumstances."

Those circumstances were that his mother was currently under the care of a private physician in Edinburgh and was likely to remain so for the rest of her life. Various family members had admitted in retrospect that Mrs. Haddon had been emotionally unstable and prone to hysterical fits for quite some time. They'd gotten worse after the death of her husband, and she'd finally lost her grip on reality with the news that Alec was to return home. Apparently, she'd been hoping that he would be killed in the war. When he wasn't, she'd paid a great deal of money to hire Lord Riddick's former groom to murder Alec.

Fortunately, the man had been as incompetent a villain as he'd been a groom. After his failed attempt at the hunting lodge, he'd clearly decided what little luck he'd enjoyed had run out and he'd disappeared. Lord Riddick had wished to run the poltroon to ground but Alec had finally talked him out of it. A trial would have drawn even greater attention to Mrs. Haddon's tragic condition and embarrassed Donella and Fergus.

Perhaps the worst part of the entire episode had been the heartbreaking scene when Alec told Fergus that his mother had attempted murder. The poor man had been stunned by the news and overcome with guilt at his mother's villainy. After stammering out an apology to Edie, he'd broken down when he also tried to apologize to Alec. He'd offered to resign his position as estate steward, but Alec had simply given his cousin a quick embrace and told him not to be daft. He'd made it clear to Fergus that no one faulted him for defending his family's honor.

It would take time, but Edie had no doubt that the friendship between Alec and Fergus would be restored. Fergus had a good heart, though he was a tad too sensitive and emotional for his own good. Edie was convinced that her new cousin needed a nice vacation in London, where he would have the opportunity to meet new people and forget about his troubles. Perhaps she could convince Mamma to take him on as a special project now that all her children were married.

"Oh, I suppose those two have redeemed themselves," Mamma said, "but I think it will be good for everyone when Donella leaves to join that convent of hers. Then everything can get back to normal."

"If life in a gigantic old castle can ever be described as normal," Evelyn said.

"Oh, I don't know," Edie mused. "It's actually rather cozy."

She knew she sounded completely silly, but she'd come to love everything about Blairgal—well, except for the drafty hallways. She couldn't help feeling how privileged she was to be a part of its history and traditions. Lord Riddick and the rest of his family had accepted her with open arms, and Edie knew how lucky she'd been to find such a gracious and welcoming home.

And to find her forever home with Alec, the most wonderful man in the world. She could barely keep from bursting into tears of joy every time she thought about a future with him by her side.

Evelyn tweaked the train of Edie's gown and stood back to admire her. "There, you're all set for your first dance with your husband. And he is a very lucky man to have you for his wife, old girl."

"Both Alasdair *and* William are very lucky men," Mamma said. "I don't say it often enough, but my daughters are the most beautiful girls in London and also the nicest."

The twins exchanged startled glances. Mamma had always doted on Edie, but she'd certainly never been prone to excessive sentimentality toward either of them, especially not Evelyn.

"Thank you, Mamma," Evelyn said. "That's exceedingly kind of you."

"It's simply the truth, my dears. Although I suppose I can't persuade the two of you to leave off your spectacles for the ball, can I?" Mamma asked, ever hopeful.

"It's my wedding day," Edie protested. "I'd like to be able to see it."

"And we're both married now," Evelyn pointed out. "No one will mind if we go about looking like a pair of fusty old bluestockings."

"Very well, although no daughter of mine could ever be termed a fusty old bluestocking," Mamma said. "Now, I suppose we'd best get out there before the men start wondering where we are."

They followed their mother out and down the long hallway toward the ballroom.

"What did you slip in her drink?" Evelyn murmured to Edie. "I've never seen her in this good a mood."

"She's finally married us all off and rather well, too. It's no wonder she's so happy."

"Rather well is an understatement when it comes to you," her sister said with a laugh. "Your new husband's family is so rich it's almost vulgar."

"I know. Isn't it splendid?"

"It certainly is."

"When you and Wolf get back from his assignment on the Continent, you must come live with us," Edie said, imitating her mother's grand manner. "I'm sure we must have an extra hunting lodge or estate hanging about somewhere that you could use."

Evelyn rolled her eyes but didn't answer, since their husbands were waiting for them outside the ballroom. Wolf stepped up, took his wife's hand, and gave her cheek a brief nuzzle. Evelyn's eyes half-closed with pleasure as she melted into her handsome husband's embrace.

"Have you sorted out all the problems of the world?" Wolf asked. "You three were certainly in there long enough."

"We were talking about you and Alec," Edie said. "And how best to drive you both crazy."

Alec, who'd been speaking to Mamma, turned to look at Edie, giving her a smile so wicked and sensual that she almost broke out in hives. He strolled over and slipped an arm around her waist, pulling her against his brawny body.

"I hardly think you two have to plot about that," he said. "You're already very accomplished at it."

She smiled up at him. "Practice makes perfect."

He dipped down and brushed a soft, delicious kiss across her lips. "Lass, you can practice making me crazy all you want later tonight when we're alone. And naked."

Her knees went weak at the seductive note in his voice, but she forced a stern expression. "Alasdair Gilbride, behave yourself. What will everyone think?"

He tilted her chin up, smiling at her. "I only care what you think, Edie, my love. You're the most important thing in the world to me and don't you ever forget it."

She melted into his arms, ready to have him carry her up to his bedroom right this second.

"Enough of that, Alasdair Gilbride," his grandfather barked as he bustled up to them. "You'll have plenty of time for that nonsense later. Now you have to lead the opening reel."

Edie choked back a laugh at the annoyed look on her husband's face. She dug an elbow into his side before he could object to his grandfather's interruption.

"Yes, your lordship, we're ready," she said.

"It's *Grandfather,* lassie," the old man said. "No need for titles now that you're part of the family."

Edie had to blink several times after that unexpected declaration, but her new grandparent was already shooing them all toward the door.

"Come along now," he said. "The pipers are in place and ready to start."

"Oh, no," groaned Mamma. "Not more bagpipes."

"Dreadful things, aren't they? Can't stand them myself," Lord Riddick said, taking her arm. "One must keep up with tradition, though. The clan expects it." He led Mamma into the ballroom with Evelyn and Wolf following behind.

Edie and Alec gaped at each other and then laughed.

"Your grandfather hates bagpipes?" Edie asked. "How is that even possible?"

Alec shook his head. "I'd forgotten that. I'd forgotten so much, idiot that I was."

She slipped her arm through his. "Like how much you love your family and how much you love Blairgal?"

He nodded. "Aye, but with your help I remembered. Thank you, sweetheart, for helping to return it back to me."

"And thank you for making me part of it. For bringing me home," Edie said, snuggling close.

His silver-gray gaze mirrored all the joy she felt now and hoped to feel for the rest of her days with him.

As the bagpipes wailed out the first notes of the reel, her husband smiled down at her. "Are you ready to greet your new family and clan, Mistress of Riddick?"

She gave him a cheeky grin. "Lead on, Master. Lead on."

*He's the man behind the mission to track down
the illegitimate children of England's Royal Princes
and help them get their due. But his deepest desire
is far more personal . . .*

Magnificent *and* stubborn. Fourteen years apart had not
changed Chloe Steele, or Dominic Hunter's love for her.
He'd been a street urchin, a boy raised at court, and
finally a magistrate, yet he'd never belonged anywhere—
except by her side. Now Chloe devoted herself
to girls threatened by scandal—like she had been.
But she was in danger, and Dominic was determined to
help—and hopefully make up for lost time . . .

Even in childhood, Dominic had made Chloe feel safe.
Now she also felt thrillingly flustered by the powerful
man he'd become, and by the longing he inspired.
Because Dominic meant not only to protect her, but to
untangle the lies that had separated them. Yet for Chloe,
surrendering to temptation may be easier than risking
a future that could ruin them both . . .

Please turn the page for a special bonus novella!

**Vanessa Kelly's
TALL, DARK, AND ROYAL.**

Chapter One

Village of Camberwell
April 1815

Dominic Hunter wheeled his curricle between the iron-mounted gates that bracketed the forecourt of the handsome Jacobean manor house. Peter, his groom, leapt down before the carriage came to a full stop at the portico.

"Stable the horses," Dominic ordered. "I don't know how long I'll be staying."

"Aye, Sir Dominic. I'll give 'em a rubdown myself."

Dominic had crammed the horses more than he normally would on the busy road from London to Camberwell because the message he'd received this morning had made him break out in a cold sweat.

Chloe is in need of your assistance. She claims to be fine, but I think it best you come immediately.

—Griffin Steele

How typical of Griffin to refer to his mother by her given name, as typical as his lamentably terse note. But

Griffin would never summon Dominic unless the situation called for it, which meant things were far from *fine*.

The fact that it was Griffin rather than Chloe asking for his help was an added irritant. After her dramatic and emotional reappearance two months ago, Chloe had subsequently adopted a calm, carefully polite manner to keep Dominic at bay. She'd spent the long years of their separation building walls around her heart, walls she seemed reluctant to dismantle. Dominic understood better than anyone the wounds Chloe had suffered. Any reasonable man would give her the time she needed to adjust to the momentous change in her circumstances. After all, for years, Dominic and Griffin had feared she was dead. To have her suddenly back in their lives was a shock for all of them.

Still, when it came to Chloe, Dominic was anything but reasonable. He wanted to blast through the barriers to reach the sweet, innocent girl he'd loved, the girl he'd spent fourteen long years searching for. That Chloe was still sweet was undeniable, and her innocent and loving heart burned bright and true as the North Star. But layered over those gentle qualities was a wary approach to life that spoke of abuse and pain and exposure to an uncaring world. Every time Dominic saw Chloe's gaze turn inward, her fawn-colored eyes growing dark with quiet desolation, he wanted to tear something—or someone—apart.

He was one of the most powerful men in England, but in the face of Chloe's pain he felt utterly helpless.

Hill, Chloe's butler, opened the door at Dominic's knock and ushered him into the old-fashioned entrance hall.

"You're expected, Sir Dominic." Concern lent Hill's aging, narrowed features a sharp look. "Mrs. Piper and Mr. and Mrs. Steele are waiting in the back drawing room."

Although Chloe's true name was Steele, she'd been living in Camberwell for years as Mrs. Piper, a wealthy but reclusive widow from Northumberland. She'd maintained that fictitious persona with rigorous discipline. It had prevented even Dominic, with the resources of the Intelligence Service at his disposal, from finding her. It baffled him why Chloe had chosen to hide when she must have known he'd do anything for her, make any sacrifice necessary to protect her. All she would say was that she'd been convinced everyone thought her dead, and she'd believed her sudden reappearance in their lives would be too disruptive.

It was the most absurd thing he'd ever heard. And he was beginning to suspect she'd convinced herself that she was more a burden than a blessing in their lives, and that her past would bring her son and her friends nothing but shame and disgrace.

"How is she?" Dominic asked.

The butler grimaced. "Mrs. Piper is being obstinate, I'm sorry to say. Told me I was an old hen to carry on so."

Dominic wasn't surprised by Hill's blunt speech. The man was more than Chloe's butler—he was a trusted confidant and had for years been providing discreet assistance in her sometimes dangerous charitable work. Dominic suspected he provided another kind of support, too, standing in for the father she'd lost a long time ago.

"I suppose if she can gripe at you, then she's not in too bad a shape," Dominic said cautiously.

"You don't know Mrs. Piper," Hill muttered.

And that was the problem, wasn't it? Dominic was afraid he *didn't* know Chloe anymore. He didn't know what she wanted and, more importantly, what she needed from him.

He followed Hill along the low-ceiled hallway of the old house, taking in the quiet. On most days when Dominic came to call, at least three or four of the girls would be rambling noisily about or taking lessons with Chloe. There were also two young women who'd recently given birth, finding shelter under Chloe's generous protection.

All told, there were currently seven girls at the manor, all either pregnant or with infants. Every single one had been abandoned by her family or forced away until after the pregnancy. Through word of mouth or the help of a mutual friend, they had found their way to the refuge of Chloe's house in the countryside.

But today, tension held the unnaturally quiet house in its grip, as if something violent had fractured the security Chloe provided for her charges.

When Hill opened the door at the end of the hall, Dominic strode through but came to a sudden halt, his heart jolting at the sight of Chloe reclining on a chaise with a bandage wrapped around her head. Justine Steele, Dominic's godchild, sat next to her holding a teacup. Lounging in a nearby armchair was Griffin Steele, Chloe's son and Justine's husband.

"What the hell is going on here?" Dominic snapped. He glared at Griffin, who had a knack for finding or, indeed, creating trouble. "How did your mother get hurt?"

Griffin let out a dramatic sigh as he came to his feet. "You have a lamentable tendency to blame me for everything, Dominic. I had nothing to do with Mother's, er, little accident."

Chloe threw aside her lap robe and stood. "Dominic, I'm fine. There's nothing for you to worry about."

But when she wobbled, Justine had to make a grab for her. In an instant, Dominic was by Chloe's side. "For God's sake, sit down." He gently lowered her back to the chaise.

Her tall, slender body felt fragile in his hands, as if the merest touch could break her. But appearances were deceptive. For all her pale, delicate beauty, Chloe had a strong will and character that had withstood years of tribulation.

"You know the doctor told you to stay off your feet and rest," Justine affectionately scolded.

"I'm not sure how she's supposed to rest with you lot fussing over her," Griffin said. "Hill has been popping in and out like a character from a farce, not to mention all the girls sneaking in. It's a bloody circus."

Justine frowned at her husband. "They're worried about Chloe."

Dominic throttled back his impulse to snap. "I would be most grateful if someone—anyone—would answer my question. Wait," he said to Justine. "First, tell me what the physician said."

"Perhaps you might try asking *Chloe,* Sir Dominic," Chloe said with pointed courtesy. "As you can see, she is perfectly capable of speech."

Dominic mentally winced. Chloe only used his title when annoyed with him. "I'm sorry, my dear. But it was a shock to come upon you looking like you'd been set upon by thieves."

Thankfully, she flashed him a wry, forgiving smile. "Apology accepted." She shifted her legs and patted the seat of the chaise. "Sit down and let Justine get you a cup of tea while I tell you all about it. Not that I wanted to drag you into this ridiculous and unfortunate episode, but my son insisted. Who knew Griffin could fuss and worry as much as any old maid?"

Her son—one of the most ruthless and powerful men in London—rolled his eyes but declined to defend himself.

"What happened to your head?" Dominic eyed the bandage wrapped around her brow.

"I bumped it, that's all," Chloe replied. "The doctor insisted I wear this silly thing and my son won't let me take it off."

Griffin narrowed his dark gaze on his mother. "*You* didn't bump your head. It was bumped for you when that bloody bastard shoved you into the wall. And you *will* keep that bandage on for as long as is required."

Dominic had been reaching to accept a cup from Justine, but his hand froze in midair. Slowly, he turned to Chloe. "Someone shoved you?"

Chloe's shoulders unconsciously hiked up a notch. "Yes, but it wasn't a very hard shove. Truly, I'm *fine*."

Dominic could hear Griffin grinding his teeth from several feet away. He sympathized, but the situation was confusing enough without him losing his temper, at least not until he'd apprised himself of the facts.

But once he tracked down the man who had dared to touch Chloe, the bastard would rue the day he was born.

"What did the doctor say?" he asked quietly, taking her long, slim fingers in his. Chloe was a lady to the tips of her toes, but her hands bore one or two faint scars and the marks of kitchen burns. As he'd come to learn, she'd worked hard over the years, first as a nurse and companion to an elderly woman, and then in running her large household. She'd been born into a genteel existence, but fate had decreed another type of life for her, and she was not a woman to shirk either work or responsibility.

Chloe gave his fingers a comforting squeeze but then carefully withdrew her hand. Dominic's heart twinged at the subtle distance she insisted on placing between them.

"You're not to worry." Her voice held a soft, comforting quality that reminded him of simpler times. Dominic's life had never been simple, but Chloe had always made it seem easy and uncomplicated. "It's a nasty little bump, but I felt only a momentary dizziness, more from shock than anything else. The doctor simply wants me to keep a cold compress on my head to take down the swelling."

Dominic gently pressed two fingers along her finely

carved jaw, turning her head slightly to examine the compress. Her skin was as soft as the inside of a rose petal, and he had to smother the urge to stroke her slim throat and white shoulder. Chloe was a year or so past her fortieth year, but her skin was still silky and unblemished by time.

One of her hands fluttered up to touch his shoulder before retreating. "Dominic, truly, there is no cause for concern, at least not about my silly head."

"I'm relieved to hear it, but clearly something is cause for concern, yes?"

Her lips pressed into a taut line, evidence of her unwillingness to answer him.

"Yes," Griffin interjected in a loud voice. "There is a great deal to be concerned about, and if Chloe insists on being so damned stubborn, then I'll get on with it."

"Really, my son, such language," Chloe huffed. "Whatever will Dominic think?"

Griffin let out a snort of disbelieving laughter, and even Justine couldn't hold back a smile.

"I know what Dominic thinks of me," Griffin said drily, "since he's made his views amply clear over the years. Although since I've married Justine his carping has diminished."

"I never carp," Dominic said, "I merely suggest. Now, I *suggest* you all stop trying to divert my attention and tell me what's going on."

Chloe sighed. "Very well, I'll tell you. As you have no doubt surmised, I had an unwelcome visitor this morning. He was the former fiancé of one of my girls."

Dominic raised a surprised brow. Chloe had gone out of her way to keep the nature of her work secure from prying eyes. Privacy was the reason she'd moved to Camberwell in the first place and had selected a manor house on a secluded country lane outside the village. The girls who came to her had an urgent need for secrecy in their desire to avoid scandal. They rarely left the manor's grounds and the house received few visitors. After the girls gave birth, Chloe found good families or sometimes relations of the girls to take the infants. That allowed the unfortunate mothers to return to their former lives, largely untainted by scandal.

It was a kindness denied to Chloe herself after the birth of Griffin.

"How did this man find you?" Dominic asked. "Did the girl you're sheltering tell him where she was staying?"

Chloe shook her head, then winced and carefully patted her bandage before answering. "No, Jane's terrified of Roger. It's one of the reasons she came to me. She broke off her engagement last month when he started to beat her. Fortunately, a family friend—my dressmaker, by a happy coincidence—was able to put Jane's parents in touch with me. She's been in my care for three weeks and has had no contact with the young man."

"You're sure of that?" Dominic asked. "Despite the abuse, young women sometimes manage to convince themselves the situation will improve. Might not Jane have sent him a message and be reluctant to tell you?"

Chloe's eyebrows went up on a delicate slant, as if she couldn't believe Dominic would question her conclusion. If he hadn't been so damn worried, he would have been tempted to laugh at her imperious glare.

"Some of them have little choice in the matter," Chloe retorted. "Most girls in Jane's condition have few options for survival."

"I know," Dominic said quietly. "Given that such is the case—"

"Such is *not* the case with Jane. Her family loves her and would keep her at home if they could. But we agreed it was safer for Jane to stay with me."

Griffin stirred. "How he found the place is a mystery, but let's put that aside for now. The point is, the swine not only found out where Jane was staying, he managed to get himself through the front door."

Chloe looked troubled. "Yes, that was unexpected. It's never happened before."

Dominic, Griffin, and Justine exchanged incredulous glances. Almost the exact same thing had happened only a few months earlier, when a group of thugs invaded Chloe's household to kidnap little Stephen, a baby under her care. That terrifying incident had forced Chloe out of hiding in order to ask for Griffin's and Dominic's help.

"Really, Mother?" Griffin asked with disbelief.

Chloe flapped her hand at him. "That situation was completely different."

"It sounds alarmingly similar," Dominic said. "I thought you'd improved your security since that particular breach."

"I have," Chloe said impatiently. "I hired the groom you recommended, and Hill's nephew has also started working for me. But Roger came alone, so I didn't perceive there to be a threat. We refused to let him see Jane, of course, despite his protestations. I tried to explain the situation to him, but he was immune to rational discourse."

"Did you confront him alone?" Dominic asked.

Again, he saw the slight hitch in her shoulders. "Why wouldn't I?"

"Because he was dangerous?" he replied with heavy sarcasm. At the moment, sarcasm was his only refuge against the frustration pulling at him. His observations over the last few months suggested that Chloe sometimes lacked a sufficient sense of self-preservation in her determination to protect her charges.

"I suppose I did miscalculate that," she admitted. "But as I said, he didn't initially seem threatening. Hill was right outside the door and my staff were within shouting distance."

She shook her head, clearly exasperated with herself. "How could I anticipate that Roger would be so foolish as to pull a pistol on me in my own house?"

Dominic carefully placed the delicate Spode teacup and saucer on the table beside him. "He pulled a *pistol* on you?" He managed to keep his voice low and steady, even though he imagined the top of his head was steaming like an erupting volcano.

"After he shoved her into the wall," Griffin cut in, his angular features pulled sharp with anger. "Fortunately, unlike my sainted mother, Hill had anticipated trouble. He and his nephew came charging to the rescue with pistols and cudgels, I'm happy to say."

Dominic pressed the tips of his fingers to his throbbing temples. "Chloe, this nonsense has to stop. You are placing both yourself and the girls in danger."

Her slender figure went rigid. "Are you suggesting this is somehow *my* fault?" She stared at him, her normally gentle eyes snapping with outrage.

"Of course not." Dominic tried not to let frustration color his voice. "But this sort of threat seems to be occurring with some frequency lately, and your security and privacy have clearly been compromised."

She continued to glare at him. Even though she looked heartbreakingly delicate, Chloe's determination and courage shimmered in the air around her. Dominic was torn between shaking some sense into her and getting down on his knees and declaring his undying devotion. She was the most magnificent woman he'd ever known.

"I will not abandon my girls or their babies, Dominic," she said. "You should know that by now."

"I'm not asking you to abandon them. I only want that you exercise an appropriate degree of caution."

Her eyes narrowed a bit more, but she held her tongue. Magnificent *and* stubborn.

"Tell me what happened next," he said with a sigh.

"Justine and I came onto the scene," Griffin said. "Young Roger wasn't stupid enough to threaten me."

Dominic's tension ticked down a notch. "Ah, then he recognized you?"

"He certainly did," Justine piped up from her seat next to Griffin. "I thought he was going to faint dead away when he realized whom he was dealing with."

She beamed at her husband with such obvious pride that Dominic had to hold back a smile. Justine had always been a reserved, proper young woman with a marked distaste for conflict and controversy. All that had changed when she met Griffin Steele.

Griffin snorted disdainfully, yet his dark eyes warmed with affection as he took his wife's hand. "Hardly, my love, but he understood the point I was trying to make."

"Punching a man in the nose will tend to do that," Justine said.

This time, Dominic did smile. "I take it you explained to this young man in your own inimitable fashion that further contact with Jane, Chloe, or any other member of this house would be most unwise."

"I did," Griffin said.

Chloe beamed at her son, her eyes shining with the love denied her for so many years. "And you did it quite splendidly, my dear. I was most impressed with your reasoning."

"Thank you," Griffin said in a dry voice. "Although I doubt it was my *reasoning* that got Roger out the door."

For the first time all afternoon, Dominic started to relax. "Then I would hope this is the end of the affair. If Roger—I begin to wonder if he has a last name—is aware of Griffin's reputation, surely he will know to steer clear of any further involvement."

When Chloe and Griffin exchanged a worried look,

Dominic felt an all-too-familiar sense of foreboding. "What aren't you telling me?"

Justine eyed her husband and mother-in-law, who both maintained an uncharacteristic and uncomfortable silence. She rolled her eyes and then gave Dominic a placating smile. "Well, Uncle Dominic, it's more about *who* Roger is, not what."

He forced himself to speak evenly. "Now I begin to understand why you've all been careful to avoid using Roger's last name. Justine, I would be grateful if you would share it with me."

"It's Campworth, Uncle Dominic." Justine grimaced sympathetically. "Yes, *that* Campworth. Roger is the nephew of Borden Campworth, the crime lord."

Chapter Two

Chloe knew it wasn't a good thing when Dominic looked stunned. For a man who dealt in the unexpected, he had a particular aversion to secrets and surprises.

"I know very well who Borden Campworth is," Dominic finally replied, dry as dust.

Oh, dear.

Chloe knew what that tone of voice meant too. Dominic was displeased, and the fault for that rested at her door.

Again.

She resisted the urge to pull the lap robe over her face and pretend that today hadn't happened. She'd spent a long night walking the floor with a fractious baby, the back of her head was throbbing from her bump, and her nerves were stretched thin as a skein of silk. Dominic's irritation was doing nothing to alleviate those conditions, either. That's why she'd resisted Griffin's decision to send for him in the first place. Chloe had known Dominic would react in his typically overprotective fashion, ordering everyone about and trying to fix everything. And as much as some part of her wished for him to do just that, she simply refused to add to the long list of burdens Dominic shouldered.

But if Griffin's *and* Dominic's reactions were any indication, Roger Campworth was indeed a problem. And that would make it Dominic's problem, since he would insist on shielding Chloe. It was one of the reasons she'd been loath to come out of hiding. It had been many years since she'd last seen Dominic, but she'd discreetly followed his career and recognized the kind of man he'd become. He'd want to take care of her, just like he took care of everyone in his life. Chloe simply couldn't permit that, not when she suspected his sense of obligation stemmed mostly from guilt—guilt that resulted from a foolish belief that *he* was at fault for the tragic mistake she'd made when little more than a child. Dominic believed he should have somehow prevented her seduction by Prince Ernest all those years ago and all the bad things that had subsequently followed.

But Chloe was entirely responsible for her own actions, and the idea that she was an object of pity or guilt to the best person she'd ever known filled her with despair.

She squared her shoulders, determined to regain control of the situation. "Surely you're exaggerating. Roger Campworth is a repellant individual, but I must believe his uncle's reputation has been blown out of proportion. And why would he even be interested in his nephew's, er, love life? I'm sure we have nothing to worry about."

Griffin snorted. "Go ahead and tell yourself that, Mother, if it makes you feel better."

Despite his annoying response, Chloe's insides glowed. Her reunion with her son had been difficult, but he'd surprised her by expending time and energy getting to know her and trying to understand why she'd hidden away for so long. Every time he called her "Mother," even in that sardonic voice of his, she felt lit from within, as if a star had fallen from the heavens and lodged itself in her chest.

"Griffin, there's no need to crab at your mother," Justine said. "She's just trying to help."

"And I'm just trying to keep her from getting murdered," Griffin retorted.

As soon as Dominic raised a hand the argument petered out. As usual, he dominated the room merely by standing there. He never raised his voice and his movements were always economical and self-restrained, but he was a tall, utterly masculine presence and could intimidate a room simply by lifting a disapproving eyebrow. He'd grown into a man of tremendous physical and intellectual power, a combination Chloe found both intoxicating and rather unnerving.

Dominic was not a cruel man, nor would he ever lift a hand to an innocent, but he was also no longer the expressive, eager boy she'd loved, one who never hid what was on his mind or in his heart. Now, he exercised iron control over his emotions, and most of the time she hadn't a clue what he was thinking, especially about her return to his life. Most days he appeared to be happy about it, but Chloe was never entirely sure.

"A little common sense would not go amiss in this discussion," Dominic said, "so let me try to inject some. Borden Campworth is a dangerous man, one of the very worst in London, as Griffin indicated."

She ignored the sudden pounding of her heart and tried to remain calm in the face of that daunting news. "I see. But it doesn't necessarily follow that Roger is just as dangerous."

Dominic's flinty green eyes widened. "He pulled a pistol on you, Chloe."

She winced. Clearly, that bump on her head was affecting her brain since she was in danger of sounding like a nitwit. "What I meant is that I don't think he intended to shoot me or anyone else. He was simply trying to intimidate me into allowing him to see Jane."

"He pushed you into a wall," he gritted out.

"Yes, he's a complete lout," she admitted. "And I'm not trying to be difficult or reckless. I just don't know much about him or his relationship with his uncle."

"Then perhaps we should ask the one person who does know," Dominic said.

Chloe clapped her hands together. "Of course! We need to talk to Jane. I don't know why I didn't think of it before."

With a rueful shake of his head, Dominic sat down next to her, reaching out to stroke her cheek. "I imagine it was the knock you took to the skull. You seem slightly rattled this morning."

His gentle touch and the affectionate tone in his deep voice almost undid her. Chloe had to clamp down on the impulse to lean into him and let the tears flow. Because she *had* been frightened when Roger pulled his weapon— more from the fury in his mud-colored eyes than from the gun barrel pointed at her chest. She truly believed he had no intention of shooting her, but she'd seen the ugly results of that sort of anger too many times, both in her life and the lives of the girls who sought her help. It was an anger that led to bruises and broken bones and lives ripped apart by fear.

Dominic withdrew his hand after a moment and stood. She immediately missed his warmth and his reassuring presence by her side.

"Justine," he said, "perhaps you could fetch Jane."

When Justine slipped from the room, Dominic went to the tea trolley to pour Chloe another cup of Earl Grey. He and Griffin fell into a discussion about a crime bill under consideration in Parliament, and Chloe knew they were giving her time to recover her poise.

As she watched the two men she loved so dearly, her heart swelled with both pride and more than a little sorrow. Griffin had overcome great adversity to build his fortune and find the woman he loved, while Dominic had matured into the finest man Chloe had ever met. She had missed all of that, left behind while they had made their way in the world without her.

That it had been her choice to be left behind offered her no comfort.

In a few minutes, Justine returned with sweet-faced, pretty Jane Clayton, her belly gently rounded in the middle stages of pregnancy. Jane was much too fine a girl to spend her life in the clutches of a man like Roger Campworth, and Chloe would do everything she could to make sure she and her baby would remain safe.

Jane's eyes rounded in dismay. "Oh, Mrs. Piper, I didn't know Roger hurt you." She threw herself to her knees, grabbed Chloe's hands, and burst into tears.

Chloe let her sob for a moment or two before drawing her up on the chaise. "Hush, Jane, I'm perfectly fine. There's no need to cry."

When Jane continued to weep, Chloe gave her a gentle shake. "That's not good for the baby, my dear. You must be calm."

Jane gave a watery sniff and nodded. Chloe gestured toward Dominic. "This is Sir Dominic Hunter. He's a magistrate, and he's not going to let anything happen to you or the baby, I promise."

The girl cast Dominic a dubious look, but he gave her an encouraging smile in return. Even dressed for driving in breeches, boots, and a plain dark coat, he was the picture of aristocratic elegance. It was not so much the style and cut of his clothing as the way he carried himself—with an innate dignity and restrained power. It had always struck

Chloe as the height of irony that Dominic, a butcher's son, had more true nobility than all the royal princes combined.

"Miss Clayton," Dominic said, "I wish the circumstances of our meeting were more pleasant, and I apologize for any distress our discussion may cause you. But we stand very much in need of your help."

It was the perfect thing to say. Dominic had a knack for reading people, and Jane was a good girl who liked to be useful.

"I'll do whatever I can to help, sir," she said earnestly.

Dominic smiled, his craggy features warming. Though he was a ruggedly handsome man in a forbidding kind of way, and often looked intimidating, it never failed to amaze Chloe how gentle and reassuring he was with women and children.

"Excellent," he said. "It would be very helpful if you could tell us about your relationship with Roger Campworth."

Haltingly, Jane told them how she'd met Roger at her father's haberdasher shop when he'd come to purchase a hat. An attractive and bold man, he'd quickly swept past her defenses. To their credit, Mr. and Mrs. Clayton had not abandoned Jane when she confessed she was with child. Despite their worries about his infamous uncle, they'd been greatly relieved when Roger announced his intention to marry her.

But relief had soured when the young lovers quarreled and Roger responded by beating Jane, leaving her bruised and terrified. When Mr. Clayton ordered Roger to stay away from his daughter, the brute had simply laughed. He'd threatened to bring the wrath of the Campworth gang down on the Claytons if they tried to prevent their marriage or deny his right to the baby.

Desperate to ensure her daughter's safety, Mrs. Clayton

had made enquiries that led her to Chloe, and she had then spirited Jane away to Camberwell in short order.

As they absorbed the ugly tale, Chloe struggled to contain her surprise. She'd known Roger Campworth was trouble, but this was the first she'd heard about his dangerous uncle. "Jane, why didn't you tell me about Roger's uncle?"

Jane's blue eyes grew teary. "Mamma and I were afraid you wouldn't take me. I'm so sorry, Mrs. Piper. I was sure Roger would never find me out here in the country."

Repressing a sigh, Chloe patted the girl's back. "I wouldn't dream of turning you away, Jane."

Dominic finally stirred. "Jane, how long have you been with Mrs. Piper?"

"Almost three weeks, sir."

He raised an eyebrow. "That long? I congratulate you on your security measures, Chloe. Evading Borden Campworth's detection for more than a few days is impressive."

Chloe didn't miss the hint of disapproval in Dominic's voice. Nor was she blind to the fact that her old friend had serious reservations about her work. But what else could she have done with her life? When she'd become pregnant at the age of fourteen, Chloe had been exiled to Yorkshire to live with a coldhearted relative. Then after Griffin was born, she'd been sent off to a school in Leeds where she'd been treated with harsh discipline and trained to be a servant. Only by the grace of God had she landed in the household of Mrs. Lamotte, a wealthy widow who took her under her wing. Mrs. Lamotte's kindness had fallen on Chloe's bruised, lonely heart like the sweetest of summer rains.

Mrs. Lamotte, a philanthropist and Quaker, had set Chloe on the path to her true calling and mission in life. Having no children or close relations, Mrs. Lamotte had left her considerable fortune to Chloe on the stipulation that she use the money to maintain a private charity to assist unmarried pregnant women. Because the kind widow had rescued Chloe from a life of shame and privation, how could she not carry out Mrs. Lamotte's plan for her?

"And what of your parents?" Dominic asked, returning his focus to Jane. "Has either of the Campworths threatened them?"

Jane twisted her fingers in her lap. "Not yet, but Roger won't hold off for long, especially now that he's found me." She started to tear up again. "I'm so afraid for my parents. I tried to make them come with me, but Papa said he couldn't close up the shop."

"Mr. Clayton has been struggling with debt these last few years," Chloe explained. "I offered to shelter the entire family, but he refused."

"Anything could happen to them, alone like that," Jane said with a heartbreaking quaver.

Chloe hugged her. "They're not alone, dear. We're going to help them, and everything's going to be fine."

Jane shook her head. "You don't truly know what Roger's like, and his uncle's even worse from what I hear."

"No, Mrs. Piper is quite right," Dominic said. "You're not to worry, Jane. We'll take care of the Campworths and make sure that no harm comes to your parents. You have my word on it."

Jane took a handkerchief from the pocket of her plain round gown and carefully dabbed her cheeks. Then she managed a shy smile for Dominic. "Thank you, sir. Is there anything you wish me to do?"

Dominic returned her smile with one so charming and kind that Chloe wondered how any girl—or woman— could help but fall madly in love with him. "For now, I only want you to rest and follow Mrs. Piper's instructions."

"That's very good advice," Chloe said past the odd

constriction in her throat. "I want you to go upstairs now and have a nap. I'll be up to see you later."

After Jane left the room, Chloe turned to Dominic. "My dear sir, who *is* this Borden Campworth? The way Jane talks about him—as does my son—he sounds a veritable monster."

"That's a tad dramatic even for me," Griffin objected. "I believe I called him a right sodding bastard."

"A regrettably accurate description," Dominic said. "Campworth runs one of the biggest criminal rings in London, dealing in extortion, blackmail, thievery, and the occasional kidnapping."

"Kidnapping?" Chloe echoed faintly.

"Unfortunately, yes," Griffin said. He gave Dominic a hard stare. "We need to do something about this."

"I'm aware of that," Dominic replied, looking imperious again. "But I need more information on which to base an effective plan of action."

Griffin's dark eyes narrowed to dangerous slits. "Then plan fast, or I'm going to take care of it myself."

Chloe jerked upright. "I don't want you putting yourself in harm's way, Griffin." Her heart thudded with sickening force at the thought of anything happening to her son.

The object of her concern snorted with disdain. "I've nothing to worry about from Borden Campworth."

Chloe shook her head. "Still—"

"There's no need to worry because I'll be taking care of Campworth myself," Dominic interjected. The grim smile curving up his mouth suggested he might even be looking forward to confronting the crime lord.

"That's just as bad as Griffin confronting him," Chloe blurted out. "Why can't Bow Street handle this, or a magistrate?"

Dominic's eyebrows went up in an incredulous lift. "Chloe, *I* am a magistrate."

"I meant another magistrate," she said, a bit desperately. "Not you."

Sitting quietly next to Griffin, Justine stirred. "Perhaps we should leave aside the question of confronting the Campworths for the moment. It seems to me the most pressing issue is getting Chloe and Jane to safety."

Chloe frowned. "I hardly expect Borden Campworth and his men to come skulking out to Camberwell. Besides, now that I know what we're dealing with, I'll take extra precautions."

"Extra precautions won't be enough," Dominic said bluntly. "You and Jane must leave Camberwell, today."

Chloe couldn't help bristling at his tone. She'd been driven from her home only a few months ago, and she had no intention of letting that happen again. Besides, who would take care of her girls and their babies if she left?

"I currently have several girls here, in addition to Jane," she said, "and I also have a two-month-old baby I need to place in an appropriate home. And then there's Stephen. Surely you are not suggesting I abandon them all to their unhappy fates?" Chloe cherished the safety of all those under her care, but Stephen, the baby she'd taken into her personal care some months ago, was particularly precious.

She knew she sounded strident, but who could blame her? She'd been forced to give up her own baby all those years ago, and she could never forgive herself for allowing that. How could she now abandon the innocents left in her care?

Griffin came to sit beside her. When he took her hand, Chloe's throat grew tight. "Mother, when we first met, you asked me to trust you and I did. Now I'm asking you to trust *me*. You need to do what Dominic says, for your safety and for Jane's."

For some unaccountable reason, Dominic scowled at

them. When she caught his eye, he wiped his expression clean.

"Did you hear what I said, *Chloe?*" Griffin asked in a pointed voice.

"Yes, my son. But I—"

He cut her off. "If Borden Campworth takes up his nephew's cause, he will think nothing of hurting you. Or worse."

When Chloe winced, Griffin gentled his voice. "How do you imagine Dominic and I would feel if that happened? We've only just found you. Do you think we want to lose you again?"

Chloe sighed. She supposed she was as susceptible to guilt and manipulation as any mother. "You're very good at that."

"What?"

"Manipulating women."

"Don't I know it," Justine muttered.

Griffin slanted his wife a roguish grin, and even Dominic couldn't hold back a smile.

"I am, but I also meant what I said. I would be . . . quite disturbed if anything happened to you, Mother."

"Very well," Chloe said, trying to capitulate with good grace. "I'm not convinced it's necessary, but I'm willing to err on the side of caution for Jane's sake."

"And for your other girls too," Dominic added. "Jane's presence here, and yours, could be a danger to them until Campworth is contained."

"Drat," Chloe muttered. "I hadn't thought of that. I certainly hope whoever speaks to this dreadful man will tell him to mind his own business."

"You may be sure I'll be doing that as soon as possible," Dominic said in a forbidding voice.

Chloe's anxiety spiked. She couldn't bear the idea of

Dominic placing himself in the line of fire any more than she could Griffin. "I don't think that's a good idea, particularly since you're quite agitated about the situation. Someone else needs to do it."

Griffin and Justine exchanged startled glances and then stared at her as if she were a lunatic.

"You think I'm agitated?" Dominic asked in a soft voice.

His quiet response didn't fool her. Still, she couldn't back down now. "I do."

"Then what would you like me to do? Knit some tea cozies and hope everything turns out for the best?" he asked.

"There's no need to be huffy about it," Chloe said. "I'm only thinking of your safety."

"Uncle Dominic, you should go with Chloe and Jane," Justine interjected. She leveled a winning smile at her godparent. "Why don't you take them to your manor house in Sussex? That way you can make sure Chloe and Jane are perfectly safe. It will be lovely there at this time of year, too."

Much to Chloe's surprise, Dominic didn't object. Instead, he regarded her with unnerving intensity then slowly nodded his head. "That's not a bad idea at all."

Griffin nodded in agreement and stood. "And I'll take care of Campworth."

Chloe had to repress a very bad word. "You'll do no such thing. Besides, I need you and Justine to look after the girls and Stephen while I'm gone. Stephen will cry himself sick without me if Justine isn't here to take care of him."

"Wonderful!" Justine exclaimed. "I've missed little Stephen very much. I'm sure Griffin would love to spend time with him, too."

Griffin looked appalled. "Yes, my heart leaps for joy at the prospect, as it does at the idea of spending an indefinite amount of time in a house full of babies and pregnant girls."

"Only two babies, dear, and you already know Stephen," Chloe said. "And it would set my heart greatly at ease if I knew you and Justine were looking after things."

"I suppose I don't have much choice in the matter," her son replied, eyeing his determined wife. "But then who's going to deal with Campworth?"

"Your cousin Aden St. George will do it," Dominic said. "He'll be only too happy to have a friendly chat with the man responsible for kidnapping his wife last year."

Justine stood up, clearly ready to take command. "Then everything's settled. Uncle Dominic will take Jane and Chloe to his manor house where everyone can have a nice little rest."

Chloe glanced at Dominic, startled by the heat in his emerald gaze as he studied her. When a satisfied smile curled up the edges of his mouth, she had the oddest feeling he had something else in mind besides "a nice little rest."

Chapter Three

Chloe walked through the old-fashioned but gracious entrance hall of Dominic's manor house, stopping to peek down one of the cross-corridors. The house was wrapped in a peaceful hush. Given Dominic's penchant for order and control, she wasn't surprised in the least.

She *had* been surprised, however, to learn he owned a country estate. Apparently, he used it primarily as a safe house for his agents. That saddened her for his sake, because it was a lovely old house that deserved to be enjoyed, and she would have preferred that Dominic used it as a retreat from the constant demands of his work.

But his life was clearly one of unending responsibility, and from what she could tell he drove himself beyond reasonable limits. Chloe understood that relentless drive because she shared it. Her work gave her purpose and made bearable the sacrifices she'd been forced to make, giving up those things that normally gave meaning to a woman's life.

Still, she hadn't had a choice in the matter, unlike Dominic. He'd *chosen* to devote himself to protecting his country and helping others, denying himself the domestic pleasures most men sought in wives and families. And she couldn't help suspecting that her unfortunate fate had played a role in his decision not to marry. The fact that Dominic remained a bachelor pleased her a great deal more than it should, and was something she was reluctant to admit even to herself.

She headed for the library, mentally reading herself a stern little lecture. Over the years, Dominic had never been far from her mind and she'd cherished the memories of their youthful, fierce attachment, clinging to it like a bright talisman during many a lonely night. But what she had felt back then was innocent affection and the loyalty of a foolish girl. The world had beaten such fancies out of her, and the time had passed where she could hope for something more than what she already had.

Especially if that something *more* was Dominic. Being with him was impossible for more reasons than Chloe cared to count—starting with the fact that she wasn't even sure how she felt about the man he'd become. In many ways he was a stranger to her, and a rather intimidating one. Better that they simply remain friends and leave unexplored the yearnings that troubled her in the dark hours before dawn.

Forcing a smile, Chloe opened the door and stepped into the library. Dominic sat behind a large rosewood desk in one corner of the spacious room, frowning down at a ledger book no doubt taken from the stack at his elbow. Mr. Cates, the butler, hovered behind him. Like all the staff she'd met that afternoon, Cates had impressed her with his quiet competence and clear devotion to his master. He and most of the others, in fact, had served Dominic in the Intelligence Service before retiring from their more hazardous duties.

Dominic looked up and smiled. "There you are. I'll be with you in a moment, my dear."

"Take your time. I'm happy to peruse your lovely books."

She wandered around the handsome room, half-listening to Dominic's rumbling voice as he spoke with Cates. The low tones washed over her, somehow both soothing and ruffling her nerves.

Pausing by one of the floor-to-ceiling bookcases that lined the room, Chloe covertly studied him. Dominic's face was aggressively male, all chiseled angles, dark, slashing brows, and a wide, firm mouth. His complexion was deeply tanned, as if he spent more time riding under the open sky than prowling the corridors of power. Deep grooves bracketed his lips, and faint white lines flared out from the corners of his piercing green eyes. Each feature was sharply distinctive, as if vying for prominence over the others. But they blended into a visage that was ruggedly noble, a face that spoke of years of discipline, sacrifice, and power. Chloe tried to reconcile that face—a mature one that wore every one of its forty-two years—with the open, youthful one she'd known as a girl.

Though too much had happened in the intervening years, she still couldn't help looking for traces of the boy who'd been her dearest friend. Occasionally she caught glimpses of that boy in the tilt of Dominic's lips or in the warmth in his eyes when he looked at her. But mostly she saw a man who carried too many burdens.

One of which, she suspected, was now her.

As if he sensed her watching him, he glanced up. His intent gaze brought a flush to her cheeks. But Chloe didn't look away. There was no point trying to hide from Dominic. He'd always had an odd knack for reading her, as if he possessed some uncanny emotional barometer that could measure her deepest thoughts and feelings.

One corner of his mouth ticked up in a wry smile. "What is it?"

She shook her head. "It's nothing. Please don't let me interrupt your work."

He studied her for a few moments, then nodded and turned back to Cates. Dominic was not one to waste words, another change she'd noted. As a lad, he'd hardly ever stopped talking, telling her about his studies, events in Kew Palace or at court, or the antics of the older princes. It had all seemed exotic and exciting to her, and she'd hung on his every word.

Chloe wished they could recapture that closeness. In so many ways, Dominic struck her as terribly alone—almost as alone as he'd been when she'd first met him as a charity case in the royal household, living on the fringes and not truly belonging to anyone.

Resuming her wanderings, she perused the spines of the impressive collection of books that lined the shelves. He had a smaller, well-stocked library in his town house in London, but the depth and breadth of this collection astonished her. She wondered if it had come with the house when he'd purchased it.

She'd just taken down a magnificent copy of Milton's *Paradise Regained* when Dominic dismissed his steward and rose from his desk. Her consciousness of him flared out like an invisible cobweb, thrumming with silent vibrations as he came near.

"Looking for a little light reading?" he asked sardonically, after glancing at the book.

She wrinkled her nose. "I suppose it's rather dull in comparison, but I do prefer it to *Paradise Lost*. I'm not particularly fond of depictions of sinners and hellfire, no matter how beautifully they're written."

"I imagine not." He took the book and slid it back onto the shelf. She'd had to stretch up to reach it, but he easily slipped it into place, his tall presence towering over her. Chloe was a long Meg, but Dominic topped her by several inches. His dominating presence flustered her in a way she found dangerously attractive.

"I'm impressed with your library," she said, trying to hide her nerves. "Did it come with the house, or did you acquire it on your own?"

He propped a broad shoulder against the bookcase, apparently relaxed but watching her with a thinly veiled intensity, as if he would peel away the years that had separated them. She didn't know whether to be alarmed or flattered by his regard, but she feared it had more to do with a misguided sense of responsibility for her than with a genuine interest in the woman she'd become.

"A little of both," he said. "I bought the house six years ago from a baronet who was consolidating his holdings. The collection was good to begin with, but I've been adding to it." The grooves beside his mouth deepened with a rueful smile. "Books are my true weakness, but I've no room in my town house for any major additions of a literary or frivolous nature. The overflow must come down here."

Chloe slapped a hand to her chest. "Good Lord, Dominic. Frivolous reading? Don't tell me you've resorted to Mrs. Radcliffe, or other novels of a sensational nature."

A wicked gleam lit up his eyes and sent a warning shiver down her spine. When he opened his mouth to answer, Chloe quickly pressed two fingers against his lips. "Don't you dare say anything outrageous, Dominic Hunter. You'll make me blush."

For a fraught moment, they stared at each other. His lips parted a fraction and she felt a whisper of hot breath against her fingertips. Chloe snatched her hand away, curling it into a fist so he wouldn't see how it trembled.

His eyes glittered with the strangest expression, but then his mouth twisted as if he couldn't decide whether to grimace or smile. "Heaven forfend I should cause you to blush, my dear."

Chloe mentally winced at the dry tone to his voice. She

turned away, somehow feeling as if she'd disappointed him. That had happened more than once these last few weeks, to her growing dismay. The worst part of it was that she didn't quite know the reasons why, nor could she bring herself to ask him.

She drifted along the bookshelves, pretending to study the titles he'd lined up with a historian's precision. "Dominic, how much time do you spend at this house?"

When he didn't answer, she glanced over her shoulder to see him standing where she'd left him. Then he slowly followed in her wake. "Usually no more than once or twice a year."

She frowned. "And yet you keep a full staff?"

The heaviness lifted from his expression. "I take it you manage all your own household and estate accounts, and quite ably too, I'd wager."

Chloe folded her hands. "Naturally."

She tried to maintain an expression of prim decorum, but Dominic's rare smiles always warmed her to her toes. She wished he would do it more often.

"Well, Madam Manager, I assure you that the house is put to good use. Not only as a safe house, but for government meetings that require privacy."

"Secrecy, you mean," she said drily.

Again, his grin warmed her. "Precisely. It's close enough to London to be convenient but well away from prying eyes."

She slowly nodded. "That makes sense, but . . ."

"But what?" he prompted, coming close. Chloe had to resist the impulse to rest her hand on his chest, seeking out his strong, steady heartbeat.

"It seems such a shame. It's a lovely house and deserves better." She tilted her head back to meet his eyes. "Don't you ever think about living here?"

His gaze bored into her, then moved around the room. "I thought at one time that I might retire here."

"And, now? Do you still think about that?"

He grimaced, clearly not happy with the turn of the conversation. "Not for a few years. I've been too busy, and . . ."

"And?"

He scowled, but seemed more embarrassed than annoyed.

"I'm hardly a good candidate to play the country gentleman, Chloe. What would I do in a place like this? Entertain the local gentry and ride to hounds? It was a ridiculous idea to begin with."

She nodded, deflated by that answer. "I understand. Country life must seem very boring, given the circles in which you move. I'm sorry we've forced you to rusticate when I'm sure you can barely spare the time. You've been very patient with us, and I want you to know how grateful I am."

His dark brows drew together in almost comical dismay. "Chloe, I didn't mean to suggest—"

She touched a hand to his forearm to interrupt. "Please don't apologize. I think I'll just go for a walk on the grounds, if you don't mind. They look quite lovely with the gardens just coming into bloom. I promise not to wander too far afield in case Jane needs me."

His lips pressed into a frustrated line, but then he nodded. "Of course. I'll be happy to show you the gardens."

She dredged up what she hoped was a firm, polite smile, one calibrated to show that he needn't worry about her. "That won't be necessary. I'm sure you have a great deal of work to do."

He took her arm and steered her toward the door. "That's true, but I'd much rather spend time with you."

She eyed him uncertainly. "Really?"

"Yes, really."

"Well, if you're sure."

He halted them before the door. "My dear friend," he said, sounding rather exasperated, "*never* doubt that I want to be with you. I've spent *years* missing you, and I'm not about to take for granted the opportunity we have to make up for lost time."

She peered at him, almost afraid to believe him. Dominic was a master at hiding his emotions, but right now he gazed at her with open warmth and affection. She wanted so much to respond, but she knew how dangerous it was to let down her guard and make herself vulnerable to countless risks. Like Dominic, she'd become skilled at repressing her feelings. The destruction of her world and the loss of everything she'd ever loved had only become tolerable after she'd walled away her emotions.

But that wall, the thing that had enabled her to function, was crumbling now that Dominic and Griffin were part of her life. And even though she was overjoyed at her reunion with them, the sense that she stood on the brink of losing control terrified her.

When Dominic lifted an eyebrow in challenge, Chloe felt her lips waver up in a reluctant smile. As treacherous as their renewed friendship could be to her guarded heart, she had no choice but to accept his return to her life and see it as a blessing and a second chance. She owed him that, at the very least.

"I should like that," she said.

"Good," he replied in a gruff voice.

He opened the door and took her hand, leading her toward the back of the house. She yielded to him and to the moment, enjoying the feel of her hand engulfed in his calloused palm. Dominic had wonderful hands—large, long-fingered, strong, and competent. Despite her best intentions, she'd wondered more than once over the last few weeks how those hands would feel upon her body.

Her naked body.

He glanced down at her. "Are you all right? You're looking rather flushed."

Mortified by her thoughts, she almost choked. "I'm perfectly fine. Why do you ask?"

He looked slightly puzzled. "As I said, you're flushed."

Chloe stifled a groan. Close proximity to Dominic obviously had a deleterious effect on her brain. "Sorry, my wits have clearly gone begging today. It must be all the excitement."

"And the fact that you were knocked on the head this morning."

Actually, she'd forgotten all about that, though it seemed as good an excuse as any. "Then a walk in the fresh air will be just the thing."

When Chloe started for the door, Dominic held on to her. "Not so fast, love. You need to put on a cloak."

"But it's a beautiful day," she protested, hiding a shiver at his casually delivered endearment. "And I'm still wearing my carriage dress."

"I'm not taking any chances with your health, Chloe, so don't argue with me." He snagged a woolen cloak from a hook by the door.

She heaved a dramatic sigh that brought a smile to his lips. Then she stood like an obedient child as he draped the cloak over her shoulders and drew it close around her neck.

"May I go out and play now, sir?" she asked.

He tipped her chin up and brushed a quick kiss on her forehead. Chloe felt the shock of that simple touch through every part of her body.

"No impertinence from you, Miss Steele," he said with mock reprimand.

She laughed as he steered her outside. No one had

called her *Miss Steele* in a very long time. When her uncle had convinced her to go along with his mad scheme to declare her dead—and wasn't *that* a decision she regretted—she'd adopted Piper, her mother's maiden name, consigning Steele to a fictional grave. Hearing Dominic call her by her proper name rolled back the years, making her feel almost young again.

He quickly led her through the kitchen garden, with its neatly laid out rows, guiding her to a gravel path that wandered along the back of the house. It led down into an old-fashioned, quaintly styled garden. Lilacs and other flowering bushes were starting to bloom, and daffodils and hyacinths danced in the late afternoon sun in a cheerful riot of color.

At first glance, parts of the garden appeared to be running wild, but then she noticed that the lawns and hedges had been carefully clipped. The grounds lacked the formal beauty of the current classical style but had a sweet, welcoming air. It was the kind of garden where children could romp, and young lovers could steal kisses under an arbor laced with blossoming vines.

They strolled along the path, engaging in idle chat about the domestic details of their lives. Though she would have expected him to be bored, he listened attentively, as if talking about her beloved rosebushes and her home-brewed recipes for morning sickness and colic were the most fascinating subjects in the world. It reminded her of their youth, when Dominic had focused so much of his attention on her. Despite his seemingly privileged position in the royal household, he'd in truth been nothing more than a lonely boy starved for affection.

Chloe had been lonely too. Her widowed father had been the kindest of men, but he'd been consumed by his duties as a royal tutor and his scholarly pursuits. Their busy housekeeper had done her best to play mother to

Chloe, but it hadn't really been enough. Not until she met Dominic, the day after her ninth birthday, had Chloe found her first true friend. For the next five years, they'd spent every free moment together. They'd read books in her father's study, roamed the gardens behind Kew Palace, and lived in a world of their own making.

Those innocent days had been the happiest of her life.

Dominic steered her to a wooden bench under a trellis covered with purple clematis. He remained standing, one booted foot on the seat and a forearm braced on his powerful thigh. He stared out over the garden, his expression brooding and almost grim.

"What are you thinking about?" she finally asked.

His gaze shifted slowly back to her as if returning from a great distance. "Do you ever wonder what life might have been like if we'd managed to run away and board that boat to America?"

She repressed a sigh, disinclined to bridge that painful topic. Looking back on those dreadful first days of her pregnancy still made her sick with shame and an incoherent sort of anger. Some days, she couldn't even sort out who her anger was directed at—herself, or almost every person she'd known as a child.

Chloe tried to make light of it. "I imagine I would have spent a good deal of time emptying my stomach all over you and anyone else nearby. I was dreadfully sick, if you recall."

A faint smile teased the corners of his stern mouth. "I wouldn't have minded. Not for you."

Returning his smile, she shook her head. Knowing Dominic, he probably wouldn't have minded if he'd spent the entire passage to America covered with the contents of her stomach.

They'd been so young and foolish to ever think they could run away, fleeing their troubles and everyone they'd known. But Chloe's father had planned to send her to Yorkshire to live with her uncle during and even after her pregnancy. The prospect of that separation had driven her and Dominic to desperate measures.

With a determination and competence beyond his years, Dominic had put their plan in motion by arranging for their journey by public coach to Southampton where they would catch a ship to start a new life. But Chloe had suffered a bout of morning sickness so severe that they'd been forced to take a room at a small inn along the way. It was there that Dominic's future guardian, Sir Anthony Tait, caught up with them and convinced them to return to Kew.

"I remember you telling me that," she said. Her heart ached at the memory. "But I wasn't strong enough for a sea voyage, Dominic. Not in my condition."

"I would have taken care of you," he said with a quiet conviction.

She stared at him, shocked that he believed their foolish plan could have worked. "Of course you would have tried, but you were only fourteen, Dominic. And neither of us had ever been farther from home than London. How could we have managed both a difficult journey and life in a country where we had no friends or means of support?"

He removed his booted foot from the bench and sat next to her. Even sitting he loomed over her, and Chloe could feel the pulses fluttering in her body.

"I'm not saying it would have been easy. I'm simply telling you I would have taken care of you and the baby. I would not have allowed anything or anyone to hurt you."

For the second time that day, tears swam across her vision. She forced them away, just like she forced away the impulse to give in to his fantasy—to believe that he could, in fact, keep all the bad things away from her.

"I know you would have tried to protect me until the last breath was squeezed from your body," she said.

The pain etched on his features tightened her chest. For one raw moment, she saw all the old sorrow in his gaze, all the heart-rending grief he'd felt over their separation. Dominic had cried that last day together, just like she had. The knowledge that she'd caused him so much pain was a burden she'd carried for a long time.

Chloe groped for his hand. "I'm sorry I was weak, Dominic. I wish more than anything that I'd been strong enough to stay with you, but I was so sick and so afraid."

His fingers closed over hers, holding her hand against his thigh.

"It wasn't your fault," he said, shaking his head. "It was mine. I should have found a better way. I should have been strong enough for both of us. Instead, I failed you when you most needed me."

She'd been staring at their interlaced fingers, trying to breathe through the pain, but his words brought her head up. "You were only a boy. There was nothing more you could have done, Dominic."

His gaze narrowed and he opened his mouth to argue with her.

"No," she said emphatically. "I forbid you to carry guilt for that wretched incident a moment longer. We were children, Dominic, and we had neither the means nor the maturity to properly deal with the situation. We should never have run away in the first place. I knew it was wrong and foolish of us."

His hand tightened briefly on hers, then he let go. She could sense how little he liked her answer.

"Besides," she added, "Sir Anthony would never have allowed us to keep going. There was no other choice but to return home to Kew."

He cut her an enigmatic glance, his face once more set in stone. "If you knew it was wrong to run, why did you agree to go?"

She clamped down on the impulse to fire up at him for making her dredge up all the old pain. Dominic was never cruel, especially to her. She might have been separated from him for twenty-eight years, but she knew that essential part of him had not changed. He obviously needed something from this discussion, and from her.

She clasped her hands together and propped them under her chin as she struggled to compose an answer. Dominic waited, so still and silent he might have been carved from the same marble as the bench. But an odd disturbance seemed to seethe in the air around him. She could imagine it lifting the hair from her neck and swirling her skirt around her legs.

"I did it for you. For us," she finally said.

His gaze held hers with implacable intensity. "Then why did you give up so easily, Chloe? Why did you give up on us?"

She struggled to find the words that might satisfy him. "Because of my father. He already felt so betrayed by my loss of virtue. How could I inflict yet more pain on him by leaving the country, never to see him again?"

Dominic's eyes blazed with emerald fire. "You didn't betray your father. Cumberland seduced *you,* not the other way around. You were an innocent."

"I'm not disputing that." Her mild response seemed to throw him back a bit. "I'm simply trying to explain my reasons."

He gave a tight, grudging nod.

"Papa was shattered when he found out I was pregnant," she continued. "His initial disappointment in me—and in *himself* for failing me—was so intense that I couldn't bear it. It made me think it might be better if I just disappeared from his life." She shook her head, still amazed at her youthful naïveté. "But running away just made everything worse for him. It brought on one of his attacks, and he never truly recovered."

In fact, her father had died only a few months later after Chloe was exiled to Yorkshire.

"It sounds as if you've been blaming yourself for your father's death for all these years," Dominic said.

She frowned at his tone. "Well, I don't know who else is to blame if not me."

He rested his forehead on his palm and muttered a curse under his breath.

Chloe's temper began to stir. "Yes, I know I've been a disappointment to you. Well, that's nothing new. I was a disappointment to my father and almost everyone else in my life. Believe me, Dominic, I've been told that more times than I can count. I don't need a reminder from you."

Dominic jerked his head up. "My only true disappointment, Chloe, is that you didn't trust me enough to reach out to me when you finally could. Christ! How could you think that I wouldn't want to see you again? You mean the world to me—you always have."

His anger and sorrow, bleached to a pale, bitter poison by time, crawled through her veins. She didn't blame him, but how could she ever explain her reasons?

"I'm sorry," she whispered. "You must think me an utter coward."

"I think nothing of the sort, and you know it. I only wish to understand why you would turn your back on the people who love you."

Frustration pulled her throat tight. "I don't think I'm able to explain it in a way that would make sense to you. I'm sorry." The truth was, some days she barely understood it herself.

He leaned into her then, his gaze hot with a need that almost stopped her heart.

"Try me," he gritted out.

She truly wanted to, but the weight of past failures bore down on her like the descending arc of an executioner's blade.

"I can't," she blurted out. "I'm sorry."

Chloe pushed him away and stumbled to her feet. Hurrying along the gravel path, she forced herself not to look back. If she did, she would surely see the evidence writ large on Dominic's face that she'd failed him once again.

Chapter Four

Dominic braced a hand on the mantel and stared down at the fire, trying to ignore the generous brandy Cates had poured out for him. As much as he'd like to get royally drunk, he wouldn't give in to temptation. Not until the threat to Chloe and Jane had passed, at any rate. Besides, getting cup-shot would hardly fix his problems with the lovely Mrs. Piper. Their stroll in the garden had started out promisingly but then turned into a debacle of his making. He knew how reticent she was about her past, and for the last month he'd respected her privacy, refraining from asking for details about her life. He'd told himself that he had no business resenting any of her decisions, either now or in the years gone by. And he'd even convinced himself that was true.

Until today. That was when all his submerged resentments had come roaring to the surface, surprising him with their force. When he thought of how he'd snapped at her, giving in to anger, he almost cringed with shame.

He scrubbed a weary hand over his face, wincing at the image of her distraught expression as she backed away from him, convinced she'd disappointed him again. She hadn't, of course. Frustrate, yes. Even infuriate. But given the person she'd become in the face of such adversity, he could only admire her. His disappointment was all with himself—for not understanding her and for failing to give her the time she needed to absorb the realities of her new life.

But even worse than his disgust with his own behavior was the heartache he felt at the knowledge that Chloe blamed herself for the fate she'd been dealt. Besides guilt over her pregnancy, she obviously felt responsible for her father's premature death, though no one who truly knew the situation would believe that. Unfortunately, his clumsy handling of the situation today had only driven her away. She hadn't even joined him for dinner, preferring instead to have a tray upstairs with Jane. For the immediate future, it seemed, his plans to use this trip as an opportunity to finally seduce the woman he loved into his bed—and into his life—must be placed on temporary hiatus.

Sighing, he picked up his untouched brandy and headed toward his desk. His collection of books held no interest for him tonight, nor would they help him get to sleep. Given that he had no chance of seeing Chloe before tomorrow, he might as well work.

Halfway through a report from one of his agents, he heard a murmur of quiet voices in the hall and then the door to the library opening. Frowning, he glanced up only to feel his mouth drop open when Chloe entered the room carrying a tea tray.

"Thank you, Cates," she said to the butler, holding the door. "I'll ring if we need you."

Dominic rose as she crossed the room, straight-backed and graceful as she carried the heavy tea service to his desk. Chloe sometimes gave an impression of fragility despite her taller-than-average height, but her slim body had a wiry strength born of years of hard work.

"Good evening, my dear." He relieved her of the tray

and put it on his desk. "I would have thought you already in bed by now."

"I generally keep country hours, but it's barely nine o'clock," she said with a shy smile. "I thought you might like some tea."

Even though she looked utterly composed, he sensed her nervousness. "You're right," he said, studying the delicate wash of pink on her cheeks. "But you were busy with Jane, and you must be exhausted."

Her mouth pulled into a little grimace. "It's kind of you to phrase it so delicately when we both know I was hiding from you."

He hesitated, caught off-guard by her blunt speech. "I'm sure you had your reasons."

She shook her head. "There was no excuse for my dreadful behavior this afternoon. I didn't stand a chance of sleeping tonight unless I came down and spoke with you."

Dominic backed up a step with mock alarm. "Oh, God, don't tell me you're going to apologize again. I swear, Chloe, you'll reduce me to a bundle of nerves if you do."

She stared at him for a second, then she burst into laughter. "Actually, I was, although I understand how irritating it can be when someone constantly apologizes. But I *do* owe you an apology, Dominic. I was a terrible coward this afternoon, and I'm so sorry for it."

"Chloe," he began, starting to feel a little desperate.

"Let me pour you a nice cup of tea," she said in a soothing voice. "Then we can talk."

He crossed his arms over his chest. "My dear, you do not need to try to manage me."

"The way you always try to manage me?" she asked drily.

"I am entirely innocent of that accusation, madam."

Trying to hide her smile—not very successfully—Chloe placed his cup of tea on the small table between the two high-backed chairs in front of the fire. With a funny little sigh that pierced Dominic's heart, she subsided into one of the chairs.

"No tea for you?" he asked.

"No, but if you don't intend to finish that brandy, you can give it to me."

He retrieved the glass from his desk. "Careful," he said after she took a generous sip. "You don't want to get drunk."

"Maybe I do," she muttered, cradling the glass in her slender fingers.

He sat in the other chair. "Are you in need of some liquid courage?"

She let out a dramatic sigh. "You've always been able to anticipate my thoughts, haven't you?"

"Chloe, you need never be afraid to say anything to me. And if anyone should apologize for this afternoon's discussion, it is I. I was a boorish, impatient fool. Feel free to box my ears if I behave like that again."

She leaned forward, her expression terribly earnest. "But that's just it, Dominic. You had every right to be impatient. I've been running away and hiding for almost as long as I can remember. It's become a habit, and not a good one."

He leaned close, too. "My sweet, no one could blame you—not after all the harm that's been done to you. I only wish I could make all that ugliness disappear."

She blinked several times, her gaze soft and misty-eyed, but then she unleashed a dazzling smile. It ripped his heart from his chest and dropped it at her feet. "I don't know what I've done to deserve so generous and kind a friend. You quite humble me, Dominic."

Christ.

She was destroying him, and yet she had no idea. That *she* should feel humbled after everything she'd suffered made him want to tear the world apart and make it over for her.

"That's simply nonsense," he said gruffly. "Now, was there something you specifically wanted to tell me?"

She smiled. "Not specifically, no. But what I'd like you to do is ask me whatever question you want. I promise to answer as honestly as I can."

His mind went momentarily blank. Then he had to struggle through a sudden swarm of questions flooding his brain.

"Anything," she gently repeated.

He sucked in a breath. There was so much he wanted to know, starting with how she truly felt about him. But he suspected he wasn't yet ready to hear that answer. "Very well. I never fully understood why you agreed to your uncle's demented scheme to fake your death after you finished your schooling."

Her quiet sigh held legions of sorrow. "Yes, I know it must seem inexplicable. But the simple answer is that Uncle Bartholomew insisted it would be best for Griffin. He was convinced that any contact with me would fatally taint my son with my fallen nature—"

"Bastard," Dominic muttered.

"Indeed. But at the time, all I had was the hope that Griffin would be spared my shame. My uncle said that if I insisted on being part of Griffin's life, he'd refuse responsibility for the both of us. I was only seventeen and would have been alone in the world. How could I possibly take care of myself and a little boy?"

Dominic straightened. "But you had me, as well as Sir Anthony and Lady Tait. They would have been happy to take you in."

She flinched as if he'd just slapped her. "Dominic, I hadn't heard from any of you for almost two years. I wrote whenever I had the chance, but after the first few replies, you never wrote again. Neither did Lady Tait. What other assumption could I make but that you had no desire to maintain contact?"

Dominic frowned. "I wrote to you every week, Chloe, without fail. It was you who stopped corresponding with me."

For an infernally long moment, they stared at each other. Then bitterness flattened Chloe's mouth into a tight line. "Uncle Bartholomew must have told the staff at my school to intercept our letters." She shook her head. "What an unhappy, angry man he was to deny me even that consolation."

Dominic spat out another, riper term for the old bastard. Chloe's eyes widened with shock, but she let out a reluctant laugh. "Well, I think I must agree with you, at least in this case."

Disbelief pushed him to his feet. "I can't believe I didn't demand that Sir Anthony take me to Leeds to see you. He said it was best to wait until you finished school before attempting to contact you again, but then we received word that you'd died of a fever." He stared down into her beautiful, haunted gaze. "Chloe, you thought you were all alone when the opposite was true."

He turned away, not wanting her to see how his hands shook with guilt-fueled rage. As he stared blindly into the fire, he heard the rustle of her soft skirts before she rested a gentle hand on his back.

"The fault lies only with my uncle, Dominic. He was a hateful, bitter man who caused us all a great deal of harm. But he's gone now, and it serves no purpose to give in to anger and regret."

Dominic slowly unclenched his hands and turned to face her. "I wish I could accept that as easily as you."

She shrugged, her calm gravity restored. "I've had many years to reconcile myself to my circumstances, Dominic. It was how I survived."

He understood that choice, at least for a young girl who thought herself alone in the world. But what about later? "You did more than survive. You ended up a wealthy woman who had a great deal of control over her fate. Once you were free, why didn't you try to take Griffin back or contact me?"

He finally acknowledged that he wasn't just angry with himself, or even with her uncle. He was angry with Chloe for giving up on him. On *them*.

She seemed in perfect control as she studied him, but Dominic sensed her mentally backing away. "Don't do that, Chloe. Don't retreat from me again."

She blinked, clearly surprised, but then she gave a cautious nod. "Yes, of course. That is what I do. I apologize. Please sit down and I'll do my best to explain it to you."

When he held his ground, she flashed him a rueful smile. "*Please* sit, Dominic. You can be quite unnerving when you loom over me in that intimidating fashion. It's not necessary to manipulate me in order to extract information."

He felt a flush creep up his neck. "Sorry, I didn't mean to do that."

She let out a soft laugh. "I think part of you wants to do exactly that, but we'll let it pass for now."

Unfortunately, she was probably right. In his line of work, intimidation and manipulation were his stock-in-trade. Chloe, however, was the last person he wanted to bully into compliance.

"I did try to see Griffin after I came into Mrs. Lamotte's inheritance," she said as they resumed their seats. "I wrote to Uncle Bartholomew, pleading for a visit. But he was adamant that I stay away. He said Griffin was perfectly happy without a mother, and that the shock of my reappearance in his life could only be harmful."

"Not an unexpected response, was it?"

"Believe it or not, I was surprised by it. I had hoped that with the passage of years, my uncle would have forgiven me. Such was certainly not the case."

The pain in her fawn-colored eyes made him want to snatch her onto his lap to comfort her. "Why didn't you push the bastard?"

"I worried that he would make a fuss and feared it might result in some ugly gossip that might reach Griffin's ears. Instead, I decided to wait to make contact until my uncle sent him away to school, which he promised to do— at my expense. That way, I would have better control over the circumstances of our meeting."

Dominic nodded. "But then he died and Griffin ran away to London."

She grimaced. "It took me a year—with the aid of a very expensive Runner—to find my son. By that time, he was working at The Cormorant and you had your eye on him. It appeared that Griffin was settled in his new life and, from what I was able to glean, he was adamant in refusing help from you or anyone else."

When he remained silent, her eyes pleaded with him. "Truthfully, I didn't know what to do. Griffin was fifteen years old and believed me dead. What would be the consequences of my sudden resurrection? Given what he'd been told about me, would he even wish to know me or face the scandal that would result if my identity became widely known?"

Her beautiful mouth twisted with a delicate sneer. Dominic hated seeing that expression on her face.

"Just think of it," she continued, "the Duke of Cumberland's former lover rising from the dead. I can't begin to imagine the public reaction to *that* bit of news. If Griffin had remained in the Yorkshire countryside, we might have been able to avoid damaging gossip. But in London . . . well, it seemed better to remain at a careful distance. Close enough to keep an eye on Griffin but far enough away to prevent him or anyone else from stumbling onto my secret."

"You were never Cumberland's lover," Dominic growled. "He seduced you once when you were little more than a child. Besides, Griffin already knew by then that you were alive, since your uncle had confessed to the entire ruse on his deathbed."

"Yes, but I didn't know that," she said in a calm tone.

Her controlled manner spiked his frustration, but he reined himself in. He knew how difficult this conversation must be for her.

"I can appreciate your logic regarding Griffin," he finally said. "But why did you never attempt to contact me? Surely you didn't think I'd gossip about your scandalous past." He invested that last phrase with heavy irony.

She let out another heavy sigh. "No. But you had moved on with your life, and I still believed you didn't know I was alive. You seemed consumed by your work and, as far as I could tell, spent a great deal of time in Portugal and Spain. It seemed wrong to burden you with my situation given the difficulties in the Peninsular War I knew you must be dealing with."

"Bloody hell, you should have been a spy. Is there anything you didn't find out about me?"

She flashed a cheeky grin. "A great deal, in fact. But I did know that you moved in the highest circles." Her grin faded. "Those circles included considerable contact with the Court of St. James and with some of the royal family."

That, of course, was at the heart of the problem. It was

the reason she'd stayed away from him and from the other people in her past. "You wanted to avoid Cumberland, and you feared knowing me would bring you into that circle."

She paused, as if running through answers in her head. "Partly," she finally said.

He leaned forward, bracing his hands on his knees. "Did you really think I would do that to you? Force you to spend a moment in that bastard's company?"

She shook her head, but her lips remained firmly closed.

"What, then?" he exclaimed in exasperation.

"I was afraid of the potential for scandal. It would have made my work more difficult, for one thing. But honesty compels me to admit that I was, quite simply, afraid of drawing so much attention. I know that makes me a coward, and I'm sure you must be terribly disappointed in me." She wrinkled her nose at him, as if trying to make light of the heartbreaking confession.

"Chloe, you have more courage than anyone I've ever known. You were betrayed and abandoned by your family and torn from those who would have protected you. Despite that, you've created an admirable life." He took her slender fingers. They were cold and shook slightly in his hand. "I would have revealed none of your secrets," he said. "Never."

She squeezed his hand. "I'm sorry I didn't trust you, Dominic, but I'd lost the knack for it, you see. I know that's not much of an excuse, but it's the truth."

"And do you trust me now?" he asked quietly.

When she withdrew her hand, his gut clenched.

"Yes, of course," she said. "But . . ."

"But what?" he prompted.

"I don't really know you anymore." She blew out a frustrated breath. "And you don't know me, not after so many years. It's disconcerting, knowing how much we've both changed."

Dominic wanted to argue that she hadn't truly changed. She was still the sweet, loving person she'd been as a girl, kind and generous to the core. But that wasn't what she needed to hear.

"What do you want to know about *me,* Chloe?"

She seemed to stop breathing for several fraught seconds. Then she folded her hands primly in her lap and looked him straight in the eye. "Have you been involved in many relationships, Dominic? With women, I mean." Though her voice ended with an uncharacteristic break, she held his gaze.

"Do you mean have I ever had a mistress?" he asked, testing her boundaries.

Her cheeks pinked a bit. "Yes, or availed yourself of other opportunities."

He frowned. "I'm not sure what you mean by that."

"I should think it obvious. My son ran a gaming house and brothel, and you were no stranger to either establishment."

His mouth sagged open. "How the hell did you find that out?"

Though she waved a dismissive hand, her cheeks were now more red than pink. "Please just answer the question."

He was torn between satisfaction at the jealous tone to her voice and irritation that she thought he would sleep with prostitutes. Still, a great many men in the *ton* did so without second thought, so he supposed he couldn't blame her.

"No, Chloe, I never slept with any of the girls at The Golden Tie or any other brothel, for that matter. Nor have I ever kept a mistress."

She exhaled a relieved breath, but then her eyes went

wide. "Do you mean to say you're a . . ." Her voice climbed into a squeaky register before breaking off.

Perplexed, he stared at her for a few seconds before understanding thundered through his brain. "Good God, Chloe, I'm not a saint."

She winced. "Of course not. I was silly to even think it, much less ask. Forgive me."

He studied her, trying to deduce the best way forward. Chloe was obviously trying to explore what might exist between them, but she was having trouble getting there, too hampered by her past hurts to see a clear path forward.

"As I said, I don't claim to be a saint," he repeated quietly, "but I've done my best not to take advantage of women."

She gave a slow nod. "I should have known that, of course. Please forgive me for assuming otherwise."

"You have nothing for which to apologize. Is there anything else you'd like to ask me?"

Chloe hesitated for a few moments, as if gathering her courage before asking the next question. "Why have you never married?"

"Because I couldn't imagine loving anyone else but you, and the news of your death simply tore me apart. Then, as you noted, I threw myself into my work. I had neither the time nor the inclination to think of marriage or a family." He paused to gauge her reaction, taking in her wide-eyed gaze. "And then Griffin told me you were still alive. After that, there was never a possibility of anyone else."

She sucked in a shocked inhalation, her gentle curves pressing against her trim-fitting bodice. Dominic's muscles coiled tight with an instinctive reaction. His life had been leading inexorably up to this moment, and he practically shook with desire and longing.

When the tip of her pink tongue swept over her lips, he

had to hold back a groan. What he couldn't hold back was the swell of his cock at the thought of Chloe, naked and wrapped around him. "Sweetheart, surely you've always known how I felt about you?"

She raised a trembling hand to her forehead. "It's been so many years, and we were just children."

"We're not children anymore."

Her nervous laughter echoed softly in the quiet. "No, we're certainly not."

But like her, Dominic was fully aware of the passage of years and what might have happened in the meantime.

She frowned. "What is it?"

"What of you?" he asked, dreading the answer. "Have there been men in your life?"

Her eyebrows winged up. "You mean lovers? Truly, Dominic, what would have been the benefit for me in that?"

He could think of a few, but clearly they had not occurred to her. "We're not all bounders and reprobates, Chloe. Some of us want nothing more than to cherish the women in our lives."

She stared at him, her body straight and unmoving, her face pale and still. But her eyes blazed almost golden in the firelight that washed over her. "Is that what you want, Dominic? To cherish me?" Her voice was a sweet mix of uncertainty and longing that arrowed straight into his heart.

"I've never stopped loving you," he rasped. "And that will never change. But now I want more. I want what any man wants from the woman he loves."

The muscles in her throat rippled as she swallowed. The tense, high set to her shoulders reminded him of how difficult this must be for her.

"I know you're afraid," he said gently. "Afraid of opening yourself up to another man after everything you've been through—"

He broke off, stunned by her sudden, dazzling smile. She slipped from her chair and came to her knees before him, resting her hands on his thighs.

"Dominic, do shut up," she ordered in a gruff little voice. "And after you've done that, please kiss me."

Chapter Five

Dominic simply gaped at her, and for several horrible moments Chloe wondered if she'd offended him. After all, a lady did not throw herself at a man's feet, all but demanding he make love to her.

But then his starkly handsome face came to life. His emerald eyes glittered with heat and laughter, and his mouth curled up in a triumphant smile. That look on any other man's face would have sent her running for the hills, but on Dominic's it made her muscles go delightfully weak.

"Your wish is my command, Mrs. Piper," he said in a darkly amused voice.

Given the hungry look in his eyes, she half-expected him to swoop down and carry her away. Instead, he lifted gentle hands to cradle her cheeks. His gaze roamed her face, lingering there, and she suddenly had to blink away tears.

"Dominic?" she whispered as her hands fluttered up to rest on his, strong and warm beneath her fingertips.

"I've waited a lifetime for this, Chloe. I want to savor every moment." But then one corner of his mouth kicked up with a rueful twist. "And I must admit to being completely terrified that I'm going to frighten you. You've been through so much, Chloe. I don't want to—"

She stretched up to press a kiss to the hard slash of his jaw. "Don't be silly. I know I'm not very experienced—" She paused when his eyebrow lifted and gave him a sheepish smile. "Well, I have *no* experience, except that one time—"

He let his forehead rest against hers. "Trust me, love, that *one time* doesn't count, at least not in this situation. And I beg you to refrain from any comparisons unless you wish to unman me completely."

Chloe had never thought she could find anything amusing in the ugly incident that had scorched the landscape of her life, but she smiled now at the aggrieved tone in Dominic's voice. She slipped her arms around his neck, touching her nose to his. "That would certainly be an unfortunate end to the proceedings."

He drew back to search her face. "I truly don't mean to make light of your past, my darling, and I would shoot myself before I did anything to hurt you. But I want tonight to be a new beginning. For both of us."

"Dominic, you could never hurt me." Her heart ached at the tenderness in his gaze. "Now, I believe you're supposed to be doing something, or do you need a reminder?"

A slow smile curled up the edges of his oh-so-enticing mouth. "Ah, yes. Kissing you."

Then his warm lips were on hers, and Chloe almost collapsed forward onto his lap. He gently teased and tasted her with a soft, unhurried rhythm. In so many ways it was her first kiss, and she'd been waiting an eternity for it. She laced her fingers around his neck, cautiously relaxing into his strength and heat.

His lips wandered from her mouth to trail across her cheekbone and nuzzle the shivery part below her ear. A slow, provocative wonder unfurled inside her. Dominic was right. This was *nothing* like the awkward, rushed encounter of her youth, a painful interlude that had left her stricken and ashamed. Even Prince Ernest had been mortified by what had happened between them, red-faced in the aftermath as he stumbled over a clumsy, defensive apology. It had been tragic and stupid, and Chloe had thought she'd never want another man to touch her again.

Until two months ago, that is, when Dominic had blazed back into her life and reminded her that she was no longer a frightened girl but a woman, with a woman's emotions and needs and a desire for love so surprising and fierce it almost frightened her.

It took her a moment to realize he'd pulled back. She blinked up at him, missing the heat of his kiss.

"I must be making a botch of this," he said, tapping her nose. "Your mind is wandering." He spoke in a light, teasing tone, but she couldn't mistake the concern in his gaze.

She broke into a smile, swept up by a radiantly clear sense of freedom that had nothing to do with money or control and everything to do with him. "Actually, you're doing splendidly. Please continue."

When he laughed, it seemed like the sun rising on a glorious midsummer morn. Over the years, she'd cherished memories of the boy he'd been—warm, open, and her best friend and staunchest defender. He was still all those things, but now he was so much more. He had become a powerful and utterly captivating man who dazzled her to the tips of her fingers and toes.

A moment later, he had her gasping as he rose to his feet in one fluid motion and lifted her from her knees up into his arms. He cradled her against his broad chest and started for the door.

"Um, where are we going?" she asked.

"To my bedroom."

"Oh, well, that's all right, I suppose." She mentally winced at her ridiculous answer.

He jiggled her as he reached for the door. "Did you really think I would make love to you on the floor of my study?"

"I hadn't thought that far ahead," she confessed.

He carried her into the softly lit hall but came to a halt at the foot of the staircase. He studied her face, his gaze so intent she imagined he would dive into her soul if he could, tearing any barriers that lingered between them.

"Is this truly what you want, Chloe? I promise I'll do anything you ask."

She nodded, rejecting the old fears that sought to hold her back. "It *is* truly what I want, but it's all new to me. I'm not entirely sure how to act."

He started rapidly up the stairs, not impeded in the least by her weight. "It's new to me too, I assure you. I can only hope you'll be gentle with me."

Startled, she let out a laugh then slapped a horrified hand over her mouth.

"What's wrong?" Dominic asked.

"What if someone hears us?" she hissed. "What will your servants think?"

"They think whatever I tell them to think. Besides, they all know how I feel about you."

She peered at him as he strode down a hall branching off from the top of the staircase. "They do?"

Dominic stopped outside the last door at the end of the corridor. "I've been looking for you for a very long time. That hasn't been a secret, at least not to my personal staff."

A stab of guilt kept her lips pressed together. She hated the suffering she'd caused Dominic and her son over the years. Griffin had given up searching for her long ago, but not Dominic. He'd kept grimly to the task, eschewing love and marriage as he searched. Though she should be flattered by his single-minded dedication, instead it saddened her and, if truth be told, unnerved her just a bit.

He opened the door and set her down, then kicked the

door shut behind him and took her gently by the shoulders. "You're not to feel guilty about that, Chloe. It was my choice, and I don't regret it."

She scowled up at him. "How did you know what I was thinking?"

"You have a very expressive face when you're not putting your guard up. Besides, I do know a little about how you think."

"Well, that's hardly fair," she grumbled, "since most times I haven't a clue what you're thinking."

He slid his hands to her waist and pulled her close, his gaze turning smoky with desire. "I would bet you can deduce exactly what I'm thinking at this moment."

When she felt the press of his erection against her belly, her eyes went wide. "Ah . . . so it would seem."

He let out a soft laugh. "Come to bed, love. I have a powerful need for you."

She blushed but went willingly when he led her across the large bedroom. She cast a swift glance around, taking in the elegant, masculine furnishings, the expensive wool carpet under her feet, and the massive, four-poster bed. With its wealth of pillows and thick, brocaded coverlet in antique gold, it looked almost decadent and rather unexpected for a man like Dominic.

For an unwilling moment, she couldn't help wondering if he'd ever shared that bed with another woman.

She squeaked when he picked her up and plopped her onto the high mattress, then bent to meet her eye to eye. "Just so you know," he said, "you're the first woman I've ever taken to this bed."

Chloe swatted at his chest. "Stop doing that!"

He laughed, then crouched down before her. "And you stop worrying." He swiftly unbuttoned her half boots and slipped them off. "Just forget the rest of the world for now.

We're completely alone at this end of the house, and no one will bother us."

She jumped a bit when his hands slid up under her skirts.

"This night is for you, Chloe," he said. "More than anything, I want you to enjoy it."

He looked so handsome kneeling before her, so focused on her, that she couldn't hold back a tremulous smile. No one had ever felt for her with such intensity—no one but Dominic. The wonder of it stole her breath. That a man like him would wait for her, would still love her despite the pain she'd caused him, was truly a miracle.

There had been precious few miracles in Chloe's life.

"I would like that very much," she whispered.

"Good."

He quickly untied her garters and slipped off her stockings. Then he went to stoke the fire, stopping to extinguish the lamp on the bedside table. Chloe hid a smile, knowing he was making every effort to preserve her modesty. It spoke to the generosity that was so much a part of his nature.

Dominic swung her legs up onto the bed and gently rolled her onto her belly. After unbuttoning her dress, he unlaced her stays and rolled her back to face him. "Time to get you out of that dress."

"I'm perfectly capable of undressing myself, you know," she spluttered, choking on laughter and nerves.

"I've been dreaming of undressing you for weeks," he said with a theatrical growl. "You're not to deny me that pleasure."

"It's a good thing I didn't know, or I would have been completely mortified."

His only response came in the form of a rakish grin. Chloe helped him pull the dress from her body but voiced a protest when he dropped it on the floor. He ignored her, intent on stripping off her stays.

A moment later, she was clad only in her chemise. Dominic sucked in a breath as he gently fingered the white lace and silk ribbon trim on her bodice.

"Christ," he muttered, "if I'd known you were wearing something like that under those spinster dresses of yours, I would have gotten your clothes off weeks ago."

Chloe propped herself up on her elbows, torn between shyness and pleasure under the heat in his gaze. "I know it's silly, but I like to wear pretty things against my skin."

"It's not silly. It's the most enticing thing I've ever seen," he rasped out. "You're going to be the death of me, Chloe."

"Not before you get your clothes off, I hope."

His eyes glittered with amusement, but then he started ripping off his clothes. Though Dominic was the most controlled and graceful of men, he practically tripped over himself in his eagerness to undress. By the time he was down to his smalls, Chloe had collapsed on the bed, nearly breathless with laughter.

He let out a mock growl of protest. "Laugh at your peril, my dear."

When he came to the bed, his body gleaming gold in the firelight, she lost her breath for a second time. Dominic was gorgeously imposing. He had muscular arms, a broad chest with a generous dusting of black hair, along with lean hips and long, powerful legs. His equally impressive erection nudged against the confinement of his smalls. The memories of the smiling, skinny boy she'd cherished for so many years evaporated as she took in the man looming over her.

"My God," she said past a tight throat. "You're so beautiful, Dominic."

He swept a hand over her body, tracing her curves before settling at the junction of her thighs. When he cupped her sex through the thin lawn of her chemise, she almost fell off the bed in surprise. "You're the beautiful one, Chloe. My sweet little goddess, so pretty and delicate."

"Thank you," she gasped, shivering as he outlined the plump flesh between her thighs. She was so tall and long-limbed that no one but Dominic would ever think to call her delicate. But with his big hands roaming her body, cherishing her with every touch, that was exactly how she felt.

"Let's finish undressing and get under the covers," he said.

He yanked down his smalls, kicking them away before helping her sit up. When he worked the chemise up over her body, the fabric rasped softly over her breasts. Her already-sensitive nipples pulled tight.

Naked a moment later, she wriggled up the bed, reaching for the covers. But he stopped her by coming down on top of her, his heavy body pressing her deliciously into the mattress.

They stared into each other's eyes. Chloe's breathing hitched as her nipples rubbed into the coarse hair on his chest. Instinctively, she arched into him, a small cry escaping from her lips as she pressed tight.

Dominic groaned and his eyelids fluttered shut. He flexed his pelvis and settled more heavily between her legs, his erection resting low and heavy across her mound and just brushing over her slit. When she pulled her legs wider, cradling his hips, his eyes snapped open. They flared with heat as he captured her gaze. Chloe went lightheaded in a jumble of nerves and excitement.

"God, you feel good," he muttered as he nudged her again.

Then his head dipped and he captured her mouth in a hot, open-mouthed kiss that soon had her reeling. As his tongue pressed between her lips in a lazy sweep, he reached a hand down to her thigh and pulled it up to rest high on his hip. That spread wide her vulnerable sex, and sensation streaked from the tight little knot of flesh to settle deep in her womb. She moaned into his mouth as delicate, wonderful spasms rippled through her sheath.

When Dominic pulled away from the silky warmth of their kiss, she sounded an incoherent protest.

"Patience, my sweet," he murmured. "I simply want to see you."

He shifted to the side, one muscled thigh pressing her lower body into the mattress. His hand settled on her belly, just above her nest of auburn curls. "So pretty," he whispered. His voice held a soft note of wonder that sent warmth cascading through her body.

Then he began stroking her, his long fingers tracing her hips and ribcage before dancing up to her breasts. Chloe lay transfixed by the sight of his strong hands teasing her body. When he cupped her breast, plumping up the rigid tip of her nipple, she froze with anticipation.

"Your tits are gorgeous, Chloe," he growled. "Even more than I imagined."

Before she had a chance to truly register that unexpectedly vulgar but exciting observation, Dominic's dark head came down and his mouth fastened on her nipple. She let out a sharp cry of surprised pleasure, then froze again beneath him.

His head came up. "What's wrong?"

She gnawed her lip, mortified. "Do you think anyone heard me?"

Dominic flashed a wicked grin. "We're alone here at this end of the house. You can make as much noise as you want."

She eyed him uncertainly. "I take it that making noise is a good thing?"

"Undoubtedly."

Then he returned to her breasts and tormented her into

a frenzy of passion. He fed greedily on her, sucking her nipples into aching points, making her moan and squirm beneath him. As he made love to her breasts, his other hand roamed her body, brushing lightly through her curls and drifting over her thighs, making her damp and hot with need. Chloe clutched at his broad shoulders and twisted beneath him, wanting—needing—so much more.

With a last soft nuzzle, Dominic pulled away from her breast. Chloe opened her eyes and fought to focus her gaze. Her fingers were clenching his upper arms, her nails leaving small red scores on his skin.

Dominic, shifting, moved off her. "Open your legs a bit more, Chloe."

Her limbs felt heavy as she obeyed, making room for him between her thighs. Dominic settled on top of her, breathing out a harsh sigh as the broad head of his erection slid between her drenched folds. She clutched at his shoulders, restless with heated desire. She'd been waiting a lifetime, and now they would finally belong to each other.

"Ready, love?" he murmured.

A shaky laugh escaped her lips. "You have no idea."

He groaned as he entered her, pushing slowly inside. "I think I do."

For long seconds, she held herself still, trying to relax as he forged past her untried inner muscles. Chloe wasn't a virgin, but she came terribly close—one adolescent encounter, and then years of spinsterhood. Years of denying her womanhood and pretending it didn't matter.

But, now, captured in Dominic's embrace, gazing into his burning emerald eyes, all that barren pain faded away. Her flesh went slick and soft around him, accepting their union. When he took her mouth in hot possession, she wrapped herself around him, the final barriers between them crumbling to dust.

Thank God.

"All right?" he murmured against her lips.

She wrapped her arms around his neck, holding close. "It's perfect."

And it was. It was perfect as he began to move inside her in a slowly building rhythm that sent coils of heat and sensation spiraling through her body. It was perfect when his breath hitched and he pulled her legs high and wide, bringing her sex tight against his pelvis. She panted as he rocked into her, faster now, and harder, driving her toward climax as he plunged into her.

And it was perfect when she threw her head back and cried out as spasms rippled from her womb in glorious waves, drowning her in pleasure. She clutched at him, resisting the flutter of her eyelids, needing to see the pleasure overtake him, too. His loving gaze bored into her, so blazingly emotional that it brought tears to her eyes. Trembling, she pulled his head down and kissed him. A moment later, he climaxed, groaning as his big body shook in her arms.

He collapsed on top of her but then slowly rolled to the side, bringing her to rest on his heaving chest. "You were right," he managed to gasp. "It was bloody well perfect."

Chapter Six

Breathless, her heart pounding, Chloe sprawled on top of Dominic. His chest rose and fell like a bellows as they lay together in a glorious tangle of limbs. It felt perfectly, wonderfully right, and her mind still reeled from the intimacy of their connection.

Even loving Dominic as much as she did, it still astounded her that sexual relations could be so . . . joyful. For her, it had always seemed an ugly, shameful business and not simply because of her past. For years, she'd cared for girls who'd been treated as objects of convenience, her entire life devoted to repairing the damage inflicted by careless, callous, and even violent men.

She should have known it would be different with Dominic. Despite everything, he still loved her, even though most men would have seen her as damaged goods.

When his hand trailed down her spine to her bottom, she twitched. The contrast between the heat of his skin and the cool air of the bedroom flowing over their naked bodies soon had her shivering. With a soothing murmur, he slowly eased out of her—Chloe had to repress a sigh at that—tucked her against his side, and pulled up the bed linens.

As she lay there, cocooned in warmth, a ridiculous

image of a kitten curling up between the paws of a giant mastiff popped into her head, and she couldn't repress a little snort. Dominic was certainly big, strong, and protective, but she was far from defenseless. She'd learned long ago that the world was a harsh place and a woman was best served by ensuring her independence and security as much as possible. That philosophy formed the basis of her work and, indeed, her life.

Dominic slipped a finger under her chin and tilted her head up to meet his heavy-lidded gaze. Muted passion warmed the dazzling green of his eyes along with what was surely a great deal of masculine satisfaction.

"I hope I'm not the object of your amusement, Mrs. Piper," he drawled. "Such disrespect will cause me to sink into a terrible melancholy."

She laughed out loud. "I doubt there is very little that could wound the confidence of the high and mighty Sir Dominic Hunter."

"I'll high and mighty you, madam," he growled, tipping her over onto her back. His kiss, as heated as any they'd shared, left her gasping.

"I swear, Dominic," she managed when he let her up for air, "I can't think when you do that."

Now it was his turn to grin. "That's the point, Chloe."

But then his smile faded. He propped himself up on one elbow while his other arm rested on her stomach, keeping her gently pinned. He looked concerned, and she lifted an eyebrow in silent question.

"Are you all right?" he asked.

"Yes, I'm fine. You needn't worry about me," she assured him.

"I do worry about you. Practically every minute of every day since you've come back into my life."

She didn't like the sound of that. "I'm grateful for your help, Dominic, but I'm well able to take care of myself."

Now it was his turn to raise his eyebrows. She couldn't blame him for his skepticism, since crime lords were beyond anything she was accustomed to dealing with. But the last thing she wanted was to become yet another item on his long list of concerns.

"I've been looking after myself for a long time, Dominic, and taking care of others who needed my help too."

He brushed a kiss on the tip of her nose. "I'm aware of that, sweet, and you have my sincere respect and admiration for all you've accomplished."

Oh, dear. That was even worse than him worrying about her. Having Dominic condescend to her, however unconsciously, made her mentally cringe.

"But you're not alone anymore," he carried on, oblivious to her growing consternation. "You have a family now, a son and a daughter-in-law. And," he said, with pointed intent, "you have *me*."

Her innate sense of caution stirred. "What exactly do you mean?"

He went slack-jawed for a few seconds, but then the lines of his face turned imperious. She'd come to recognize that expression as one he adopted when about to start issuing orders.

"I mean that as your future husband I will support and take care of you, and I will deal with any problems you encounter from now on."

Chloe froze. Leg-shackling Dominic had not been on her mind when she'd started this. She'd only wanted to be with him—to feel happy and cherished for once. To feel like a woman in love.

But marriage? There were so many complications involved in marriage she didn't know where to start. Fool that she was, she should have known that it was *exactly* what Dominic had wanted and planned for all along. That

was another thing she'd learned about him—he always had
a plan.

Too flustered to address that subject head-on, she fastened on his second point. "What do you mean you'll deal
with my problems from now on?"

"The problems associated with your charitable work, of
course," he said, stroking her cheek.

She forced herself not to nuzzle into his hand. "I wasn't
aware I had any problems with my work, aside from the
temporary one posed by the Campworths. But once that's
resolved, I will be returning to Camberwell."

His eyes narrowed with a touch of irritation. Still, his
touch was gentle as his hand cupped her cheek. "It's entirely reasonable for you to wish to oversee your Camberwell establishment, but it's not practical for us to live there.
If you don't think my town house in London is large
enough, we can look around for something bigger, perhaps
in Mayfair."

"Why would I want to live in London?" she blurted out.

"Because that is where your husband lives, of course."

She pushed his hand away and sat up, clutching the bedclothes to her chest. Dominic stayed propped on his elbow,
his big body relaxed, but the hard set to his mouth and jaw
relayed a different message.

"Dominic, you are making a great many assumptions.
Leaving aside the question of marriage . . ." The dangerous spark in his gaze had her stumbling over her words.
"That aside, I have no intention of giving up Camberwell
and moving to London. First of all, my work is too important to me, and second of all, I couldn't *possibly* live in
the city."

She ended with a wave of her arms, which caused the
linens to slip and expose her breasts. When Dominic's gaze
dropped down and lingered, she struggled to cover herself

up. The fact that he had whipped a hand over to keep the linens trapped around her waist wasn't helping.

"Your work is too dangerous, Chloe. The last few months have clearly demonstrated that," he said, sounding somewhat distracted. "I'll find someone to manage the day-to-day operations in Camberwell. I have a few retired agents who would fit the bill quite nicely and would enjoy the work."

She glared at him as she gave up the struggle for the bed linens. "Truly, Dominic, hardened spies managing an establishment for vulnerable girls and their babies?"

He shrugged as he ran a finger over her belly trying to delve lower under the bunched fabric.

"Stop that!" She planted a hand on his chest and shoved him onto his back. Then she scrambled out of bed, casting a desperate look around for her dress. It lay in a crumpled heap at the foot of the bed, so she snatched up Dominic's dressing gown from the chair beside her and wriggled into it. She had to wrap the belt twice around her waist to secure it.

By the time she was decent, Dominic had pulled himself up to a sitting position, a scowl on his features and his arms crossed over his brawny chest. He obviously wasn't the least bit concerned about his near nakedness, since the bedclothes fell low on his hips, exposing his flat belly and the arrow of dark hair leading to his groin. He looked so sinfully enticing—even with that thunderous brow—that Chloe had to fight the urge to throw off the dressing gown and crawl on top of him.

"Chloe, I'm certain we can find someone suitable to take up your work in Camberwell. I don't understand the problem."

His perplexed frown signaled that he truly didn't understand how delicately she managed things. It had taken years to develop channels of communication and a method of operation that preserved the privacy of the girls who came to her, protecting them and their babies and helping them to move back to their old lives or establish new ones. Strangers simply could not take it over—not without probably destroying everything she'd worked so hard to build.

But there was no point in explaining that further since, for Dominic, that wasn't the issue. For him, the issue was their marriage.

She mentally composed herself. "Dominic, it's very kind of you to offer marriage—"

He actually growled at her turn of phrase.

Chloe ignored him. "But I don't think you've considered why that course of action is either desired or in *your* best interest."

"What the hell are you talking about?"

"You are a magistrate," she said patiently, "and a highly placed member of the government. You know it's not appropriate for a man of your position and standing to marry a woman like me."

His expression suggested she'd taken up howling at the moon. "Chloe, I'm the son of a butcher. There isn't a drop of noble blood in my veins."

"You were raised at court and you have the ear of both the prime minister *and* the Prince Regent." When he started to object she held up a hand. "You can protest all you want, Dominic, but you know it's true. I am not the sort of woman you should marry, either by inclination or breeding."

"May I remind you," he said through clenched teeth, "that you are the daughter and granddaughter of gentlemen. Your maternal grandfather was a well-regarded magistrate and one of your great-uncles was a dean at Cambridge. When it comes to *breeding,* yours is significantly more distinguished than mine."

"And I am also a disgraced woman with an illegitimate child."

"Whose son has royal blood running through his veins."

"I don't need you to remind me of that," she snapped. When his eyes widened at her tone, she sighed. "I'm sorry. I didn't mean to be rude."

"You need never apologize to me, my love." His stern features softened. "Why don't you come sit with me," he said in a coaxing voice. "There's no reason to stand there—your feet will get cold."

Oh, she was tempted, but she knew he was trying to wheedle her into agreeing with him. She regretfully shook her head.

Dominic ran a frustrated hand over his jaw. "Chloe, no one need ever know who you are or that Griffin is your son. As far as the world is concerned you are Mrs. Piper, a wealthy, respectable widow from Leeds who engages in charitable work. We can say you're an old friend of mine, which is certainly not a lie."

"But the rest of it is. Are you suggesting that we lie on the marriage license or to the minister who would conduct the ceremony?"

He waved that obstacle away. "Of course not. But there is more than one vicar who owes me a favor and would be happy to keep our confidence."

"I'm sure," she responded drily. "But you must realize that the only reason my fictional persona withstands scrutiny is because I live so quietly. As the wife of Sir Dominic Hunter, I would be vulnerable to speculation and gossip."

When his nostrils flared, he looked rather like a bull contemplating a charge. Dominic was the kindest, most generous man in the world, but he was also one of the most stubborn she'd ever encountered. He'd been that way as a child, as well. It had helped him survive the trials of life in the royal household, but it was a formidable obstacle for anyone trying to win an argument with him.

"For heaven's sake," she said, "I am sure there is more than one person in the world who would try to use my past against you. They might even try to blackmail you."

He looked mortally offended. "Anyone foolish enough to try would fare very poorly, I assure you."

"No doubt, but the damage to your career and to our lives would be considerable. I truly think you underestimate the level of gossip and disgrace such a scandal could generate. How could our marriage hope to survive that?"

Well, that tears it.

By the look on his face—and the fact that he'd thrown back the covers and leapt from the bed—Chloe had finally pushed him too far. His big feet thudded to the floor and he stalked up to her like an outraged Zeus descending from Mt. Olympus.

A very naked Zeus.

"Chloe, you have nothing to be ashamed of in *any* part of your life. You are the best woman in England, and the person who says otherwise will regret it."

She tore her gaze from his magnificent, half-aroused body, fixing it somewhere over his shoulder. "I cannot possibly have a rational conversation until you cover yourself."

He barked out a disbelieving laugh but obliged her by snatching his breeches from the floor and yanking them over his long legs. Chloe forced herself to avert her gaze when he arranged himself and buttoned up his fall.

"There, does that assuage your offended sensibilities?" he asked sarcastically.

If the subject hadn't been so serious, Chloe would have been tempted to laugh. It seemed farcical to stand around half-naked, snapping at each other like spoiled schoolchildren.

"Thank you," she said, trying to recapture a shred of dignity. "Now, as I was saying—"

"Chloe, just hush a moment," Dominic interrupted in a gentle voice. He took her hand and raised it to his lips. That simple touch, knowing what she now did about the pleasure he could bestow, sent a shiver coursing through her.

"I love you," he said. "Nothing could ever change that or diminish my feelings for you. I truly believe that you're unduly worried about what might happen if . . . *when* we marry. Of course there is always the possibility of discovery, but I believe the risk to be minimal. Besides," he added with an encouraging smile, "even if your past were to be discovered, I can manage it. *We* can manage it. It's old history, my darling. No one will really care."

She peered at him, anxiety ghosting through her like an icy wind. Dominic had more insight into the *ton* than she did, but she was hardly naïve in the ways of scandal in the highest reaches of society. News of London gossip was an invariable fact of life even in a quiet village like Camberwell. Dominic would surely stand fast against even the ugliest of it, loyal to her to the end. But that sort of loyalty, combined with his pig-headed conviction that his power made him all but untouchable, could be disastrous for his career and their relationship.

"And what of my feelings?" she asked, trying a different tack. "Because of your position in society, I would be an object of interest and scrutiny. How am I to live with that, given my situation?"

He shook his head. "I don't understand. I already told you that I would shield you from *ton* gossip."

"I'm not just talking about them."

"Then who?"

"The one who hurt me. And never mind how I might react once the father of my child recognizes me." Dominic flinched, but she kept ruthlessly on. "How will *he* react once he discovers you've married me? Unless your relationship with Prince Ernest has undergone a dramatic improvement since the last time I saw you together, I can't imagine he would look upon our marriage with favor."

"Do you think I care for a moment what that bastard thinks?" he growled. "It's none of his damn business."

His response mystified her. "Dominic, he's the brother of the Prince Regent. He can make a great deal of trouble for us."

His eyes sparked green fire. "Ask me if I care."

Chloe wanted to shake him. "Tell me, how do you bear it? You and Ernest always loathed each other. How can you stand his company, or has your enmity diminished over time?"

She hated pushing him like this, but it was the only way. He *had* to realize how impossible this was.

"We avoid each other whenever possible," he said in a cold voice. "It's not that hard to do."

"Well, I'm afraid I don't possess your ability to pretend that the past didn't happen."

His head jerked back as if she had slapped him. "I may not show it, Chloe, but my loathing for the man has colored a great deal of my life. After losing you, encountering him on a regular basis has been an ugly cross to bear. If he wasn't a royal, I would have beaten him to a pulp long ago."

Turning from her, he stalked to the fireplace. He braced a hand on the mantel and bowed his head to stare into the flames. Chloe followed, a piercing regret doing its best to crowd out the joy she'd found in his love.

Carefully, she rested a hand on his back. "Dominic, you move in the highest circles of the land, which would mean that I, on occasion, would have to as well. Even if Prince Ernest didn't recognize me, would you force me to keep company—however brief and formal—with the person who ruined me?"

He cut a sharp glance over his shoulder. "I would never

force you to do anything. You don't have to associate with anyone you don't want to."

"Unless I lived the life of a recluse, I don't see how it could be managed. And there are others to consider besides ourselves. What of Griffin? All your hard work to restore his reputation would be destroyed if our connection was discovered."

Under her hand, his muscles bunched with tension. "I refuse to accept such a notion. Besides, Griffin is the last person to give a damn about that sort of thing."

"Perhaps. But Justine certainly would care, as would I. The gossip about their marriage has yet to die down even as it is." She removed her hand. "Dominic, I cannot and will not bring disgrace onto you or my family. The very thought of it makes me ill."

When he turned to her, his face was stark with dismay. It killed her to have to disappoint him again, but it was far preferable to the havoc their marriage would wreak upon his life.

Dominic grasped her shoulders. "Chloe, do you love me?"

The pleading look in his eyes had her choking back tears. "Of course I do."

"And did finally acknowledging that love—being with me—make you happy?"

Happiness . . . something she hadn't felt for years. Not until Dominic and her son came back into her life. "Yes," she whispered.

The tenderness in his lopsided smile made her heart throb with a harrowing combination of elation and sorrow.

"Then what is there to be afraid of?" he asked.

Nothing . . . everything.

She hardly knew how to answer, so she remained silent.

His hands dropped to his sides. "Chloe, I can make this work. You must learn to trust me."

More than anything she wished she could, but trust was a commodity she'd given up on many years ago. Even Dominic, as strong and powerful as he was, couldn't fundamentally change the circumstances of their lives.

"You must not ask this of me, Dominic. It is too much."

While he stood frozen before her, she went up on tiptoe and pressed a kiss to his hard, disbelieving mouth. Then she clumsily snatched up her clothes and fled the room.

Chapter Seven

With a grateful sigh, Chloe accepted a cup of tea from Justine. "I don't know what I would have done without you, my dear. I owe you and Griffin a considerable debt of gratitude."

Her daughter-in-law smiled. "No thanks are necessary. The girls were very little trouble, and we adored spending time with little Stephen."

"*Adored* might be a tad strong, my love," Griffin responded with a roll of his eyes. He was lounging across from them, looking entirely at home in Chloe's drawing room.

Chloe and Jane had arrived in Camberwell only an hour ago. According to the report Aden St. George had sent to Dominic yesterday, Borden Campworth had been mightily displeased to learn of his nephew's actions. Apparently, Campworth had no desire to run afoul of Dominic—or Aden, for that matter—and had instructed Roger to leave Jane alone. In Aden's judgement, that made it safe for Chloe and Jane to return home and Chloe had immediately begun making plans to do so.

Unfortunately, those plans had not gone over well with

Dominic, who clearly thought she was trying to avoid him. He'd tried more than once to revive a discussion of marriage, intent on convincing Chloe of the error of her ways. She, however, had refused to rehash a subject that held no chance of a positive resolution. No matter how much she might secretly long for it, marrying Dominic was too great a risk—both to her security and her heart.

It was risky for him, too, even though he was too stubborn to see it. The scandal of her past would eventually rear up if they married, with significant repercussions for him. Dominic would be obliged to ignore the malicious gossip or continually defend her character, and God only knew how the Prince Regent and his brothers would react. She and Dominic might be able to weather the storm, but the damage to his career—and their relationship—would be severe.

Despite the aching regret she felt every waking moment, Chloe knew she'd made the right decision. Though she hoped Dominic would come to understand, right now it was up to her to make the only appropriate decision for both of them.

"What a shame Uncle Dominic couldn't come in for a visit," Justine said. "I would have loved a chat."

Griffin cut her a cheeky grin. "I, however, am remarkably grateful he was too busy. You know how much he loves to lecture me. I am a never-ending source of disappointment to the man."

"It must run in the family," Chloe said without thinking.

Griffin and Justine exchanged startled glances.

"In any event," Chloe hastily added, "Dominic sent his apologies. He simply has too much work on his desk after a week away from London and was quite eager to get home." She let out a sigh at the memory of Dominic's brusque, decidedly unsentimental good-bye in the carriage.

"Is something wrong?" Justine asked her after a lengthy pause.

Chloe mentally shook herself and smiled. "Good heavens, no. I'm so pleased to be home and very curious as to what has been going on in my absence. You must tell me everything."

Justine exchanged another dubious glance with Griffin, but then nodded. "Of course. If you—"

A quick tap on the door interrupted her. Hill entered, looking concerned. "It's Mrs. Clayton, ma'am. Jane's mother. She's begging to speak with you."

"Naturally," Griffin muttered. "A little peace around here was too good to be true."

Chloe rose. "Bring her in, and you'd better fetch Jane, too."

"Oh, dear," Justine said. "Whatever could be the matter now?"

"Perhaps it has nothing to do with Campworth," Chloe replied. "It might be some sort of family emergency."

"We couldn't possibly get that lucky," Griffin said.

Chloe hushed her son as Hill returned with their visitor.

"Do come in, Mrs. Clayton." Chloe extended a hand. "Please have a seat and let me pour you a cup of tea."

Mrs. Clayton was a short, sturdy-looking woman with a pleasant face. Her expression tight with worry, she took the offered seat but refused the tea. "Mrs. Piper, there's no time for beating around the bush. My poor family is in a fierce amount of trouble." She then burst into tears at the exact moment Jane walked into the room.

Chaos reigned for a few minutes, but repeated reassurances from Chloe and Griffin that no harm would come to the Clayton family finally restored peace.

Haltingly, Jane's mother explained that Roger Campworth had paid a visit to her husband's shop that morning.

Mr. Clayton had tried to face him down, claiming that Jane was under Sir Dominic's protection, but that had only infuriated Roger.

"That awful man shook my poor husband like a terrier shakes a rat," said Mrs. Clayton in a quavering voice. "Mr. Clayton is no coward, but he's getting up in years and he's no match for a bully like Roger Campworth."

"What does Campworth want?" asked Chloe as she patted the distraught woman's hand.

"He wants Jane to come live with him. Says she's carrying his child, and she's got no right to keep it from him."

Jane's lips quivered. "I can't go back to him, Mamma. He'll beat me!"

"Of course you're not going back to him," Chloe said firmly. "You're to stay right here."

Mrs. Clayton grimaced. "Thank you, ma'am, but my husband . . . I'm worried fierce about him. Roger said he'd beat him black and blue if Jane didn't come home with me today."

"This has gone on long enough," Griffin said as he came to his feet. "I'll ride into the city and fetch Dominic. Then we'll both pay a visit to Borden Campworth and his idiot nephew."

Chloe clenched her fists as she struggled to contain the fury coursing through her body. She'd spent her life trying to protect women from men like Roger Campworth, mostly by hiding them away and living in secrecy. But despite all the subterfuge, danger had still invaded her household, threatening everything she believed in.

Something else had to be done.

"This isn't Dominic's problem," she said. "It's mine, and *I'm* going to take care of it."

They all gaped at her, but Griffin found his voice first.

"Mother, you cannot take on Borden Campworth yourself. He's one of the most dangerous men in London."

"I understand, but I will not be cowed. Nor will I continue to shield myself behind the threat of Dominic's power."

"It's a bloody convenient threat," her son protested.

She shook her head. Dominic considered her work too dangerous for her to continue, and this incident would only serve as confirmation. If they had any sort of future together, even as friends, she had to prove she could manage her own affairs. She had to prove to him that she was his equal. She would not live in fear, and she would no longer hide from vile men like Borden and Roger Campworth.

She would no longer hide from anyone.

With a mental jolt that sent her to her feet, Chloe realized how sick she was of hiding. She'd spent most of her life doing just that, sacrificing the things most important to her. Her son, Dominic, and the freedom to be who she really was—Chloe Steele, a woman who'd made mistakes but still deserved to have a life, not one lived in the shadows.

A woman who, finally, had a real chance at creating a future built on love instead of shame.

Griffin waved a hand in front of her face. "Have you even heard a word I've said?"

Chloe smiled at her son. "I did, and I agree with you. Borden Campworth *is* a dangerous man, which is why you're coming with me."

"Last chance to turn back," Griffin said.

The long-suffering resignation in his voice told Chloe he had no real expectation she would do any such thing.

"We've come this far," she said, eyeing the dilapidated

tavern that squatted like an ugly toad in a back alley of St. Giles.

The Crow and Cock was at the heart of Campworth's territory and, according to Griffin, was the best place to start looking for him. But now that they were actually here Chloe had to admit to a certain level of unsettled nerves, and not simply about Campworth. Dominic would be furious that she was taking such a risk, but what else could she do? She had to prove to him as well as herself that she would not be intimidated by bullies, whether they were louts like Roger Campworth, criminals like his uncle, or royal princes.

"You don't have to do this," her son said as he took her gloved hand. "You don't have to prove yourself to anyone. Not to me, not to Dominic."

Chloe had to blink away tears of gratitude that she'd been given a second chance with Griffin. "No, but I need to prove this to myself."

He studied her with a gravity he didn't often show but which she recognized in herself. Then a wry smile curved up his lips. "All right, Mother. We'll do it your way, but let me go in first. And remember, if I say it's time to leave, then we leave. Understand?"

"Yes, dear," she said meekly.

He shook his head and pushed through the tavern door. Chloe followed but halted just over the threshold, giving her eyes time to adjust to the gloom inside.

When her vision cleared, she saw a low-ceilinged room, sparsely furnished with battered tables and chairs. A long oak bar took up one end of the room. A coal fire burned in the grate, and spirit lamps on the bar and one of the tables threw off a dim but adequate light. Though it smelled of dampness, sweat, and stale beer, the room was relatively clean and not nearly as frightening as she'd expected.

Until, that is, her gaze caught and held that of a man

sitting at the table with the lamp. The man's cold-eyed, calculating stare, his unexpectedly elegant and expensive suit of clothing, and his indefinable sense of power told her that she was looking at Borden Campworth.

Two hulking men stood behind the crime lord, eyeing Griffin with consternation.

"Griffin Steele," Campworth said with a harsh drawl born of a life spent in the stews. "Haven't seen you in St. Giles for a time and then some. But I suppose you're so busy with your nob's life that you've forgot where you come from."

"I never forget anything, Campworth," Griffin replied. "You do realize that, don't you?" He sounded bored, but only a fool would mistake his meaning.

"My apologies," Campworth said, showing his teeth. "Who's your friend?" He let out an unpleasant laugh. "Getting tired of your wife already, I suppose."

Griffin glanced over his shoulder at Chloe. She knew he would never reveal their relationship without her permission.

"I'm his mother," she said, stepping forward. She felt rather than saw Griffin's jerk of surprise. "And I've come to talk to you about your nephew, Roger. He is causing me a great deal of trouble."

Campworth's brows arched. Then an irritated comprehension tightened his blunt features. "Steele's mother? You're the woman who took in that brassy little piece, Jane Clayton."

"Correct, on both counts."

The crime lord let out a disgusted snort. "Not only do I have to put up with threats from Dominic Hunter's rabid dog underlings, I'm to have Griffin Steele crawling up my arse, too? Christ, what did I do to deserve that?"

"You failed to keep your nephew under control," Chloe

replied. "He continues to make threats against the Clayton family, and I won't have it."

Campworth barked out a harsh laugh. "Oh, you won't, will you? I'm trembling in my boots, I am."

"You should be," Griffin said. "You may take anything my mother says as my word as well."

Chloe couldn't help beaming at her son. "Thank you, my dear. That's very sweet of you."

"You're welcome, Mother," Griffin replied politely, even though his dark eyes glinted with amusement.

"Oh, Christ," Campworth muttered. "I need a drink."

"Mr. Campworth," Chloe said in a stern voice. "I must insist that your nephew leave Jane and her family alone. I will hold you responsible if he does not."

"Oh, you will, will you?" he growled, slowly coming to his feet. Borden Campworth wasn't a tall man, but he had a hulking, intimidating presence. "The girl carries Roger's brat, and he wants to do right by her. What the hell is your problem with that?"

"I should think it obvious. Your nephew is a brute and a bully, and Jane wants nothing to do with him," Chloe said. "I must insist that you and Roger honor her wishes."

"Why should I honor the wishes of a tart? Or you, for that matter," Campworth said with a sneer. "If you're Steele's mother, you're obviously a whore, and I don't listen to whores."

"You will, however, listen to me," Griffin said in a voice gone suddenly hard as stone.

"Never mind, dear," Chloe said as she extracted her pistol from her reticule. She pointed it at the crime lord. "Mr. Campworth, if you do not agree to my demands, I'll have to shoot you. And then I suppose I'll have to shoot Roger, too."

For the second time that day, every person in the room gaped at her. And for the second time, it was Griffin who found his voice first. "Good Gad, you're as bad as my wife," he exclaimed as the door to the tavern opened behind him.

A shaft of sunlight streaked across the floor, only to be blotted out by a large, looming shadow. Chloe heard a swift, heavy tread of boots behind her and then a voice that raised the hairs on the back of her neck.

"No," Dominic said, clearly furious. "She's worse."

Chapter Eight

Dominic handed Chloe down from the carriage, resisting the temptation to hoist her over his shoulder and storm up the steps into his town house. She was obviously feeling as put out as he was. She'd spent the short trip from St. Giles silently fuming and casting him irate glances. Why *she* should be annoyed with him, when he'd saved her pretty arse from all kinds of trouble, was a mystery.

When the servant sent by a quick-thinking Justine had come hammering on his door, Dominic had been plowing through a mountain of correspondence and obsessing about Chloe. Those last few days in the country had been a disaster. Chloe had barely spoken to him and had spent as little time in his company as possible. Although he understood her fear of discovery and scandal, he couldn't abide the prospect of letting her slip away from him again.

Especially now that he'd finally taken her to bed. Making love to Chloe had been everything he'd dreamed about for long, lonely years, shaking him to the core and ripping from him any pretense of emotional control. The idea of not making Chloe his wife was now absurd. Nor would he settle for some sort of clandestine affair he knew would chip away at her self-worth. She deserved more than that. She deserved to stand in the light of day, honored and respected by all who knew her, without a hint of scandal or approbation attached to her name.

But how could he give her all she deserved and yet still protect her privacy? Dominic had been pondering that thorny problem when his butler ushered in the messenger from Justine bearing news that Chloe had gone to beard Campworth in his den. That had sent Dominic bolting for St. Giles, furious, terrified, and determined—once and for all—to get the situation with Chloe under control.

"Well, I'll let you two talk this out on your own," Griffin said after stepping down to the pavement. "I'll take a hack to Camberwell."

Dominic turned and leveled him with a glare. It must have been a fairly effective one to make Griffin take a hasty step back.

"I think not, you young idiot," Dominic snapped. "You'll accompany us inside and explain exactly why you agreed to that insane venture."

"Really, Dominic, there is no need to talk to Griffin that way," Chloe said. "He was only doing what I asked him to. Besides," she sniffed, "everything turned out rather well, if you ask me."

Flabbergasted, Dominic stared at her. Even Griffin seemed rather taken aback by her insouciance in the face of what could have been an exceedingly bad outcome.

"Only because I arrived before things got completely away from you," Dominic replied from between clenched teeth.

When he recalled the fury on Campworth's face, the man's disbelief that anyone—much less a woman—would hold him at gunpoint, Dominic broke into a cold sweat. If he had arrived even a few moments later, God only knew what would have happened.

Fortunately, his appearance had brought Campworth and his goons up short, especially when Dominic had stated that Chloe was his affianced wife. Chloe had started to sputter a protest, but Griffin had hissed something that silenced her impending outburst. She'd glared blue murder at Dominic but held her tongue while he ordered Campworth to keep his swinish nephew away from Jane Clayton and her family. If he failed to do that, Dominic stressed that he would make it his personal and unending mission to bring Campworth's criminal empire crashing down around his ears.

At that point Campworth had capitulated, rattled by the prospect of bringing on the wrath of Dominic, the Intelligence Service, and half the departments in the Home Office. He swore to keep his nephew under control if he had to *beat the living shite out of him to do it*, as he so charmingly phrased it.

Dominic had then marched an irate Chloe out of the seedy tavern, while Griffin had tried—not very successfully—to quell his amusement. He was ready to throttle the both of them.

The butler let them into the house, his eyes widening with surprise as he caught the hat and coat Dominic tossed at him.

"We'll be in my study," Dominic barked as he steered Chloe to the staircase. "See to it that we're not disturbed."

"Really, Dominic, there's no reason to be so rude." Chloe sounded slightly out of breath as he pulled her up the stairs. "I don't know why you're making such a fuss."

Dominic's eyes almost crossed with frustration that she would take her safety so lightly, and the fact that he could hear Griffin trying to smother another laugh didn't improve his temper in the least. He herded them into his study and shut the door with a decided bang.

Griffin strolled over to the drinks trolley and poured himself a brandy. "Mother, can I get you something to drink?" he asked politely.

"No, thank you, dear. But perhaps you could pour one for Dominic. He seems to need it."

Grinding his back molars, Dominic stalked over to the fireplace. He braced both hands on the mantel and stared down into the glowing coals in the grate, inhaling deep breaths in an effort to remain in control. Chloe had a knack for blasting through his defenses, pulling his most volatile emotions to the surface. That obviously wasn't going to change anytime soon, so he might as well start learning to manage them.

Mentally fortifying himself, he turned to face Chloe and her son. They stood side by side, Chloe the picture of composure while Griffin held two tumblers of brandy. A faint, sympathetic smile lifted the corners of his mouth. Superficially, mother and son looked nothing alike—until one noticed the identical determined tilt to the jaw, the high, carved cheekbones, and same direct gaze. And as angry as he was with them, Dominic couldn't suppress a flare of happiness that Chloe and Griffin had finally been reunited.

"I assume," he said, "that something happened at Camberwell to send you two haring off on that mad folly?"

Chloe pursed her lips, clearly not liking his characterization, but she nodded to Griffin who proceeded to outline the events of the afternoon.

"I take it," Griffin said, finishing up, "that my ever-practical wife sent you a message as to our whereabouts?"

"She did, and you can be grateful for that. God knows what would have happened if I hadn't arrived when I did."

"I'm sure Mr. Campworth and I would have reached

some sort of accommodation," Chloe said. "It was very kind of you to come, Dominic, but it was entirely unnecessary."

Her tone made it clear that she didn't find his interference *kind* at all.

"Christ, woman," he finally exploded. "Are you daft? I can understand the need to deal with Campworth and I can even understand sending your reprobate of a son, but you had no business going there. What you did, putting yourself in grave danger, was entirely unnecessary. It's *my* job to take care of men like Campworth, not yours."

Chloe propped her hands on her hips, scowling at him. "I disagree. You clearly believe you're doing me a service by interfering in my work, but I assure you such is not the case."

"I'm not interfering in your work, I'm trying to keep you alive," Dominic roared.

Her eyes popped wide. He couldn't blame her, since he rarely lost his temper and never yelled. But Chloe's return to his life had upset his mental equilibrium in ways he was only starting to realize. Some days he barely recognized himself.

Chloe recovered from her surprise and marched up to him. She jabbed a forefinger into his chest—hard. "Now you listen to me, Dominic Hunter, I've had quite enough of your—"

"For God's sake," Griffin broke in. "Will you two please shut the hell up? You're worse than a pair of squabbling children." He took Chloe by the elbow and steered her to one of the club chairs in front of Dominic's desk. "Sit, Mother," he said sternly.

Much to Dominic's surprise—and Chloe's, he suspected—she did.

Then Griffin turned his irritated gaze on Dominic. "Take the other chair, Dominic."

Dominic momentarily debated refusing, just to see how

Griffin would react. Then he shrugged and took the seat next to Chloe, curiosity overriding his anger.

The young man stood before them, his arms crossed over his chest as he disapprovingly eyed his elders. As usual, Griffin looked more like a highwayman than a gentleman, with his dramatic black garb and long, clubbed-back hair. But Dominic's reluctant protégé had come a long way on the difficult road to slaying his personal demons and reclaiming the life that was rightfully his. Dominic would never have a son, but Griffin was the closest thing to it. He couldn't help feeling something akin to a father's pride and affection.

Such an expression of emotion would appall Griffin. But it was there nonetheless, and Dominic intended to do everything he could to cherish Chloe and her family.

Griffin shook his head in disgust. "You've been circling each other for over a month, and Justine and I can hardly stand to be in the same room with the two of you. You're so bloody cautious with each other that one would never know you were once the best of friends. These days, you're barely polite strangers. I'm not entirely sure what the problem is with Dominic, but you, Mother, have been wallowing in guilt long enough."

Chloe's shoulders went up around her ears. "I'm sure I have no idea what you're talking about."

Griffin's brows lifted in a sardonic tilt. "Mother, you're so patently transparent it's laughable. Rarely does a day go by that you don't apologize to me for all your *past failings,* as you put it. Yes, you made mistakes, and we all agree it was the height of foolishness to hide yourself away for so many years. But we know why you did it." He switched his attention to Dominic. "Don't we?"

Dominic met Griffin's challenging gaze, and in that moment, all his half-formed theories and tangled emotions about Chloe suddenly sorted themselves with stunning clarity.

"Yes, we do," he replied. "Your mother was punishing herself for the past, for the shame she imagines she brought to her family and her good name. By denying herself the company of those she loved, she hoped to cleanse herself of those imaginary sins."

"They were *not* imaginary," Chloe said in a tight voice. When she twisted in her chair and looked at Dominic, the sorrow in her eyes made him want to weep. "That shame all but killed my father, and I hurt you too, Dominic. And how can I forget the damage I inflicted on Griffin by abandoning him?"

Dominic took her slender fingers in his. "My love, you were an innocent girl who was taken advantage of by one who knew better. No shame attaches to you. The fault was all Cumberland's."

Like a child, she rubbed the tears from her cheeks with her free hand. "You warned me about him. I should have listened to you."

"I grew up with the swine, Chloe. I knew him a great deal better than you did. But it doesn't matter. Not anymore. *He* doesn't matter."

"Perhaps, but how can I be forgiven for what I did to Griffin?" Chloe stared earnestly at her son. "I was a coward to let my uncle take you away from me. I should have fought for you. I should never have given up so easily." She shook her head in self-disgust. "I was afraid, and I let that fear rule my life."

Griffin let out an exasperated breath then hunkered down before her. "It pains me to resort to mawkish sentimentality, but you need to know that I have forgiven you. You were, in your own illogical way, trying to protect me. Besides, if not for the choices you made, I likely never would have met Justine. And that, my dear mother, would have been the greatest harm anyone could have inflicted on me."

Chloe let go of Dominic and took her son's hands. "You truly feel that way?" she whispered.

Griffin nodded. "Truly. And since I have forgiven you, surely you can learn to forgive yourself."

He leaned forward and brushed a kiss on her forehead, then rose to his feet and directed a scowl at Dominic. "As for you, for God's sake stop trying to control everything and everyone. I know that's like telling you not to breathe, but my mother has proven she can manage her own business. As I've discovered with my own wife, being overly protective rarely works."

Dominic was torn between irritation and laughter that Griffin had the nerve to read him a lecture. "Anything else?" he asked drily.

"Yes. You've spent years looking for Chloe, running around like a bloody knight chasing down the Holy Grail. Now, she's finally here, and you've got her, so make the right decision." Griffin glared down his arrogant nose at him. "Or else you'll have to answer to me."

"Oh, really?"

"Yes, really."

"Very well, then I will," Dominic replied.

Griffin eyed him suspiciously, then nodded. "About time. Now that I have you two sorted out, I'll be on my way."

"I don't understand any of this," Chloe complained. Still, she surreptitiously wiped away a few tears, and her eyes were shining with love as she gazed at her son.

"Dominic will explain, Mother," Griffin said as he pulled on his gloves. "I'll see you back in Camberwell."

With a nod to Dominic, he strode from the room. They heard a murmur of voices out in the hall, and a minute later the slam of the front door. Then silence fell, broken only by the solemn tick of the mantel clock and the hissing of the coals in the grate. The late afternoon sun shafted through the windows, casting a soft benediction of light that reached into corners and dissolved shadows with its warm glow.

Dominic finally allowed all the accumulated tension of the last few days—of a lifetime, probably—flow away on a great, invisible river. The answer was now so clear. It had been there all along, from the moment Chloe walked into his study two months ago.

"I don't fully understand what you and Griffin were talking about," Chloe said in a hesitant voice. "I wish you would explain it to me."

Dominic reached over and scooped Chloe out of her chair and onto his lap. She squeaked and clutched his shoulders, her big eyes round with surprise and, perhaps, a little apprehension. Right now she looked so much like the girl he'd first come to love that his heart ached. He couldn't wipe away the pain of the intervening years, but he would do his damnedest to make sure her future—their future—was rich with love and happiness.

As he cradled her against his chest, he felt a profound gratitude that she was safe in his arms. "In a minute, love. First, I want you to tell me why you were so insistent on confronting Campworth without me."

She winced. "I'm sorry I upset you, but I had to prove to myself—and to you—that I had the courage to face down a man like that. To face down *any* man, even someone like Campworth, or . . ." Her voice faded for a few seconds, but then came back on a clear note. "Or like Prince Ernest. Because Griffin was right. I *have* been living my life in the shadows for too long. If I couldn't stand up to Campworth and confront my fears, then I didn't deserve to have either my son or you in my life."

Dominic stroked her cheek. "I understand, and I admire

your courage. But you put yourself in harm's way. You know that Campworth is a very dangerous man."

She gave him a surprisingly cheeky grin. "That's why I brought Griffin with me. I knew Campworth would be loath to pick a fight with him. Plus, I did have my pistol."

Dominic groaned and bowed his head. "Don't remind me."

She huffed out a little chuckle but then put her fingers under his chin, tipping his head up to hold his gaze. "Dominic, do you still wish to marry me?"

He didn't hesitate. "More than anything I have ever wanted in my life."

She drew in a full breath, as if for courage. "Then I accept."

His heart jerkcd hard against his ribs. "Do you mean that?"

"Yes."

Dominic wanted to leap to his feet, spin her around in his arms, and then carry her off to bed. But he reined in the delirious impulse. "I will do my best to protect you from gossip and scandal, Chloe, but there are no guarantees."

She nuzzled her soft mouth against his in the most perfect of kisses. "I know that," she said when she pulled back. "But I'm done with hiding away like a frightened child. I'm only worried about the impact on your reputation and work."

"There's no need to worry, love. My reputation will be just fine." He leaned in to kiss her again, but she stopped him by putting her fingers to his lips. "There's more, isn't there?" he asked in a tone of mock resignation.

Though she flashed him a contrite smile, he saw the determination in her gaze and felt the tension in the rigid muscles under his hand where it rested low on her back. "Yes. I'm sorry, but I must make it clear that I will not give up my work in Camberwell. I understand that decision won't please you, and I'll do my best to work around it, but I will be spending at least part of every week in the country with my girls and the babies."

"I suppose that's an inviolable condition?" He moved his hand in a soothing stroke along her spine down to her bottom.

Her cheeks flushed pink, but she still managed to dredge up a scowl. "It is, and don't try to distract me with *that,* Dominic. It won't work."

He exhaled a sigh. "Such a pity. In that case, I have no choice but to agree to your terms."

"You do?" She sounded astonished.

Dominic let out a rueful laugh. "I suppose I deserve that, given what an unthinking brute I was the last time I asked you to marry me."

"No, I understood that you simply wanted to protect me."

"I still do," he said, "which is why I will be moving out to Camberwell with you. I am well aware of your ability to manage your own affairs, but I would like to believe you could benefit from my assistance. Just think of how many more girls we could help by working together."

As she gaped at him, Dominic had to repress a laugh. "And, my darling, you do have a tendency to attract a rather unsavory sort. Just think how handy it will be to have me around the next time a nefarious crime lord or murderous aristocrat starts skulking about."

"But what about your own work? How can you manage your government business from Camberwell?" She frowned. "Dominic, it would hardly be a good idea to have spies coming and going at all hours of the day and night. It would be very disruptive and possibly dangerous for my girls."

"I agree, which is why I'll be retiring."

She almost slid off his knee.

"Careful," he said with a laugh as he grabbed her by the waist.

"Dominic . . . I . . . why would you do that?"

"Because I love you and because you're the most important thing in my life. I lost you once, Chloe. I'm not going to let that happen ever again."

She stared at him, looking anxiously hopeful. "Are you sure? What will the Regent or the prime minister think about that?"

He shrugged. "I don't give a damn what they think."

"But—"

He silenced her with a kiss, ruthlessly taking her mouth. She melted against him, trembling in his arms. By the time Dominic pulled back, his hands were shaking with passion and need.

"Chloe, I've given most of my life to the Service and to my country. I'm proud of my work and have no regrets. But I used it as an escape, too. I used it to forget my pain and to find purpose in my life. Now I have another purpose—loving you, helping you with your work."

"Will it be enough?" she whispered.

"It will be more than enough. And it's time, anyway. I'm not young anymore, and I find myself increasingly weary of the work. It's right to hand it off to a younger man."

She unleashed a smile so luminous that it made him light-headed. "I'm so happy you feel that way," she said, throwing her arms around his neck.

Dominic held her close. His heart and mind seemed to be undergoing a quiet revolution, absorbing the change in his life with an almost prayerful gratitude. He had never thought this day would arrive, and yet here it was. Though he could never truly be ready for it, he would spend the rest of his life doing his best to be worthy of Chloe.

She rested against him for a few minutes, as if she also

needed time to take in such a momentous change. Then she stirred and sat up with a thoughtful look on her face.

"What is it?" he asked.

"I'm thinking about Griffin, and how ironic this is."

"Ironic in what way?"

"Well, it was Griffin—or my pregnancy, rather—that initially drove us apart. And then his birth sent me into exile, for lack of a better word. Through no fault of his own, his very presence is what kept us from each other."

Dominic paused for a moment, then let out a laugh. "And it's because of Griffin that we found each other, too."

She nodded. "Yes. Because of who he is, I was able to reach out to him for help when I truly needed it. And," she added with a sly grin, "because he's so outspoken—"

"You mean disrespectful."

"In some ways, yes. But that quality allowed him to tell us the truth about where we were going wrong. Who knows if we would have ever found our way to each other without Griffin?"

"Good God," Dominic said, rather appalled. "Do *not* tell him that. He's swell-headed enough as it is, and if he thinks he's responsible for bringing us together . . ."

"I'm sure he already does," she added with a suspicious quaver in her voice.

"Ah, well, he's your son, so I suppose I'll have to put up with him."

She laughed. "I do hope there will be at least a few compensations."

Dominic flashed her a wicked grin. "Oh, I can think of one or two you can show me right now."

And with laughter on her lips and joy in her eyes, Chloe did just that.

Epilogue

Lyme Regis
June 12, 1815

My dear son,

*I was pleased to receive your letter and your
assurance that all is as it should be in Camberwell.
Dominic and I are so grateful that you and Justine are
caring for my charges while we are on our wedding
trip, and I promise to make it up to you as soon as we
return. You have my word that you will not have to
hold another colicky baby or manage any more
hysterical young females until Christmas, at the very
least. You are kindness itself, dearest Griffin, and no
mother could ask for a finer son.*

*We are comfortably situated in a manor house not
far from the Cobb, with lovely views and the
invigorating scent of the sea air. After our stay in
Bath, with its round of social engagements, I confess
to a feeling of relief at the slower pace of life in this
seaside town. Some might call it dreadfully flat, but
we were so busy in Bath that we had barely a moment
to ourselves. Many were eager to ingratiate
themselves with Dominic—and with me, if you can*

believe it. I suspect some were being polite for his sake, but I'm pleased to say that most people were nothing less than gracious and welcoming.

Still, this is our wedding trip, and I was longing to spend time with my new husband—without distractions!

There is another reason why I'm relieved to be quietly situated. I have been suffering from a slight stomach indisposition. There was never any real cause for concern, but Dominic insisted I see a physician. Such a fuss over nothing, or so I thought. You see, my son, it would appear that I am increasing, and sometime around Christmas I will be presenting you with a little brother or sister! You can imagine my astonishment to find myself with child at my age. Dominic was rendered entirely speechless for almost two minutes—a rare event, as you know. After I recovered from my own surprise, I admit to having felt some concern as to his reaction. But I needn't have worried. The dear man is overjoyed, as am I. He says it is a just reward from Providence after our many trials.

I now count myself as the luckiest of women, with great blessings in my life—you and Justine, my dear husband, little Stephen, and now this unexpected joy. The doctor assures me that I am disgustingly healthy and have nothing to worry about. We discussed returning to London, but Dominic wishes me to rest for a while longer before starting the journey. There is no need, but I'm happy to let him coddle me.

You should see our return to Camberwell by the end of the month, at the latest. I will write before our departure, and I look forward to seeing you, Justine, and Stephen very soon.

> *With love,*
> *your excessively happy mother,*
> *Chloe Hunter*

Dear Reader,

Thank you so much for reading *How to Marry a Royal Highlander*, the final book in my Renegade Royals series. My heroes, the illegitimate sons of England's royal princes, have finally claimed their heroines and rightful places within the world of the English *ton*.

But is this really the end of the Renegade Royals? I'm happy to report that it's not! I'll be continuing their adventures in a new spin-off series, one with a bit of a twist. This time, I'll be telling the stories of the female Renegade Royals, the illegitimate daughters of England's princes who must fight even harder than their male cousins to find love and happiness in British society.

The new series is called The Improper Princesses, and the first story features a remarkable young woman named Gillian Dryden. Gillian is the daughter of the Duke of Cumberland, and was raised in Italy after her mother married an Italian count. Gillian loved her stepfather, who treated her like his own child. After he was murdered by bandits, Gillian turned into something of a vigilante, determined to avenge his death.

Think of a Regency Sydney Bristow from *Alias*!

Needless to say, Gillian's dangerous activities are hardly considered proper. Along with Sir Dominic Hunter, the leader of the Renegade Royals, Gillian's family decides it's time for her to return to England and find a respectable husband. As you can imagine, that's something of a challenge. Not only is Gillian a wild child, her scandalous background makes her a less than attractive marriage prospect. No man in his right mind would want to marry her!

Enter Charles Leverton, the Duke of Walcot. He's brainy, sophisticated, and powerful, and is the perfect man to tutor Gillian and help her become a proper lady. Needless to say, Walcot is horrified by the prospect—until he meets Gillian. She may be wild and unconventional, but she's also beautiful and smart, and the most intriguing woman he's ever met. Gillian may resist his efforts to turn her into a perfect lady, but what Walcot wants, Walcot generally gets.

My Favorite Princess will be released in 2016. I'll be updating my website with news, contests, and excerpts from the new series over the next few months, so be sure to stop by. You can find me at www.vanessakellyauthor.com.

I'd like to thank my readers for their support of my Renegade Royals—it means the world to me. I hope you'll join my Improper Princesses for even more adventures!

Happy reading!

Best,
Vanessa

Books by Bestselling Author
Fern Michaels

___The Jury	0-8217-7878-1	$6.99US/$9.99CAN
___Sweet Revenge	0-8217-7879-X	$6.99US/$9.99CAN
___Lethal Justice	0-8217-7880-3	$6.99US/$9.99CAN
___Free Fall	0-8217-7881-1	$6.99US/$9.99CAN
___Fool Me Once	0-8217-8071-9	$7.99US/$10.99CAN
___Vegas Rich	0-8217-8112-X	$7.99US/$10.99CAN
___Hide and Seek	1-4201-0184-6	$6.99US/$9.99CAN
___Hokus Pokus	1-4201-0185-4	$6.99US/$9.99CAN
___Fast Track	1-4201-0186-2	$6.99US/$9.99CAN
___Collateral Damage	1-4201-0187-0	$6.99US/$9.99CAN
___Final Justice	1-4201-0188-9	$6.99US/$9.99CAN
___Up Close and Personal	0-8217-7956-7	$7.99US/$9.99CAN
___Under the Radar	1-4201-0683-X	$6.99US/$9.99CAN
___Razor Sharp	1-4201-0684-8	$7.99US/$10.99CAN
___Yesterday	1-4201-1494-8	$5.99US/$6.99CAN
___Vanishing Act	1-4201-0685-6	$7.99US/$10.99CAN
___Sara's Song	1-4201-1493-X	$5.99US/$6.99CAN
___Deadly Deals	1-4201-0686-4	$7.99US/$10.99CAN
___Game Over	1-4201-0687-2	$7.99US/$10.99CAN
___Sins of Omission	1-4201-1153-1	$7.99US/$10.99CAN
___Sins of the Flesh	1-4201-1154-X	$7.99US/$10.99CAN
___Cross Roads	1-4201-1192-2	$7.99US/$10.99CAN

Available Wherever Books Are Sold!
Check out our website at **www.kensingtonbooks.com**